Louise Voss has been in the music business for ten years, working for Virgin Records and EMI, and then as a product manager for an Independent label in New York. More recently she has been Director of Sandie Shaw's company in London. She lives in south-west London with her husband and daughter. Her first novel, *To Be Someone*, is also published by Black Swan.

Louise Voss can be contacted on www.louisevoss.com

Acclaim for
ARE YOU MY MOTHER?

'An exhilirating emotional ride through love, friendship and loss'
New Woman

'A heart-warming story which covers the complicated and emotional themes of being orphaned and adopted and searching for birth parents'
Hello

'Strong characters, a meaty plot and a satisfyingly unexpected twist transforms Emma's journey of self-discovery into a very good read'
Woman and Home

'Utterly believable ... Highly emotional ... it's also a complete tear-jerker'
Heat

'A poignant, often funny insight into what really shapes the people we become'
Woman's Own

Also by Louise Voss
TO BE SOMEONE
and published by Black Swan

ARE YOU MY MOTHER?

Louise Voss

BLACK SWAN

ARE YOU MY MOTHER?
A BLACK SWAN BOOK : 0 552 99903 2

Originally published in Great Britain by Bantam Press,
a division of Transworld Publishers

PRINTING HISTORY
Bantam Press edition published 2002
Black Swan edition published 2003

1 3 5 7 9 10 8 6 4 2

Set in 11/12pt Melior by
Falcon Oast Graphic Art Ltd.

Black Swan Books are published by Transworld Publishers,
61–63 Uxbridge Road, London W5 5SA,
a division of The Random House Group Ltd,
in Australia by Random House Australia (Pty) Ltd,
20 Alfred Street, Milsons Point, Sydney, NSW 2061, Australia,
in New Zealand by Random House New Zealand Ltd,
18 Poland Road, Glenfield, Auckland 10, New Zealand
and in South Africa by Random House (Pty) Ltd,
Endulini, 5a Jubilee Road, Parktown 2193, South Africa.

Printed and bound in Great Britain by
Clays Ltd, St Ives plc.

Dedicated with love to my mother, Veronika Jackson,
and in memory of my father, Hugh

Acknowledgements

Thanks to everybody who spent time in helping me with research for this novel: Louise Crockart, Ruth Paveley, Grace Banks, Brian Sharp; and DC Wendy Thomas and DS Ian Goldsborough of Shoreditch CID.

Thanks to all my friends for their continued support, particularly Marian and Tony Baines, Mark Edwards, Louise Harwood, Sharon Mulrooney, Claire Harcup, Clare and Richard Jackson, Linda Buckley-Archer, Stephanie Chilman, Jacqui Hazell and Jacqui Lofthouse.

Thank you very much to my editor, Selina Walker, for all her patience and hard work; and to everyone at Transworld, especially Larry Finlay, Diana Beaumont, Marina Vokos, and all the sales reps, particularly Trish Slattery. Also to Richenda Todd for sorting out my wobbly timelines!

Extra special thanks to my agent Jo Frank, for everything, as always. And also at A.P. Watt; thanks to Linda Shaughnessy, Vicky Cubitt, and Rob Kraitt.

Finally to my family: Matt and Gracie – I can't even begin to express how grateful I am to them.

PART ONE

1

'No, don't look right at the camera. Look at me. Just imagine that it's you and me, having a normal chat. It's not an interview. I'm just asking you questions, like a mate would, over a drink. OK? Ready? Right: let's start with you telling me why you've decided to look for your birth mother, after all these years.'

'But you already know that. I told you last week.'

'Emma. Pretend you haven't told me anything yet.'

'Well, I suppose I – um . . . oh, damn it. Sorry.'

'Don't worry about the pauses, I can edit them out afterwards.'

'. . . I'm sorry. I can't get the words out. Didn't I tell you that I'm really . . . what's that word which means you can't speak? Inarticulate. I'm really inarticulate under pressure.'

'Emma, there's no pressure. Ignore the camera.'

'But I don't want to be on TV! Turn it off. I've changed my mind.   My rash is coming up. I'll be all blotchy . . .'

'Let's try again in five minutes. I'll make us some coffee.'

But would I ever be able to tell Mack about all the

things that mattered, even if he didn't have a digital video camera stuck in my face and a deadline for his commissioned documentary on adoption? The real reasons that, after nearly thirty years and a couple of half-hearted earlier attempts, I'd decided to launch a proper search for the woman who gave birth to me? I wasn't sure that I even knew myself. I supposed it was the sum of many small parts, some more dramatic than others.

I tried to see if I could list them. Something had happened between me and a homeless man on a tube train. Something even worse happened to my relationship with my boyfriend, Gavin. Something shifted, a subtle slide, between my sister Stella and me. My job was in danger of becoming stale. I was depressed; perhaps I had been for some time. Maybe it was like global warming: the signs had been there for years but we'd all been ignoring them. It was too big, too scary. Of course I'd always been curious about my natural parents – in my situation, who wouldn't have been? But my yearning had been painted over, again and again, by the simple daily brush strokes of coping; working; bringing up Stella by myself. It was a rhythm which left no room for anything more than idle speculation – there may have been another 'me' underneath the layers, but I just didn't have the time or the emotional resources to strip them off and see. Until now.

'Ready to try again? Take a deep breath.'

'OK. Well, there was this man on the tube a couple of weeks ago, and he reminded me of a book I used to read to Stella when she was little – oh, that doesn't make much sense, does it? Oh hell, I'm even irritating myself here. Sorry. Bet you wish you'd picked someone else for your documentary now.'

'No, Emma, I want it to be you. I told you: you're a survivor, it's a great story. And what we uncover might be even more exciting. However much you waffle at the

beginning, that's what'll come across. I know you. Trust me.'

On that day in October, when the man flung himself through the closing doors of my carriage of the tube, I'm sure mine wasn't the only stomach to give a sudden sick lurch. The faces of all the other passengers registered shadowy panic too, before they hastily dropped their eyes back to their books and newspapers. I delved into my bag for any reading material I could find, which turned out to be a leaflet on how to treat verrucas. I'd picked it up for Stella at the Health Centre last time I was there for the baby-massage class.

As the Central Line train prepared to depart from Shepherd's Bush station, the man started to rock, bouncing from side to side off the red bars which flanked the doors. We could all smell him now, as the nostril-flaring stink of unwashed body crept stealthily around the carriage, an accusatory weapon. I felt myself blush, as if the smell activated the blood rushing to my cheeks.

The man was staring at me, and I blushed even more deeply, feeling the old, hated rash of embarrassment sweep up over my chest and neck. I forced myself to think of something to distract me; to stop me feeling so flustered.

I thought about the twelve massages I'd done that day. I loved being an aromatherapist, but I hated the on-site part of it – it was such hard work. My forearms were getting so muscly that I was beginning to resemble Popeye.

I glanced up. He was still staring.

Don't look, Emma. Think. Where was I? Oh yes, how nightmarish the on-site clients were. They were mostly surly advertising executives who treated me like something they'd scraped off the bottom of their shoe. I suppose because I found it quite hard to make small talk with strangers, and I didn't naturally have what people call a 'bubbly' personality anyway, they just thought of me as a non-person. They never thanked me at the end of a session, and often carried on doing business while I worked knots out of their sweaty backs, barking dictation at hovering secretaries in muffled voices, their cheeks squashed into the black leatherette doughnut of the massage chair's face rest.

Still, I was on my way to a big night out that night, so I told myself to forget about the narky execs. The Who in a special, one-off charity concert, at the Royal Albert Hall, with my beloved. And even better, I'd nipped home first to drop off my massage chair – nicknamed the Bastard – to ensure that Gavin and I wouldn't have to participate in a threesome with its bulky black shoulders and spiky limbs. It was transported in a black vinyl holdall, the whole thing resembling an occupied bodybag, which took up the space of another commuter and invariably made me deeply unpopular during rush hour. Plus, it weighed a ton. Going anywhere on the tube with it made me cringe, and it meant that Gavin couldn't give me a lift home afterwards on his bike.

I decided that I shouldn't moan about it so much. It made it sound as if I hated my job, and really, I didn't. I loved massage. It was one of the few things I knew that I was naturally good at: aromatherapy; disco dancing; playing the recorder. Sex, too, according to Gavin. But massage was what I did best. And the aromatherapy I did from home was a completely different kettle of fish to the on-site.

The clients who came to the flat were mostly women, whom I sent away afterwards limp and grateful, heaven-scented with essential oils. After I'd done the initial consultation, where we sat at my desk and they told me about their aches and pains, I'd mix up the oils best suited to their moods and symptoms, and then, after that, it was as if my hands took over. If the clients wanted to talk, I was happy to talk back to them, learning about their husbands, kids, cars, money worries, beauty treatments – and if they didn't, that was fine too. In fact I preferred it, because then I could concentrate solely on getting the energy flowing between us, through me, into them, which was what made for the most effective massage. Long after they'd gone home again, their words of praise and relaxed delight lingered like the oils themselves around the rooms of the flat.

I wished I had some oils on me right then, in the train – lavender and rose would have been nice. The man's smell was making me feel queasy, and I didn't dare look to see if he was still staring at me. Then, abruptly, he began to howl.

In such an enclosed space, the sudden and abrasive noise caused everyone's heads to shoot sharply upwards to the source, eyes wide with surprise and embarrassment. It was a deeply emotional sound; the brittle veneer of commuter respectability unique to British public transport – where someone blowing their nose too obviously was cause for people to tut in disgust – made it seem alien and incongruous.

Or maybe vanilla, I thought. Vanilla oil was so soothing. Apparently it was the scent most similar to the smell of breast milk. I very much doubted that I personally had ever been breast-fed, so maybe it wouldn't have that much effect on *me*.

The man, still howling, was shaking his head as if a bee had flown into one of his ears. He'd stopped looking at me, thankfully, and I studied him surreptitiously. He was probably in his late twenties, with wild hair and dirt-darkened skin. He was wearing a battered old leather jacket with a can of Tennant's sticking out of the pocket, and his eyes rolled around uncontrollably in different directions, like joke eyes. I thought his face looked as if it had been formed from the same leather as his jacket; they were the same shades of exhausted brown. I felt sad for him, that someone so young had got himself into such a state.

The twelve people in my part of the carriage employed a variety of reasonably predictable reactions to the man's behaviour. Most looked away hastily, staring at the floor or edging their bags and briefcases more firmly behind their calves. A very expensive-looking man opposite examined his immaculately manicured fingernails. The student next to me turned up the volume on his Walkman as far as it went, making the tinny *kerchink kerchink* sounds even louder and tinnier. A woman with sticky-thick plum lipstick and big hair fiddled with her fringe and blushed and, next to her, a couple of Spanish teenagers held hands, whispering and giggling nervously. A doughy young tourist opposite stared impassively ahead of her, and I wondered idly what on earth would possess someone that plump to wear a garment emblazoned with the logo 'Fat Face'.

The man finally stopped howling. I read my verruca leaflet with great interest as he approached, his stink hovering around him, almost visible in its pungency.

He jerked his arm up and pointed at Mr Expensive with a trembling, dirty finger.

'You – yes, you, Tony Blair, you make me sick, you smarmy git! Well, at least this time you won't wriggle out of it. You're gonna die down here with the rest of us, under the ground, forgotten, cattle, no one will let us out of our cages, the ground is splitting, earth's pouring in, look, we'll be buried alive . . . YES, YOU – I'M TALKING ABOUT YOU. It's all part of the plan, to subdue us. You're all too stupid to realize it, but it's obvious – we can't get off, this cage is locked, they just say we can leave to screw with us! You know we'll all die down here, don't you?'

At that exact moment, with a sickening crunch, the train shuddered to an unscheduled stop in the middle of the tunnel. The lights flickered, then came back on again, but the engine died, and for a minute there was silence.

The man leaned forward and stuck his head in Mr Expensive's face. 'DON'T YOU?' Mr Expensive recoiled with disgust and fear.

Nightmare. I couldn't wait to tell Gav about this, I thought. Nervously I checked that my Who tickets were still in my pocket: stiff, shiny, sixty-pounds-per-head, been-looking-forward-to-it-for-weeks tickets.

My reflection in the window opposite was distorted and long, and I appeared to have another identical upside-down head growing out of my own. With my hair tightly scraped back in a long ponytail and my glasses, I thought that I looked like some sort of weird and disapproving governess. At least the denim jacket and big hoop earrings made me appear a bit less of an old fogey. I had a horrible image of the man grabbing my earrings and pulling, and my hands instinctively rose to fiddle with them, leaving the verruca leaflet in my lap.

Unfortunately this seemed to draw the man's attention to my reflection, and he wheeled around, snarling, and stood directly in front of me. Sweat beading my forehead, I quickly moved my gaze upwards until I met his eyes. They had stopped rolling and, as we stared at each other, the only conscious thought going through my head was how green they were.

It would have been an insult to him and to all homeless people if I were to say that I knew how he felt, because of course I'd always had a nice place to live. But once, when Stella and I were first alone, I believed I had an idea of what it was like to feel that lost.

The tension grew and grew until finally the man looked down, darted forward, and with one swift movement grabbed the verruca leaflet from my hands and ripped it in half. I jumped out of my skin and, briefly, felt like crying: that breathless sweaty feeling behind the eyes and in the throat. Then he turned, seized a book – Terry Pratchett – from the hands of the student with the Walkman, and threw it forcefully up and behind his head.

It hit the forehead of the woman with the plum lips with a smack, leaving a red graze. She started to whimper loudly, covering her face with her hands.

Through the pounding of my heart, I still managed to be impressed at how exactly her nail varnish matched her lipstick. The urge to cry left me, and I was strangely not at all scared. I looked at my watch. It was only six o'clock. Masses of time. I'd been planning to do some shopping in Kensington High Street first, although now I had this idle thought that perhaps the man was right, perhaps we *were* all going to die down here? I thought that the synapses in my brain must not have been firing properly, for the very next second I found myself wondering if I could afford that lovely three-quarter-length denim skirt I'd seen in French Connection the week before. Money, whilst not desperately tight, wasn't exactly plentiful either, and the tickets had been my big indulgence for the month.

There was a stunned silence from everyone else. Then the Spanish girl began to cry for real, snuffling and burying her head in her boyfriend's shoulder, lost in his outsize designer jacket. On the only visible part of her face was a thin, plastered-down and lacquered sideburn which had been sculpted into a delicate serpent.

The man stared briefly at the outburst of emotion erupting behind him. Then, once more, he locked eyes with me. At that moment, it was as if I woke up. My trancelike musings on nail varnish, foot complaints and denim skirts vanished, and I was hit with the sudden revelation that we were the same, I and this disturbed man. I felt an overwhelming wave of empathy for him. I saw myself sitting on benches at midnight, cold and miserable; and ten years on, I felt the same, only less cold. *I* had no more idea of my own place on this strange planet than he did – possibly less – and unless I took steps to find it, then I could see myself ending up in a similar state, standing on a tube train incandescent with rage, ranting at Tony Blair or London Transport – random victims, innocent or otherwise. New clothes and Who tickets: they were like trying to stick Band-aids on a severed limb.

Perhaps this was an exaggeration, but the point was, in that split second, I realized that for years I'd been drifting, sacrificing everything to make sure Stella was OK: that she was fed, watered, educated, loved. I had been subsuming my own needs to care for my little sister – and what about me? Who'd been looking after *me*? Not Gavin, not really. In fact, nobody. Not one single person. This was an alarm bell. This man was telling me that things had to change. That I really had to *do something about it* before it was too late and my life slipped by, measured only by a succession of nameless backs, burly or weedy, in marginally differing striped shirts.

Actually, that wasn't true. I didn't quite subsume *all* my needs to take care of Stella, not at first. There was this one lapse, after Mum and Dad were killed, ten years ago. I did something terrible, something which helped me identify with the man on the train. I'd never told a soul, but in those first few months of bewildering bereavement, I used to wait until Stella was asleep – eleven, twelve o'clock – and then I would let myself out of the house, leaving her alone in there. The thought of her slight figure motionless under a Barbie duvet, the only living thing in the house, made me nearly physically sick with guilt – but I had to do it.

It started with a craving for air, a longing to escape the stuffy confines of our recycled grief as we sat each night, wordless, on the sofa, our eyes empty squares of flickering escapism. When Stella had finally, silently, trailed off to bed, I used to go and stand in the back garden, breathing in the dirty night air, listening for town foxes and cats being penetrated, wishing I could scream like that too.

One night, before I knew what I was doing, I'd slunk like an intruder along the passage at the side of the house, unlocked the gate, and I was out. A rush of exhilarated freedom filled my lungs for a second, and I found myself walking away. It was eleven-thirty, and most of the houses in our street were sealed for sleep, but a few had lights in bedroom windows. I stared at these, willing myself to be able to see in, to see parents getting ready for bed, to catch a glimpse of a mother stroking her daughter's forehead and kissing her in her sleep. I could still feel the imprints of Mum's kisses branding my own forehead; feel the memory of love, nurture not nature, but still as strong.

That first night, I was only out for a few minutes. By the time I reached the end of the street, I raced home again, my footsteps metallic on the empty pavements, hurling myself back through the gate and into the kitchen, assailed by the stillness of the dead house, but relieved that all was still quiet. For the rest of that night I stayed downstairs and played my recorder, softly, immersing myself in its tinny breathless parp: my other prop in times of crisis. I never read music, just played along to songs on the radio, picking out melodies and bass lines, mindlessly creating muzak in my head. It went a small way towards drowning out some of the guilt and grief. Until the next time I sneaked out again.

I knew that if social services ever found out – found out about the wandering, I mean; my recorder playing wasn't *that* bad – I risked losing Stella. She was only nine years old; she would be taken into care. But as time went on, I reasoned with myself that if I *didn't* get out on my own at night like that, I would explode, and possibly hurt Stella in some other way. I wrote a note for her which I left on the kitchen table at nights, just in case she woke up and couldn't find me – although that never happened. Stella slept as if in a coma. *Stella – gone down to the 7-11, back in fifteen minutes, don't worry xx*. During the day, I hid this note under the lining paper of the kitchen drawer.

I was rarely out for more than twenty minutes, and I always took a rape alarm with me. Some nights I even dressed up – not short skirts and high heels, but just a bit of mascara, black trousers and a swirly hairdo – so

I could pretend that I was an ordinary nineteen-year-old, coming home from an ordinary night down the pub. On those nights I walked briskly, purposefully, clutching my empty handbag firmly under my arm.

I walked down to Ealing Broadway, glancing in the windows of a few bars and pubs to see people drinking and having fun. I saw girls laughing and flirting, leaving lipstick imprints on their wine-glass rims, and I wanted to press my own lips up against the glass of the windows. I wanted to leave my mark somewhere.

Sometimes I even saw girls I'd been to school with. Half of me wanted to go in and talk to them, but the shy part of me knew that I never would. It was enough, really, just to see that life was going on without me. I realized that this sounded horribly self-pitying, but it was true.

I could've got a babysitter for Stella, and gone out for real, if I'd really put my foot down. But she was so clingy, those first few months, that if I even tentatively mentioned that my friend Esther had rung to invite me to a party, Stella's eyes would get huge with panic, her voice instantly thick with tears, and she'd whisper 'please don't leave me'. And that would be that.

Other nights I just meandered about, up and down the residential streets near our house, my head dragging with grief, stumbling and blinded by the tears that I couldn't shed in front of Stella. I'd walk to the nearest bench and sit down, pulling my knees up under my chin, not caring who saw me crying. I wanted to be rescued; I didn't care who by. I wanted someone to take the burden off my shoulders and the decisions out of my hands.

There was no way I'd ever tell *that* to the camera, though.

2

'So, tell me about this book you used to read Stella. What's it got to do with the man on the tube?'

'It was called Are You My Mother? *It's a really sweet book, about this baby bird who hatches just after his mother's gone to look for some food for him. He jumps out of the nest and goes to find her, only he doesn't know what she looks like, so he goes up to all these different animals and asks them if they're his mother, but of course none of them is. In the end he gets so desperate that he's asking aeroplanes and ocean liners and, eventually, this big scary digger . . .*

'Oh no. I can't believe that even telling you about this is choking me up. It's a kids' book . . . That's ridiculous. Sorry. I'm a bit emotional at the moment, what with one thing and another. Can we stop for a bit?'

I probably hadn't given *Are You My Mother?* a thought for fifteen years. It was Stella's favourite book when she was three years old. I read it to her every single night for months, over and over again until the words were printed indelibly on my mind. I could still remember most of them, the same way that you

24

remember all the lyrics to certain pop songs even though you never consciously learned them in the first place.

At that stage, Stella couldn't read, but familiarity had branded the text into her head too. She used to recite every sentence along with me, verbatim, cackling and squirming with a toddler's heartlessness at the subtle pathos of the story. If I ever tried to miss out a single line, or, God forbid, skip a page, it provoked a storm of protest.

Mum had worried when the book first came into our household, a birthday gift from Stella's rather tactless godmother. Mum even took me aside and asked if I was OK about it, since I was the one who'd have to read it – I was, officially, on permanent bedtime-story duty.

'I could get rid of it, Emma darling, really,' she'd said. 'I could just put it in a bag for jumble before we've even read it to her, and she'll never miss it, not with all these other presents.'

I was touched by Mum's unwarranted concern; until she mentioned it, I hadn't thought twice about its subject matter. After that, though, I did feel a bit funny the next few times I read it. I supposed, subconsciously, I did identify with that poor lost baby bird when I was thirteen years old. Although back in those days, I had Mum and Dad, so why would *I* need to look for my real mother?

In the book, of course, it all worked out in the end. The scary digger picked up the bird in his scoop and popped him back into the nest, just as the mother flew home, worm in beak. Mum used to snort through her nose at this part of the book. 'Typical,' she said. 'The mother comes back, completely oblivious to the fact that her baby's even left the nest. She'd be appalled if she knew what he'd been up to, talking to all kinds of strangers and getting himself in trouble! He should have just stayed put and waited patiently.'

That was one of the things I really liked about Mum.

For a scientist, she got really passionate about things. Sometimes we used to actually act out the entire plot of *Are You My Mother?*, after I'd finished reading it. Stella would be curled up as the egg, and I'd pretend to sit on her. I'd fly away and look for a worm, Stella would hatch out, and Mum would put on silly voices for all the animals she approached in her search. If any of my friends had ever seen me participate in this little charade, I would have had to kill myself. Obviously.

After six or seven months of daily recitations and numerous dramatic productions, even Stella eventually got sick of *Are You My Mother?* To my great relief, she gradually stopped declining the offers of other bedtime books, and we got into, successively, *The Diggingest Dog*, *Hop on Pop*, and *The Tiger Who Came To Tea*. By the time she was four, she could read herself and she didn't need my services so much any more. Instead, more often than not, she read to her two imaginary friends, Gunk and Marmalay, the ones who lived inside the lamp-post on the pavement. They were allowed into the house just once a day, so that Stella could read them a bedtime story.

Things had changed so much since then. Now, seeing that desperate, abandoned-looking man howling on a tube train, staring at me as if I might just be his salvation – well, it made me realize that, like the baby bird, it was time I did a little searching of my own.

The train eventually vibrated back into life with a reluctant whine. After a further few seconds it hauled itself down the remainder of the track to Notting Hill, and the doors slid open. I stood up, still gazing into the green eyes in front of me. Then I bent down and picked up the two halves of the verruca leaflet, just because I can't stand litter in trains.

Finally, and maybe because on all those cold nights walking around I'd so passionately wanted someone to do this for me, I took the man by the hand and led him out of the carriage at Notting Hill station. Before I even had time to think about it, I'd escorted him calmly up the escalators to the main ticket hall. Passengers descending the opposite escalator sailed past us in a blur of incredulous features and unsubtle stares as the man keened and wailed, his dirty hand clasped in mine. I gazed grimly at the caked-in grime between the metal corrugations of the escalator stairs, stabbed with a sudden desire to scrub them out with a toothbrush and make them shiny and new again.

Back in the bowels of the tunnel, the doors slammed shut and the train continued on, oblivious to the small but life-changing event which had just occurred on board.

It was the most out-of-character thing I had ever done in my whole life.

3

*'What did Stella think of you leading this man off the
tube? Was that when you told her about wanting to
look for your birth mother?'*

I couldn't tell Stella about the man straight away. What
with the shock of everything else that happened that
evening, it took me a couple of days to summon up the
energy to relate the story at all. And it was much,
much longer before I told her about the decision
regarding my mother.

When I finally mentioned the encounter on the
train, Stella looked at me with an expression of such
distilled horror that it was almost comical, and I
wished I'd kept quiet.

'You're out of your *mind*!' she screeched, rolling the
stud which pierced her tongue around and around her
mouth, as far as its bolt would allow it to travel, teasing it against her top teeth so it stuck out between her
lips like a metal full-stop at the end of her sentences. I
thought it was a good thing the stud was screwed
down on both sides, otherwise she'd definitely have
swallowed it.

'I mean it, Emma, that is the most insane thing I've

ever heard. What the hell got into you? Men like that on trains, ranting away, they're unbalanced. They *kill* people, Emma. He could've had a machete under his coat, or anything. He might not have realized you were trying to help him; he could easily have lashed out at you! It's that Care in the Community thing, isn't it? It just doesn't work, and you might have ended up as another statistic, and *then* where would I be?'

I was torn between being impressed that Stella was even aware of the Care in the Community scheme, and irritated by her selfishness.

'Oh cheers, Stell. I'd be dead, but all you're worried about is where that would leave you. Well, I'm touched by your concern but, as you can see, I'm fine. I just felt sorry for him, OK? I'm not saying I'd do it again, but it felt right at the time. Don't give me a hard time about it. I've got enough else to worry about.'

Stella suddenly leaned across and hugged me wordlessly. She smelled of teenager's make-up – cheap sparkly tubes of things – and, even in late autumn, she smelled of summer. It occurred to me that her freckles probably contained slow-release sunshine. Our mother had freckles like that too. Stella looked more like her every day.

The man and I had eventually got up to the relative safety of the ticket office. A flower stall blazed a riot of colour in the tunnel leading to the exits, and I gulped down the beauty of fresh green leaves and velvet petals: yellow, orange, crimson, blue, the blessed shades of life. Every other person passing through the station seemed to be staring, riveted, at me as I stood frozen to the spot, just by the turnstiles. I tried to drop the man's hand but he wouldn't let go. I felt as if he and I were at the centre of that time-lapse cinematography where we stood still and everyone else whizzed past us in a blur of speeded-up film. The man seemed to be simmering quietly, seething with some sort of suppressed emotion. I was afraid to imagine what.

In a funny kind of way he reminded me of a pregnant woman. Through my association with GP surgeries and ante-natal clinics, I'd massaged quite a few over the years, and some of them exuded a definite air of panic. I supposed it was the sensation of being out of control, all those hormones whirling around, carefully maintained bodies suddenly exploding in all directions. It must be awful if you didn't want the baby, and just about bearable if you did. It was always a shock to me, how many pregnant women felt so ambivalent about it.

Of course, I thought, he probably doesn't have a ticket. He didn't look strong enough to vault over the turnstile, and now a small cluster of uniformed London Underground officials had assembled at a safe distance, clearly wondering whether to intervene or not. I was still holding his hand – for all they knew, he might be mentally disturbed and I his carer. I felt as if this was true, but tried to swallow the thought, for that implied even more of a responsibility towards him. He smelled so bad that my eyes were watering, and I found myself taking tiny little huffing breaths through my mouth to avoid having to inhale him.

I felt fearful for myself again: never mind the smell, what if he pulled a knife on me? He'd been threatening enough in the tube. I looked away from him, and caught the eye of one of the guards under his blue peaked cap. I shook my head infinitesimally, just enough to tell him, no, it's OK, I'll handle it. But please don't go away, just in case.

'Are you hungry?' I said eventually, trying to keep the quaver out of my voice. 'Do you want some money for a sandwich or something? Because I've really got to get going. I'm late meeting my boyfriend.'

He growled at me, and I nearly wet myself. The thought of Gavin, clean, smelling of bike oil and aftershave, appeared like a mirage in my mind and I clasped the mental picture to me.

Then he said, 'Yes please, I'd love a sandwich,' obedient as a child.

'If you let go of my hand, I can get you some money,' I said, desperately. The fearful heat of our combined palms had created a sticky vacuum between our hands, and his huge thick curved yellow fingernails were beginning to dig into my flesh. I began to wonder if we'd have to be surgically separated and, without waiting for him, I wrenched my hand away. It took every single ounce of self-restraint I possessed not to wipe my liberated hand on my coat.

With trembling fingers, I got a ten-pound note out of my purse and thrust it at him. He promptly scrunched it up in his palm, really fast, and pushed it into a pocket somewhere – I didn't see where, but wouldn't have been at all surprised if it was his body which had pockets rather than his clothes.

'Bye bye then. Thanks, girlie,' he said, turning directly towards the gaggle of uniformed officials, as if resigned to his fate. Suddenly I couldn't bear the thought of him being escorted into an office, patronized and probably prosecuted.

'Have you got a ticket?'

He shook his head, and I could have sworn I saw the look of the baby bird from *Are You My Mother?* in his eyes: that combination of naked vulnerability and a pinch of bravado.

'Here. Have mine.' I handed him my one-day travel-card, making sure that the guards didn't see me do it. I'd just have to pretend I'd dropped mine when I got to my stop. As a rule, I was almost ridiculously law-abiding but, compared with the embarrassment I was currently enduring, a scolding and even a fine did not seem worth worrying about.

I might have been imagining it, but there seemed to be an element of triumph in the way that he pushed the ticket into the machine, claiming it again as he walked into the yielding turnstile under the stern eyes of the three guards. I watched him go with a strange mixture of relief and something approaching a bizarre pride, as if he were my child off to school on his own for the first time.

I headed left, towards the tunnel leading to the District and Circle line, just as a gruff but strident voice stopped me.

'Hurry now, darling, or you'll be late for work. I'll see you tonight for dinner, OK?'

Surely not. But yes. I looked over my shoulder and there he was, leaning on the far side of the turnstiles, waving coquettishly at me with his horny yellow fingernails. Colour, deep and painful, flooded my cheeks and chin and ears. But as I turned away again, worse was to come. A full-on, no-holds-barred yell of '*I LOVE YOU*' echoed around the tunnel as I hurried away for the last time, a flurry of light sniggers whispering in my wake.

4

'Tell me about you and Gavin. How did you meet?'

'What's that got to do with anything? I don't really want to talk about him at the moment, actually.'

'Don't be defensive, Emma. I'm just trying to build up a picture of your life. It's helpful to have lots of background information – I can always cut it out later if there's too much.'

'Oh, right. Sorry. It's just . . . well, there's something I haven't told you about Gavin yet.'

How did we meet? I didn't have to struggle to remember that, I'd been thinking of little else other than Gavin for the past couple of weeks; since the night of the man on the train, and The Who. Certain songs remind you of certain times of your life, and only that morning, on my way to work, I'd heard some music thumping out of a souped-up Ford Mondeo crawling round Shepherd's Bush Green in rush hour traffic. The rhythm, even muffled, was familiar: Stereo MC's *Connected*, one of the best albums around to dance to in the early nineties. That was what Stella and I had been dancing to right before I met Gavin.

Stella and I did a lot of dancing in those days. We

hadn't been getting on too well before then, around the time that she hit adolescence like a sledgehammer and suddenly I became the embodiment of Satan. I had no idea how to handle a nubile teenager – even at thirteen, Stella knew exactly how beautiful she was, and the power that her looks allowed her to wield. It frustrated the hell out of her that it didn't work with me, though.

We had such ferocious rows, mostly about money, that I just wanted to get up, walk out of the flat, and never come back again. Or else slam her head repeatedly against the kitchen counter until she saw sense. I felt so resentful – how many other twenty-three-year-olds had to bring up a stroppy teenager? It wasn't fair.

More often than not, we both ended up having tantrums, usually climaxing in Stella threatening to call her social worker and get herself fostered 'anywhere but with you'. That was the cut-off point, where even Stella knew she'd gone too far; the collapsing-into-each-other's-arms-and-sobbing point. I was proud of myself that I never once suggested that I'd call the bloody social worker myself. Mum had always told me that I was tenacious, and Stella proved it.

So, thankfully, when I started taking her to parties with me, it all changed again. Things were beginning to settle down anyway – finally. I'd finished my aromatherapy course and met a few new people. Plus, we'd sold the house and moved into the flat, so money was no longer such a worry. Stella was very young for adult parties, but, I figured, by bringing her out with me, I could keep an eye on her, rather than worrying about what she was up to at home on her own. It empowered both of us, in a funny sort of way. She helped me to be less shy, and I bestowed on her the 'grown-up' status she craved.

I tried my best not to let her smoke or drink or any-thing – not that it was really a druggy crowd, other than the odd late-night joint going around.

Aromatherapists were mostly too holistic to want to get out of their skulls on Class A drugs, and they weren't those kinds of parties anyway. They were more your spliff and lager brigade. Anyway, Stella didn't care what they did or didn't do. She was just so chuffed to be there, and to be able to tell her schoolfriends that she'd been out till five a.m. on Saturday night.

My friends used to play things like entire Prince albums at their parties, or James Brown. And the Stereo MC's record, of course. Hearing it again, coming out of that car, reminded me so clearly of that party.

Stella and I had completely hogged the dance floor for the entire length of the extended mix of 'Connected'. We were a team; we had all the moves. It was the sort of dancing that risked you looking a prat if you did it in a nightclub, but which was just perfect in a stranger's front room, trying not to bash your elbows on their mantelpieces or your shins on their pushed-back coffee tables. The sort of dance where it was impossible not to grin manically the whole time you did it, not because you knew you looked stupid – the opposite, in fact. We grinned because we knew we looked cool as hell. It was mostly funky disco, with a few sub-Supremes steps and a touch of jive thrown in; over the years of practising in our bedrooms, we'd refined these moves until all the cheesiness was eliminated and it was casual, hip. Heads turned, nodding along in unison, and because we were both doing it, I didn't feel remotely shy. It was so liberating. And Stella could have been in Steps by now, I really thought that she could.

I had no idea whose party it was, or why Gavin was there. It was in this big mansion-block flat off Baker Street, up millions of stairs and past several bicycles chained to the banisters. Stella noticed Gavin straight away, she said he was leaning against the bookshelf drinking a beer, talking to a much shorter man and that he couldn't take his eyes off me. Although I was sure I remembered him eyeing up both of us.

35

After we had finished dancing to the next record – The Clash, 'The Magnificent Seven', surprisingly good to dance to – we'd gone into the kitchen, pink-faced, breathless and giggly, and Gavin had followed us in. The first thing he asked, gallantly, was what we wanted to drink. The second thing was, 'Would you like to buy a Barbour?'

I'd raised one eyebrow at him – or at least tried to. It probably came out more like a squint. 'A *what*?' I said.

'You know, a Barbour. Waxy green jacket thing Sloanes wear.'

'Do I *look* like a Sloane?' I said, all kind of cool and frosty. It was a good eight years since it had last been considered even remotely trendy to wear a Barbour, unless you were a Hooray Henry.

'Well . . . no, actually. Thing is, I'm a bit desperate. A bloke in Canary Wharf flogged me thirty-five of them when I was drunk. They're in the boot of my car now and I've got no idea what to do with them.'

This was Gavin all over. It later transpired that he hadn't even come to the party in his car, so in the unlikely event that I *had* wanted a knock-off Barbour, he wouldn't even have been able to sell me one. It was all talk with him.

Then he asked me where I was from.

'Shepherd's Bush,' I replied, and he laughed.

'No,' he said. 'I mean originally. You look kind of Spanish, or South American or something. Where are your parents from?'

It was the first time anybody had asked me that out-right. I hesitated.

'Um. They're English,' I said, managing not to add *I think*. I knew that I'd been adopted in England, and my adoptive parents were both British but, although I'd often wondered, I hadn't enquired about the nationality of my birth parents when Mum and Dad were alive.

'People always said that I looked just like my dad, though,' I added, on safer, if less biologically pertinent, ground. As a child, it had been a source of much hilarity to me when old ladies in the street would take in Dad's and my similar dark brown hair and eyes, and short stature, and comment upon our likeness. If only they knew, I'd think with something approaching glee at our shared secret knowledge of their ignorance.

' "Said?" '

'Pardon?'

'You said, "said", in the past.'

'Yes. He died. In fact, both my parents are dead.'

'Oh. Sorry. Then why did you say "they're English", in the present?'

I sighed. I hadn't really wanted to get into all this, not in a first conversation. 'It's complicated. I was talking about my birth parents when I said they were English. I don't know if they're still alive, because I'm adopted. My *adoptive* parents are dead, and people used to say I looked like my adoptive father, which was mad, because he wasn't even my real dad.'

'Right,' said Gavin, looking as if he wished he'd never asked.

At first I thought that Gavin wasn't very good looking. He was skinny and a bit bald, with a funny curving mouth, and it seemed to be Stella who was the most obviously impressed by his charms. They got on so well that I began to worry that he had his eye on her, and was wondering if I should drop in the fact that she hadn't even done her GCSEs yet. And then after a few minutes he began to grow on me, too, and within the hour I'd decided that his curved lips were the most appealing part of him.

'I *love* your eyelashes,' he said. 'Would you consider giving me a butterfly kiss?' He held out his hand to me, wrist-first as if to receive a free perfume sample, and, self-consciously, I fluttered against the warm, smooth skin of his palm, with Stella making puking faces behind Gavin's back. His hands smelled so masculine, a mingled memory of slapped-on aftershave and engine oil.

'They used to call me Elephant Girl at school,' I muttered, immediately worrying that he'd think this was because I had a weight problem, or a thick skin, instead of being a reference to my implausible lashes.

Gavin laughed. 'You're far too sexy to be even remotely elephantine, even with those eyelashes.'

Notwithstanding the dodgy Barbours, he was by far the nicest bloke I'd met in a long time. After that butterfly kiss, he gradually turned his attention away from Stella and began to concentrate on me. The conversation wasn't just empty flirting, either, but turned into interesting discussions which began with politics – at least as far as my wobbly political opinions allowed – and traced a winding path around to music, books and films, ending up with a lively debate about whether *Four Weddings and a Funeral* was any good or not. Gavin dismissed it as 'girly crap' and said that *Pulp Fiction* was an infinitely better movie, but for a change I stuck to my guns and didn't back down.

'I like girly crap,' I said proudly.

It was the best conversation I'd had in months; best of all because it concluded with a long, luxurious, open-mouthed kiss, pressed up against the coat cupboard in the hall. Stella, disgusted, had wandered off to find someone else to dance with and, for once, I didn't worry about who.

I naïvely assumed that because Gavin had mentioned the Barbours in the boot, he'd be able to give us a lift home, and I could pick up my car in the morning, but around midnight he'd looked at his watch, like Cinderella, and muttered about having 'a bit of business' to see to. He took my phone number and gave me his, produced a large motorcycle helmet, kissed me effusively on the mouth again, and vanished into the night. By which time I was three glasses over the limit.

I'd repaired back to the dance floor to find Stella, bliss floating around me like a chiffon scarf, and told her we'd get a cab home later. At three a.m., however, to my horror, I realized I had left my wallet at home. With a view to finding somewhere to crash out, we conducted a thorough recce of the flat, but by that time not one single vaguely soft surface remained unclaimed. Beds, sofas, chairs, even the rugs on the dusty wooden floors were taken by semi-comatose bodies.

So we'd clattered off down the many flights of stairs in our party sandals, Stella so tired that I could tell she was fighting an urge to hold my hand. I remembered trying to get comfortable in the car; then peering over the passenger seat to say goodnight to Stella, who was already asleep, stretched out in the back. The sight of her made me feel horribly guilty at my lapse of responsibility, so I turned back again. Removing my contact lenses, I sat them neatly in front of me on the dashboard, reclined my seat and snuggled down under my spread-out cardigan.

As the tiny transparent blue bowls glinted wetly in the night, caught in the light of a street lamp above, I thought of Gavin's smile, and the way my insides had turned liquid when he kissed me.

5

Six years down the line, I still went weak at the knees when Gavin kissed me. I soon discovered that he was by no means a settling-down, 2.4 kids kind of a guy, but I think I probably intuited that, right from when he offered me a knock-off Barbour. I did sometimes wish that he would come to the garden centre on a Sunday with me, or even offer to cook once in a while, but a spark of some sort was still there between us. That was the main thing, I told myself.

For ages, I had no idea at all what he saw in me. He was an ex-hardcore skinhead punk, a Bristol bootboy, all shady dealings and brushes with the law; whereas I was nicely brought up, quiet, and had never so much as whipped a Sherbet Dib-Dab from the corner shop as a kid, for fear of being caught. Over time, I began to wonder if it was my innocence which appealed to him; my malleability, the way that I could blend, chameleon-like, into most situations. I never embarrassed him in front of his friends, and rarely gave him a hard time about his impossible unreliability. That I let him get away with it makes me sound like a total wimp, and perhaps I was. He was the only serious boyfriend I'd ever had; my first true love.

On the night of the man on the train, we were

supposed to be meeting at seven o'clock, outside the main entrance of the Royal Albert Hall. The gig started at seven-thirty sharp, with no support act, so this was a vain attempt on my part to get him there on time. I'd tried to get Stella to be on standby, in case of a no-show from Gavin, but she wasn't interested, especially when I let it slip that the tickets were really expensive.

'*How* much? And the *who*?' she said, predictably. 'Never heard of 'em.'

'Yes you have, Dad used to play their records constantly. Surely you remember? "I Can See For Miles"? "My Generation"? "Magic Bus"?'

But Stella just shook her head and looked at me as if I was mad. 'Emma, I was nine years old when Dad died. I was into MC Hammer, not some crumbly old bunch of hippies that he liked.'

'Mods, Stella, they were Mods.'

'Whatever. Enjoy the gig. I hope Gav turns up on time.'

'He'd better,' I said, doubtfully. 'I've drummed it into his peanut brain that he absolutely has to be there otherwise I will kill him. Surely he won't dare stand me up.'

Famous last words.

I loved The Who, although Dad's predilection for the band was the main reason I wanted to be at the gig so badly. One of his lifelong ambitions was to see them play live, and he'd never achieved it, so I felt as if I was going on his behalf. I suppose this made me rather more emotional than I would have been under normal circumstances. The fact that I also had heinous PMT didn't help, either. My breasts were practically fizzing with hormones, and before Gavin was even late, little stabs of irritation were already shooting around my brain, fighting for supremacy with delayed shock from the encounter on the tube.

When I finally arrived at ten to seven, the first thing I did was dive into the Ladies and wash my hands, lathering them with so much soap that the whole sink filled up with cheap off-white bubbles. I would have given anything for a nail brush, but had to content myself with rubbing my now-clean hands with paper towels until the paper flaked off and disintegrated. I imagined it taking away the clammy stench of the train man's dirt-sticky hands, but I still felt tainted. In the mirror above the sink, I looked greyish. The other women in the toilets seemed to be giving me a wide berth, and I wondered if the man's undesirability had rubbed off on me too.

Feeling marginally better, I trailed back outside to wait for Gavin. There were hundreds of people milling about; mostly thirty- and forty-year-old ex-Mods who'd dug out their target T-shirts and moth-eaten parkas for the occasion. The Royal Albert Hall loomed above us, dignified and ornate. If a building could look disgusted, then it certainly did. If it was up to me, it said in the elegant curve of its walls and the soft red decorated brick, none of you riff-raff would be allowed in. Ladies in crinolines and gentlemen in top hats, please. Not you grubby youths in your *anoraks*.

As I stood waiting, I listed in my head the reasons that I loved Gavin. Every Valentine's Day for four years he'd sent me red roses. He cried at soppy movies, his bristly head drooping on my shoulder. He listened endlessly to the sorry sagas of my trials with Stella's teenage upbringing, and offered to whip out the nunchakus to deal with anybody she might be having trouble with at school, teachers included. He bemoaned the rapid spread of his bald spot – hereditary – and the ebb and flow of his waistline – alcohol indulgence; plus, he was utterly supportive of my aromatherapy business. In fact, he was still my most loyal customer. I could never resist the look of melting adoration in his eyes when, after a hard day on the run from the Inland Revenue or the local constabulary, he persuaded me to give him an Indian head massage or a Reiki session.

Gavin was self-employed, as a . . . well, a sort of . . .

a sort of person who consulted others on how to avoid the Inland Revenue, I supposed. A kind of professional Dodgy Person. Actually, he helped people who wanted to set up restaurants and things; for a percentage of the profits, he sourced properties and arranged finance and wooed investors. That was the official story, anyhow. And for someone with such a dislike of the bourgeoisie, he was surprisingly well connected. Local businessmen and posh totty kind of adopted him as their token rough diamond.

When Gavin had money, he was incredibly generous, and took me and Stella out for very expensive meals at Pharmacy or the Atlantic Bar and Grill, where he seemed to know everybody. He was constantly nodding and waving and nipping over for improbable little chats with anorexic ladies dressed in Burberry. If he was skint, however, although he would still take me out for dinner, it was more likely to be to a Pizza Express where, as a finale to the evening, he sometimes dragged me out without paying the bill, the angry shouts of the waiters ringing mortifyingly in my ears. Mum and Dad would have hated him, and I wondered why this still bothered me.

Twenty minutes later I was still standing outside the Royal Albert Hall, cold, pissed off and faintly nauseous. I had stopped thinking about Gavin's good points, and drifted into some less favourable descriptions.

If I ever visualized the demise of our relationship, I always assumed that it would have something to do with his penchant for standing me up. It was the one thing which had always annoyed me most about him, even more than his dodgy dealings and questionable ethics. I had been in so many restaurants on so many occasions, sitting alone at the table, getting progressively more fed up and miserable.

There was an episode of *The Simpsons* where the teacher, Mrs Krabappel, went on a blind date to a smart restaurant, dewy-eyed and hopeful in her best dress. But Bart Simpson had set the whole thing up as a hoax, and Mrs K. was stood up. You saw her sitting expectantly at the table sipping a drink, surrounded by the other diners, then slumping slightly down in her chair, the candle burning lower, her hair gradually becoming less coiffed; until finally hours had passed, the restaurant was empty, and waiters were putting the chairs on the tables and sweeping the floor around her. The candle had burned out altogether and Mrs Krabappel's head had drooped down onto her folded arms in despair. I always identified completely with that scene.

At seven-fifteen I rang Gavin's mobile – God knows why, because he always turned it off when he was late for something, to avoid getting yelled at. I left a crabby message on his voicemail. At seven-forty-five I left a really nasty second message, saying he was an asshole, I was going in without him, and I'd leave his ticket on the door although it would serve him right if I flogged it to a tout.

By the time I was ushered into my seat, I'd missed the first three songs, and I was fuming and upset. After the couple next to me had glanced over at me once or twice, I realized that I was muttering to myself.

I eventually simmered down enough to pay full attention to the music, only to be hit by an overwhelming sensation of missing Dad. I visualized him in Gavin's empty seat, cheering and probably jumping up to dance, infecting everyone around with his enthusiasm whilst almost certainly embarrassing the pants off me. The feeling hit me in the stomach, almost taking my breath away with its intensity, and when they played 'Won't Get Fooled Again', I nearly cried. There is a sense of desolation particular to being amongst thousands of other people enjoying themselves, and I resented Gavin's absence even more. At least if he turned up I'd have a shoulder to cry on.

I decided that the encounter on the tube had probably affected me more than I thought. But it wasn't just the man on the train, or missing Dad, or Gavin's flakiness, or even the PMT which upset me that night.

It was the teenagers with cancer, in aid of whom the concert was being held. There was a small brave gaggle of them in the audience, wearing matching T-shirts advertising the Teenage Cancer Trust, some with head-scarves or baseball caps covering balding heads, a few with steroid-puffy faces. They looked bemused a lot of the time, probably never having heard of The Who until a few weeks earlier. The less-well ones had to keep sitting down, assailed by the loud guitars and ecstatic punters, old – to them – people who knew all the words to these boring – to them – songs with end-less twiddly guitar solos. Whatever their music of choice was, it almost certainly wasn't this. None the less they clapped gamely, and smiled a lot, and cheered, when they weren't looking tired or bemused. I couldn't take my eyes off them.

About halfway through the show, by which time I'd given up all hope of Gavin arriving, there was a hiatus in the proceedings. The doctor who founded the Teenage Cancer Trust came on stage to be presented with a cheque for a million pounds by the band. He gave a little speech of thanks, and when he announced that 'some of his cancer sufferers are in the audience tonight', a couple of the group of teenagers leaped up and punched the air in recognition. The well-meaning, middle-class crowd didn't know what to do – wanting to applaud their bravery, but aware it wasn't at all appropriate to cheer somebody just because they had cancer.

I couldn't stop wondering how these kids felt. Were they gazing at the thousands and thousands of healthy adults surrounding them, only a tiny percentage of them as unlucky as they were, and thinking *it's not fair*? Were they wondering if they too would ever get old enough to come to a concert at the Royal Albert Hall in celebration of a band whose records they adored thirty years ago?

Suddenly my own gripes seemed unutterably trivial in comparison. Hormones – I was lucky that they were at least predictable. Missing Mum and Dad – well, yes, that was a loss, but it was nearly ten years ago, and I had my whole life in front of me. As for Gavin – I needed to stop moaning about him and decide whether to accept him, warts and all, or not. I *knew* he was unreliable, always late, dodgy – but, hell, no one was perfect. Stella was always trying to make out that the reason I didn't ditch him was down to my own lack of self-esteem, but she read too many teen magazines. She had no idea, yet, how much you had to compromise in life; she was still young and beautiful enough to believe that she should have the best of everything, all the time. And as a matter of fact, I thought Gavin was good for me, on the whole. He was often sweet, generous, fun and, as far as I knew, faithful.

Pulling myself together, I resolved henceforward to give him more of a break. He would almost certainly have had a reason for not showing up at the gig – after all, he loved The Who as well. He was the best thing that had ever happened to me and surely, if I met him halfway, then he'd be less cavalier about standing me up in future. He was a true original, and I was lucky to have him.

So after the final encore, I bounded out of the Albert Hall, my ears ringing, on an adrenalin high from being at a great concert, thankful that Stella and I were both fortunate enough to be alive, healthy, housed, happy enough, and that I had a bloke who loved me. As I delved in my bag to get some money to throw into the Teenage Cancer Trust collection buckets, I noticed that there was a message on my phone. I dialled in to retrieve it, and it was Gavin.

'Yeah, Emma, listen. I'm sick of this. My bloody car got towed away and I've had to go and get it from the bloody pound, and it's been a nightmare. The battery on my mobile ran down after your message so I couldn't call you back. But you never cut me any slack, do you? I can't always be there at your beck and call. I was looking forward to the gig too . . . Anyway, what with one thing and another, I've had enough. I think we should call it a day. I don't need this kind of aggro. I'm sorry, babes. We had a good time but we both knew it wasn't going to last for ever. I'll ring you next week and we can sort out our stuff. I mean it; it's over. Sorry. Bye.'

Breathless with shock, I hailed a black cab and went straight round to his house, letting myself in with my spare key, where I found him spliffed up in front of a video of *The Sweeney*. Despite his socked feet resting on the coffee table in a manner indicating extreme relaxation, his resolve was even stronger than in his phone message. I made a fool of myself, crying and begging, practically, but he was unmoved.

'I can't handle this any more,' he said. 'We're a habit, babe. You can do better than me.'

Did he mean that he could do better than me, too? My less-than-robust sense of self-worth crumbled even further as, with more than a few tears, I waited for a minicab to take me home.

'Can't I stay? Just tonight?'

'I think it's better this way, honestly, babes.'

He hugged me, and his smell was still delicious: spliff, aftershave, warm skin, taking me right back to the smell of his palm at that party where we first met. I felt shocked, battered by the day's events, devastated at the sight of Gavin's socks and the knowledge that I might never feel his arms around me again, or the rub of stubbly skin underneath his chin.

As my cab pulled away from the kerb at an only slightly more sedate speed than the Sweeney's, I realized that I hadn't even told Gavin what had happened with the man on the train, let alone the decision the encounter had inspired in me. A good story left untold, I thought, staring out at the slick

47

streets of a drizzly Thursday night. I wondered if I would really go for it; if I would really ever try to trace my birth mother. I could certainly have done with a mother right then and there, next to me on the dirt-faded and torn tartan upholstery of that geriatric minicab, enveloping me in unconditional love and reassurance. Hugging me. Telling me that it was all going to be all right.

6

'Some adopted people believe that they have no identity, no place in the world. Did you ever feel that way? If so, can you pinpoint what prompted it?'

Being adopted always gave me stabs of sadness, especially on my birthdays. The thought that the person who'd given birth to me had just moved on, and possibly even forgotten about me. But it was a self-indulgent sadness, really – I *had* parents who loved me.

It was never any great secret. I had always known I was adopted, although I didn't have any recollection of when or how Mum and Dad had first told me. It was just something I grew up with, like the dusty smell of orang-utan hair, or the omnipresent flakes of tobacco from Dad's pipe. Mum had always let me know that my birth parents were very young, not married to each other, and simply unable to give me the kind of life they felt I deserved. This knowledge did take some of the sting out of being given away, but only some of it. It felt like a real sting; a bee sting – tweezers easing it out a little way until it snapped off and stuck obdurately in my flesh.

But I couldn't have asked for better parents than Mum and Dad; I mean, I really *liked* them, most of the time. As a kid, they gave me as much of a sense of identity as they possibly could have done. And I'd certainly much rather have had Dad and Mum as adoptive parents than my friend Esther's real but miserable and uptight kin, who'd slap her round the legs for even thinking about cheeking them, and only gave her half the pocket money I got.

Plus, if being given away at birth was part of the Grand Scheme of Things for me, I was relieved that I hadn't ended up in some sad, badly funded children's home: too many kids crowding round a television trying to get a sense of stability from the Saturday morning cartoons. Wetting the bed, crying at night, underperforming at school; never having money for new clothes or records.

Yes, I'd been one of the lucky children. I never felt that I had no place in the world, not even when Stella came along and I no longer had Mum and Dad to myself. I'd thought I'd feel excluded, but my parents' joy was infectious. Stella's birth became the most unexpectedly wonderful thing that had ever happened to our family.

She arrived slightly prematurely, quite unusually for a first child, and – as usual – took us all by surprise. On that particular rainy Wednesday Dad had, as a rare treat, taken me on a shoot with him. In her late-pregnancy befuddlement Mum had copied down Dad's contact number at the studio with a seven where an eight should have been. She couldn't remember the name of the company who'd hired him for the shoot, or the location of the studio, or even when he'd said he'd be home. Consequently, she ended up enduring the intense eight-hour labour alone.

Meanwhile Dad, to his eternal remorse, had not bothered to check in with Mum from a payphone that day – he'd thought about it at lunchtime, but hadn't been able to locate any two- or ten-pence pieces amongst the fluff of his trouser pockets, and I'd searched equally fruitlessly along the vinyl seams at the bottom of my Holly Hobby purse. The baby wasn't expected for another ten days, so he had carried on with the business of photographing a lissom lady clad in pink legwarmers, ballet shoes and a selection of up-to-the-minute dancewear for the brochure of a west London dance studio.

I sat patiently on a stool just outside the brightly lit enclave of big umbrellas, wide shiny screens and jumble of black cables snaking around the edges, and watched my father as he called out 'Lovely, super, smile darling, chin up, head down, a tiny bit to the left – beautiful!' all the while clicking, clicking, clicking away with his big camera, deftly twisting it in every angle.

The model smiled continuously, which did quite impress me. Later that day, when I'd begun to get bored, I surreptitiously tried it, and discovered for myself that it wasn't easy. I held my lips up and apart in a rictus of bared teeth and appled cheeks, and timed myself on the second hand of my Snoopy watch; my smile only lasted one minute and eleven seconds before I had to relax my aching cheek muscles.

At that point I had to go outside and have a pee. The model's make-up bag was spilling open on the edge of the sink in the tiny bathroom, and my fingers twitched with the effort of not trying her sticky bright pink lip-gloss and the brick-red blusher. I managed to resist, instead contenting myself with stroking my cheek with her huge soft brush. It felt like the velvety inside of a foxglove.

When I returned to my stool, I passed the by now thoroughly dragging time by mentally awarding points to the different styles and colours of leotard worn by the model. Top marks went to a V-necked black-and-coffee striped number, quite low-cut over the model's narrow hips. The stripes themselves were V-shaped too, fitting neatly and strikingly together in a pattern that reminded me of the parquet floor in our living room.

Dad loved getting this kind of job. He was quite new to fashion photography, as most of his work up to that point had been for a local solicitors' firm, by whom he was employed to photograph skid marks on roads after car crashes, scars left by industrial accidents or slip-shod surgeons, or – his least favourite – uneven bits of pavement over which old ladies stumbled and injured themselves. This was all supplementary income for his other business, of selling 'make your own camera' kits. He had designed two models, the Victortec and the Victortilt, and a factory in Birmingham manu-factured the parts, which he then sold in kit form to camera enthusiasts via small ads in the back of *Amateur Photographer*. Unfortunately there were not an awful lot of people with the time or the inclination to make their own cameras, so Dad was beginning to concentrate more on the freelance photography work. His regular appointments with cracked pavements helped pay the bills, but to be in a real studio with a real model was his idea of heaven.

'It's just so much more creative,' he said to Mum on many occasions.

That particular shoot had ended at six o'clock. I was weary from sitting still for so long, and my eyes were scratchy from the bright lights and the flash gun; but I felt so proud of my father and his important, glamorous job.

I was bursting full of stories to tell Mum about the day, but we had returned to a cold, empty house and a note shoved through the letterbox from Mrs Polkinghorne, the arthritis-ridden elderly lady next door: *Barbara in labour, ambulance has took her. I'd of gone too only me knees is playing up again. She says please hurry up when you get back. Florence.*

The next thing I remember was rushing down long hospital corridors, the thwack of the thick plastic

52

doors echoing behind us, and my hand sweatily clutching Dad's. Dad was in such a state that he had forgotten the original plan, which was to leave me next door at Mrs P.'s, eating Battenburg and listening to descriptions of her operations for the duration of the labour; and just to present me with my new brother or sister once he/she was a neatly swaddled *fait accompli*. There was no way that I was going to remind him. This was a momentous day, and I didn't want to miss a second of it. Dad had, however, remembered to bring his camera, and its heavy black case bumped against my side as we ran.

We were lost in the hospital labyrinth within minutes, Dad too fazed to read the signposts, and me too young and flustered to follow them. We began frantically asking everyone who passed by: 'Maternity?' 'Maternity?' 'Maternity?' until a porter who looked exactly like my headmaster frowningly directed us, and we set off again at a trot, too fast for my short legs. I remember the *swish swish* of my marigold-yellow elephant cords rubbing together at the thighs, and the mingled tones of exasperation and excitement in Dad's voice: 'Keep up, Emma! The baby could be here at any moment!'

But by the time we reached the Maternity wing, Stella had already arrived, and was lying pinkly and complacently alone in a huge bassinet next to an empty bed. Dad actually grabbed hold of a nurse, leaving a small crumpled damp mark on the sleeve of her immaculate uniform.

'Where is she? Where's my wife – Barbara Victor? My wife. Is everything all right?'

The nurse fixed a smile to her face, although far less enthusiastically than the leotard model had earlier, and gave Dad a look that even I could easily interpret as Oh no, another panicking daddy. That's all I need.

'Everything's fine, Mr Victor. Mother and baby are both doing well. We just had to pop your wife up to theatre for a few stitches, that's all. Nothing to worry about. She'll be back in a tick. Would you like to see your daughter?'

I had already identified Baby Victor, as confirmed by the words on the plastic shackle around her tiny ankle and, while Dad was talking to the nurse, lifted my sister out of the bassinet, scrutinizing her miniscule toenails and reverently touching the sprout of pale hair on her crown.

'You were in, and now you're out,' I whispered. After all those months of watching my mother's belly lift and distort, sudden violent punches and karate chops, I had half expected the baby to emerge looking like Hong Kong Phooey.

Actually I hadn't known what to expect, but it wasn't this beady-eyed little person not much bigger than a Tiny Tears.

'I'm sorry,' said the nurse, striding over, lifting Stella out of my arms and placing her into Dad's instead, giving me, I thought, an unnecessarily hard stare. 'It's immediate family only until visiting hours. This young lady will have to wait in the visitors' reception.'

Dad didn't hear her at first. Tears were rolling down his face, riding bumpily over his stubbly cheeks. 'This is her? This is my baby girl? God, she's incredible. Oh Emma, isn't she wonderful?'

'Yeah,' I muttered, glaring back at the nurse.

'Immediate family only, please,' the nurse repeated, her arms crossed across her chest.

I looked defiantly past her and up at a TV on the opposite wall. The sound was turned down, but the picture showed Toyah mutely performing, her flat carroty hair bouncing horizontally along with her manic posturing.

'Can we call the baby Toyah?'

Dad ignored me, still unable to tear his eyes away from the bundle in his arms. The nurse looked twice at the time on the upside-down watch pinned to her apron.

'Mr Victor, I hate to be a spoilsport, but I must ask

54

that this young lady comes back at the designated visiting hour. Immediate fam—'

Dad looked up briefly from his in-depth examination of Stella's fingers. 'Emma is immediate family. She's our daughter. This is her new sister.'

The nurse looked confused. 'I'm sorry. I wouldn't have been so insistent, it's just that I understood that Dr Victor was a first-time mother.'

After another long pause, Dad grinned at me. 'No,' he said. 'Dr Victor was already a mother.'

I beamed back at him, and at my little sister in his arms, her conker-sized fists punching the air. The nurse arranged her features into an apologetic expression. 'Well,' she said. 'You might as well sit down and wait, then. She should be back any time now.'

The three of us sat and waited. I could hardly breathe, terrified that I might be wafting germs into the baby's face. Meanwhile, in his simultaneous elation about Stella and anxiety about Mum's wellbeing, Dad's expression was changing so frequently that he reminded me of the toby jug we had sitting on a high shelf at home. When it was a good day in the Victor household, the jug was placed smiley-side out, but if there had been bad news, Mum turned it around so that its droopy pottery lips formed a mournful frown. If someone had put that jug on a potter's wheel and spun it around, it would have resembled Dad's face.

'Don't worry, Dad,' I kept saying, patting his arm. 'She'll be fine, the nurse said so.' She must have tripped and fallen, I thought to myself, to need stitches. I'd had stitches once, when I went flying over a low chain-link barrier in Tesco's car park.

The lines at the corners of Dad's eyes were rigid with tension – until Stella opened her pink mouth and yawned noisily, and then the same lines relaxed into joyous creases. 'Would you look at that?' he said, with as much awe in his voice as if the newborn Stella had just recited the first two verses of 'The Rime of the Ancient Mariner'.

I could not keep my hands off the velvety skin on Stella's pliant skull. It was the softest thing I had ever touched. Even the dancewear model's make-up brush seemed like a Brillo pad compared to this.

'Dad, did the baby really come out of Mum's *bottom*?' I remember whispering, whipping my hand away from Stella's head with the sudden realization of where it might have been. It occurred to me that all the facts of life I'd been given must just have been elaborate wind-ups; Stella's head was far too big to come out of any hole that I'd ever been aware of. Perhaps pregnant ladies developed trap doors that swung down when the time came, like the one we had in our loft.

'No. Well, yes. She came out of her . . . hmm . . . vagina. Mum's told you about vaginas, hasn't she?' For the first time since arriving at the hospital, Dad sat up and gave me his full attention. 'Hey, weren't you supposed to stay at Mrs P.'s until the baby came?'

I looked pityingly at him. 'Well, yes, but the baby's already come, hasn't she? And I was with you, not Mrs P. So do boys have vaginas *underneath* their willies then, or what?'

The ward doors opened, and we both looked up to see Mum being pushed through in a wheelchair. Her face was ashen-white, her hair was a flattened, matted mess and, worst of all, she was crying hysterically. Dad practically flung Stella onto my lap, and ran over to her.

'Darling, oh my darling, what's the matter?'

Mum couldn't speak. Tears just flooded down her face, and she shook her head. Fear sat like a brick in my gut. Something must have gone terribly, terribly wrong. Perhaps Stella wasn't ours at all. Or perhaps Mum had needed an emergency stomach removal.

The nurse who was wheeling Mum up to her bed beckoned to a passing orderly, gesturing to him to close the curtains around us. He complied, averting his eyes from Mum's grief, and, with a practised flick of the wrist, wrapped our family up around the bed like an overwrought but well-intentioned birthday present for Stella. The nurse and Dad together levered Mum out of her wheelchair and steered her onto the bed, gently lifting her legs for her and swinging them under the blanket.

Dad just held her, rocking her back and forwards, the same as he did to me when I had a nightmare, and she was still crying. I could only watch in mute panic. Was Mum going to die? He looked over the top of her mussed-up head at me, and made 'clear off for a minute' faces. I hesitated, torn between a wish to stay and help calm her down, and a strong desire to go away until Mum came back to normal again.

As I reluctantly handed Stella over to our parents, I whispered in her minuscule ear, 'Mum's not usually in a state, you know, but she had an accident and needed stitches. Don't worry. I'll pass you over to her for now, but I'll be back in a minute.'

'Good girl.' Dad fished fifty pence out of his pocket. 'Go and see if you can find a vending machine to get yourself something nice, and pop back in ten minutes, OK?'

After some considerable flailing along the nylon walls around the bed, I eventually found the opening in the curtains and slipped through, pretending to walk out of the ward. As soon as I was out of their line of vision through the chink I'd left in the curtains, I doubled back again and round the other side of the cubicle. The lady in the next bed was asleep, her mouth wide open and her breath stertorous, so I was able to eavesdrop undetected.

Mum was still crying, but talking low-voiced at the same time, her words all tumbling over each other as if she wanted them out of her body as fast as possible: 'Oh my God, Ted, it was unbelievable, as if the delivery wasn't bad enough, which it was, it was horrible; they had to give me a drip because I kept throwing up so I had all this fluid inside me, and

57

when she was born I ripped –' I felt, rather than heard, Dad wince – 'but they said I didn't need stitches which was a relief only then I was dying to pee but every time I tried there was just all this blood, so eventually they tried to put a catheter in me and they kept jabbing it in, but there was so much blood they couldn't see what they were doing, and it was agony and I was screaming and you weren't there, and eventually they said they'd have to stitch it up so they could get the catheter in, and they took me to theatre and gave me two injections, one on each side, and that hurt even more but it still didn't stop me feeling the needle and thread going in and out and it was sooooo painful, worse than the delivery, and I thought my bladder was going to burst too, and *then* they put the catheter in and apparently I weed out eight pints of liquid and it took fifteen minutes . . .'

Eventually Mum's crying subsided and then petered out, but I was still frozen with horror on the other side of the curtain. I couldn't comprehend the details of what she'd been through, but it was plain that she had been suffering unspeakable agonies. She had told me, beforehand, that having a baby hurt quite a lot, but I had never imagined that it could cause her *this* much grief.

I didn't really understand why she seemed so upset about the stitches, either. My stitches had hardly hurt at all, and I'd had seven. Injections: fair enough, those were agony. But, in a way, I thought she was over-reacting somewhat, which was most unlike her.

Then she said something else, which made me forget about stitches.

'Imagine going through all that agony and then just giving the baby away afterwards. I don't know how people do it. I don't know how *she* did it. I mean, that's the only thing that makes it worth while, isn't it, the end product?'

Mum was talking about my birth mother. I couldn't believe it at first, and then when I took in the enormity

58

of what she was saying, I interpreted it in my own ten-year-old and less than rational way: that my birth mother had hated me so much that she was prepared to go through agonies like that, and then *still* didn't want me.

My heart pounding, I slunk out of the ward, loitered for a couple of minutes outside, and marched back in again, empty-handed. To my relief, the atmosphere was more normal when I stuck my head back through the curtain. Dad had taken his camera out of the bag and was checking light levels and arranging a red-eyed Mum and the sleeping Stella into a Madonna-and-Child-type pose.

'Sorry, darling, I didn't mean to scare you,' she said thickly to me. 'I'm fine now, honestly. It all got a bit much, and the wretched stitches really hurt. So what do you think of your sister?'

'She's lovely,' I replied wistfully. 'So where *are* your stitches, Mum? I can't see any.'

Dad and Mum exchanged looks and smiled, Mum blushing.

'I'm sitting on them, sweetheart. Pass me my hand-bag, would you? If Dad's going to take our pictures, I at least want to have some lipstick on and my hair combed. Then come and sit up here and be in the photo.'

As I squeezed onto the pillow next to my mother and new sister, twining my arm around Mum's neck and donating my cheesiest smile, my earlier anxieties faded away. Even if my birth mother hadn't wanted me, maybe it had still worked out for the best. At least the most amount of pain *I* had ever caused Mum had been when I ran over her bare foot on my tricycle and broke one of her toes.

'All my girls together,' Dad said, squinting through the viewfinder at us, zooming us in and out for our place in the photo album. 'Smile!'

7

After Gavin dumped me, I didn't go out for four days. Everything made me cry: the film of dirt on the roof of my car; my inability to erect the rotary washing line in our tiny shared back garden; the pathos of the boy selling dusters at the front door, and my meanness for not purchasing one. It would have been easier to list the things which *didn't* make me cry. In between the storms of tears I played my recorder constantly, for hours on end, lying on my back trilling mindlessly away with the radio tuned to Virgin. It didn't matter what the song was, I had a stab at them all: 'French Kissing in the USA', 'Jackie Wilson Said', 'Papa's Got a Brand-new Pigbag'. I played and played until my lips began to tremble so much that I couldn't purse them enough to blow, and tears rolled down the brown plastic and into the fingerholes. Poor Stella, it almost drove her mad.

I made Stella phone the individual Human Resources directors of the four different companies where I did my on-sites, and tell them all I was ill.

'This is weird,' she said, replacing the telephone. '*Me* calling in sick for *you*. Do you want me to write you a note excusing you from games, too? You used to write me fantastic notes to get me off PE, do you remember? "Stella has a doctor's appointment. We think she has Dutch Elm Disease." Or, "Stella is unable to play lacrosse today. She gets too upset when her legs go purple and blotchy in the cold weather." '

I didn't crack a smile. 'I never wrote anything that irresponsible.' I picked up my recorder. 'Brass in Pocket' had just come on the radio, and that was a great tune to play along to.

'Oh please, not again,' Stella begged, sitting down on the side of my bed, and then crawling in next to me, like she used to when she was much younger. 'At least wait until I've gone out.' She wrinkled her nose at the inexorable web of rejection and stale despair I had weaved for myself in my pit. 'It's a bit smelly in here,' she added.

'Get out, then. No one asked you to climb into my bed.'

Stella rolled over and propped herself up on one elbow. 'I'm so worried about you, Em. I've never seen you like this before. Please get up. You're scaring me.'

I stared resolutely at the ceiling. To be honest, I was slightly scaring myself, although there was a secretive and subtly liberating element to this excessive wallowing. All our tragedies prior to this had been shared, and I'd always had to put Stella first, to hold it all together for her sake; but the grief of losing Gavin was all mine.

Eventually I turned to face Stella. In marked contrast to my unkempt and grey self, she looked fresh and dewy, dressed and ready to go to college, her hair in two blonde plaits under a checked bandanna. She looked like an advertisement for milk.

'Has he rung?' I hated myself for asking.

Stella tutted, rolling her tongue stud. 'What, do you think I wouldn't tell you if he had?'

'I don't know. You might not, if you thought it would upset me even more.'

'Would it?'

'Oh shut up, Stella. I don't know. I don't know anything any more.'

Stella nudged me affectionately. 'Come to the pub tonight.'

'No, thanks.'

'Come on. It'll do you good to get up and out. It's only me and Suzanne and a couple of mates from college. I'll ring Mack and invite him too, if you like.'

'No! I don't want to see Mack.'

'Why not?'

'Because he never liked Gavin and he'll be all smug and *I told you so* about it.'

'No, he won't. He's your friend – he'll cheer you up.'

'I don't want to see Mack yet. There's nothing he could say to make me feel better. And if you see him, don't tell him, OK?'

Stella sensed me weakening. 'OK. But you'll come to the pub with us? I promise you, Emma, I'm going to keep bugging you until you give in.'

I surveyed the scene around me with weary disgust: the frowzy sheets; the inevitable balled-up tissues, the sections of old weekend papers strewn across the bed – papers I hadn't had the chance to read before, since I'd been too busy having a relationship with my boyfriend. Now time stretched endlessly ahead of me, winding off into a misty grey void whenever I closed my eyes. I supposed that I should try to fill up at least a couple of hours of that infinity with something. I couldn't stay in bed for ever – I had a worrying suspicion that I might be getting a bedsore. Either that, or it was just an enormous spot growing on my bottom. Knowing my luck, it would turn into a boil and I'd have to go to hospital to get it lanced, which was what happened to one of my aromatherapy patients. She said it was hideously embarrassing, because suddenly a whole roomful of medical students appeared and crowded round to watch the ignominious event . . .

'Oh, all right then. I suppose so – just for an hour or so.'

Stella kissed me, relief lighting up her face and making her skin even more peachy. 'Good! Right, better go, otherwise I'll be late for my life class, and Yehudi always moans at us if we're late. Will you be OK?'

'Of course,' I said haughtily, rolling my eyes at my bunny slippers, which were peeping out from beneath the bed looking, I imagined, relieved that they might get a night's respite from being the footwear of choice.

'See you this evening, then. I'll bring us back a Chinese first, if you don't feel like cooking. Oh, and Emma?'

'What?'

'You will wash your hair before we go out, won't you? You look like Neil from *The Young Ones.*'

'Thanks a bunch,' I said morosely, rolling back into my stale pillows and pulling the duvet over my head.

Two minutes later I was fast asleep again. I seemed to be unable to do anything other than sleep, cry and play recorder. I dreamed that my birth mother bustled into my bedroom, clucking and matronly – so matronly, in fact, that she wore an old-fashioned nurse's uniform, with the funny starched white tricorn hat and the red cross on her apron distorted by the contours of her huge Carry-On-esque breasts. Worryingly, she looked exactly like Frankie Howerd. She tidied away all the detritus of my misery, the sweet wrappers and sodden tissues, and managed to change the sheets to crisp fresh ones, executing brisk hospital corners, with me still in the bed.

Then she sat down and stroked my forehead, whispering words of encouragement in my ears: proper, heartening advice and not merely placatory clichés like 'there's plenty more fish in the sea'. I felt the heavy weight of her bowing the mattress next to me and, gratefully, I reached out to her. But when I opened my eyes, there was nobody there. All was silent, except for traffic noises from outside the window and the sound of a pigeon tap-dancing on my windowsill in the watery mid-morning sun.

I wanted to do it. I wanted to start searching for her – far more thoroughly this time than my last attempt, eight years previously. It wasn't that anybody could ever replace Mum and Dad, because they couldn't; but just to have someone, something of my own, some answers about my past. To stretch the iridescent walls of my bubble to accommodate more than just me and Stella.

I got out of bed, my warm feet silent on the wooden floor, and gingerly opened the curtains. The pigeon jumped, and eyed me balefully for a second, before sailing off, affronted.

'You've got a nerve, to be annoyed with *me*,' I said, as it swooped across the road to perch in the gutter opposite. 'Crapping all over my windowsill.'

Vapour trails criss-crossed the wide pale sky like scars, and I wished that I could fly away somewhere too. I turned back into my bedroom and gazed miserably at myself in the full-length mirror. Even without my glasses on, the blurry reflection showed me what a state I looked. Stella was right, I *did* currently resemble Neil from *The Young Ones*, lank, Nana Mouskouri hair, droopy lips and shoulders, pasty complexion.

It was funny to think that Stella was a baby when *The Young Ones* was first shown on TV. She seemed to like it even then, undulating gently in her bouncy chair as she stared with startled blue eyes at the television screen. Years later, she and her friends almost wore out the video of it, laughing hysterically, but with a certain cultivated post-modern irony to their amusement.

The hardest thing about searching for my birth mother would be telling Stella. I had never even admitted to her that I knew my birth mother's name; that I had found it in a letter, shortly after Mum and Dad were killed.

I was nineteen – Stella's current age, although she was

nine at the time – when they died. With a single knock on the bathroom door, everything changed.

I was in the bath, getting ready for a night out, and it was Annette, a friend of my mother's, who had knocked tremulously on the door. She was babysitting Stella that night, because Mum and Dad had gone to a wedding in Wiltshire. I was surprised and a little irritated to see her face wavering psychotically at me through the swirly frosted glass – babysitter turf was strictly downstairs on the sofa, in front of the television. She sounded odd, too, almost as if she was crying, but since I'd just lathered my hair into a wig of suds and couldn't hear her all that clearly, I decided that she probably just had a bad cold.

'Emma, there's . . . someone here to see you.'

'I'm in the bath. Tell him I'm not ready yet.' I'd told Simon, my newish boyfriend, to come round for me at eight, and it was only twenty-five to.

There was a pause. 'It's not your boyfriend. You'd better get out. Please.'

Irritated, I dunked my head under the water, rubbed off the shampoo, then sat up, causing a small soapy tidal wave to whoosh up to the end of the bath.

I was running late, but I'd wanted to wash my hair anyway. Simon was taking me to a disco, his best friend's eighteenth birthday party, at the function room of an Ealing hotel. We'd only been going out for a month, but I'd already brought him home to meet Mum and Dad, so I knew I was keen. I had endured that ordeal the previous week, and Dad had been his usual embarrassing self, the conversation going something along the following lines:

DAD [*in mock-pompous voice*]. Now tell me, young man, are your intentions towards my daughter entirely honourable?

SIMON [*blushing to the roots of his hair and studying his Doc Martens with great interest*]. Um . . .

MUM [*slapping Dad on the arm*]. Oh, for heaven's sake,

Ted, leave the poor man alone. Take no notice of him, Simon, he's pulling your leg.

Simon had been mortified, but touchingly awestruck that Mum had called him a man. He went on and on about what a cool mother I had, until I wanted to suggest he took *her* out for a date instead.

Grinning at the memory of Simon's discomfort, I wrapped a towel around my slick wet body and opened the bathroom door. Annette stood there, with an expression on her face unlike anything I'd ever seen before, and the smirk dropped away from my lips. She appeared waxy, greenish, terrified. I thought for a fleeting second that she'd looked more normal when viewed through the frosted glass.

'Are you all right?'

'Oh Emma. I just got here and then . . . please come downstairs, straight away.' She grasped my bath-warm arm with her fingers, cold and red from the walk from her house to ours. She was still wearing her overcoat. It was March, but cold, cold weather.

Alarmed gooseflesh broke out all over my body, a chilly sort of fear.

'What is it? Is it Stella?'

She shook her head, tightened her grasp on my arm and frogmarched me, dripping, along the landing to the top of the stairs. I looked down the staircase and saw through the banisters the top of a policeman's hat. When I turned back to Annette she was crying, silently but indisputably.

I ran down the stairs two by two, clutching the towel to my breasts, almost tripping at the bottom and half skidding on the wooden hall floor, until coming to a halt at the policeman's feet. If I hadn't been so frightened it might have been funny. The policeman took off his hat and held it awkwardly by his side, twitching it slightly as if it were a Salvation Army tambourine. He looked at about retirement age: craggy, with bloodshot, basset-hound eyes and a bald spot, old and tired after too long being the bearer of bad news.

'What's happened?' I croaked. 'Where's Stella?'

Swiping a hand across her face, Annette pointed to the closed door of the sitting room. 'She's in there, watching a video. She's fine. She let me in but didn't see . . . *him* arrive, PC . . . what's your name?'

Now she sounded almost cross, as if he were a troublesome schoolboy.

'PC Fletcher,' he supplied.

'Yes. Well. Why don't we all go in the kitchen and sit down? I'll make some tea.'

I resisted the urge to shout at her: 'Stop behaving like you own the place. You're just the babysitter! Whatever this is, it's nothing to do with *you*.'

None the less, the policeman and I sat down, awkwardly, across from each other at the kitchen table. Annette had taken off her coat and filled the kettle but now continued to stand at the sink, motionless. She was quite plump, and from behind she resembled a joint of meat tied up with string: bulges popped out on either side of her bra strap, her waist, and the place where her knickers cut into the sides of her hips.

'Look, whatever it is, please can we get on with it? I'm going out in twenty minutes' time and I'm not even dressed yet.'

The policeman cleared his throat, but when he spoke, it was to Annette's back.

'Could you fetch Miss Victor – Emma – a dressing gown or something? She looks cold.'

Annette turned then. 'Where is it?'

'On the back of my bedroom door,' I replied automatically. When she'd left the room, the kettle still not switched on, the policeman looked me in the eyes. I felt dizzy. It was all I could do not to put my fingers in my ears and start singing *la la la* to drown out what was coming.

'I'm so sorry,' he began, as I knew he would. I stared mutely at him, elbows on the table, fist holding up the towel, my whole body now shaking.

'Can you confirm that Ted and Barbara Victor are your parents' names?'

I nodded, feeling sick.

'I'm so sorry ... They've been involved in a car accident on the M3.'

I nodded again.

Annette returned with a dressing gown, but in her panic she had gone into my parents' room and unhooked Dad's bathrobe, a navy towelling one with a fraying cord and pockets stuffed with tissues. She draped it over my bare shoulders and the smell of him filled my nostrils.

'Are they dead?'

PC Fletcher reached across the table and patted my hand. 'I'm afraid they are, yes.'

'Do I have to identify their bodies?' It was all I could think of to say. I had an unbearable mental image of me in a cold stainless steel room, with someone pulling separate drawers out of the wall containing Mum and Dad's broken remains, toes tagged.

I felt a tickle on my shin, and looked down to see a cluster of bubbles sliding down over my ankle and onto the floor. I watched them trace their slow path, spotlit into a shifting beautiful iridescence, more tenacious than life. Just hours earlier, Dad had changed the bulb which now illuminated them.

The policeman cleared his throat again. He spoke as quietly as if he were trying to hypnotize me. 'That won't be necessary. All we'll need you to do is to confirm that these items belonged to them.'

He pulled a clear plastic ziplock bag from his pocket and put it on the table. It contained two sooty-looking objects, which on closer inspection turned out to be Dad's wristwatch and Mum's moonstone necklace.

'Why are they all black?' As soon as I said it, I realized why, and spots danced white before my eyes. It was all I could do not to throw up or pass out. I was aware of my senses distilling down into one pure sensation: not grief or anger or any emotion, just the feeling of my hand still clinging to the towel. My parents were dead but I must not let this policeman see my boobs.

The PC beckoned to Annette. 'I think you'd better call a doctor,' he said. 'Get her something for the shock. And if you could make that tea, that would probably be a good idea too.'

Mum's make-up bag was still sitting on the end of the kitchen counter, from where she had transferred a few key items into her sparkly clutch bag before she left: lipstick, comb, powder. When dizziness made my head droop onto my chest, I got another waft of the post-shower aftershave and soap smell off Dad's bathrobe, so I jerked upright again. I didn't realize I was crying until the tears ran warm down the chilled damp skin of my cheeks.

'Who can I contact for you?' PC Fletcher had flipped out a small notebook and had his pen poised, desperate for something to do.

One small part of my brain tried to consider this, but I couldn't think of anyone at all. Who was it appropriate to call in these situations – my ex-headmistress? The milkman? Ghostbusters? Where were all our fucking *relatives*? The cousins we could move in with; the apple-cheeked grandparents; the sympathetic uncles and aunts. But there was nobody. Mum was an only child. Dad had one brother, but he'd last been heard of living in a commune in the Hebrides and hadn't been in touch for years – I couldn't remember ever meeting him, and Dad never spoke about him. It seemed that they'd had some sort of terminal falling out. None of Mum or Dad's parents was still alive. Stella's godmother Maggie, the one who'd given her *Are You My Mother?*, had married an Australian and emigrated to New South Wales six years earlier. I didn't even have a godmother, and had always envied Stella hers, even if she did live on the other side of the world.

Stella. Someone had to tell Stella. I so didn't want it to be me.

Even though I hadn't given my birth mother a thought for months, I suddenly longed for her to appear, like a substitute or an understudy, to fold me up in her arms and tell me she'd take care of me from now on. But unlike my own parents, I didn't even know if she were dead or alive. And Stella still had to be told.

'Stella,' I whispered. Annette came over then and put her arm around me, but I shook it off.

Telling Stella was twenty times worse than I could have anticipated. I'd gone into the sitting room, alone, and over to where she was curled up on the sofa, half watching *Sleeping Beauty* – or, as she called it when she was a toddler, *Sweep 'n Booty* – on video whilst simultaneously sewing another hexagon onto the patchwork quilt she and Mum had been working on for months. Her cat, Ffyfield, was draped across her lap, almost covered by the quilt, one paw stretched luxuriantly out like the arm of a sleeping child.

I picked up the remote and clicked off the video, expecting sudden black silence – the soundbed to the words with which I was about to ruin her life – but instead, the TV came back on, a close-up of Robert Smith from The Cure, my favourite band, performing their new single on some chat show. Under normal circumstances this would have had me riveted, and although I did think, Oh, look, it's The Cure, I then immediately thought, So what, I have to tell Stella our parents are dead.

'Annette's here. I let her in just now.' Stella glanced up at the television. 'And by the way, I was watching that video, if you don't mind.'

I turned off the TV properly this time, and sat down next to her, unable to believe what I had to say. 'Stell, something terrible's happened.'

She looked at me then, and I broke down, keeling over on the sofa, pressing my face into the edge of the colourful quilt on her lap, causing Ffyfield to jump up in panic and bolt across the room. I shouldn't be doing it like this, I thought. I ought to be strong for her. It all seemed totally unreal. Preposterous. I wanted to be excited about the prospect of going to a party with Simon, or of seeing Robert Smith on telly, red-lipped and bashful. Not this.

'What?' Stella tugged at my hair in panic. '*What?*'

I managed to sit up again, reaching out for her, hugging her narrow shoulders towards me and pushing her head into my chest so that I didn't have to look in her eyes.

When I told her, I felt her whole body go rigid. Then she elbowed her way free of my embrace and stared at me, her small white face twisted with horror.

'No!' She screamed and hit me, hard, catching my ear and the side of my head. Before I could grab her, she leaped up and began clawing at her own face, clawing and ripping at her skin, and then at the quilt she'd spent so many countless hours on. I just about managed to grab the scissors from her sewing basket and kick them out of the way under the sofa before she lunged for them. She was howling like a banshee, screaming gibberish. PC Fletcher and Annette rushed in just as Ffyfield shot out of the door, his tail upright and bushy, like an oversized squirrel's.

By the time we managed to calm Stella enough to stop her screaming, we were all sobbing and shaking, apart from the PC, who was red-faced and a little breathless. Pieces of torn-up patchwork carnage lay everywhere, like twisted metal and broken glass on a blood-stained motorway verge. For the first of many times to come, I regretted passionately that Stella and I hadn't been in that car too.

8

The letter from my birth mother just turned up in my hand, during the uniquely painful exercise of clearing out my parents' things: all those years of household paperwork, crammed into dozens of shoeboxes all over their bedroom. The social worker who'd handled Stella's case, Janice, more or less insisted on coming round to help me, since left to my own devices, I'd never have done it. I would have just shut the door behind me and let it all stay in there, gathering dust.

Janice and I had waited until Stella had gone back to school to start the sorting, and it took ages; several days of squatting on Dad and Mum's crushed-strawberry pink bedroom carpet, surrounded by a printed inventory of the Victor family, with Janice valiantly trying to cheer me up with stories of her days in a punk band and her pink-haired struggles with the Establishment. I barely even answered her, just noticing that the more animated she became, the more her meagre breasts bobbed around underneath her threadbare CND T-shirt.

It was a teeth-grittingly gruelling thing to have to do, but eventually we were nearly finished. Under Janice's expert guidance, everything that needed to be kept was sitting in piles on the floor, waiting to be filed, and everything else thrown away. I had to be ruthless because we were moving to a flat in Shepherd's Bush – I already had an offer in on the house. My parents had taken out life insurance, but I wanted to be extra certain that there would be enough money in the bank to pay for the rest of Stella's education. Plus Janice had gently suggested that a fresh start might be the best way forward. We would only rattle around in that great big house by ourselves.

It did mean, though, that however much I instinctively wanted to keep them, there would not be room for all the accumulated years of paid electricity bills or blotchy kindergarten paintings. I kept just a few mementoes: photographs, obviously, and Stella's swimming certificates. Birthday cards from Mum and Dad to us, often funny cartoony caricatures of us all, drawn by Dad himself. And one poignant little note which Dad had scribbled to Mum on the back of an old Christmas card. The black ink of the biro showed up only intermittently on the shiny card, so that in places you had to look at the indentations made by the pen in order to read the words. He must have written it when I was in the room, not wanting to risk my overhearing him if he'd whispered it. It said, *What do you think of E's new boyf? I think he looks like Betsey – is that why she fancies him?* Underneath, in Mum's neat writing, it said, *Shut up – I think he's cute.*

Dad had replied, *Shd I be jealous? I know how much u like hairy red-heads w/ long arms . . .*

The two subjects of this written conversation were Simon Cartwright, the boy who was meant to be taking me to an eighteenth-birthday party on the night of their accident; and Betsey, an orang-utan who was the main focus of Mum's Ph.D. Dad was right, too: I'd never noticed how much Simon actually *had* resembled Betsey.

Simon had only been to the house once, the week prior to the crash, so this note had added poignancy for me because it was written just days before Mum and Dad died. Simon never made it through the front door on his second visit – he had apparently turned up in the middle of the chaos that night, just after I'd broken the news of the accident to Stella. I didn't know whom he spoke to or what they told him, but I never heard from him again, nor did I try to contact him. It was as if he'd never existed – which I think was another reason I kept the note.

All Mum's research notes had to be dealt with too, reams and reams of them; and Dad's business accounts, which were floating around, stuffed haphazardly into plastic bags or just loose in piles. I found about three thousand of the leaflets he'd had printed up, containing the instructions for construction of the Victortec and Victortilt (Mk II) cameras which he made in kit form; and I put them all out for recycling except a handful. Mum's notes I parcelled up and posted to her university faculty – let someone else make a decision about something, I thought.

As I cleared and quietly cried, simultaneously filing and keening while Janice rabbited on relentlessly next to me, I supposed that at the back of my mind was a flicker of hope that I might suddenly stumble on a great cache of correspondence pertaining to my own heritage. Or at least my absentee birth certificate, which I'd never seen. But there was nothing, until I unearthed the letter: one limp, unprepossessing sheet of paper, so crumpled up already that I nearly threw it away without a second glance.

Luckily I did give it a second glance, and when I realized what it was, my heart beat so fast that I thought I was going to faint.

It was dated two months before the accident.

Rose Cottage
Teffont
Nr. Salisbury
Wilts.

Dear Barbara and Ted,

*It's been a while since I heard from you. I haven't been
well again. I do respect your wishes not to tell Emma
that I'm asking after her, but I would so like to know
how she is. Please send me a little note to let me know
what she's going to do now that she's left school. She's
in my prayers every day.*

Yours sincerely,

Ann

PS I might be leaving here soon.

Ann. A good name for a mother, was my first
thought. Frustratingly, there was no surname, which
meant that she and Mum must have been in correspondence prior to this. I'd felt a momentary flash of
anger at Mum for excluding me from the woman who
was at the core of my identity. Then I reread the words,
about ten times, while Janice was blithely launching
into an anecdote about her band opening for Adam
and the Ants in 1979. There was something a bit weird
about the note, I thought. As if Ann was not saying
everything she wanted to say – or maybe that was just
how I wanted to see it. But it seemed a little abrupt,
somehow.

At least she had included an address – I could write
to her. Even if she had already moved, perhaps the
current occupants of the house would forward my
letter. Eventually Janice noticed the shock on my face,
and the way my hand was shaking as I scrutinized the
flimsy piece of writing paper, holding it up to the light
in the vain hope that there might be another secret

message to me contained within it, written perhaps in lemon juice or invisible ink, the way they used to do in Enid Blyton, the Secret Seven or the Famous Five. I had so badly wanted to be in the Secret Seven when I was nine.

'Are you all right? What have you found?' Janice asked, sitting back on her heels and pushing her curly hair out of her eyes.

'It's from my birth mother,' I said, in a strangled-sounding voice.

Janice rushed over and gave me one of her carefully appropriate social-worker hugs. She smelled of womanly sweat and Body Shop White Musk, and her arms felt bony around my shoulders. Not motherly at all, but then that was probably intentional.

'Wow. How do you feel about that?'

She was always asking me how I felt. It bugged the hell out of me, because what could I say, during those terrible days, except what I always said: 'Shit.'

'Shit,' I said. 'Her name's Ann. I didn't know that.'

'Are you going to contact her?'

'I don't know. Not at the moment, probably. Too much – you know – on my plate.'

With that, I left the room, climbing gingerly over the 'To File' piles of documents on the carpet where Dad's slippers used to be, Janice's Post-it notes stuck pink and bossy on top of each stack.

I ran into my own bedroom and shut the door behind me, ignoring Janice's gentle tap and call of 'I'm just out here if you need me.' Smoothing out Ann's note with the flat of my palm, I placed it carefully between the pages and the hardback cover of my old Brothers Grimm fairytale book, and slipped it under the bed, the words already etched on my brain.

I tried to process what information I could from the few words Ann had written. She referred to herself in the singular, not the plural: *I might be leaving here soon.* Surely, if she was half of a couple, she'd say 'we'? She could be single, widowed, or divorced. I was torn between hoping, selfishly, that she hadn't had any more children, so that if we ever met I'd be even more of a prize to her; and wishing that she'd gone on to have a big family so that I'd have a whole slew of new relatives to get to know.

Other than her address – Rose Cottage, Teffont, near Salisbury, Wiltshire – the fact that she said her prayers, and that sad little line *I haven't been well again*, the letter volunteered little personal information about my birth mother. Even her writing style gave nothing away. It was a neat, small, almost childish hand, but the spelling and grammar were faultless. From these scant facts, I constructed an awful vision of her as a kind of grotesque Baby Jane figure, kneeling at the foot of her bed in a short baby-doll nightie, hair in rollers, big eyes cast heavenwards, praying for me. On the bedside table, in my fevered imagination, were clusters of pill bottles of different shapes and sizes. I couldn't visualize her face, but it was pale and wan with regret and ill health. I hoped she wasn't seriously ill – what if she had cancer or something? By the time I found her, it might be too late.

Later, after Janice had tramped off home in her Doc Martens, I searched every other place in the house where more letters might have been hidden. There was definitely nothing else in Mum and Dad's bedroom, since Janice and I would have found it, so I resorted to leafing through the pages of all the books on the bookshelf, and in the shoeboxes at the bottom of the wardrobe in the spare room. But I found no more correspondence from Ann.

I couldn't stay angry at Mum and Dad for not letting me in on the secret of Ann's identity – I was sure that if I'd asked, they'd have told me. Instead I channelled my rage towards Ann herself, feeling quite scornful of her naked need. Serves you bloody well right, I thought. *You* gave *me* away. You gave up your rights to me. Why *should* my mum tell you anything about me?

None the less, a few days later, I sat down and wrote to her. Just a little note, telling her about Mum and Dad's deaths, and the address of the flat we were about to move into. No pressure, playing it cool, my pen shaking with the effort of not betraying the emotion I felt at writing a real letter to my real mother.

A couple of weeks after we moved into our new flat, the letter, opened and resealed with sellotape, was returned to me. Ann's puny, inadequate, three-lettered little name was crossed out, and our address written carefully on the front, next to a message reading: *Return to sender. No forwarding address.*

I was so furious that I kicked a chunk out of the bathroom door, splintering the wood, leaving little glossy chips of frustration on the hall carpet, and a lot of fabricated explaining to do to Stella about how the hole got there.

But I couldn't afford to do anything further about it at that point. I had been granted status of official foster carer to Stella, and felt that I now had to maintain at least the appearance of being a responsible, mature adult. Not a kid who went around kicking in doors.

The circus of social workers, probate solicitors and estate agents finally packed up and left town, and Stella and I, in our new flat with big windows, a small kitchen, and a damaged bathroom door, had no choice but to try and pick up the pieces of our freshly orphaned lives.

9

In the first year the two of us were alone together, the feeling of dreadful responsibility for Stella nearly suffocated me. She cried constantly, and I envied her for the ability to do so – I didn't have the luxury of wallowing. I was nineteen years old, and suddenly I had a double funeral to organize, a big house to sell, a small griefstricken sister to look after, and a future in tatters – I had to turn down my place at Exeter University and find a job instead. Not to mention the shock of finding the correspondence from my birth mother, and the rejection I felt when my letter to her was returned – although, really, that was the least of my problems.

I handled the first few months OK, I believe – although I don't remember much of it. I know Mum and Dad's friends and neighbours rallied round, and Janice the social worker was fantastic, but the burdens were still on my shoulders. It was me who lay awake every night obsessing about selling the house and buying a new place; about whether a flat in a mansion block or a conversion would be better, or whether a garden was preferable over a parking space; if I would ever pass my driving test, having failed twice already.

The list of things to worry about was endless, a

Yellow Brick Road of problems twisting out of my sleep-deprived mind and off into the horizon. I developed spots and psoriasis, migraines and stomach complaints, bit my nails to the quick and pulled my hair out in clumps.

I could have dealt with all that, though, as long as I was looking after Stella properly. But gradually, Stella's welfare began to be just another yellow brick. I loved her fiercely and protectively, as ever, but felt I couldn't cope with the pressure of her constant tantrums and often downright nastiness to me. I knew, of course, her behaviour was born out of grief, but I began to lose sight of her as a real person. She became just another trial sent to wear me down.

The turning point came when we moved house; it was bound to be an emotional time, leaving the home in which we had both grown up. I'd already given ten binbags full of Mum and Dad's clothes to charity, sold two sofas and a wardrobe, and flogged all Dad's cameras to the camera shop in Acton. I was feeling utterly drained, and Stella had barely spoken at all for a week. A callous 'SOLD' board stuck wonkily in the privet hedge outside was a brusque reminder of the collapse of our happiness. Stella kept the living-room curtains closed all day so she didn't have to look at it.

The day before the move, we had said our individual goodbyes to the secret freckles of the place. For me, these were my refuges in times of crisis: the larder, and the cupboard under the stairs which tapered to a warm dark hideyhole at the end. Stella, I knew, had cried in the attic where she and Mum used to do most of their sewing, and in the utility room where Ffyfield's bowls and litter tray still stood — Ffyfield had run away shortly after the night of the accident, and never been seen again.

Finally, by some unspoken agreement, we convened in Mum and Dad's bedroom and climbed together into the cold bed, still made up with the same sheets and duvet cover I remembered Mum changing on the morning before her death. I'd found the old ones in the linen basket after the funeral, and I couldn't bring myself to wash them for weeks.

We lay there in silence for some time, looking at the same ceiling our parents had woken to every morning. As we clutched our hands together, united in our grief, I had felt an overpowering wash of love for Stella.

On either side of the bedroom window stood two large antique Chinese vases, facing each other stolidly, a pair which Dad had inherited from his grandmother. They had been there all my life, but because Stella and I were banned from going near them in case of accidental breakage, I didn't remember ever really studying them that closely before – we both just took them for granted, the way you do with familiarized beauty, whether in objects or loved ones.

Lying in the chilly bed holding hands with Stella, when I should really have been packing up my wardrobe, I stared at the vases. They were really old, and, I noticed with wonder, really, really beautiful. The glaze was cross-hatched with delicate brown hair-line cracks, the white background faded to an eggshell grey. And the *figures*. They were painted in the traditional blue associated with Chinese designs, but these were not the bland poker-faced stick figures found on willow-patterned plates or tea sets. These were people, a whole village-worth of characters: victorious warriors on horseback; plump peasants with sparkling eyes and rosy cheeks; sexy matrons greeting their loved ones home from wars; friends; children; generals; workmen. These people had stories to tell, they had a past as fascinating and mysterious as that of the vases themselves. I had never realized they had personalities like that.

I kept staring from one vase to the other. It was completely quiet in the bedroom, the evening sun casting a mellow dappled glow around the room as it filtered in through the leaves of the trees outside.

'Look at the vases, Stell. They're so beautiful,' I

whispered. Stella peered over the edge of the duvet and followed my gaze.

'It looks like they're moving round and round,' she said slowly, as transfixed as I was. 'Like on a merry-go-round.'

She was right. I don't think either of us would have been surprised if the figures had become animated for our entertainment, moving in a graceful circle around their vases like carved horses on candy-striped poles, slowly congregating in different groups, chatting, blushing, asserting, moving on.

'You know, like in *Mary Poppins*,' Stella added, and I did know exactly what she meant: when the merry-go-round horses detach from their circular base and sail off across the fields. We lay and imagined what it would look like if the figures on one vase suddenly floated across to visit their kin on the neighbouring vase – a translucent rainbow's arc of the moving figures. The energy fields between the two would carry the townsfolk there and back, an animated and magical highway whose traffic left behind an empty ceramic landscape.

'The vases wouldn't look the same, though, without the people on them,' I started to say, but suddenly I was too choked to speak. When I looked around, I saw that Stella had fallen asleep, curled up in the centre of the bed in the way she used to as a special treat, when she was a toddler.

By the time I eventually got out of the bed, leaving Stella to doze, it was dark outside. Feeling a leaden depression, in tandem with a faint foolishness at the flight of fantasy, I turned on a bedside lamp and brought one of the vases into the cone of yellow light to inspect it more closely, tipping it carefully upside down to examine the base. A deep carved Chinese signature decorated the bottom, which I traced like Braille with my fingertip. I felt as though I could rub the sweat of the artist who had just completed this tableau: a more alive thing than my parents. The lettering looked triumphant; bold and deep and almost clumsy in comparison to the intricate decoration around the sides.

As Stella slept on, I finished the rest of the packing, leaving the bedclothes on our parents' bed until last.

The next morning, an hour late, two removal men came and took the vases away in their white van, together with the few essential pieces of furniture we'd be able to fit in our new flat.

In my complete inexperience of moving house, however, I had been less than discerning in my choice of movers. They had advertised themselves on a card in the window of the newsagents – not Bodgit and Scarper exactly, but similar. I'd hired them because they were far cheaper than any of the other quotes I received. One of them kept staring at me and scratching his head, as if he were asking, 'Do your parents *know* that you're moving all their furniture out of here?' Whenever I caught him doing this, I glared at him through narrowed eyes, daring him to try it.

When the vases and I were reunited at the new place, however, I found out exactly why the movers had been so cheap. I heard the Chinese villagers before I saw them – a flimsy crushed cardboard box being loaded off the van, its contents clunking and rattling together. I couldn't bring myself to believe the worst until I opened the box, in which both vases had been lain together, no bubblewrap or protective polystyrene, just a few of sheets of thin white paper serving no useful shield at all. I cursed myself for not supervising better – I had just assumed that the men couldn't be so stupid as to pack them that badly – and then I cursed the men.

Scenes of carnage met me when I lifted the flaps of the box: felled generals, weeping widows, headless horses and screaming children. Blue chips of blood everywhere; no survivors. For a fleeting moment I wished I could have helped them escape, that through the power of my imagination they could have been evacuated to safety as the cattle trucks pulled out; trailing despondently away to an unknown future, clutching all their belongings in wrapped shawls tied to the end of long sticks over their shoulders; leaving just creamy shards of what had been their home for hundreds of years. But it was too late.

'Sorry, miss,' the boss said half-heartedly as I yelled and ranted and almost kicked him. 'You should've said if you wanted proper packing; it's extra, see.'

But, as terrible as that day was, the loss of the vases came to crystallize the realization which I had been avoiding for so long: my responsibilities weren't just abstract yellow bricks of things to worry about at night, but real life-and-death ones. I alone could be the one to alter the course of Stella's life throughout her rocky climb to adulthood, and I alone could make her path harder or smoother.

Fortunate, then, that it was only the two vases which got shattered. It made me see that it could as easily be Stella. If something happened to her, it would be my fault. The realization was both appalling and strangely energizing. I'd already been fortunate to have been considered mature enough to get custody of her; and now I had to make sure that she grew up to be someone Dad and Mum would have remained proud of.

10

Against my better judgement, I did go to the pub with Stella that night. Obediently, I washed my hair first, standing in the shower miserably singing 'I'm gonna wash that man right out of my hair', without meaning a word of it, just letting the water sluice off my body, and wondering what Gavin was doing at that precise moment. I wanted to keep him *in* my hair, to keep the memory of his touch on my scalp.

Our local pub had just been refurbished, with much subtle arty lighting, huge abstract canvases on the walls and leviathan sofas. Stella thought it was fantastic to have such a trendy bar so nearby, but I missed its previous incarnation as a dingy public house with dark walls, scuffed wooden tables and warped dartboard.

When we sat down with our drinks I wondered out loud what had happened to the pub's previous clientele: to the old men in shabby clothes with a silent dog under their chairs, or the odd brash divorcee who didn't set her sights too high.

'They probably put them all in the skip with that foul sticky carpet,' Stella replied. She never had been known for her sentimentality.

Stella's mates turned up soon after, and I began to

wish I'd stayed in bed. There was Suzanne, whom I knew very well – she and Stella had been best friends for five or six years, through school and on into their fashion-design course at Ealing. She was fine: sweet even, with her big eyes and small dreadlocks. She reminded me of Annabella Lwin from Bow Wow Wow, but whenever I said that, she and Stella always looked blankly at me. 'Before your time,' I'd mutter, feeling old, even though it was really before my time, too.

But Dan and Lawrence were so young that Dan still had stickers of dance acts peppering his backpack and a chain looping from the pocket to the belt buckle on his oversized jeans; and Lawrence was officially and very self-consciously a Fashion Victim: Hilfiger, Firetrap, Paul Smith and Diesel all fought for supremacy about his undernourished-looking person. He had the kind of strut only ever seen on a teenager with a seventy-pound haircut.

I wondered if Stella had slept with either of them. She slept with far too many men. It made me feel queasy and worried, although what could I say? I was convinced she wouldn't be like that if Mum and Dad were still alive. But she wouldn't listen to me, the boring older sister. I just hoped I'd drummed the safe sex message into her head enough.

There was an older guy there too, Charlie, who I suspected had been invited as a kind of consolation prize for me, although he only seemed to have eyes for Stella. He was a graduate student with a rugby player's physique and a braying Sloaney voice; I took an instant dislike to him. What on earth was he doing hanging about with these immature nineteen-year-olds, I wondered; and then realized that he was probably thinking the same about me. His eyes were mean, and he was drinking too much.

'What course are you on then, Em?' Charlie asked me, immediately looking away as if he couldn't be bothered to hear the answer.

I loathed being called Em by anyone other than

Stella. 'I'm not a student. I'm Stella's sister. I'm an aromatherapist, and a massage teacher,' I said haughtily to the back of Charlie's fat head.

Lawrence overheard. He swooned with mock lust, and nudged Dan. 'Cool – she does massage.' They winked at each other in a Benny Hill-ish fashion, and I had to pretend to laugh, although this was the tediously predictable male reaction which often greeted the announcement of my profession. I sometimes thought that I might as well have business cards which featured me topless, brandishing a whip.

After ten minutes I was bored rigid. I wish I could have joined in the conversation, but it was too difficult. Half the time I didn't even understand what they were talking about, and when I did, every time I opened my mouth to talk, someone else had already launched in, and before I knew it, the topic of conversation had evolved into something else.

I hadn't always been quiet, though. In the right circumstances, particularly if alcohol was involved, I'd been described as 'a right laugh'. It was like unbunging a drain. Once I started to flow, I flowed – only not just a few days after being dumped.

I gazed towards the door, tuning out their voices, willing Gavin to appear and take me away from all this, until the irritating tone of someone's mobile phone interrupted my thoughts. It would have been so nice if my own mobile was programmed full of the numbers of friends whom I could just call up and invite to join me. I tried to picture it. *Come on down, if you're not doing anything. I'm just here with Stella and her mates, but they're, you know, so young. It would be great to see you. I could do with a decent chat about something other than Gilles Peterson; no, he's not a weatherman, he's a DJ.* But my phone only had five numbers programmed into it: 'Home', 'Stella Mob', 'Gav', 'Train Enqs' and 'Health Cent'.

It wasn't that I had no friends. I did have quite a few once, but apart from Mack, whom I saw quite a bit of

– partly because he was a neighbour, partly because he secretly fancied Stella, and mostly because we just kind of clicked – I'd seen them only intermittently over the past few years. Between work, Stella and, most of all, life on Planet Gavin, I just didn't seem to have any spare time. Doing aromatherapy from home meant that most of my appointments were in the evenings, after the clients finished work, and so whenever I had a night off, I only wanted to see Gav.

Plus, he'd been very much a one-woman man; as in one bird, but loads of mates to drink pints and smoke spliff with. His idea of purgatory would have been to sit around a dinner table with other couples, discussing how nice the hanging baskets outside the Royal George were; or bemoaning the trials of finding somewhere local to recycle plastic milk containers. Gavin was more of the 'ducking and diving, dodging and weaving' school of social behaviour, which I had found exhilarating to begin with, then occasionally exciting, and eventually completely frustrating and something he should have grown out of at twenty. Still, he loved me – or so he said. I could forgive him a lot for that.

I wondered, for the millionth time that week, why he'd stopped loving me. If he ever really had loved me. If I was even lovable.

The students were still talking about nightclubs and DJs, and I listened half-heartedly for a few minutes before tuning out again. They might as well have been talking in a different language. Stella went clubbing most weekends – she did all her dancing without me these days. Which was as it should be, since she was grown up now, and had her own friends. Besides, I felt too old to be out till four a.m., gurning manically and spinning on my head. I was much happier curled up on the sofa with Gavin, watching a video. Or at least, I had been.

'Do people still spin on their heads?' The words in my brain were suddenly on the outside, without me

88

realizing I'd said them aloud, cutting right through an animated discussion about Fatboy Slim's last album. Everybody stared at me.

'What?' Stella wore an expression comprised of equal parts indulgence and embarrassment, and I felt as if it was I who was the silly younger sister, out of her depths in this big grown-up conversation.

'Um, you know, I suppose it started with the break-dancers in, what, eighty-three, eighty-four, didn't it? They literally used to spin on their heads, and then it came to be like an expression for what kids did in discos . . .'

Cringing, I heard the words 'kids' and 'discos' jarring discordantly around the table. I felt about eighty-five years old. I looked at Charlie, the other 'older' person present, for support, but he appeared to be counting the bubbles in his pint of poncey European lager.

'No,' said Stella. 'Nobody spins on their heads any more.'

'I think I'll just go to the loo,' I said, standing up and cracking my knee against the edge of the low table. 'Excuse me.'

More than anything, when I was fifteen, I'd wanted to be able to breakdance. I used to beg Mum to let me rip up the lino in the kitchen so I could carry it around with me in an unwieldy roll, ready to lay down on any sort of surface and do my stuff. I could do a passable back spin, but the first time I tried a swan-dive, where you dived on your front and then slid back up as if nothing had happened, it had been a disaster. The lino I was practising on was still attached to the kitchen floor, so there had not been a lot of available space. I'd banged my head so hard on the side of the fridge that I nearly knocked myself out.

So my breakdancing skills were never honed enough for public display (and I'd have been far too shy to perform, anyway) but it was around that time I began to teach Stella some of the disco moves we later evolved into our own dance routines. I realized that I missed going dancing with Stella.

When I emerged reluctantly from the ladies' again, I saw from across the bar that Stella was holding court, talking animatedly, more than half-drunk, waving her slender hands with their heavy silver rings in the air and then momentarily stilling them while she pulled out a cigarette from the pack on the table in front of her. Her hair looked incredible loose around her shoulders, its artfully snaky blonde waves like a sculpted Pre-Raphaelite.

Suddenly, everyone round the table, except Stella, who was still occupied with her smoke, raised their heads and watched me come towards them. Through some strange and unpropitious coincidence all the conversations at the other tables around them dropped in volume, allowing me to hear Stella's words quite clearly, despite the cigarette flapping between her lips as she held a lit match to it:

'. . . Well, she's not my real sister, she's adopted. Oh, and guess what, she plays the recorder! And when she was a kid, her best friend was a gorilla called Betsey!'

It seemed to me, approaching as if in slow motion, my cheeks flaming, that the whole bar turned to see who this strange, adopted, monkey-loving, recorder-playing weirdo was. The lack of reciprocal laughter from her friends alerted Stella to the fact that she'd been rumbled, and she leaped up awkwardly as I got back to the table.

'I was just telling them about Betsey, Em. It's such a cool story.'

Through her sugary-liquor flush, Stella's face turned peaky and anxious as she watched me gather up my coat and bag from the depths of the leather sofa.

'Nice to meet you all,' I said, putting one arm into the sleeve of my coat, 'but I've got to go now.' Stella rushed to help me with the other arm, but I violently shrugged her off. I turned to leave, then turned back to the sheepish-looking group of students. 'Oh, and by the way, Betsey wasn't a gorilla. She was an orang-utan.'

I don't know why Stella said Betsey was a gorilla. Our mother had been a zoologist who spent years working on a Ph.D. on the behavioural patterns of orang-utans – not gorillas, or chimps, or baboons: orang-utans. I think I was as much hurt by Stella's lack of respect for our mother's research as by the insulting nature of her comment about me.

Mum had based her research project at London Zoo, over time becoming friendly enough with the zoo-keepers to obtain permission for me, aged five, to play with a baby orang-utan called Betsey, so she could observe Betsey's reactions. Thus was the start of a beautiful friendship, although Mum used to joke that the Ph.D. should have been about me rather than Betsey, as I'd learned to swing on an old car tyre tied to a tree, and deftly peel bark from branches.

Nobody, not even Mum, ever really understood my relationship with Betsey. It went much deeper than the novelty of being allowed in the orang-utan enclosure, with the general public standing outside: the divorced fathers laughing and pointing me out to their enthralled toddlers; kids' noses pressed enviously up against the thick glass, while Betsey and I climbed on dead tree branches together and fed each other bananas.

For almost five years, until Stella was born, Betsey really was my best friend, my most loyal companion. She showed me unconditional, straightforward devotion, unswerving in its constancy, never prey to the fickle fluctuations marking the relationships of the other little girls in my primary school. Betsey never cared about stunt kites or Mousetrap or Wonder Woman, or that you couldn't join the most popular club in the third year unless you owned *Voulez-Vous* or looked like Anni-Frid or Agnetha. And even with Mum and Dad long gone, it was Betsey I remembered with crystal clarity, not my parents. The hairy gentleness of her long sinewy arm around my neck, the sweet acrid smell of orang-utan pee on the straw in the cage; her liquid brown eyes and tender rubbery nostrils.

I couldn't even remember what Mum smelled like. Not even a hint. Not perfume, not skin, not even the heavy scent of sleep after all the countless nights I spent cocooned in bed between her and Dad, in those years when I was still an only child; Dad grumbling and fidgeting in his sleep, Mum's arm flung protectively around me as I lay stretched out in a contented, mattress-hogging sleep. Even their faces had faded, apart from as pictured in the one-dimensional reminders framed on the mantelpiece.

No, when I dreamed of my losses, they were almost always personified by the ugly beauty of big yellow teeth, and thick pinky-orange eyelids, and gentle long black horny-nailed fingers, like a simian pianist.

What was more, I'm almost sure I wouldn't have become an aromatherapist if it weren't for Betsey. Although she couldn't speak to me, she responded by touch. If I'd had a bad week at school, or felt poorly, Betsey seemed to know before I even told her. I would sit cross-legged and talk to her about it, sometimes sniffing as I relayed my current tale of woe: Patricia Jackson hadn't let me have one of her Blackjacks when she'd given everyone else one; or I had to have a filling at the dentist; or, Dad had shouted at me for writing my letter to Father Christmas on the back of his passport application form. Betsey would put her head on one side and then she would stroke my arm, or my shoulders, searching for non-existent fleas, grooming me firmly, but with what felt like such love that my childhood grievances or pains would gradually dissipate into a wonderful relaxed catharsis of security.

It felt exactly the same as when Mum used to stroke my forehead when I had a headache, except that Betsey could keep going for ages. The first time Mum saw me keeled over, fast asleep in the straw, with

Betsey still petting me, she thought something terrible had happened, and rushed into the cage to rescue me. I'd woken up in her arms with a bleary, blissed-out smile on my face.

Outside the bar, I heard Stella's stricken voice behind me, reedy in the cold night air. 'Don't be cross, Emma, I only mentioned you were adopted because Lawrence said we didn't look at all alike.'

'It was the *way* you said it. So you don't think I'm like a real sister to you then? And what the hell did you mean by saying "guess what, she plays the recorder"? So what? It might not be the trendiest of instruments, but it relaxes me, OK? You made me sound like a complete freak. Well thanks a bundle, Stella. Now at least I know what you really think of me.'

Stella grabbed my arm again, but I shook her off. 'Get lost, Stella. I've had enough of you and your boring little friends.'

Two men with crew cuts and sports shirts, each carrying a laptop computer case in one hand and a bottle of lager in the other, walked past and sniggered. 'Girls, girls,' said the shorter of the pair. 'How about a nice bout of naked mud wrestling to sort out your differences? It can be arranged, for a small fee.'

'Mind your own business, assface,' hissed Stella. They too were the sort of men who would extract an unnecessary amount of comedy mileage on learning that I did 'massage' for a living. I began to walk away, but she followed me.

'I'm really sorry, Emma. It was so tactless of me, specially after this whole Gavin thing, too. I promise I'll never tell anyone you're adopted again, not unless you say it's OK. Or that you play the recorder. And of *course* you're a real sister to me.'

Stella curled her fingers into my palm, her rings clicking against my one signet ring, left to me in Mum's will. 'Friends again?'

I didn't answer, and wouldn't take her hand. Stella, unaccustomed to conciliation, lost patience. 'All right then, St Emma, have it your own way. God, some people can't accept an apology. If you think my friends are so boring, why don't you go out and get a few of your own? In *fact*, why don't you just go and get yourself a bloody *life*? You know, things could be much worse – you've only been dumped, but you're still lying round the flat like a total martyr all day! It's just lame.'

'Fuck you,' I said, and wheeled around towards home, walking so fast that I caught up with the two would-be mud-wrestling organizers. I barged recklessly past them, almost daring them to say something else to me, but they must have caught sight of my expression, because they wisely refrained.

In the distance I could hear a penitent wailing, '*Em-ma, I'm sorreee, come baaaack*', but I didn't turn around.

11

I hated arguing with Stella. We hardly ever fought these days; not the way we had ten years earlier. Although, having said that, I was perhaps finally starting to realize that there was a fine line between keeping the peace and being trampled on.

She did try to come in and see me when she got in from the pub, but I'd locked my bedroom door and pretended to be asleep. I was just too tired to deal with it all. I decided I'd accept her apology in the morning.

But her words had hit home. I made myself get up the next day – I had to go back to work at some point, and that day was the start of three new baby-massage courses, so I couldn't very well not turn up. Gavin had dumped me, I'd had a row with Stella, and it looked like rain, and yet somehow I kept seeing the face of the man on the train, the terrible confused expression of somebody who was not in control of their own life. I just kept thinking: I don't want to become like that.

However much I missed Gavin, it was time to pull myself together. I had things to do: more constructive things than locking myself in my room with a descant recorder. I had a mother to start looking for.

Stella was in the bath, so I sat alone at the breakfast table with a bowl of Special K and my novel, *Temples of Delight* by Barbara Trapido, propped up against the teapot. It was the first day since Gav and I split up that I'd even had the inclination to read a book, so I took that as another good omen.

Ten minutes later, I rinsed my cereal bowl under the hot tap and upended it on the draining board, again noticing the muscle definition in my arms. My bulging body-builder forearms were the things I hated most about my appearance, and I wondered if it would put off any prospective new boyfriends – not that I wanted a new boyfriend, not yet. It felt weird, to have to view myself through the eyes of a stranger, to see how I rated for sexual attractiveness after so many years of being spoken for.

I mentally listed my attributes and flaws, trying as usual not to compare myself unfavourably to Stella. I didn't mind wearing glasses, because I knew I had nice eyes – people raved about my eyelashes, and it always embarrassed me. And my body was OK. Not perfect, a bit too pear-shaped for my liking – if I wore my hair scraped back off my head, I thought I looked like a pin-head – but I could just about get away with little tops and tight trousers. I wished I were tall, though, like Stella. We had roughly the same measurements, but she appeared much slimmer because of the extra four inches she had on me. Still, she had to go swimming twice a week to stop all the alcohol she consumed turning into chins and love-handles and wobbles, whereas the physical effort of my massages kept me fit. Not to mention the added strain of having to heft the Bastard around with me on the tube the whole time.

At least I didn't need to take the Bastard into town that day. Three hour-long classes of teaching neurotic new mothers how to soothe their windy Baby-Gap-clad bundles into a state of perfect baby relaxation – much nicer than businessmen's impervious backs. I prided myself on the success of those classes; I loved the way that a roomful of fractious hollering could simmer down into contented gurgles – and that was just the mothers . . .

Stella was still in the bath, and I wondered if she was trying to avoid me. I stood outside the bathroom for a moment, not barging in like I normally did, just knocking softly on the door.

'Can I come in? I need to clean my teeth.'

It's funny how arguments impose a spiky formality on even the closest relationships. I waited a moment, then heard a watery swoosh.

'All right,' she said faintly, grumpily.

I opened the door and went in. Stella was lying in the tub, staring straight ahead of her with a set expression on her face, bubbles hiding her body and bearding her chin, her blonde hair piled up messily on top of her head. She looked red-faced, but I knew that was because she always ran the water in at much too high a temperature. Wordlessly, I went to the basin and began to clean my teeth, relishing the sharp minty taste of a new day. It was true that I was feeling better – but I was still waiting for another apology.

'Right, I'm off, then,' I said, in between spitting out mouthfuls of water. I replaced my toothbrush in the bathroom cabinet, noticing as I did so Gavin's old spare toothbrush lying next to a box of Nurofen and a pink plastic razor. I picked it up and looked at it, its yellowing splayed-out bristles somehow reminding me again of the man on the train.

'Won't be needing this any more,' I said, dropping the toothbrush in the mini swing bin next to the toilet, and trying not to think about how much I missed Gavin's warm clumsy body and his lame excuses. The reflection of my face loomed smearily in the bin's stainless steel top. All the surfaces in our bathroom were smeary. Neither of us was very adept at keeping them polished, but we couldn't justify the expense of a cleaner.

Stella turned her head and looked at me for the first time, sweat beading her forehead, her cheeks an unbecoming aubergine sort of colour.

'I didn't mean what I said last night.'

I went over and sat on the edge of the bath, getting a damp patch on the seat of my jeans. 'Thing is, you were partly right. About me needing to get a life, anyway.'

'I'm sorry, Em. I was so stupid to say that thing about you not being my real sister. Of course you are – the words came out wrong, that was all. I really hate it when we fight.'

She reached out a bubbly hand for my dry one, and her skin felt soft and almost slimy, like wet soap. Very different to the man on the train.

'Me too.'

'So do you forgive me?'

'Yeah. Just don't tell everyone about my private life again. And don't bloody tell everyone about Betsey, either, it makes me sound like such a freak. I was only a kid at the time.'

'I know. Sorry. I was a bit pissed. I won't do it again, I promise.'

I stood up, clearing a porthole in the steam on the mirror, partly to check my make-up, and partly so I didn't have to look at Stella when I told her of my decision to trace my birth mother.

But no words came; just my breath, misting up the mirror again, obscuring my face. I *would* tell Stella soon of course; I had to. Just not yet. I so desperately wanted her to be supportive, and happy for me; but I was so afraid that she might not be, that it might be too great a threat.

Stella sat up in the bath, sending a splash and a slow wash of bubbles sliding over the side of the tub and onto the wooden floor. The skin on her chest and arms was seared red from the hot water, the level in the bath delineated on her body by the sudden contrast of white above it.

'Love you, Em.'

'I love you, too.'

Absently, I wiped the rag-rug bathmat over the

spillage on the floor. I'd bathed Stella as a kid so often that it would almost have felt natural to lift her out by her armpits and towel her off myself. It was the job that I always chose over the dishes or tidying my bedroom, when Mum gave me options of household chores. Stella used to create such complete fantasy worlds for herself when she was in the bath: re-enacting the whole of *The Wizard of Oz*, or *The Little Mermaid*. I still half expected to find naked waterlogged Barbies in the bath after Stella drained it, what was left of their lustrous blonde locks matted and greasy from over-enthusiastic soapings.

'I'd better go, or I'll be late. I'll see you this evening, then. Have a good day at college.'

'Thanks. Bye, Em.' She sank back under the bubbles again, sighing with the relief of redemption.

I would tell her soon, I decided. Just not yet.

12

Percy, our elderly neighbour from the flat below, was at the communal front door, shakily picking two full milk bottles off the step as I squeezed past.

''Ello, Susan love, 'ow are you? 'Aven't seen you since the Boer War!'

'Hello, Mr Weston, it's Emma, remember? I'm fine, thank you.'

'Funny that, me daughter's called Susan, too.'

Not funny at all, quite logical really, I thought. It occurred to me that a rainstorm would intensify the awful smell which emanated from his health-hazard of a flat. I generally tried to avoid thinking about what might be the cause of it, but it was hard, particularly as he often left his front door open. Once, when Percy was out in the back garden, I'd dared Stella to go and peek in. Stella had held her breath and stuck her head round into the kitchen, where, she'd reported back, there were piles and piles of dinner plates stacked up on every available surface, literally hundreds of them.

''E's gorn,' said Percy, who was clad in just an untucked dirty white shirt, voluminous trousers, and worn felt bedroom slippers.

'Who has?'

'In a bit of an 'urry, wern 'e?'

'Who?'

'That man wiv the big shoulders. Your sister's young man.'

'Mr Weston, Stella doesn't have a young man, not at the moment. And you shouldn't be out in this weather without a coat,' I said, looking at his bare bluey-purple hands. 'You'll freeze.'

He shrugged. 'Ain't no one to talk to in there,' he said, and my heart went out to him. I was in danger of being late for the baby massage, but I managed to endure five minutes of listening to Percy tell me the same story over and over again: a gruesome anecdote about the operation on his varicose veins, how they had been pulled out of his calf like a drawstring out of an anorak, until I thought that I was going to die of hypothermia and boredom. By the third time of telling, I was jigging from foot to foot, and my compassion for Percy's loneliness had condensed into a stew of frustration. Eventually I had to interrupt.

'I'm sorry, Mr Weston, I've got to go to work now. Take care of yourself, all right? Bang on the ceiling later if you need any shopping, won't you?' I refrained from adding *And turn your TV down to a sensible level*, and wrenched myself away down the path.

As I turned into the street I noticed the irritating tinkling of wind chimes from the garden two doors down, and wondered if the noise was filtering through the bathroom window and getting on Stella's nerves as she lay in her leisurely bath. It must be great to be a student. Partying every night, rolling up to lectures once a day, if that. My own college course had only been nine months, and far too intensive for that kind of behaviour.

The weather didn't look too bad, just blustery and chilly, the wind whipping up dead leaves into mini tornadoes but no actual rain. Head down, I hurried on, concentrating on the gum-blackened spots on the pavement; the dark morning making everything even more depressing.

Stella and I had loved this area when we first moved here: the puny but fiercely protected trees growing at intervals out of the concrete; the people in the little parade of shops who soon knew our names; the clusters of children – Indian, Jamaican, Vietnamese – who played on their bikes and skateboards on the pavements every day after school. It was much more of a community than the haughty detached villas where we had our previous family home. That wasn't to say that we preferred it, though. It was just different; a complete change when we most needed one.

The two old ladies from the charity shop for the blind on the corner were battening down the hatches for the storm, carrying armfuls of other people's unwanted possessions back into the shop from where they'd only just finished displaying them on the pavement. I was never quite sure if those two were sisters or not, but they both had doughy faces with nicotine-stained grey hair, and wore shapeless polyester trousers and nylon blouses, which looked distinctly as if they were gleaned from the racks in the shop. I envied them their companionship. The sight of them always made me wonder if Stella and I would still be living together as old maids when we were that age. Perhaps we were just stuck together for life, too rooted in habit and tragedy to ever break apart.

'In for a storm,' said the taller of the old ladies, clutching a bald canary-yellow baby's blanket and a worn-out saucepan to her chest.

'Yup,' I replied. 'Better get going before the rain starts.'

A bolt of lightning flashed over the rooftop of the Bush Theatre as I waited to cross at the lights, and the back of my neck prickled with gooseflesh as thunder clapped cymbals over my head. I put up my collar and hurried on as the first fat raindrops plopped down around me; praying that the man wouldn't be there, waiting for me, inside the tube station.

I made it to Covent Garden, and the health centre,

thankfully unaccosted, with two minutes to spare before the start of my class. There was just enough time to get changed and dry my wet hair underneath the hand drier in the ladies'.

I carried my coat and bag over to Joanne in the health visitor's office. Joanne was sitting behind her desk, talking on the telephone, saying: 'Mmm, mmm, mmm, yes, I know, but I think the problem here is less the poo's *consistency* than the fact that Archie's doing it on the *floor . . .*' She made a face at me, and I managed to smile back. *Can I leave my stuff here?* I mouthed, pointing at the space behind Joanne's desk, and Joanne nodded and continued her conversation.

'Mmm. Well, I'm afraid you're going to have to let him know that this isn't acceptable behaviour . . .'

The waiting room of the health centre now resembled the end of the Mothercare January sales, with every type of pushchair – double and single buggies, three-wheeled all-terrain models, hoods up, hoods down, tartan, polka-dotted and tiger-printed – all parked in a disorganized jumble through which I had to fight my way to reach the room where I was holding my class. Judging from the number of buggies, I had a pretty full house. I took another deep breath and opened the door.

The seventeen mothers inside, already seated in an uneven circle on the carpet, did not even notice my arrival at first. They were all too deeply engrossed in their conversations about cracked nipples, episiotomies and sex-starved husbands; and, once again, I felt an outsider, the only one who hadn't earned the milky badge of endurance that they wore with such pride on their shoulders.

I managed to insinuate myself into a small space between a big hearty Sloane who was busily laying out a Burberry changing mat, and an anxious-looking older mother with circles of milk staining the front of her T-shirt, whose baby had a soft brush of jet black hair standing vertical on his otherwise bald head. Yikes, that's an ugly one, I thought uncharitably.

I cleared my throat. 'OK, shall we make a start, then? My name is Emma, and I will be teaching you an invaluable skill: how to give your baby a wonderful, self-affirming start to a healthy life. Babies, just like ourselves, respond extremely well to touch. I'm sure you're all aware of how much a good cuddle can help a fractious baby; you do it instinctively. Massage is just an extension of this, with many extra benefits for your baby's health.'

The mothers stopped talking, and the breastfeeding ones unsuckered their babies' greedy mouths from their breasts. There was a momentary glimpse of a selection of engorged nipples, followed by a hasty pulling-down of blouses and T-shirts, and they all laid out their children on mats or towels in front of them, with their heads towards the centre of the circle.

'If you can just undress your babies, please.'

I watched as they lovingly manoeuvred tiny arms out of equally tiny jackets, some hand-crocheted, some designer, but mostly Baby Gap; stripped minute cotton vests over floppy heads, and peeled blobs of towelling sock off little purple feet. None of the babies was as cute as Stella had been.

Every time I conducted one of these baby-massage classes, I was reminded of the secretive creases of Stella's new body. I could still remember the whiff of unwashed skin from underneath her chin, where the crease was so deep that drops of old milk would some-times collect and fester, unnoticed by all, until its presence was announced by a sourness, like an infant version of body odour.

In the other classes, where the babies were a few months older and the mothers more confident in their massage strokes and undressing techniques, I saw the progression of Stella's own growth. How, when she learned to sit up and look around, she finally grew a neck, so the creases got more accessible. How her tiny wavering peeled-prawn fingers matured into strong and scratchy grabbing hands; and she developed a huge and proud pot belly, like a miniature Buddha. When she lay back in the bath to have her wisps of hair washed, this tummy had stuck out above the bubbles and a small puddle of bath water collected in the dip of her belly-button. If she leaned forward for a toy boat or a duck, her chest compacted into a little baby-fat cleavage. Stella's cheeks got bigger and bigger and shinier and shinier, and she learned how to do a nasty fake simper, with a wrinkle of her nose and a gracious incline of her head. Her real smile was so much nicer – she had an unforgettable dolphin mouth, with lips which drew apart and up exactly like velvet stage curtains swishing open at the start of the opera.

Stella had always been beautiful, and she'd always known it. All the babies in my classes seemed like pale imitations.

I wondered why I felt so maternal towards Stella. Had it always been that way? I remembered her birth again, and the way I'd had such a feeling of pride that anyone would think I'd given birth to her myself . . . had I not been ten years old, of course. She was a big, squashy, smiling, living Tiny Tears, and I treated her as such. Although perhaps the maternal feelings had only been established once she became my actual responsibility. Once I became all she had left.

As I talked, I watched the mothers and thought about what made a mother a mother: was it nature or nurture, birth or death, love or responsibility? There was nothing these women wouldn't do for their babies. They were gagging to learn how to massage them, cure their wind, soothe their cries – not just to make their own lives easier, but to make their babies happy, so they'd grow up stable and confident and loving.

My own birth mother had never done this. She'd never gone to the department store and agonized over which model of pram to buy, fingering Aircell blankets and bunny mobiles – not for me, anyhow. Even if there had been such things as baby massage courses in 1971, my birth mother would not have signed me up. All she had done was to push me out of her and then move on, without me.

As I guided the women through the basic strokes and feathery fingertip movements, watching them lovingly rub almond oil into their babies' tiny chests, I wished someone with great big gentle hands would come and smooth away the fist of misery in my own chest. I wondered what Gavin was doing, if his dark nervous hands were stroking someone else's body now, hesitantly, uncertainly, but thrilling with the touch of new flesh.

The babies' faces seemed to be glowing in the reflective light of their mothers' love; and I reaffirmed the decision which I'd been wavering about since meeting the man on the train.

I really *was* going to try and trace my birth mother this time, not just half-heartedly as I had before. Last time I'd given up at the first hurdle, partly because Stella needed me, and partly because I felt it somehow unseemly to go out and find a new set of parents to replace those I'd lost. Every time since then that I'd considered the prospect anew, Stella had manifested her continued need of me: boy trouble; funds needed for orthodontia; that dreadful time when she was accused of stealing from her Saturday job at Sainsbury's. There had always been some crisis which chased any thoughts of my birth mother out of my mind.

Until now. The previous night's row in itself had demonstrated several further things: Stella did not need me any more. She could fight her own battles; she was nineteen, an adult. No longer a helpless baby kicking on a changing mat; a spoilt toddler; or a woebegone ten-year-old orphan in a droopy black taffeta dress. I'd done what Mum and Dad would have wanted. Stella had never been taken into care, or abandoned by the system, like that man on the train. I personally had seen her through first periods and GCSEs and ill-advised party outfits.

Surely I too had every right to look for a bit of mothering, now that I had the chance.

13

'When you were at school, did the fact that you were adopted make you feel you were different from your classmates; and if so, was this in a positive or a negative way?'

Most of the time, it didn't make me feel different. I had a mum and dad, same as everyone else.

Actually, for a long while it was Betsey who made me feel as if I was set apart from the others. I believed – probably mistakenly – that people were more impressed by the fact that I had an orang-utan as a playmate than the fact that I was adopted. Until one particular school trip to the zoo. After what happened on that trip, I really began to wonder whether I was special at all.

I can still see the pink slips of paper which Mrs Meades handed out to the class that afternoon, in the five minutes of pre-bell subdued hysteria; the pink slips which heralded the most eagerly anticipated event of my entire primary school career. As my slip skidded across the lid of my desk, carrying with it the faintest scent of Mrs Meades's Sea Jade perfume, I remembered catching sight of the words, and a thrill of excitement had rushed so fast up to my chest that it felt as if my school tie would roll up of its own accord.

Form 3Y will be going by coach to the orang-utan enclosure of London Zoo on October 23rd. To coincide with our forthcoming project on primates, Dr Barbara Victor will be giving a talk on her work with orang-utans. Your child will need a waterproof and a packed lunch. Cost £2. Please sign and return the slip below to confirm your permission.

After school I catapulted myself and my satchel through the front door, waving the form and yelling, 'Mum, Mum, you didn't tell me it was definitely happening!'

Mum was studying at the kitchen table, surrounded by piles of books and notepads, her huge glasses teetering on the very tip of her nose and several blotches of fountain pen ink decorating her fingers. She was still wearing her flowery vinyl apron, which her pregnant belly had pushed out so far that it almost touched the edge of the table in front of her. A delicious smell of baking scones drifted around the room.

'Well, I didn't want to tell you until all the details were worked out. Besides, it wasn't up to me to let you know. I won't be there as your mother, I'll be there as Dr Victor.'

'I know, I know, but isn't it brilliant? I can't wait for them all to meet Betsey. Do you think she'll do that thing where she pretends to clean my glasses? I hope she doesn't wee on my foot again, though, that would be so embarrassing. Will you come on the coach with us?' I flung myself at her, wrapping my arms around her middle, the vinyl apron forming a cool slippery barrier between us. Laughing, Mum lifted the apron up and stuck my head underneath it so that my face rested on the familiar warmth of her taut stomach instead.

'Hello, baby brother-or-sister,' I mouthed against her, pressing my cheek firmly down in the hope of feeling a kick.

'No, I'll probably just meet you there. I want to take the car so I can go to the library afterwards. I hope Wayne will be better by then – his flu's been dragging on for weeks. The vet came again yesterday.'

I nodded sympathetically, still buried under the apron, although I was somewhat scared of Wayne. Wayne was Betsey's father: five feet five, with a seven-foot arm span and an impressive beard, and he did not much approve of my friendship with his daughter. Having him lying feebly on the straw in the next cage was considerably less nerve-racking than having him swinging along the fence which separated us, yelling at me, as he usually did.

'Are you making scones? Can I have one?' I emerged back out into the warm scented kitchen, cheeks flushed and hair coming adrift from the bobble securing my ponytail. Mum adjusted it for me, and stroked my face.

'Yes, darling. I made them for you. Get the jam out of the larder please, and we'll have one together.'

The twenty-third had dawned clear and cold. A coach, with long droopy wing mirrors like Denis Healey's eyebrows, wheezed up to the school gates at eight-forty-five, and we were allowed on, jostling and sniggering, to stake our places by the great big windows, all the better to make faces out of. While most of my classmates piled towards the back, satchels and lunchboxes bumping along the seats, I, without hesitation, took the prime position at the front nearest the driver.

The driver was a tiny little man, no bigger than most of us nine- and ten-year-olds. He had an unlit cigarette tucked behind his ear, as if to prove that, despite his size, he *was* old enough to be in charge of this large vehicle.

110

I felt so bursting with pride that my feet barely seemed to touch the steps as I ascended. This was my day. Darrell Hawkes tried to pinch me as he went past, but I stuck my nose in the air and ignored him. Whereas we were all togged up in macs and anoraks and duffel coats, Darrell wore nothing warmer than a T-shirt which bore a peeling decal reading, 'If I said you had a beautiful body, would you hold it against me?' His nose dripped like a faulty tap, he really did eat worms – I'd seen him do it – and he already had a criminal record for shoplifting. Everybody hated him.

My friend Esther climbed on last, late as usual. 'Can I sit with you?'

I hesitated. I had been entertaining a swottish hope that Mrs Meades would ask that question, so that I could fill her in with more details of my intimate knowledge of the primates we were about to visit. But Mrs Meades had already settled herself across the aisle, her register sticking out of the top of her big plastic shopping bag, and her legendary enormous furry boots filling up the entire space between her seat and the back of the driver's booth. People stopped in the street and stared at those boots when she wore them. They were luxuriantly, opulently furry, like two well-groomed Persian cats. The whole effect was of a strange hybrid, half teacher, half yeti; something that might have escaped from a zoo in a Roald Dahl book.

'OK,' I said to Esther, who scrambled up onto the seat next to me and opened her lunchbox, pulling out a packet of Skips.

'Want some?'

'Yes please. Are you looking forward to seeing the orang-utans?'

Esther shrugged. 'Yeah. Though I'd rather see the elephants. Orannatans are boring.'

I felt as if she had just insulted my family, and so when she proffered the Skips, I took a much bigger handful than was strictly polite. The truth was, whilst acting like some kind of junior primate specialist, I had somewhat played down the closeness of my actual relationship with Betsey. I'd instinctively felt, even from a young age, that it might make me a target for ridicule to my classmates. Any form of difference was frowned upon amongst the pupils of Linley Road Junior School. You could be viciously prodded in the playground for not knowing all the words to 'The Big Ship Sails on the Alley Alley O'; or for wearing glasses, as I'd discovered to my cost on the day that I first got mine. I'd been in the first year then, and so mortified that I had actually walked into the classroom backwards.

So, regardless of how proud I was of my enduring friendship with an orang-utan, I was also aware that if I overplayed it, it could be a potentially ostracizable offence, on a par with poor Rosemary Thatcher's burns.

Rosemary was in 3R. The day before she joined the school, all the teachers had had a quiet word with their classes, telling us that we were to be nice to her. That a terrible fire which had started in a chip pan in her house, when she was little, had left her with some scars. I had imagined that these would be long white scars like the ones found on pantomime villains and picture-book bank robbers, but the scars on Rosemary's face weren't like that. Her whole face was a red weal, with twisty pink bits around her eyes, nose and mouth. She looked as if she had been dropped into a pot of boiling water, and my stomach shrank and contracted every time I saw her. I was consumed with the urge to befriend her, but every time I saw her sitting alone on a bench, the one furthest away from the portable goalpost in the playground where the big boys congregated, I just couldn't think what I could possibly say to her. Her aloof distance scared me as much as her boiled cheeks.

So although most of my fellow third years knew that I went to the zoo a lot because my mum worked there, none of them really had the whole picture, not even

Esther. I had decided it was time to change all that. I hugged myself in anticipation of the awe on their faces when they saw me walk amongst the orang-utans issuing commands, like a lion-tamer subduing the mighty beasts in a circus ring. Well, if I was lucky, Betsey would give me a cuddle. 3Y would be so impressed that not even Darrell Hawkes would ever consider teasing me about it. I prayed Betsey would be generous with her affections and not having an off day.

The coach pulled away, the tiny little driver swinging the immense steering wheel around and narrowly avoiding a row of parked cars as he eased his way out onto the main road. He clicked on a radio, and speakers filled the interior with a high, breathy, squeaky woman's voice – I later found out that it was Fern Kinney, singing 'Together We Are Beautiful'. He sang along, only about two octaves lower and out of tune. 'Together we are beautiful! Oh, so beautiful!' he growled, his fag dropping ash onto his stay-press trousers as we barrelled along the ring road. His legs were so skinny that the trousers seemed all crease and nothing else.

I didn't speak much to Esther after that. She ate the remainder of her Skips, and I gazed out of the window unseeing, dreaming of the moment of glory when I was to be the only one allowed inside Betsey's cage, and my classmates would realize that I was the special one, the lucky one, the chosen one.

On arrival at the zoo, we traipsed in a straggly crocodile towards the orang-utan enclosure, my hot dry hand resting in Esther's Skip-sticky one, Mrs Meades's boots stroking each other as she strode noise-lessly in the lead.

Mum was already there, a white lab coat straining at the buttons across her bump. 'There's your mum.' Esther was finally beginning to sound impressed. And not before time, I thought.

With only a tiny cursory wave of acknowledgement to me, Mum led us all around the outside of the enclosure, pointing out the orang-utans' habitat, discussing their diets and exercise preferences, and touching on their mating rituals. Darrell Hawkins of course sniggered uncontrollably at the mere mention of the word 'mating', but my mother was a trouper, and took no notice.

'That's Wayne over there,' I said in a loud stage whisper to Esther, unable to control myself any longer. 'He's had the flu, but he's better now. He's Betsey's dad.'

Mum half smiled, half frowned at me to be quiet. Then she gathered us all around her, and announced, 'OK, children, we're going inside now. There's rather a lot of you, so please try and be quiet so you don't overwhelm or frighten them.'

We filed inside the big stable-like building, thick glass separating us from the orang-utans. Wayne was still wandering around outside, but Pru and Maisie, Betsey's sisters, were loping about, occasionally sitting down and tearing off a leaf to nibble, their long legs folding beneath them like collapsible pushchairs. There was no sign of Betsey.

I shot a look at Mum. *Where is she?* Mum pointed at the sleeping quarters and raised her eyebrows, but I shook my head back. I didn't think Betsey could be in there; she rarely slept during the day. A faint uneasy feeling began to creep over me. Mr Jenkins, the zookeeper, wouldn't allow me inside their house unless it was just Betsey and I together – the other ones weren't nearly so friendly with me.

Mr Jenkins appeared in the doorway, his shiny pate and buck teeth gleaming under the spotlights of the enclosure. Like Mrs Meades and her boots, he resembled some sort of composite from the natural world: half egg, half chipmunk. He smiled goofily at Mrs Meades, perhaps recognizing a kindred spirit, but she didn't notice, as she had got a small faecal-stained piece of straw snarled up in the fur of one of her boots, and was clearly trying to work out how to extract it without touching it. Then Mr Jenkins spotted me – largely because I was waving frantically at him – and beckoned me over. My chest puffed up with pride, and I pushed my way through the group and over to his side.

'Hello, young Emma,' he said. 'I'm sorry, love, but Betsey's a bit under the weather today. She's coming down with that flu that's going around.'

'Where is she?' I was torn between concern for Betsey, a sense of crushing disappointment, and enjoyment of my classmates' curious faces.

'She's in bed, love. Best leave her alone—'

Just then, I saw Betsey's skinny red arm stretch out from her straw boudoir, followed by a pair of bleary eyes as she cautiously began to emerge.

'There she is, Mr Jenkins! Oh, please can I go and see her? Please, just for a minute?' Hopping anxiously from foot to foot, I turned around to appeal to Mum. 'Mummy, please?'

Mum made a 'leave me out of it' face. By now my class were riveted, and I was desperate. This would be my only opportunity. I rushed up to the glass and knocked on it, waving madly across at Betsey. It was true, she didn't look well. Her eyes had a sorry, dead appearance, and her hair was lacklustre. She grinned faintly at me, but it was nothing that anyone else would've noticed. Then she sat down and listlessly picked a few fleas off her thigh.

Mr Jenkins frowned sympathetically at me. 'I'm sorry, Emma, but the answer's no. She's been in a very bad mood all morning, and I'm getting the vet over to take a look at her later. You don't feel much like playing when you're poorly now, do you? Same with Betsey. Pop back in again next week, and I expect she'll be right as rain again.'

Next week! Next week was no good. Next week, my entire class wouldn't be watching as I demonstrated my Dr Doolittlesque empathy with our closest animal relatives. I burst into tears. My class began to titter awkwardly, and Darrell Hawkes chanted, *sotto voce*, 'Em-ma Victor loves the monkeys, Em-ma Victor loves the monkeys . . .' He started to lope in a circle around me, his bare goosepimpled arms hanging down in bracket shapes in front of him, making chimpanzee noises and occasionally beating his puny chest. Mrs Meades gave him a clip round the ear, but the damage was done. What I had most feared had come to pass: I was now an object of ridicule.

Mum led me outside by the elbow and told me to pull myself together, I was making a big fuss about nothing and embarrassing myself. She gave me a cuddle, though, and made me blow my nose, but it didn't make any difference.

When we got on the coach to go home again, Esther went and sat near the back with Julia Pidgeon. Julia, unfortunately, lived up to her name, with a fat stomach, skinny legs, and the worst pigeon-toes I'd ever seen, and I knew that Esther didn't even like her that much. They both played tenor recorder in our recorder group, and there was always a lot of argy-bargy going on around the trembling skeleton of their reluctantly shared music stand.

Perilously close to tears again, I wandered further on down the aisle in search of a seat, but they were all taken except one empty one next to Rosemary Thatcher.

'Hello,' I said nervously, thinking that at least now I'd be able to talk to her properly. I slid in next to her, still sniffing, but feeling a little bit better. Perhaps Rosemary Thatcher would be my new best friend – the tragedy and romance of her marred beauty and otherness had always been far more appealing to me than boring old Esther. The most exotic thing about Esther was her frilly ankle socks. 'Can I sit here?'

Rosemary muttered something which I couldn't hear, and looked away.

'They're really brilliant, aren't they, orang-utans? Did you know that they can swing distances of up to thirty feet? I wish I could do that, don't you?'

Rosemary turned back to me, her disfigured face impassive, staring at me out of her slits of eyes. 'Go away, Emma Victor,' she said. 'You're weird.'

Getting up without a word, I fled down to the front of the coach again, curled up in a window seat in the five-row oasis of emptiness between Mrs Meades and the first lot of children, and wept hot, silent, bitter tears all the way back to Acton.

Betsey didn't want me. Esther didn't want me. Even Rosemary didn't want me. All the magic was gone – for ever, I thought. And when the baby arrived, I knew it would be much, much worse.

14

But, of course, I was wrong. However strong my love for Betsey had been, it wasn't a patch on how I felt for Stella, from the moment I first saw her.

Betsey had died a few weeks after that fateful zoo trip, carried off by the same flu her father had contracted. I'd been utterly grief-stricken for days and, despite completing a terrific project for Mrs Meades – a sort of posthumous biography of Betsey – my classmates remained unimpressed. I'd thought my life was over – until the first time Mum picked me up from school accompanied by Stella in her pram. All the girls in my class coochy-cooed over her so rapturously that, by association, I began to feel special again. My next project was entitled 'My Little Sister', in which I showed everyone photographs of Stella in the bath; and even Rosemary Thatcher managed a smile at the sight of her.

And now here we were, nineteen years later, my little sister and I, on a wintry Sunday afternoon. It was the weekend after our row and, even though we'd made up, the peace was a fragile gossamer one, flimsy with hidden truths and unspoken secrets.

I looked across at her as she talked without

listening, kneeling on the floor, her hair snaking across her face and her long fingers flicking over the pages of a large illustrated book. I tried to remember the sight of her lying pinkly in that pram at the school gates, but found that I was having trouble imagining a time when Stella couldn't talk. It's funny, I thought, how the people you love can drive you so far round the bend.

The wind was howling with such volume around the window frames that Stella had to raise her voice to be heard above it, which irritated me even more, since I was trying to finish *Temples of Delight*. She was browsing through a book of eighties fashions for a project she was doing at college; wittering inanely and endlessly in the way she only ever did with me, and had been doing since she was two years old. It still wound me up – it was like being trapped underneath a waterfall.

'I sometimes think,' she said dreamily, 'of all the clothes I've ever made, in my whole life, from dolls' clothes to those awful naff things I made in primary school – you know, poncey blouses and that time I tried to make jeans, and that weird holey jumper that actually looked really punk, do you remember the one? I just wonder if one day someone will try and track them all down for a complete retrospective of my career – wouldn't that be hilarious?'

I tsked at her. 'Dream on, Stella. I don't think any-one's ever going to exhibit the dresses that Vivienne Westwood made for her teddy when she was six, so I imagine you'll be safe.'

Stella flicked through the pages until something caught her eye. 'Ooh, look, it's those belts. Suzanne and I were talking about them the other day – do you remember them, Em? Sort of canvas webbing, they came in lots of different colours and the buckle end always dangled down, and on men they were supposed to be like penis extensions. Look.'

I ignored the stretched-out book being thrust under my nose. 'Stella, I'm trying to read. Leave me alone.'

Stella was getting annoyed too. 'They're coming back in again. I just wanted to know if you'd ever had one, that's all.'

'No.'

'Did you have any legwarmers then?'

'Yes, I had legwarmers. Pink ones.'

'Suze and I were watching *Fame* reruns on cable the other night, and it was so crap. I couldn't believe that they were actually supposed to be talented. *I* could play the viola better than that skinny bird, and they're all so ugly!'

'She played the cello, not the viola; get your facts right. I'm going to finish my book – in peace.'

I marched out of the room, picking *Temples of Delight* off the arm of the sofa on my way. I'd always secretly thought that the cellist from *Fame*, all eyes and cheekbones and long delicate fingers, was absolutely the most beautiful woman ever, and had yearned to look like her. But remembering back I supposed that her character, Julie, had been a bit wet really. Funny how people's ideas of beauty changed, I thought as I flopped down onto my bed. Stella was right, none of them would really be considered that gorgeous these days: not that dopey Bruno with his big soppy eyes, or cheesily hard Leroy and his shiny pecs, even that little black girl, the main one. Irene Cara. She was cute, but there'd been a whole gaggle of that type of girl on TV in the early eighties: the blind one in the Lionel Ritchie video, Jennifer Beals in *Flashdance*, the female cast of *Cosby*. However much they said eighties fashions were back in again, you still didn't see that shaggy, permed winsome look any more. Thankfully.

I wondered in which era I might have been most fashionable – with what length hair, what style glasses? I had the sort of hair which always looked scruffy, no matter what I did to it. It wasn't wavy enough to be curly, but too kinky to be entirely straight. I got the odd blonde highlight, but nobody ever seemed to notice, even in my dark hair.

I was a little envious of Stella's mad hairstyle, even though it would be a bit too high maintenance for me. She had to groom and style and pamper it, constantly putting gunk in it to keep the waves in place. Anyway, she thought *I* was lucky – my hair might not be all that special, but my eyes were lovely. I knew I ought to have shown them off a bit more. They were my best feature, and I looked better when I wore my contact lenses; but they were so scratchy in my eyes. People always assumed that I hid behind my glasses; only Stella understood that I actually wore my glasses when I felt *more* confident, not less.

I often wondered if I'd be more confident if I had blood relatives around to compare myself against: a genetic map charting my future, so I could know whether I'd still be good-looking at fifty, or whether the crumbling would accelerate out of control. Whether I'd get leaner with age, or whether at forty my bum would drop. And, much more seriously, whether there were any nasty surprises lolling around in the undergrowth, like a hand-grenade with its pin pulled out: breast cancer, Alzheimer's, diabetes. I didn't like surprises.

For a second the man on the tube came back to me, his eyes green and sparkling, the only clean part of him. I wonder how he came to be so alone, where *his* family were?

I still hadn't done anything concrete to begin my own search. Although my resolve was still strong, it seemed like such a momentous task. Come on, I told myself. Think. Be logical. You've always been a logical kind of person. It was on all your school reports: *Emma has a very logical mind and methodical approach*. Supertramp's *Breakfast in America* was one of the first albums I ever bought, because it had 'The Logical Song' on it.

Much to my irritation, however, every time I tried to think how to go about finding my mother, the face of

Julie from *Fame* loomed repeatedly into my consciousness instead; her dreamy eyes, the elegantly skinny knees sticking out from the long, broderie anglaise-festooned skirt on either side of the big shiny cello, the upward tilt of her chin as she sawed resolutely away. But try as I might, I just couldn't remember the actress's name. It was on the tip of my tongue for days.

The doorbell rang just as Stella was getting out of the shower the following Saturday morning. I wasn't yet awake, but the sound penetrated my dream, and before I was even aware of moving, I found that I'd hauled myself out of bed and was standing squinting blearily out of the window. Even without my glasses on, I recognized the thinning halo of hair and the toes of the red All Stars which was all I could see of our visitor.

'It's Mack,' I called, groggily, rubbing my eyes.

'Oh crikey. Shall we pretend we're out?' replied Stella, tying her towel more firmly around her breasts as she came into my room.

'No. Don't be cruel to him. Anyway, I haven't seen him for ages,' I mumbled.

Besides being a mate of mine, Mack was also the self-appointed handyman of the Victor household. He lived four doors down from us, and Stella had sussed him as a potential free Mr Fixit when she spotted him screwing up a security light outside his front door. One quick burst of the Stella charm was all that was required, with the odd top-up when she felt particularly sorry for him; and Mack was now at our beck and call – replacing washers, mending hairdriers and, once, escorting off the premises a particularly mammoth spider which even I couldn't face. But the best corollary of all this free DIY was that he and I had become good friends.

I was very fond of Mack. At first, I'd wished that Stella found him fanciable, since he was so clearly taken with her, and occasionally entertained the faint hope that they would get it together. Not married or anything, but I did think it would be good for her to have a long-term relationship, to stop all this ... *gadding about*, as Mum might have said.

But despite my encouragement, Stella remained adamant that he was too old, his hair was too weird, and he was too much of a nerd. She wasn't even impressed by his very credible job as a freelance television producer – mostly because we'd never seen any evidence of him actually doing any work, and were both beginning to wonder if he was making it up. Eventually I realized that Stella was right. Mack was lovely, but just wasn't attractive, not in that kind of way.

'All right then, but will you answer the door while I get dressed?'

'But I'm not dressed, either.'

'I know but, with all due respect, it's not your legs he's going to be looking at, is it?'

'God, you're so vain. Well, I suppose it's time I got up. I've got a massage at twelve-thirty.'

Stella disappeared into her bedroom, dropping her towel en route to reveal the tiny owl tattoo on her pert fashion-student's bottom, as I came grumpily out of my own room, pulling on a thick jumper over my short pajamas.

'Mum would have a fit if she could see you now, with your tongue and that ... thing on your bum. She'd say I wasn't looking after you properly.' I felt cross, although now that I thought about it, Mum had been pretty laid-back. I seemed to be trying to squeeze triangle-shaped memories into round holes of truth. How odd.

Stella confirmed what I'd been thinking. 'She wouldn't have had a fit. I bet she'd have been totally cool about it. Plus I bet she'd think you've done a great job taking care of me.'

Her voice was muffled as she struggled into a very tight silky polo-neck, then jeans, a glittery belt, and thick red hiking socks. Unexpected tears stung the backs of my eyes as I plodded, touched by Stella's remark, down to the front door.

'Hi, Mack, sorry I took so long. The intercom's broken again.'

'Hi, Emma. Well, I'll have a look at it for you if you like, but I don't know much about them. Guess what, I brought something for you.'

'Really? What? Come in.'

Mack's pale hair bounced around his head as he walked up the stairs. If it had been longer, he would have looked like one of those fibre-optic lamps, so that if you switched him on he'd light up purple and crimson and turquoise.

He thrust an HMV bag into my hands. 'You said you'd never got around to buying it on CD.'

I opened the bag and extracted a copy of *The Head On The Door* by The Cure. 'Oh wow, fantastic. This'll bring back memories. Thank you so much, Mack, you really shouldn't have done. Make yourself at home, and I'll put some coffee on.'

Mack looked pleased. 'It was nothing, really. It was on sale in HMV and I just remembered our conversation, that's all.'

Stella came into the room at the tail end of the conversation, clutching her make-up bag, and clocked that gifts were being distributed.

'Hi, Mack,' she said. 'What's that?' She pointed at the CD I had left on the kitchen counter.

'Hello, Stella. You look great. Oh, that's just a little present for Emma.'

'Right.' Stella was very put out. I knew just from the tone of her voice that she was thinking, Well, where's mine then? She could be so spoilt sometimes, I thought. As if I'd expect any friend of *hers* to bring me a gift.

'Mack,' I said, 'did you ever watch *Fame*?'

'Oh, you're not still on about that, are you?' Stella turned her back on Mack and went over to the microwave to apply lipstick, using its shiny reflective door as a mirror.

'I think it was before my time,' said Mack, obligingly racking his brains. 'Why?'

'I'm trying to remember the name of the actress who played the cellist. I think she was in *Footloose* too. It's bugging me.'

'Er, sorry, I don't have a clue.' Mack was momentarily crestfallen, then suddenly brightened. 'Look it up on the Net. I'll find it for you, if you like.'

His face lit up at the brilliance of the idea, and he cantered down the hall to our secondhand computer in the living room, which he had recently sourced, delivered, set up and installed software on. 'Great, thanks, Mack,' I called, following him in with two of the three coffees I'd made. Beyond a knowledge of basic wordprocessing – i.e. that clicking on the little square at the edge of a document made it bigger – and Solitaire (6 games won, 251 lost), our new computer was a bit of a mystery to me. I could just about write up invoices and do correspondence for my aromatherapy practice, but, shamefully, I was probably the only person left in the developed world who hadn't yet got to grips with the Internet. I hadn't had the time or the inclination and, frankly, I found it all somewhat sinister.

'OK, now, here we go. Let's do a search on *Fame* and maybe, let's see, the eighties.'

Mack was all businesslike and nerdy, an overgrown lead character in some Hollywood teen movie about the boy-whizzkid who taps into the Pentagon's computer and disarms a few nuclear warheads, in between rounds of *Tomb Raider* and saving his parents' marriage. I still marvelled that he did anything as glamorous as make television programmes.

The search proved not to be very helpful, mostly mentioning Irene Cara's hit of the theme tune rather than the TV series itself. We switched to a different tack, tracking down the film of the series instead, but it turned out that the skinny cellist wasn't even in the movie version. Eventually we got a result by searching for *Footloose*.

'Here it is!' I shrieked, peering through Mack's hair at the screen, and accidentally inhaling a few fine strands. 'Look, cast list! Um ... Kevin Bacon, blah blah blah ... LORI SINGER! How could I forget that name? Lori Singer, Lori Singer – great. That's such a load off my mind.'

'Any more for any more, before I log off?' Mack asked.

'What do you mean?'

'Do you need anything else finding out while we're on-line? The World Wide Web is your lobster – and I know what a technophobe you are.'

'Oyster,' said Stella. She had finished her make-up and joined us, out of joint curiosity and boredom.

'I knew that, too,' said Mack haughtily. 'Hey, let's look *you* up.' He tapped in Stella's name. After a brief pause the results came up: *Your search has found 12 mentions including 'Stella Victor'.*

'Fab,' she cried. 'Is that really me?'

Mack scrolled down. 'Haven't you ever looked yourself up before? I thought that's what everyone did as soon as they got an Internet connection.'

'Nah. I was waiting until I'm famous. More gratifying then. Still – twelve mentions? That's not a bad start.'

Stella wasn't joking. She dreamed of seeing her face on posters in the Underground; perhaps publicizing her flagship store, or promoting her new autobiography. The line 'A Little Orphan With Big Talent' would probably feature. She once admitted to me that she got prematurely annoyed and offended at the mere thought of some lout sticking a blob of chewing gum on the part of the poster corresponding to the end of her nose, or a drawn-on moustache. She sulked for days when Stella McCartney got the job as designer for Chloë – *she'd* wanted to be the first famous fashion designer called Stella.

Mack laughed. 'I have to warn you, though, most of these mentions will probably be duplicates or sites with people called Stella and Victor in them.'

Stella's name came up, legitimately, in two documents: one mentioning her runner-up status in a group project she'd done at college last term, and the other as an alumnus of her old school.

'Wow. I'm on the Web, therefore I am. Well, it's a start, I suppose. Your turn, Em. Go on, Mack.'

'No, don't bother, Mack, please. Why don't we try Mum and Dad? I bet Mum's got loads of mentions for her dissertations, and there might be something about Dad's cameras. Barbara and Ted Victor.'

I suddenly wanted to see their names on the wavy screen, to feel that they still existed, even if only in cyberspace. They did both come up on the search, several times, but the contexts and references were so tedious that after trawling through a couple of sites which had published their research papers on, respectively, 'The Endangered Habitat of *Pongo pygmaeus abelli* (the Sumatran Orang-utan)', and 'Design and Construction of the Victortilt (Mk II)' – reproduced without permission, I noted, on an amateur photographer's website – the novelty soon wore thin, and Stella told Mack to log off.

I, however, remained staring at the blank screen, struck with a gigantic realization. I absolutely could not believe that I had never thought of it before. It was so incredibly, glaringly *obvious* . . . I'd have to ask Mack to help me, though. I wasn't sure which of those search engine thingies to use, and I couldn't ask Stella. Not yet. But at least it would be a start; the start I'd been putting off making for two weeks.

Thanks, Lori Singer, I told her, and imagined her like an angel, smiling beatifically at me and playing me a special little aria on the cello, glad that she could have been of assistance. Because, the thing was, I already knew my birth mother's surname.

After finding that letter with her Christian name and

address on it, ten years ago, I'd phoned up the reference library in Salisbury, where a lovely old librarian with a tweedy-sounding voice had gone and looked her up for me on the local Electoral Register. I later found out exactly the same information by the more straightforward method of sending off for my birth certificate, but at the time I hadn't realized you could do that, and I'd been utterly elated at my discovery. I had sent my own letter again, bursting with renewed hope and unbearable anticipation, this time with her full name on the front – Ann Paramor – and 'PLEASE FORWARD'; but once again it had been returned to me, either stubbornly or blithely unopened, and all my earlier resolve had crumbled away, defeated.

I turned to Mack. 'Are you busy tonight? Do you fancy coming round to watch *Men In Black* on TV with me? There's beer in the fridge, and Stella's going out, so I could do with the company.' I could ask him then, I thought. When Stella's out.

'Aren't you seeing Gavin tonight?'

I narrowed my eyes at Stella when Mack wasn't looking, willing her not to say anything, but she was engrossed in a copy of last month's *Company* magazine, and didn't seem to have heard.

'No. So, are you up for it, or what?'

'Sure. I'll come round at about eight then, shall I?'

15

Stella was leaving to meet Suzanne at the pub just as Mack came back that evening. She was dressed in one of her own designs: a PVC and cotton miniskirt with trapped rose petals, and her legs flowed out like solidified golden syrup from underneath it.

'Inspired by natural forms,' she remarked smugly, as she noticed Mack's pale-fringed eyes tracking over her cinematically.

'So I see,' he replied, not meaning the skirt at all. I gave him a look, which was lost on him until Stella had left the flat in a cloud of CK One, banging the front door behind her, my exhortations to be careful hanging in the air, mingling with the perfume.

'She's very easy on the eye, your sis,' he said wistfully. 'It's such a pity she's so young.'

'Yeah.' I flipped the top off a beer and handed it to Mack. 'I really worry about her,' I said abruptly.

'Well, you shouldn't,' he replied, taking a long swig and putting his palm over his mouth to suppress a little burp. 'Stella's old enough and—' He evidently realized that by no stretch of the imagination could the expression 'old enough and ugly enough' ever be applied to Stella, so he stopped. 'Old enough to look after herself,' he concluded. 'I mean it, Emma. She'll do whatever she's going to do, and she'll be fine. She's not stupid. In fact, Stella is one of the most self-possessed women I've met, even at her age. She knows what she wants.'

'She's had enough practice where men are concerned, I suppose,' I said, changing my mind about the cup of tea I was making, and helping myself to a beer as well. Perhaps if I drank less tea, I too would be going out on dates as often as Stella.

The stupidity of the thought made me laugh. Stella had men of all ages falling at her platform soles, and it had everything to do with her blonde hair, porcelain skin and Kate Moss body, and bugger all to do with how much tea she did or didn't drink.

'She's ten years younger than me but she's still probably been out with more than twice the blokes that I have. And she and her mates are so *experienced*. They talk about all this stuff that I hardly even know about. God, for all I know, she might even be *doing* it!'

Stella and Suzanne behaved like men, as far as I could see: strutting about, proud of their sexuality and the discerning manner in which they erroneously believed they distributed it. The picture I had of them, flitting around from one preternaturally hormonal boy to another like two bumblebees bouncing around inside different flowers, nothing in it for them except the thrill of fresh pollen dusting their noses, could have scared me witless, if I let it.

'Doing what? Having sex?'

'No – although I know she is. I meant, doing all the stuff that they giggle about. Frottage. Watersports . . .' I couldn't think of anything else.

Mack laughed. 'I'd say it's extremely unlikely. Since when have teenagers ever done more than about five per cent of the things they discuss? Give yourself a break, why don't you? She's an adult. What she gets up to in the privacy of her own room is really none of your business.' His face assumed a wistful expression, and it was not difficult to imagine what he was thinking.

We adjourned to the living room. 'Have a seat. The film doesn't start till nine,' I said, waving an arm towards our plum sofa, where we sat in silence for a few minutes, drinking our beers and listening to the traffic noises outside the window. The sound of cars passing reminded me of the suck and crash of waves on a shore.

'Haven't you had many boyfriends then?'

'No. A few flings here or there before Gavin, but he's been the only serious one . . .' I tailed off. I still didn't know why I hadn't told Mack about Gavin finishing with me. I suppose I felt it was too humiliating to admit. If Mack had been a girl, I'd have told him like a shot, but ours wasn't really that sort of friendship. I had a sudden craving for a close girlfriend or two: that combination of fan club, personal shopper, shrink and punchbag, all with a shared secret vocabulary, that Stella had with Suzanne.

'Stella must have started young, to have been out with twice as many boys as you.'

'Actually,' I said, pulling a scratchy little feather out of the sofa cushion, 'we started at the same age. Thirteen. The difference was that I didn't get another date for about four years after my first one, and she's had a different boyfriend approximately every month since then.'

'Well, at least with all that experience you can be sure she won't let anyone try it on with her. Innocence is probably the biggest danger, especially combined with drop-dead beauty like Stella's.'

'Whatever,' I said, morosely.

Mack glanced at me, and realized that perhaps he'd been extolling Stella's physical virtues a little excessively. 'So, tell me about your first-ever date,' he said, nudging me into a smile.

'God . . . Well, he was called Pat Short, which was a bit unfortunate because he was this teeny little second year from the boys' grammar. He looked like he ought to have a catapult and a copy of the *Beano* sticking out of his back pocket.'

Mack laughed, stretching back on the sofa and sticking his red All Stars out in front of him. I really hated those All Stars. No wonder he couldn't pull, I thought bitchily.

'Where did you meet?'

'In the children's library. I was getting some more Dr Seuss books out for Stella. I don't know what Pat's excuse for being in there was – he probably thought that all those miniature tables and chairs might make him seem bigger. He slipped me a note.'

'How romantic.'

'Wait – you haven't heard the best bit. It said something like "Do you want to go out with me?" and it was signed "Hawkwind".'

Mack spluttered into his beer. '*Hawkwind?* As in the band? I thought you said his name was Pat?'

'It was. He just liked Hawkwind, that's all. Of course, I'd never heard of them, and so I thought some tall, gorgeous, nut-brown Cherokee was writing me notes, but when I looked around, all I saw was this undersized schoolboy with National Health glasses like mine on. He was sort of gurning at me and staring at my boobs like he had X-ray vision, so then I realized it must be him.'

'Did you have boobs at thirteen?'

'Yes, actually. The trouble is, they stopped growing when I was fourteen.' I cupped my hands over my chest protectively, trying to imagine that they were Gavin's hands on my bare breasts, like that Janet Jackson album cover. I felt my nipples harden at the thought – it was an odd sensation, to be simultaneously aroused and depressed. I wondered, yet again, what Gavin was up to that evening.

'So then what?'

'Oh, well, to cut a long story short, we went to see *Footloose* together, but I left before the film had even begun.'

132

The date had been a disaster from the start. It was just after Easter, and, to save having to buy overpriced jelly babies in the cinema, I'd brought with me the large box of Maltesers I'd been given as an Easter gift: Mum and Dad had laid on an Easter egg hunt in the garden for Stella, and the Maltesers were a tacit acknowledgment of the fact that I was too old to hunt under bushes for my chocolate.

Once we had paid – individually – for our tickets, Pat had led me, with an authority belying his size, straight to the back row. We sat down, with him on my left, and I crinkled the cellophane off my Maltesers. As I offered the box to him, two things happened.

Firstly, he immediately slid his right arm around my shoulders, before the previews had even started. He was clearly aiming for my right breast, but unless his arm were suddenly to grow about eight inches, he didn't stand a chance. But he kept trying, valiantly pressing himself closer and closer to me until he was practically squashing me into my seat. I could smell the Brylcreem in his thick blond hair, and the warm teenage funk of Right Guard unsuccessfully disguising armpit sweat.

The second thing that happened was that his left hand began robotically stuffing Maltesers – *my* Maltesers – into his mouth. He reminded me of a game Stella had at home, called Hungry Hippos, where you had to make four primary-coloured hippos leap up and swallow as many yellow balls as you could, as fast as you could.

I recoiled in horror from this dual onslaught. Every time I tried to move either myself or my box of Maltesers, his relentless hands would follow, squeezing and cramming. It felt as if those hands had some kind of inbuilt homing instinct, since he never once looked at me or spoke to me. His eyes remained fixed on the screen. I closed the lid of the box, but his fingers slid beneath it. Then I placed the box on the floor by my feet, but he reached down and pulled it across to beneath his own feet. Before *Footloose* had even begun, I'd had enough. Ripping his arm away from where it was draped, tentacle-like, across my back, I stood up.

'If you want them all that much, why don't you just *finish them*!'

I dumped the box and the remaining six Maltesers over his head, where one stuck, unnoticed, in the Brylcreemed thatch, and pushed my way past the rest of the snogging couples in the back row, stepping on toes and kicking over buckets of popcorn. Pat Short gazed after me, open-mouthed, but made no attempt to follow.

When I got home I shut myself in the larder, sitting down on the hard concrete floor next to a sack of King Edwards, and sobbed without restraint. Dad heard me, opened the door, and squeezed in next to me.

'Aren't you supposed to be at the pictures?'

He hugged me to his chest, and I thought how different it felt to Pat's skinny insistent grip. I pushed my face into the warm cotton of his shirt.

'He . . . he . . . put his arm around me.'

Dad stroked my hair. 'Don't worry, chicken, I'm sure you told him what's what. But, on the other hand, who wouldn't want to put their arm around a gorgeous girl like you? Is that why you're back so early?'

Agonized, I lifted up my head so I could look him in the eyes. My glasses were partially steamed up with tears, making him seem edgeless, less substantial. 'No, Dad, I left because he . . . he . . . he . . .'

'*What?*' Now Dad was beginning to get worried. I could tell he was ready to go round to Pat Short's house and give him a good kicking, and I felt delighted. 'What, darling? Tell Daddy. It's OK. Shhh, tell Daddy.'

Taking a deep breath, I stammered, '*Daddy, he ate all my Easter Maltesers,*' before collapsing into a fresh storm of sobs. When I surfaced again, Dad's mouth was twitching. He bit the inside of his lip, and swiped a hand roughly across his face, as if trying to wipe away his grin. Then he tousled my hair, gave me another hug, and stood up, his hand resting on the shelf between a tin of peaches and a box of Quaker Oats.

'Come on, chicken. Let's go and have a cup of tea. You know what, I think Mum might just have one Easter egg left over. Shall we go and have a look?'

I never saw Pat Short again.

'Well, I don't know why you're looking so sad. It sounds like you had a lucky escape.'

'I was just thinking about Dad. He was always so good like that. You know, looking after us. We were his little girls.'

'Do you still miss him?'

'Massively.'

I stared out of the uncurtained window into the smoggy brown city night, trying to picture Dad's face, but I couldn't remember it, not as the face I'd known. I could only picture him from the photograph on the mantelpiece: big sideburns, hamming it up for the camera, frozen in a youth that had bypassed him two decades before. Those same twenty years in between were the years I'd been his daughter; seen him every day, bounced on his lap and cried on his shoulder, but now it was as if he hadn't even existed. Tears filled my eyes and I turned my head away so Mack couldn't see.

Now, I thought. *Tell him now*. Tell Mack you're adopted, and you need his help to look up your birth mother on the Internet. For Christ's sake, just do something to stop this hideous wallowing.

I wanted to tell Mack everything: from how much I loved it when people used to comment that I looked just like my father, right up to meeting the homeless man on the tube, and the feeling that I had to let go of Stella, and do something for myself. Tell him about all the confusion that was tangled up in my head, tormenting me.

But when it came to the crunch, I just couldn't. The

135

clarity and purpose I'd derived from finding Lori Singer that morning had trickled away, and I just felt too tired to explain the whole messy story. So yet again I copped out.

'Stella was thirteen when she went on her first date, too. Needless to say, hers was a completely different kettle of fish.' Furious with myself, I tried to inject a note of levity into my voice.

'How come?'

I wasn't sure whether Mack was being sensitive in playing along with my forced story, or whether he really hadn't noticed that I was upset. The latter, probably, I thought.

'He was five foot eleven, fifteen years old, already shaving. Richard Something, his name was. He picked her up in a cab, took her to a film, then to Pizza Express for dinner.'

I could still remember Richard standing there in the hall, gravely helping Stella into her coat and shaking hands with me, as I'd scrutinized him with extreme suspicion.

'Don't worry, um – Miss Victor. I'll look after her,' he'd said, and I had fought back the urge to grab him by his Stussy lapels and yell, 'You'd better, you jumped-up adolescent oik, or I'll remove your grillocks with a steak knife.'

Instead I'd just said, 'I'll pick you up from the restaurant at ten o'clock, Stella, OK? Have fun', and then spent the next four hours anxiously pacing the hall and wondering if I could get away with disguising myself and sitting at an adjacent table in the restaurant, to make sure he was behaving himself with my sister. Even back then I knew that it probably wasn't necessary to be so excessively over-protective, but I couldn't help it. It was as if I had to take on the combined protectiveness of Mum and Dad, plus an extra couple of ladlefuls to compensate for my own lack of experience in those situations. Was ten o'clock the right time? Should it be earlier? Later? Should I have offered to collect her or not? I remember wishing there was an Adolescent Dating Manual to which I could refer.

And here I was, six years later, still worrying about Stella.

'Come on then,' I said abruptly, hauling myself out of the sofa. 'I'll get us some more beers. The film's about to start.'

'Emma?'

'Yeah?' I held my breath, waiting for Mack to ask me what was really wrong, to offer me a shoulder to cry on, to tell me everything would be OK, and he'd help me trace my birth mother.

'What *is* frottage, anyway?'

I'd just have to ask Mack to help me with that Internet thing another time, I thought as I lay in bed later. When I'd had a bit more time to think about what I might be getting into. When I'd got a bit more energy.

To try and get myself to sleep, I was softly playing my recorder along to 'In the Army Now' by Status Quo, which I'd found on Radio Two. Not out of choice – I'd had a little browse through the radio stations, but most of them were broadcasting hard house, which was nigh on impossible to play along with.

I began to fall asleep still propped up on my pillows, loosely attached to my recorder; wondering vaguely what a psychiatrist would make of me, in bed alone with my lips around a long brown tubular instrument.

16

The next day, after Stella had gone to Camden to look for bargains, I got dressed, conducted a perfunctory hoover of the flat, and sat waiting in the spare room for my twelve o'clock appointment to arrive.

A stick of incense burned a trembling finger in the corner, and the crisp sheeted surface of the massage table was covered with a fresh strip of white paper from a large roll, similar to the sort found in doctors' surgeries. I hoped the effect was less clinical, however, thanks to the stack of fluffy lavender towels on top of the paper, the gentle ambient music floating over small wall-mounted speakers, and a bronze statue of Buddha in the fireplace. I was proud of this room. It was the only room in the flat that ever got hoovered right up to the skirting board.

The twelve o'clock client was late, but I hadn't really noticed how late. I'd been fetching a new bottle of sweet almond oil from the cupboard in the corner when I suddenly had to stop and sit down, as if my head could no longer support the weight of my thoughts.

Of course I'd always been curious about my birth mother, but only in an idle, abstract kind of way; I had always found it hard to believe that I could have been any happier with my real parents than I was with Mum and Dad. They were loving and mostly attentive and, besides, I didn't have anyone to compare them to. But, even as I thought this, I began to remember all the niggly little things I'd whitewashed over in the redecoration of my memories after their deaths.

The great prickly lump, like a conker shell, permanently in my throat at the thought that they couldn't possibly love me as much as they loved Stella. The way that Mum carried photographs of us both in her wallet, but while mine was a fuzzy snapshot of me in a snowsuit, from a distance, Stella's was a crystal-clear close-up, showing off each individual eyelash. The way that they gave Stella her own cat, when I'd always wanted one.

Hang on, though. Did I ever actually *tell* them that I was desperate for a cat? Surely I must have done – what child holds back from nagging their parents for their heart's desires? But on the other hand, perhaps my memory was a little wobbly. Perhaps I hadn't actually *realized* how much I wanted one, until Ffyfield strolled into Stella's chubby arms, rasping a reluctant kiss onto her irresistible cheek. After having an orang-utan in one's life, a pet cat might have seemed a little lame; so it was hard to be sure.

I lay down on the carpet and put my feet up against the wall, like an inverted bracket, to give my body a few minutes' extra relaxation before I had to massage. I'd found Lori Singer, just like that. Of course, Lori Singer was famous, and therefore much more likely to be on the Internet, but if Mack could find two bonafide mentions for Stella, who wasn't at all well known – much to her chagrin – then there must be a little bit of hope for me, too.

They were bound to have . . . what were they called? Plots? Pages? No, sites, that was it . . . sites for adopted people looking for real parents. Mack kept saying how you could find out anything on-line. It was the Information Superhighway. I heard on Radio Four that you could adopt a vegetable patch on the Internet, for God's sake. I stared at the ceiling, noticing how yellowish the paintwork looked in contrast with the pristine white walls. It upset me, the thought that clients might be lying there while I worked on their feet, thinking how badly the ceiling let the room down.

But I wouldn't have time to do anything about it in the near future, not with the other, much more pressing, issue at hand. I needed to phone Mack, immediately, and ask for his help. The only problem was, I couldn't remember where I'd put the piece of paper with his new mobile number on it. He'd said something about helping a colleague in an edit suite all that week, even on a Sunday, so I knew he wouldn't be at home.

I crept into Stella's bedroom, on secretive tiptoe even though she was out, and began to rummage for her filofax, in the vain hope that she might just have written the number down when he gave it to us. He was the only person who possessed a spare set of keys to our flat, and Stella locked herself out so regularly that she needed all his contact details to programme into her mobile.

The filofax could have been anywhere. There was so much stuff packed into the bedroom that it was hard enough to see the floor, let alone one small fur-covered address book. I gazed around despairingly, resisting the temptation to sweep all Stella's junk into several bin-bags and take it down to the two old ladies at the blind shop. They'd be in for a surprise if I did. Stella's outlandish clothes were all over the place, draped over a tailor's dummy by the window, or untidily shoved onto hangers on wheely rails down the side of the room. Feather boas, skimpy little vest tops, studded belts and sequinned long skirts jostled with hooded sweatshirts and a variety of decrepit leather and suede jackets bought at street markets.

Her designs lay around everywhere, in varying

stages of completion from paper to uncut fabric to the finished article. The bed in the middle was covered with bits of sari material and several yards of gingham. Her bedroom looked like a theatre dressing room or a photographer's studio, or an indoor version of the market stalls she frequented every Sunday morning as religiously as church.

It was Mum who'd first taught Stella to sew. By the time she was nine, Stella's success in the craft was on full view in the Victor household: in the neatly stitched embroidery on all our pillowcases; the casual jersey dresses she could almost make by herself; the jumpers she knitted for Ffyfield. It was the one thing in which Stella really excelled – her teachers were gratifyingly amazed when she would appear in school, yet again, with a homemade zip-up jacket or pearl-buttoned shirt or halter-necked top.

'I made this,' was practically her catchphrase. She courted the compliments with the subtle fervour of a medieval lady being wooed by her knight.

Ten years earlier, Mum had tried to teach me the same skills. We began, in the same way, with knitting. Unfortunately, Mum hadn't realized that the fact that I was left-handed would be such an obstacle, and within two abortive lessons had concluded that it was impossible to teach someone in a mirror image of how one learned it oneself. I could knit one row of stitches perfectly, if in slow motion: wrap the wool over the end of the needle, poke the other needle through – but after that I was lost.

'Sewing,' Mum had said. 'That'll be easier – it doesn't matter which hand you use. Come on, Emma, let's make a skirt for you!'

And I was thrilled, caught up in the excitement of going to the department store and choosing a pattern from the Little Miss Vogue collection; watching some beautiful cotton material being unwound in lush folds to be cut into skirt lengths on the counter, with the peculiarly satisfying dark metal sound of the scissors shearing through it; then buying all the matching accoutrements: zips, buttons, thread.

Disillusion crept in at the pattern-cutting stage. Even with Mum showing me where to cut, all the black lines and arrows and triangles on the horrible flimsy paper confused me, and I got it hideously wrong. The pattern ripped, or crumpled, or I found I'd cut it out a size too small . . . and that was the *easy* part.

'Relax, Emma darling. Your shoulders are up round your ears.'

'I can't *do* it!'

'You can. I promise, you can. Look, just tack these two bits together – no, these two, and then sew the waistband on. It's easy.'

'Mum! It's *not* easy . . . Why is the waistband all thick in the middle?'

'Ah. Good question. How did that happen? Here, give it to me and I'll redo it. You carry on tacking that seam.'

By the time the fabric was eventually, with many pricked fingers and tearful expostulations, cut out, pinned together, and sewn up, my disillusion had turned into extreme frustration. This escalated to utter loathing of the finished product, with its wonky, gappy seams, ill-fitting zip, and too-tight waistband, despite Mum's best attempts to put it right. What was intended to be a simple A-line skirt looked more like a tea cosy. The skirt would never be worn, and I felt like a failure every time I noticed it, scrunched up at the back of my wardrobe.

So of course Stella would be brilliant at it, a natural. I would come home from school to find her and Mum at the kitchen table, their heads together, silent in amicable concentration, embroidering intricate flowers along the bottom hem of a perfect little maroon taffeta skirt, and it would give me a feeling like pinking shears trimming around the lining of my stomach. Without even speaking to them I'd stomp up the stairs to my bedroom, listen to my Cure records at full volume, and contemplate dying my fringe pink.

By the time Stella was twelve, all she ever talked about was becoming a fashion designer. The job was made for her. Designing clothes was a doddle – and not only would she get huge amounts of money for doing it, but she could also parade up and down a catwalk in triumph, the world's press at her feet and the standing ovation of the glitterati in her ears.

Lifting a purple lacy Wonderbra off the edge of a picture frame on Stella's mantelpiece, I gazed at a photograph of Dad and Mum on their wedding day. Their expressions were carefree, almost smug, and it was such a very sixties photograph, with Dad's huge tie and Mum's white crocheted minidress and floppy-brimmed hat. The steps of the register office filled up the rest of the frame, dotted with confetti and good wishes. Poor things, I thought. The couple in the photograph had no idea of the trauma in store for them when they later tried to have the family they longed for. All those nights of pre-marital courtship, when they'd been tipsily suggesting names for their children.

Mum had, laughing, told me about this once. Before they were even officially engaged, they'd decided they wanted at least three or four children. They would be called Olly, Molly and Polly. Next might come Dolly, 'the show girl, obviously; and *then*, if we can face having any more, we'll have Solly – *and he'll be the Jewish one!*' Mum had wheezed, slapping her thigh with hilarity.

I never understood this joke, not for years. In fact, it made me feel uncomfortable and inadequate. They'd envisioned five children, and all they got for nine whole years was me, short, skinny, second-hand, and suffering from regular migraines. It was a bit like wanting the Swiss Family Robinson and getting that sour-faced Mary from *The Secret Garden* instead.

I replaced the photograph on Stella's mantelpiece,

catching sight of her furry zebra-print Filofax across the room as I did so, half-hidden beneath a pink Stetson. Better still, she actually had written in Mack's new mobile number, which I copied onto my palm in black felt-tip pen.

It was a measure of how completely I'd forgotten about my twelve o'clock massage – if I'd massaged anybody then, they'd have ended up with Mack's phone number in black streaks down their back. As I wrote the last digit, I wondered why on earth I didn't just walk out of the bedroom with the Filofax and replace it later; but somehow the whole operation had assumed a kind of furtive secrecy. I didn't want Stella to know I'd been in her room at all.

I went back into my bedroom and dialled Mack's mobile off my palm.

'Hi, Mack, it's Emma.' I noticed that my foot was jigging up and down.

'Emma! How are you? Is everything OK?' Mack sounded surprised, but then, I never usually rang him during the day.

'Yeah, everything's fine, thanks. I'm really sorry to bother you. I just wondered if I could ask you a favour.' I winced, thinking how often this was the reason I contacted him.

'Oh, yes, look, I'm sorry I never got around to bleeding those radiators when I was over last night – are they still banging?'

Poor Mack. I made a mental note to buy him a really nice present for all the odd jobs he'd done for us recently. 'No, no, not that sort of favour. Actually, it's sort of a long story. I need some information, and I wondered if you could help me look it up on the Internet. All that Lori Singer stuff gave me the idea. I meant to ask you last night, but I . . . forgot.'

'Sure. No problem. Want me to pop around again tonight? I'm playing squash but I could—'

'No . . . listen, would it be OK if I came over to yours tomorrow? This sounds kind of weird, and I'll explain it later, but . . . I don't want Stella to know what I'm up to.'

There was a pause. In the background I could hear a voice in a thick Northern Irish accent shouting, 'JUST REBOOT IT! RIGHT NOW!'

'Well, this edit will be finished, so I said I'd go and see my mother tomorrow, but I'll be back in the evening if you want to come over then. Although aren't you seeing Gavin?'

'Um . . . no. No, that would be fine.' I felt so uncomfortable that I had to clamp the receiver to my ear to prevent myself slamming the phone down, and pretending that the conversation wasn't happening. Once it was done, it couldn't be undone. I was going to have to look for her, and no more prevaricating.

'Come round at about eight-thirty then.'

'Thanks, Mack. If that's OK?'

The same background voice could be heard again: 'Oh, you complete *tosser*!' Then there was the sound of a muffled murmur from Mack, as he put his hand over the receiver. When he returned, he was brisk and abrupt. 'Yeah, sure, Emma, that's fine. Listen, I've got to go now. There's a bit of a crisis going on here with a machine that they need help sorting out. See you tomorrow, then. Bye.'

I hung up, slowly, my foot still jiggling uncontrollably. There was an unpleasant squeamish feeling in my stomach, and sweat was prickling at my forehead, as if I'd started something I might not be able to finish. Still, it made a change from the dull ache of missing Gavin.

As I replaced the cordless telephone on its stand, I noticed the light flashing on the answering machine. I pressed the button to hear my twelve o'clock massage's angry voice calling from a mobile phone, traffic noises audible in the background. '*I've been standing on your doorstep ringing the bell for five minutes, which was a waste of time, since you obviously aren't even in . . . Well, just forget it. I'll go* to the Sanctuary in future if I need a massage – so much for stress relief! It's a joke.'

Bugger, I thought, closing my eyes so tightly that little shards of colour splintered off into infinity behind my eyelids. The intercom must be playing up again. Sometimes you couldn't buzz people in, but this was the first time the damn doorbell hadn't worked either. And how could I not have heard the *phone*?

Something poked me in the belly as I leaned forward, so I straightened up and investigated. It was the plastic bottle of sweet almond oil which I'd forgotten I had put in my trouser pocket when I went to look for Stella's Filofax. It felt squashy, inviting.

As if in a dream I walked into the kitchen and over to the sink, uncapping the bottle and squeezing the woody-scented oil all over my hands so that it dripped through my fingers and fell golden on the white enamel. I stared at my coated hands, thinking of how much flesh they had touched and caressed, taut peachy baby flesh, old baggy diseased skin. But they had never touched the skin of any of my own flesh and blood – at least, not to my knowledge. I poured more and more oil out of the bottle, trying to get it to act as a protective covering over the fear which was making my hands shake.

A picture of the baby bird in *Are You My Mother?* came back to me again: his disconsolate face and wide-open beak as the snorting digger picked him up in his scooping metal maw and carried him off, squawking, into the unknown. Help had come from an unlikely quarter for that baby bird, and it had been the digger who'd saved the day. It had deposited him right back in his nest, where the embrace of his real mother's warm wings and a fat, juicy worm awaited him.

It had to be worth a try, I thought, as the last of the oil dripped like honey from the bottle and swirled slowly away down the plughole, leaving a pale greasy skin on the bottom of the sink.

17

The following night, I had to endure what seemed like hours of Stella and Suzanne giggling and gossiping all around the flat: face-packed and tweezing, coiffing and buffing, the entire contents of Stella's wardrobe alternately on each of their bodies and then discarded on the bedroom floor, running in and out of my room because my full-length mirror was, allegedly, more flattering than Stella's.

'Honestly,' I said, trying not to sound too disapproving. 'It's Monday night. I thought you were only going to the pub?'

'We are,' retorted Stella, adjusting the ring in her bellybutton under a very short crop top. 'Gotta look our best, though, haven't we?'

'Why? Who's going to be there?'

Stella pouted exaggeratedly in front of the mirror, before unscrewing a tub of gel and applying it to her individual curls, with a movement akin to a Victorian twirling his moustache. 'Oh, you know, the usual crowd. Dan and Lawrence. Suze fancies the pants off Dan—'

'*Stel-la!*' came an aggrieved shout from the bathroom. I called out to her, 'Don't worry, Suzanne, your secret is safe with me,' before turning back to Stella.

'And what about you? Who are you after?'

'Oh,' said Stella, airily. 'I dunno. I quite like Charlie, you know, the one you met that night—' She stopped abruptly, not wanting to remind me of exactly which night.

'Not that older one, the rugger-bugger? I thought he was awful. There was something really *sinister* about him.' I remembered Charlie's small lascivious eyes following Stella's every move, and felt a wobble of unease.

'No he isn't! He's really sweet, when you get talking to him. I like older men – they've had so much more experience. Know what I mean?' Stella danced around me, running her hands over her own breasts and down her thighs in an effort to rile me. It worked.

'That's not funny, Stell. You're only nineteen. Besides, if you want an older man, why not Mack? I'm sure he's got a crush on you, and he's a sweetheart.' But I said it very half-heartedly, knowing what her response would be. I couldn't say I blamed her, either.

Predictably, Stella made a gagging face, and then pretended to yawn noisily. She looked like a puppy, clowning around, velvety-skinned and sharp-toothed, and my heart constricted with love and fear for her.

'Rightyho, I'm ready.' Suzanne emerged from the bathroom in a tight eighties-retro stripy dress with a big flower pinned on her left breast, trainers, and with her little dreadlocks coralled into a shock on top of her head. She looked bizarre and, I thought, bloody awful.

'Babes! You look awesome. Let's go, shall we? See ya, Em; wouldn't wanna be ya!'

'Bye. Let me know if you're going to be too late,' I replied, weakly, feeling a sudden urge for a cigarette even though I hadn't smoked for nine years.

As soon as the door slammed shut behind them I stripped off my jeans and put on a pair of tights and my purple satin Whistles skirt, combed some semblance of order into my hair, and burrowed about in my make-up bag to find my expensive lipgloss. It felt as if some sense of occasion were required: I was dressing up for the possibility of my real mother.

Squeezing several dropperfuls of Rescue Remedy onto my tongue, I took a deep breath and left the flat, less than ten minutes after Stella and Suzanne. On the way downstairs I saw that Percy's door was open, and heard the sound of his TV blaring from inside. I almost stopped to check if he needed anything, as I sometimes did, but at the last minute the prospect of the terrible old-unwashed-man smell made my stomach heave, reminding me too horribly of the man on the tube. On top of the fearful churning at the thought of what Mack might unearth, it was too much, and I crept on past.

Inside of another minute, I was descending the six steep and broken concrete steps leading to Mack's basement flat; steps so narrow that my feet had to go on sideways, and so perilous that I wondered how he managed not to break a limb every time he went down them. Maybe that was why he always wore Converse All Stars, I thought, for their good grip.

Mack must have seen me coming because the door swung open just as my finger was hovering over the doorbell.

'Hi, Emma, come in,' he said. 'You look gorgeous.'

'Oh, I might be going out later. I like your hair, by the way.'

Mack had had quite a radical haircut. His blond wisps had all been clipped off close to his head, creating a sort of fuzzy-gangster look. The semi-skinhead image reminded me a little of Gavin, except that Gavin could have stepped out of *Lock Stock and Two Smoking Barrels*, and in comparison Mack just looked like a little boy whose mother had given him a buzz-cut. I imagined that there'd have been no need to sweep up after she'd finished, because Mack's hair was so fine that its trimmed ends wouldn't show on the floor.

'Come in. Would you like a drink? Beer, wine, tea?'

'A beer would be lovely, thanks.' I stepped inside Mack's flat, thinking, as I always did, how much more tasteful it was than I would have imagined, with its enormous maroon crushed-velvet sofa and cream walls. Today there was also a vase of gerbera daisies on the mantelpiece, and Coldplay's *Parachutes* swelling out of hidden speakers. When I'd first met Mack, his red All Stars had erroneously led me to assume that he'd have had a flat full of pink inflatable armchairs and posters of S Club 7. I'd been gobsmacked when he said he was a TV producer. I thought people who worked in television were *cool*, and Mack so obviously wasn't.

He handed me a half-empty can of Old Speckled Hen and a half-filled glass. 'Why don't you sit down and tell me all about it?'

'Thank you, doctor,' I joked as I sank into the velvet sofa, nursing my beer.

Mack perched himself across the room on an office chair, in front of a desk groaning with expensive-looking computer equipment. He swivelled round to face me. I noticed that he wasn't wearing his All Stars, and his feet were in odd socks, one navy, one black. He looked so different without them.

'I don't think I've ever told you that I'm adopted,' I began, abruptly.

Mack's expression remained unchanged. 'No, you haven't. But Stella did, one night when I came over to see you and you were out. She and I had a bottle of wine together and she told me all sorts of things about you two and your family.'

I rolled my eyes. I vaguely remembered Stella mentioning that evening, and had felt miffed that she'd been muscling in on my mate when she had so many of her own. Plus I'd been worried – in those early days – that she might try to seduce him, and that it might somehow jeopardize Mack's and my burgeoning friendship. She'd never told me that they'd talked about me being adopted, though.

Bloody Stella. Was there anybody she hadn't told?

'I suppose she also told you that my best friend used to be a gorilla.' Much to my irritation, I was unable to keep a small tremor out of my voice.

Now Mack did look surprised. 'No. Really? Surely you'd have told me if you were abandoned in a jungle as a baby and brought up by wild animals, or anything wacky like that, wouldn't you?'

'Yes, I'd have told you and no, of course I wasn't. It's just that when Stella tells people I'm adopted, she tends to follow it by saying . . . Oh well, it's a long story. And it was an orang-utan, not a gorilla – Stella always gets it wrong. Our mother was doing a Ph.D. on them when I was a kid, that was all.'

'So you've decided that you want to trace your birth mother.' Mack stared intently at me and I looked away, studying the perfect depth of colour in the petals of the orange gerberas.

'Yes. I've been thinking about it for a while, and then the other day when you looked up Stella, I thought, I'm sure there's a way to trace people on the Web. I could just about have a stab at doing it through a search engine, but I hardly know anything about the Internet. I'm sure you would know ten times more.'

'And what about your birth father? Do you want to find him too?'

'Well, yeah, of course. But his name wasn't on my birth certificate – there was just a blank space. I don't think I've got any way of tracing him unless I find her first.'

'Haven't you told Stella about this? Don't you think she'd be supportive?'

I gritted my teeth. 'I know what she's like; she comes across as all streetwise, like she doesn't give a damn, but I'm all she's got left. She used to have nightmares that I'd die too, or leave her on her own. Of course, I know she's older now, and that's why I've waited this long; but I don't want to get her all worried that she

151

might be about to lose me too, unless . . .' I tailed off, realizing how it sounded.

'. . . unless she really *was* about to lose you.' Mack swivelled awkwardly in his chair every time he spoke, making it seem as if it was the chair which controlled his responses, sending answers through his backside, up his spine, and through his mouth. 'But why do you think she might lose you?'

'I don't! You said it, not me. She'll never lose me. But I know how she thinks, and if I find my birth mother, and end up having a really good relationship with her, Stella will feel incredibly threatened. But I have a right to know about my natural parents, don't I? I can't spend my entire bloody life not doing things which are important to me just in case I upset Stella! Surely you can appreciate that?'

Thinking about Mack's chair made me wish that the bulk of the velvet sofa would soak up my own frustration, but it merely sagged uncommunicatively beneath me. I felt an urge to punch it, or throw my beer on it, or something. What the hell did Mack know about anything?

'I've been trying to tell her,' I said in a more conciliatory tone of voice. 'But I can't find the right time, or the right words. So I've decided to make a start without her knowing. That way, if it all comes to nothing, she won't have had anything to worry about.'

To my surprise, Mack came over and sat next to me. He looked into my face, taking me in with his pale blue eyes. I wondered what it would be like if we fancied one another, and tried to imagine us a couple. But the idea of kissing him was as preposterous as the idea of kissing old Percy from the flat downstairs.

'I'm sorry. You're right – of course you're entitled to find out. I don't mean to be negative, it's just that there's something I've never told you, either. I know more about this than you might think. You see, I'm adopted too.'

I gaped at him. 'I've never met anyone else who was

adopted before,' I said. 'Why didn't you tell me, if you knew that I was?'

He grinned, a little sheepishly. 'Stella made me promise not to let on that I knew. And besides, I hadn't told her about me, either. Like you, it's not something I tell many people.'

I had so many questions that I could barely think where to start. 'So when you saw your mother today, was that your real mother, or your adoptive one?'

'Emma, I only have one real mother: I had a birth mother, and then I had a real mother. The one who brings you up, and loves you, and looks after you – that's your real mother.'

'But have you ever met your birth mother?'

'Yeah. I lived with her until I was three. Then she got sent to prison for blinding someone in a fight in a pub – she pushed a broken pint glass in this woman's face because the woman called her a slapper. She killed herself when she was inside. She was an alcoholic and a drug addict. She didn't know who my father was, apparently. When she first went to jail I was fostered by a lovely older couple from Cheshire, and they later adopted me.'

I was stunned. 'I'm so sorry. I had no idea.'

The Coldplay CD ended and was automatically replaced by Pink Floyd on the radio. Mack stood up. 'Nothing to be sorry about,' he said abruptly, 'unless I'd stayed with my birth mother. Now *that* would be a reason to feel sorry for me. Another beer?'

He walked noiselessly out of the room in his odd-socked feet, whistling a note-perfect rendition of Dave Gilmour's guitar solo at the end of 'Another Brick in the Wall', and returned immediately with two more cans.

'How will you feel if you find that your own birth mother is someone like that?' He gestured for me to pass over my empty glass. 'I promise you, Emma, this isn't something to take on lightly. You've got to be prepared for the worst. I mean, it'll be wonderful if it

153

turns out great – although then you risk Stella getting hurt – but it might not. If you want my opinion, I think that before you go ahead you should get some counselling. We could look up on the Net where you could go.'

Pink Floyd changed into Tom Robinson's 'War Baby', a song which had been on the radio a lot when Stella was a baby. Dad, always the purveyor of terrible puns, used to sing 'Sore Baby' whenever she fell over and hurt herself: 'Sore baby, talking about the Third World'. I used to poke him in the side and say, 'Da-ad! Stella can't talk about the Third World. She can hardly talk at all!' The Third World sounded like something off *Star Trek*.

'I've already done that, I did it ten years ago. I've read the books – well, a few of them. I've had the advice. I know what I'm supposed to feel and do, I've just never had the time, or the nerve, to actually do it before.'

I watched Mack pour the frothy amber ale into my glass, and it reminded me of the almond oil with which I'd anointed myself the previous day. 'I'm still not sure I've got the guts for it. If there was some way that I could – oh, I don't know – *not go all the way*. Like, if I could just find out what she's like first, without having to commit myself—'

'Or find out if she's even still alive,' Mack interrupted.

'Yeah. *Then* I could decide whether or not I want her to know who I am.'

'That's a bit . . . selective, isn't it? Appearances can be deceptive, you know. She might seem really eccentric, but be a lovely person and you'd never know. Or what if she turned out to be disabled, or mentally ill, and you felt obliged to look after her, or—'

I put my hands over my ears. 'Stop. I take your point.' I flopped against the back of the sofa, staring at the plastic ripples of the fake ceiling rose until the awful panicky feeling passed.

'No,' I said eventually. 'I need to do this. I want to look at it as an experiment – in life, if you like, something that I do for myself. I don't want to pay a detective or go to an agency. But equally I don't want to spend years and years getting obsessed with tracking her down, and having no success. I already know her name and where she used to live. I've got my birth certificate – although it doesn't really tell me all that much more, except that I was born in Wiltshire.

'Anyway, if I can't find her, or I do find her but decide not to take it further, then I'll let it drop – for good. I'll look at it as a "not meant to be". Stella will be none the wiser, and nor will my birth mother.'

'What if you find her and she doesn't want to have a relationship with *you*? She might have a husband that she hasn't told about you.'

'I think she does have a husband, or did – she was down on the Electoral Register as a Mrs. But there wasn't anybody else listed as living with her – at least, nobody over eighteen, anyway. And unless things have changed drastically since then, she does want to know me. I wouldn't do this if I wasn't sure of that. Look.'

I delved into my handbag and pulled out the letter, putting it in my lap to smooth out the already-smooth memories of creases, before passing it over to Mack. 'I found this after Mum and Dad died, just before I went for counselling. It doesn't have her surname on it, but I looked it up on the Electoral Register of that year via her address. It's Ann Paramor.'

Mack read the letter, absently stroking his newly shorn head as he did so, in a way which made me think of Stella's mate Lawrence. I wondered idly if I would see Lawrence tomorrow morning, a towel around his waist, nipping into our bathroom. But, I supposed, at least Lawrence would be preferable to that Charlie, anyway.

'Wow.' Mack handed back the limp sheet of Basildon Bond. 'So why didn't you contact her then?'

'I did, a couple of times. She'd moved house and not

left a forwarding address. I must have just missed her.'
I folded up the letter and left it on the sofa cushion next to me like a place setting. I tried to imagine Ann Paramor sitting there, joining in the conversation, but all I got was the same old image of a praying woman on her knees in a frothy nightie.

'After that, I just kind of gave up at the first hurdle. It was all too stressful. Stella was so young, and she needed me. I suppose I hoped that Ann Paramor would write again, but when she never heard back from Mum, she must have assumed that Mum wanted her to stay away.'

I paused. It felt so strange, all these secrets rolling out of me, although the consumption of one and a half Speckled Hens did make it easier. 'I can't believe I'm telling you all this.'

Mack smiled. 'I'm flattered. Besides, what are mates for? And don't think you'll get away scot free either, because later I'm going to quiz you about whether you think your gorgeous sister might deign to go on a date with an older man . . .'

I snorted, jokingly, but my heart sank. 'Oh, Mack, I'm sorry, but you really aren't her type.'

He looked at me dolefully. 'Yeah. I guessed as much already. Oh well, no harm in hoping, is there?'

I hastily tried to change the subject. 'So, about the Internet stuff: will you help me?'

'Of course. If you'll do something for me in return.'

His eyes slid over to the corner of the room, where his expensive digital video camera lay zipped up in its black canvas case, like the newborn offspring of my giant Bastard. I felt envious of the fact that the tools of *his* trade were so portable.

'Did I tell you that I've been commissioned to make an hour-long documentary as part of a new BBC series on families?'

I was simultaneously irritated and proud of him. It was great news for him, but why was he talking about his work now? 'Wow, Mack, that's great. No, you didn't.'

'Well, I have been. They liked my short film last year on teenagers and the Internet, and approached me with a view to doing something similar for this new series. But when I told them that I was adopted, and that I'd like to make a film about how adopted people find their place in the world, they were even more enthusiastic. So, you see, this is perfect timing. I'd been feeling that my own story wasn't interesting enough for a full hour, and I was thinking about asking this other guy I know from football, who's also adopted, but now, here you are, with your story. The idea of filming someone who's actually searching is much more appealing to me.'

I was flabbergasted. 'What – me? Be in a documentary?'

'Why not? I could film everything we do to try and track down your birth mother, and then if you meet up with her, you could let me film that, too—'

'Not bloody likely – you must be joking! I can see it now: "Hello, I'm your daughter, and this is the film crew!" This is personal, Mack, I can't believe you're even suggesting it.'

Mack stayed calm in the face of my increasing agitation, although I saw him look longingly over at his video camera again.

'Don't even think about it,' I said.

He spun around on his chair even faster. 'Oh, Emma, please? It's the most brilliant subject – such human interest. I promise I'd do it sensitively. And if you didn't want me to film you all the time, I'd set you up with a camera so you could talk directly into it. You know, like a video diary. If we find your mother, of course I wouldn't have to film the *actual* reunion. We could pretend you were meeting for the first time, after you already had.'

I could have hit him. A faked reunion had to be one of the tackiest, most horrible things I'd ever heard. There was no way I'd be involved in something like that. Besides, the whole prospect of being on camera was anathema to me – I couldn't even bear to have my photograph taken. But, I thought immediately afterwards, it would be kind of nice to have someone really pulling out the stops to help me look . . .

'So are you saying you won't help me unless I let you film it?'

Mack tutted. 'No, of course not. I'm not that callous. I just think it would be fantastic. And the fact that you've approached me for help, before you even knew about what I was doing – well, it just seems like such a "meant to be". Plus, I genuinely think it would be good for you, too. Feeling that you're not alone in it. Confronting your fears and doubts; getting them out in the open. And don't forget, if for whatever reason we end up drawing a blank, then who knows? Maybe your birth mother will see it and get in touch.'

'We-ll,' I said, wavering slightly. 'Can I have some time to think about it?'

'Sure. And in the meantime, let's have a quick preliminary look on-line.' He swivelled around and switched on his computer. 'We'll check out some on-line phone directories, and do a general search first, to see if we get anywhere. She might just have registered on some reunion site for adopted kids and birth parents. And I want to print out some info for you, as well. I know you said you had counselling, but that was a long time ago. I think it would be a good idea for you to have a little refresher course.'

Pompous arse, I thought, feeling a momentary flash of irritation. I wondered if he was hoping we'd draw a blank, so that he'd have more material for his documentary.

'Do they have special sites for adopted people, then?'

'Oh yeah. Mostly based in America, but she could still have posted a message on those, asking about you, and that means her name might show up in a general search. We mustn't overlook the obvious.'

I finished my beer and, standing on unsteady legs,

tottered across the room, taking the first steps towards my birth mother in eight years. As I stood next to Mack's chair, I felt as if we were posing for an Edwardian family photograph: the husband seated, mutton-chopped and suited up, the obedient wife in crinolines behind him, resting her hand on the patriarchal shoulder, staring into a five- by four-inch box camera – exactly the same as the ones Dad used to make . . .

'Emma?'

I jumped. The camera once more became Mack's grape iMac, and Mack was shaking his head in mock-exasperation. 'Anybody in there?' He passed a hand to and fro in front of my eyes.

'Sorry, I was miles away. Oh God, I don't know. Perhaps I am being too hasty. Knowing that I'm only going to give this one shot, it's like . . . I don't know, maybe I'm rushing into it. It was so easy, really, last time, finding out her name. What if it's that easy this time?'

Mack swivelled again. 'Well, I doubt that it will be. It's a huge help that you know her name and an old address, and you're lucky that it's quite an unusual surname. But anything could have happened since your folks died. She might have moved abroad, or died herself, or remarried . . . It's a shame you don't have a street number. If you did, you could go back to the Electoral Register for that year and look up the names of her neighbours and contact them, too.'

'I did think of that. I suppose I could go to Teffont and ask around,' I said doubtfully. 'What are you doing now?'

Mack had been tapping away at his keyboard, and now a document entitled 'Preparation Before Contact' filled the screen. His printer rattled into action, churning out onto several sheets of A4.

'I just keyed in "adoptees + preparation" and this came up.'

159

I pulled the paper off the printer. Glancing over the piece, I laughed when I read the first point:

1. THE FANTASY. Let go of any lifelong image, any fantasy of your birth mother. No one can live up to a fantasy . . . Be sure you are ready to accept her as she is because she's probably not what you wanted, expected, or fantasized her to be.

'That's a relief, then,' I said out loud.

'What is?'

I read out the paragraph to Mack, and then told him about the babydoll nightie and the compulsive praying.

Mack laughed too. He sounded like his printer when he laughed: brisk and staccato. 'It's so important to be prepared. Even if you only have a negative image of her, it's still a preconception, and you're going to have to try and get rid of all of those, otherwise whoever you find will be a shock, one way or another.'

He sounded as if he was already rehearsing for what he'd say on camera, and then he more or less confirmed it. 'If you do let me go ahead and film this, we'll have to do all this again. I wouldn't want to miss out any of the stages.'

'*If* I let you go ahead,' I said darkly.

Mack scrolled down a list of sites, and clicked to enter another one. I noticed, for the first time, that his mouse mat was a reproduction of Edvard Munch's *The Scream*, and I felt warmer towards him again.

'Oh, here, this one looks good. Most of these are American sites, so the legal stipulations might not be quite the same. The advice will still be sound, though. I'll just run off a few more articles, and that should be enough for you to take home and get stuck into. In the meantime, let's do a couple of quick searches now. If nothing comes up, I'll have a think about what else we can do, and get back to you in a few days, and you give me a ring when you've thought about the documentary idea. Is that OK?'

I was overcome with a sudden affection for him: silly hair, pomposity, *Scream* mouse mat, and all. 'Of course, that's fine, although I'm not making any promises. Thank you, though, Mack. Really. I'd never have done this on my own – probably not even if I *could* figure out the Internet.'

I squeezed his shoulder and he blushed, flapping his arm at me in a self-deprecatory manner. 'It's nothing. Glad to help. I just want to make you aware that you have to be prepared, that's all.'

' "Be prepared". Did you know that's the motto of the Brownies?'

The graphics on the computer screen changed, and Mack sprang into action, ignoring my question. 'Right, here we go. Here's a directory site. I'll type in Paramor, Ann. I think if you leave the area box blank it searches the whole of the UK.'

I held my breath as he typed in the information and hit the RETURN key. The tiny little circle on the screen, which indicated that you had to wait, ticked interminably around and around, until finally the pronouncement was made: 'SORRY NO MATCHES WERE FOUND.'

I was disappointed, but also faintly relieved that the moment of truth was not instantaneous. I realized that Mack was right, I did want the chance to read up a bit more on what to expect.

'Fine. Thanks again, and I'll leave you to the rest of your evening now. I need to get home and start on my reading.'

Mack looked at my satin skirt and high-heeled boots. 'I thought you were going out?'

It was my turn to blush. 'Well, I was considering it, but I'm a bit tired, actually. I'll probably just have an early night. I've got a lot to think about.'

Mack separated himself from his twirly chair and showed me to the door, helping me into my coat in a gentlemanly manner. I gave him a goodnight peck on the cheek, and climbed back up the basement steps, gingerly picking my way past a dropped packet of chips lying crushed and slimy outside his building.

When I got home, I went straight to my bedroom and lay flat out on the bed, still wearing my coat. Closing my eyes, I did a mental exercise I had once learned in a healing workshop. I imagined myself inside a circle of light, which was attached to another one, containing the praying image of my mother in the babydoll nightie. In my head, I drew a figure of eight three times around both circles. Finally I got a large imaginary pair of scissors and snipped the two apart, watching the circle containing my caricature of a mother begin to float up and away, like a huge bubble. I hoped that once I'd finished the exercise, I would no longer have any preconceived ideas about who Ann Paramor might be.

Then I began the exercise again. In the bubble this time was a television, whose screen was filled with an image of my own face, to try and get me over the craven panic that the thought of being filmed induced. It seemed only fair that I should do Mack a return favour for all the help he was going to give me, but I just wasn't sure if I could face the prospect of being on TV.

I fell asleep before the second bubble had even cleared the rooftop of the house in my imagination. The sound of my own snoring woke me up several hours later, cold and stiff, with Mack's printed sheets scattered all over the floor, and my overcoat rucked up uncomfortably beneath me.

18

'This'll be the first real scene, I think – you looking in the envelope. Then I'll cut in some of that stuff we talked about before. Maybe we can have you in voice-over for some of the sequences – kids playing on swings for when you talk about your childhood, and so on. So, whenever you're ready . . .'

Earlier on the same dark, freezing evening when Mack filmed me opening the envelope, I'd bumped into him in Sainsbury's. But I hadn't even noticed him until he tapped me on the shoulder, because something very strange was occurring in my line of vision, right there in the Pet Foods aisle.

It was that baby bird, the one from Stella's book. There it was, in front of me, hopping along the faux-marble tiled floor. I couldn't believe it. It meandered nonchalantly up Pet Foods, swelled a few deep breaths into its peanut-sized lungs, and leaped up to perch on the baskets of various single women shoppers as they stopped to browse. Its legs were the thinnest black twigs imaginable, as if they should have gobs of cherry blossom on the ends of them, like fluffy slippers, instead of sketched and fragile branches of feet.

'Are you my mother?' I thought I heard it say to an elderly woman with grey bags under her eyes, who was bulk-buying Pedigree Chum for Small Dogs. Even though the bird had jumped right onto the front of her shallow old ladies' trolley, she still didn't appear to have seen it, although it was perfectly visible to me.

I watched it jump down – for, of course, it hadn't yet mastered the art of flight – and approach a dreamy pregnant lady, who was pushing her trolley with straight arms because her stomach stuck out so far. She didn't see it either, even though it cocked its head winsomely to one side and chirped its question again, clambering up the mesh of her trolley and over her cereal boxes.

So this is what it feels like, I thought. I really am going mad. I turned away and blinked owlishly a few times, taking off my glasses and rubbing my eyes, as much of a cartoon myself as the baby bird was. That was when Mack tapped me on the shoulder.

'Got something in your eye?' He was idly scrutinizing the Whiskas, picking up a tin of what looked like chicken, inspecting it like a weightwatcher reading the fat content of a sticky toffee pudding, and then replacing it again as he waited for me to answer.

I glanced surreptitiously behind me, but the bird seemed to have vanished. 'Hi, Mack. No, I'm . . . fine. I think it's gone now – whatever was in my eye, I mean. Since when have you had a cat?'

'I haven't. I'm catsitting for my mate while he's on holiday. It's a nightmare. Brian spends all night charging up and down the hall, and he won't eat, either.'

'Is that why you're looking after his cat for him?'

'Emma, Brian *is* the cat.'

'Oh, right, of course. Sorry.' I laughed, and listened with gratitude to Mack banging on about Brian, feeling more grounded by the minute, until I decided that maybe I was just overtired or something.

'. . . I had no idea that cats were so much hassle. I'm exhausted. He either sleeps on my head, or scratches and yowls at the bedroom door if I shut him out, the little bastard. In between the galloping, of course. Anyway, it's great to see you – I was going to ring you when I got home from here, actually. I've got some information for you.'

'Really? You've found something out? What?'

'Come round and I'll tell you. I need to get this on film. I'll be home in about half an hour.'

I leaned on the handle of my trolley, absently pushing it back and forwards in tiny little ice-dance movements of excitement. 'Brilliant!'

Maybe the baby bird was a – what were those mythological bringers of news called? A harbinger? Maybe it was telling me that I was finally on my way.

'Told Stella yet?'

For a moment, I thought he meant had I told Stella about the bird.

'No, I've only just . . Oh. No, not yet. I'm working up to it.'

Mack gave me the sort of look I imagined Brian might get after sharpening his claws on Mack's chick-fur scalp. 'I still think you should let her in on it.'

'I know you do. And I will. I'll see you round at yours in half an hour, then. If I'm going to be on telly, I'd better go home and get some slap on first.' Not to mention try and recover from my unexplained hallucinations, I thought, waving over my shoulder at Mack and hurrying away before anything else untoward occurred.

In the end, of course, I had relented. I was to be the sole subject of Mack's documentary, on the strict understanding that there would be absolutely no on-camera reunions, faked or otherwise, and I could pull out if I was in any way unhappy with the way things were going. I'd given it a great deal of thought, and on balance, the appeal of having Mack's assistance and shared responsibility in the quest outweighed the horrific prospect of being on TV. Also, I secretly rather liked the idea of being part of a team, helping Mack create something, hopefully, of profound benefit for his career.

And now here I was, staring transfixed at the envelope lying on Mack's kitchen table. I wasn't even self-conscious that the camera held to Mack's eye was registering my every expression. To my surprise and relief, he'd been right about that; after the first few sessions, I had almost succeeded in pretending that the camera wasn't there at all. I no longer dried or fluffed, or any of those terms which sound laundry-related, but which actually apply to public performance. I still had absolutely no wish to see myself in the finished product though.

'Sure you want to go ahead with this?' he asked, as my hand wavered over the envelope. This was typical of Mack, to bother putting it in an envelope and sealing it. Anyone else would have just handed me the sheet of paper. Still, I supposed, it was for dramatic effect.

'Well, it'd be pretty hard to resist having a look at what's in this envelope, even if I didn't. But yes, I do want to go ahead. I've read all the stuff, and I'm ready, for whatever we find. I don't want her to know I'm looking for her until I find her, though. Then I decide. And if none of the names you've tracked down – assuming you have – turn out to be the right Ann Paramor, then I'm going to put it all behind me, stop wondering, and forget about it – her – once and for all. It'll be a shame for your documentary, but that's the way it's going to be. Reading all those articles you printed off for me has made me even more certain: I don't want it to take over my life. I don't need to know badly enough to spend years and years searching, and possibly never get an answer. If I don't find her within six months, that's it.'

Mack snorted faintly, but I chose to ignore it, instead taking a deep breath. 'So shall I open it, then?'

'Go on, then,' he said. 'It's like the Oscars, this, you

166

know, the bit where you have to make an embarrassing speech and cry all over your Versace frock.'

I flapped the envelope gently up and down in front of me, rapidly losing my nerve again. God, I was such a coward. It was only a piece of paper. What on earth would I be like if I ever came face to face with the actual woman? Out of the corner of my eye, I caught a flash of yellow, and started, but when I looked more closely I realized that it was just a sponge lying beside Mack's kitchen sink.

'Are there many of them? Ann Paramors, I mean.'

'Just a few. Open it, Emma, for God's sake. The suspense is killing me, and I already know what's in there!'

A few. He had really found a few people with my mother's name! I realized that I had begun to doubt that there would be any Ann Paramors at all, after drawing a blank on the on-line phone directory. I took another deep breath, almost hyperventilating, and ripped open the envelope.

It was a single sheet of A4 , on which was a very short typed list:

Paramor, Ann: 39 Dewhurst Gds, Nottingham, NG8 4FX
Paramor, Ann: The Old Forge, Ellesmere Road, Shrewsbury, Shropshire
Paramor, Ann B.: 8, Back Lane, Tiverton, Devon
Paramor, Ann H.: 7 Andover Road, Harlesden, London NW10
Paramor, Ann S.: Lowgill, Iwerne Minster, Dorset

I stared at the word Paramor so many times that it ceased to be a word, or a potential parent, or a red herring, but was instead a hieroglyph, an abstract pattern; wallpaper, plastering the inside of my mind with Paramors. I felt excitement and nausea spiral up inside me, and accidentally jogged Mack's camera with my elbow as he was slowly panning down the list over my shoulder.

'Wow. I don't know what to say, Mack. Did you get all these off the Internet then?'

'Actually,' he said, so sheepishly anyone would have thought he'd been looking for pornography, not parents, 'I started to use the on-line phone directories and things, but the really comprehensive ones are all based in America, or else you have to pay for them. Then I found some information about this CD-ROM you can get. It's based on the Electoral Registers as well as the phone books, and so it lists people by their Christian names and surnames. I just went down to the library and –'

'You went to the library for me? That's so sweet of you!' It was undeniably great to have all this research done on my behalf. I momentarily forgot that he was actually doing it for his documentary.

Mack fidgeted with embarrassment, as if he wished he had his computer chair to twirl on. 'It was nothing . . . Anyway, where was I? Oh yeah, I just did a search on Ann Paramor and these came up. Unfortunately there's only a phone number listed next to two of the addresses, but it should be easy enough to check them all out.'

I flung my arms around Mack's neck and hugged him, and for a moment our ears pressed together. I felt a rush of heat transmitted from his earlobe to mine.

'Oi! Mind me camera,' he grumbled good-naturedly as I pulled away, adjusting my glasses. 'It's not going to look very professional if the picture's wobbling all over the place.'

'Sorry. I'm just so excited that I've got something concrete to work with now. You're fantastic. Let's have a drink to celebrate.'

Mack looked at his watch, and then switched off the camera, placing it carefully on the table next to him. I could see the sweaty imprint of his hand already evaporating off the side of it.

'Actually, I can't stop. I've got footie practice tonight. Why don't you decide which one you want to try and contact first, and we'll go on Saturday? Oh, and if you want something to do in the meantime, could you ring Directory Enquiries, and see if you can get any more phone numbers? I don't think I'd need to film that, although when you actually phone them up, I'd like to be there.'

'Sure,' I said, beaming at both Mack and the mothers in my hand.

19

No time like the present, I thought as I unpacked the shopping I'd dumped in the kitchen before running over to Mack's. I felt light, elated, almost euphoric, as I loaded up the freezer with already-defrosting oven chips, and fish fingers in slippery wet cardboard containers, which I half expected to wriggle out of my grasp and escape in a flash of silvery fins across the quarry-tiled floor, as if excitement was animating my groceries as well as myself.

'Directory Enquiries first, then maybe just call one of the numbers,' I muttered, as I stuffed empty plastic bags into the kitchen cupboard which seemed to exist for that sole purpose, until it was full to bursting and we threw all the bags away. Stella and I had never got to grips with the local council recycling scheme, and it always made me feel guilty. Mum had been very eco-minded, with her composting and recycling. She even went through a brief phase where she used to bring Betsey's family's manure home for our garden. Orangutan shit made excellent mulch, but after a while the boot of our car started to smell so bad that Dad and I made her desist.

I felt a pang of missing Betsey, wishing it could have been her I'd seen in Sainsbury's and not a stupid little bird. Why didn't one get a choice of hallucination? It wasn't fair.

No, I decided. I musn't phone up any of the Anns yet, not after I'd told Mack that I'd wait until he was there to film it. But now the ball was finally rolling it was too tempting, like being seven and alone with a massive pile of Christmas presents all addressed to me. I'd have to make do with calling Directory Enquiries for a start. Double-checking that Stella really was out, I dialled 192. As I pressed them, the digits played a tinny synthesised rendition of the first three notes to the tune of Big Ben, before it struck the hour.

'Which town, please?' droned the operator, sounding bored witless.

'Ann Paramor,' I replied, not listening properly. This was getting to be a very bad habit – not listening to people when they spoke to me. Perhaps it was a trait I'd inherited from Ann Paramor . . . It would be so nice to know.

'Which *town*, please?' said the voice, with more animation.

'Oh, sorry. Well, there's one in Devon, one in Nottingham, and one in Shrewsbury.'

There was a pause. 'Thank you, madam, but I'm afraid I can only give out two numbers at a time. You'll have to ring back for the third. May I have the address of the first one?'

As I read out the first address, I felt like a baby bird myself, unable to fly, teetering on the wire rim of a supermarket trolley. I couldn't see over the top, but I knew that it was a long way down.

My two calls to Directory Enquiries yielded two more telephone numbers, the Nottingham and Shrewsbury ones, making a total of four out of five. By now I was hooked. Adrenalin pumped through me and I could think of nothing else but those five Anns.

I rang Mack's mobile and left him a message. 'Hi, it's me. I know you're playing football, but when you've finished can you phone me? I got two more numbers from Directory Enquiries but it's doing my head in not to be able to call them yet. Can't wait for Saturday – we should go to the London one first, don't you think? If you get a chance to come over before Saturday so I can make a start phoning them, that would be great. Anyway, talk to you soon.'

He rang me back a couple of hours later.

'Have you got any massages on tomorrow?' Mack asked. I could hear a lot of loud male braying and what sounded like heavy rain in the background.

'No, I haven't. Why? And where are you?'

'In a changing room, surrounded by a lot of naked men. Sorry about the noise.'

Even in my birth-mother-preoccupied state, I couldn't resist the mental image of weedy Mack sitting on a wood-slatted bench talking to me on the phone whilst great strapping hunks paraded naked around him, dripping wet, towelling themselves off, their muscly buttocks round and perfect punctuation marks at the base of their broad-shouldered, tapering torsos . . . mmm. It was months since I'd last had sex. Well, weeks, anyway.

'Any *nice* naked men there? You know, ones I might be interested in?' I asked, casually. I'd finally managed to confess to Mack that Gavin and I were finished and, as Stella predicted, Mack wasn't the least bit 'I told you so' about it. Just sympathetic and tactful.

He laughed, obviously picking up on my mental picture, but the sarcastic tone of his snort was a clear indication that the other members of his football team were probably not the Adonises I was visualizing.

'Not even slightly. They all make *me* look macho. Besides, haven't you got enough on your plate at the moment? That's why I was asking you about tomorrow. If you're desperate to get on, we could do it then. I was going to give myself a couple of days' holiday to redecorate my bathroom, but I think I'll just end up emulsioning Brian to the wall

172

if I stay in the flat with him for that long.'

All thoughts of male flesh evaporated instantly. 'Really? Brilliant, thanks. That would be great.'

'I'll come round at ten, then, shall I? I've got a little gizmo that I can plug into your phone to record both sides of the conversation for the film, if you can wait till then to ring the Harlesden one.'

'Oh. OK. I suppose so. But I'm dying to do something. Want me to look up her address in the *A–Z*?'

'Yeah, why not. You'll have to drive, anyway, because I'll be filming you, and I'm a pretty crap navigator.'

'Mack?'

'Mm?'

'So what happens when we call them?'

'Up to you, really. I suppose you're just establishing that they really do live at the addresses we've got for them – you'll have to make up an excuse for why you're ringing, unless you just come right out with who you are—'

'God, no way! I don't want them to know anything until I've visited them, and I'm sure we've got the right Ann. Then it has to be face to face.'

'That's what I thought. Well, we'll just have to visit them all until we find the right one. I hope they don't mind being filmed – we'll have to ask them first, of course. People can be funny about that kind of thing. I mean, look how nervous you were at first.'

'Come on, Mack, you PONCE,' yelled a voice extremely close to the receiver. 'Get a MOVE on, we're missing out on SERIOUS DRINKING time here!'

'I'll let you get back to your male-bonding exercise, then. Have fun at the pub,' I said hastily, as another image sprang to mind, this time of Mack in an headlock, some hairy knuckles kneading his skull through its ill-protecting sheath of fine wispy hair. Honestly, men. Maybe I was better off without one.

'See you tomorrow, then, Emma.' His voice did sound somewhat muffled.

* * *

Two minutes later I was lying on my bed, tracing a path with my finger along the arteries and veins of London in the *A–Z*, plotting our route to Harlesden. Stella burst into the room, rosy-cheeked and icy-fingered, bringing with her a blast of cold air from the front door and down the hallway. I quickly flipped the *A–Z* shut.

'Brrr, it's brass monkeys out there. Any supper left over?'

'I haven't eaten yet. I'll cook us something, if that's what you're hinting at.'

'Wouldn't mind. I'm starving. What are you looking up in the *A–Z*?'

Without waiting for an answer, Stella tipped the contents of her backpack out on my bedroom floor, the damp towel, fogged-up goggles and chloriney black Speedo one-piece.

'The bloody pool was packed. I only managed forty lengths before I got sick of people crawling up my legs or sticking their feet in my face.'

She scooped up her wet things and dumped them into the fraying wicker laundry basket in the corner of my room.

'Don't leave them in there, Stella; put them in the machine, or they'll start to smell. Oh, come here, I'll do it.' I extracted the laundry and went into the kitchen to put on a wash.

'Yes, *Mummy*,' said Stella, and I heard a creak and a rustle as she flopped down on my double bed. Then a thwack and a curse, as the back of her head seemed to collide with something. Oh, shit, the *A–Z*.

I rushed, too quickly, back into the room, still carrying Stella's togs. Stella was rubbing her head and examining the scrap of paper on which I'd scribbled 7 Andover Rd, Harlesden, NW10. Her wet hair had left a stringy damp patch on my blue duvet cover.

'Give me that,' I said, snatching the piece of paper out of her hand, furious with myself for drawing

174

attention to it. Stella looked at me, and then at the *A–Z*, whose page-marker ribbon was stuck in between the pages showing the Kilburn, Willesden and Harlesden areas. I considered grabbing the book, too, but it was so old that it would immediately have disintegrated. Dad used to use that *A–Z* to get around to his photographic assignments, and it was so out-of-date that it didn't even contain the Hanger Lane Gyratory System.

'Whose address is that?' Stella sat up. 'We don't know anybody in Harlesden.'

'No one you know.'

'Oh, come on, Em, tell us. Have you got a new boyfriend?'

'No . . . no. It's just . . . an old friend.'

'Who?'

'If you must know, it's Esther's new address, you know, who I went to school with. I might go and see her, so I was looking it up. We were talking on the phone the other night.'

This part at least was true. I had found a card from her the other day, stuck in between Van Morrison and Stevie Wonder on our CD shelf: a doleful snowman surrounded by glittery silver snowflakes, and I'd thought it might be nice to get in touch with her again. It would be wonderful to have a girlfriend to talk to about this whole birth-mother thing.

Since Gavin, many of my girlfriends had fallen by the wayside. I suppose it was that classic situation where, when you got together with a new boyfriend, you weren't interested in seeing your old friends. Their jokes and habits and routines seemed dull in comparison to the electric shock and adrenalin rush of your lover's soft, dry lips brushing yours, and the thrill of staying in bed all day, having sex and eating pizza.

Their names were still in my address book, and there was the obligatory and pointless Christmas card. The one in my hand was a perfect example: I knew before I even opened it that it would say *Dear Emma,*

Happy Christmas, love Esther – or Jo, or Jacqui; substitute as applicable – *PS We must get together soon!*

However, I was just as guilty of negligence as the Esthers/Jos/Jacquis. I found it one of the hardest things in the world to ring up someone I hadn't heard from in months and suggest going for a drink – I couldn't shake a horrible sneaking suspicion that the reason I hadn't heard from them for that long was because, actually, they didn't like me. Just because we were friends once didn't mean we were honour-bound to be tied together till death did us part. People changed.

Anyway, Esther was such an old friend that I'd told myself not to be paranoid, and to phone her. So, later that evening, when Stella was watching television and painting her toenails, I'd taken the telephone into the kitchen, closed the door, and dialled Esther's number three times before I allowed it to ring, as if I were plucking up the courage to phone someone I really fancied, instead of puny little Esther, with her fondness for Bananarama and frilly ankle socks, and her secondary school propensity for dating the ugliest boys in West London.

Predictably, Esther had sounded embarrassed to hear from me. There were several awkward silences, and some self-conscious chit-chat about her new house, her twin baby boys, and her new-found passion for upholstering things. I furrowed my brow at the mental image of Esther upholstering everything in sight: doors, wardrobes, husband, babies . . .

But Esther, I felt like saying, I need you. I'm looking for my birth mother and the only person I've really got to talk to about it has a camera shoved constantly in my face. I've been dumped by my boyfriend. For the first time in my life I'm keeping a seriously big secret from my sister, and I feel shitty about it. You were the only one who was there for me after Mum and Dad died. You were the only one who still came over to play records and watch

EastEnders with me. Everyone else had buggered off to university without giving me a second thought; but you were there for me that night we sat up late, drinking wine, and you held me when I cried hysterically, railing helplessly against the unfairness of my predicament. It was you who closed the door so that Stella wouldn't wake up and hear me. You who made me black coffee and handed me streamers of toilet paper to blow my nose on.

But I didn't say any of those things. Instead, there was another pregnant pause.

'I'd better go,' said Esther, without suggesting that we meet up, or even speak again soon. 'Someone needs changing.'

There were no sounds of a baby crying in the background, and I couldn't help wondering if Esther was imagining that I, in fact, was the person who needed changing. I hung up, miserably, wishing I hadn't bothered.

Stella narrowed her eyes. 'Oh, was that her you were talking to while I was watching *Top of the Pops*?'

'Yes.'

'Because I distinctly heard you ask how she'd settled into her new house . . . in *Amersham*.'

I was speechless for a moment, rumbled. I opened my mouth to confess, about all the Ann Paramors and Mack's help and everything – God knew it would be good to have someone to confide in – but then I remembered lying in our parents' cold bed holding Stella's hand the day before we moved house, and the broken vases. How could I tell her that I was about to go and find a new mother, when she had none? It felt wrong. Although not wrong enough not to proceed with my search.

'Just drop it, Stell. It's not important.'

'Oh well, then. Suit your bloody self.'

Stella stomped out of the room and into her own bedroom, and all I heard from her for the next hour was the

Red Hot Chili Peppers blasting out at top volume. Even when I text-messaged her to say that there was a toasted cheese sandwich and a bag of crisps (mistexting it as CHEES UOASTY & CRIPS) sitting in the hall for her, Stella only stuck her head out long enough to grab the plate and retreat again.

'Well done, Emma,' I told myself. 'You handled that *really* well.'

20

Mack came over as soon as Stella had left for college the next day, trailing around after me with his camera like a persistent four-year-old playing Grandmother's Footsteps, even though I was only making tea. As I stood with my back to him, mashing a teabag against the side of a mug, I could feel his presence behind me, the camera lens like a gun barrel aimed at my spine. I made a mental note to check my rear view later, with the aid of two mirrors, and then thought, What's the point? I could hardly go all prima-donna-ish on Mack's documentary, like Mariah Carey insisting on only being shot from the right side of her face. It would be vanity in the extreme.

'Right, I'm ready,' I said, although Mack had been filming for a good ten minutes already. 'Let's do it.'

I sat down on the edge of the sofa and dialled the number of Harlesden Ann, as Mack zoomed in for a close-up of my shaking fingers.

The phone rang. And rang and rang, until the anticlimax of nobody answering made the ringing tone echo round and round my head. Mack was panning around the living room now, trying to find things to film as a backdrop to this endless, tortuous ringing. He focused for ages on a photo of Stella and me with our heads together, Stella a chubby baby on my lap. Her blonde curls looked almost white against my own dark hair, and she was so wreathed in smiles that I could almost hear her gurgle.

Mack checked the sound levels again, and then turned his camera round to another picture, this time of Mum and Dad on holiday. Dad had hilariously tight striped trunks on, and Mum was wearing the stringiest bikini I'd ever seen. They looked dashing and sophisticated. I noticed, as if for the first time, what an exact replica Stella's body was of Mum's, down to the small breasts, long hipbones and concave stomach. The picture had been taken when Mum believed her belly would always be flat like that, flat and as empty as a pecked-out snail shell.

Still no answer. I imagined the phone's ring racing out of the front door of 7 Andover Road, Harlesden, down the street, searching for Ann Paramor. *Phone*, it was insistently calling. *Your daughter's on the phone. Quick!*

There was a click on the line. 'Sorry,' said a snooty British Telecom voice. 'Your call has not been answered.'

I slammed the phone down and leaped up off the sofa, almost kicking over my mug of tea.

'Yes, thank you. We had noticed,' I said to the red eye of Mack's camera. I had to turn my back on it for a moment: my breathing was so shallow that I felt as if someone was ironing my lungs.

'I'll try the next one,' I said, turning back and forcing my fingers to dial the next number, the one in Iwerne Minster, Dorset.

A different ringing tone this time, more sonorous, making me think of a butler padding silently down a long tiled hallway. Perhaps I was of noble birth. Perhaps Ann Paramor was a duchess. What did they call the daughters of duchesses?

The phone stopped ringing and I almost didn't notice. There was a lengthy pause, and just when I was wondering if I'd been cut off, the quaveriest old voice

I'd ever heard came onto the line. It made Percy sound like a spring chicken. 'Helllllllo?'

I stared at Mack, my eyes wide with shock. I felt absolutely terrified – of what? That she was the right Ann Paramor, or that she wasn't?

'Is Ann Paramor there, please?' I said, matching the quaveriness shake for shake with terror. I waited for the old lady to say, 'Yes, hold on a moment, I'll get her for you,' but instead the reply came, 'Ann Paramor speaking. Who's calling?'

Relief swooshed down my body and pooled at my feet, making me think of how kids at school used to put blotting paper in their socks to see if it made them faint. It never did.

From out of nowhere I heard myself say, 'I'm doing a survey on . . . modes of transport, and I wondered if you could spare me a couple of minutes to answer some questions?'

Modes of transport? Why hadn't I just hung up? I shook my head and made an agonized face at Mack, who rolled his eyes and twirled a finger next to his ear, almost making me laugh out loud. This was so unlikely to be the right Ann Paramor, but now I'd got this far, I supposed I might as well make double sure. Maybe she sounded older than she was. Maybe she'd given birth to me when she was fifty, or sixty. It happened . . .

'Yes, dear, just let me sit down a moment.' There was a pause, and then the soft sound of something expanding, and a sigh.

'Right, then, dear, how can I help you?' Thankfully she didn't seem in the least interested in who the ostensible survey was for.

'Er, yes. Would you mind first confirming your age for me please?'

'I'm ninety-six next birthday. The twentieth of April. Hanging on for me telegram, I am.' There was a creaky, wheezy chuckling noise.

No, even by the wildest stretch of the imagination,

you could not be my mother, I thought. But I ploughed on, regardless. 'And you live in . . .' I pretended to be consulting my imaginary clipboard, '*Eye-Werny* Minster', struggling over the unfamiliar place name, whilst simultaneously wondering why on earth I was still talking to this old lady.

The creaky chuckle chuffed down the telephone line. 'No, dear, I live in *You-Urn* Minster.'

'I'm sorry,' I said, barely holding it together. My fingers were itching to slam down the phone, to run away and hide with a combination of embarrassment and wicked hilarity. 'Of course, Iwerne Minster. Anyway, I'm afraid that actually I've called you by mistake. You're not within the age demographic of this particular survey after all. I do apologize for taking up your time. Thank you so much for your cooperation anyway. Goodbye.'

Sweat beading my forehead, I hung up, thinking that maybe this plan wasn't so daft after all. As long as I pretended to be Gavin, who could fib for England, I'd be fine.

'Well, that's not bad,' I said to the camera. 'One down, four to go. We can cross *her* off.'

I drew a thick black magic marker through Paramor, Ann S., Iwerne Minster, and dialled the Shrewsbury one, feeling slightly calmer this time.

An answerphone clicked in straight away, and we heard a brusque voice. '*Hi, this is Ann. I'm away until the tenth of January, so unless it's a business enquiry please don't clog up my machine with messages. The next fair I'm doing will be in Olympia, Earl's Court, London from the second to the fourth of February. Thank you.*'

'Oh my God,' I said to Mack. 'That could really be her. She sounds the right age. Did you think her voice was like mine?'

Mack looked pityingly at me. 'Emma, she had a Yorkshire accent. And her voice is much deeper than yours.' He took in my crestfallen face. 'Although that doesn't mean anything, of course. You're right, she did sound about the right age. But what was all that about a fair?'

'Maybe she works in a fairground, you know, like those blokes who spin the Waltzers round until you're sick.'

Mack laughed, and I had a brief mental picture of Shrewsbury Ann as a heavily tattooed dirt-brown woman with bulging biceps and a fag hanging out of her mouth, growling, 'Scream if you want to go faster.' The voice almost fitted, and it made a refreshing change from the Mommie Dearest image of her in the frothy nightie.

'Well, it's easy to find out,' said Mack, marching over to the Yellow Pages and handing it to me. I looked up Olympia, phoned the number, and within minutes an automated voice informed us that there would be an Holistic and Spiritual Fair held there on 2–4 February 2001.

'Miss Marple eat your heart out!' I said, grinning triumphantly at Mack. 'We just saved ourselves the cost of petrol up to Shropshire. Put it in your diary – we're going to Olympia.'

And assuming we ruled out all the others first, I thought to myself, then I could be meeting my birth mother in less than three months. My stomach swooped up with excitement.

'OK. This is the last one we've got a number for – the Nottingham one. Let's give this one a go, and then we can go to Harlesden.'

It was another answering machine, but this time a much less helpful one. A mechanical message, just saying, 'There's nobody here to take your call. Please leave your message after the tone.'

I put down the phone.

'Aren't you going to leave a message?'

'Of course not. I can't ask her to ring me back without explaining what I want. And I'm not using that stupid transport survey excuse again. She's probably out at work – I'll just try her again another time. So, can we go to Harlesden now?'

Mack refused to remove the camera from his eye at all, saying he wanted to capture the entire journey. All well and good artistically, I thought crossly as I took yet another wrong turning, but a bit of bloody navigation wouldn't go amiss. I was feeling too nervous to concentrate properly on the directions I'd written out in advance.

About forty-five minutes later, we eventually pulled into the correct street in Harlesden. Andover Road turned out to be a long, straight residential terrace, unadorned by greenery of any sort whatsoever, except for a dead ficus plant, still in its pot, lying like a corpse in the gutter. The number on the front door nearest us was 266.

'Down the other end, then,' I said, changing up into third gear and revving the engine out of sheer nervousness. Mack finally detached himself from the video camera to rotate his aching arm.

'Cramp,' he said, flexing his fingers. The camera's eyepiece had left a faint circle around his right eye, as if he'd been wearing swimming goggles with only one lens. He started filming again, adding in David Attenborough hushed tones: 'And here we are. Andover Road. Home of one of our primary targets.'

I wished he wouldn't be so flippant. My birth mother might live in this road.

The houses were identical in size and age: terraced two-up-two-down cottages, although many had looming dormer windows signifying a loft conversion. Most had white UPVC windows, and a few were stone clad, or painted in improbable colours – pastel green or nasty blancmange pink. Mack opened the passenger window and was holding the camera out, capturing the mosaic terrace as I drove along it.

An amiable-looking mongrel loped along the pavement, staring at the eye of the camera as if his lifelong ambition was to be on the telly, and two stout Indian ladies in saris stopped their conversation to stare suspiciously at us.

Right at the far end of the street, just before an incongruous butcher's shop – the only retail outlet in the vicinity – I began to slot the Golf into a space between a brimming skip and a rusted mini with a missing wheel, opposite number seven.

'What do you do when you see a spaceman?' Mack asked suddenly.

'Reverse into it, man,' I replied automatically, craning back over my shoulder to make sure I didn't hit the skip. I might be terrible at remembering jokes, but I wasn't *that* terrible. 'Not that this is any time for jokes,' I added, turning back around to get my first proper look at the house in question. Then I wished I hadn't.

'Hmm,' said Mack, zooming out to take in the neglected and sorry façade of number seven.

I took off my glasses and cleaned them on the hem of my shirt, bending forward to do it so that I could look away. When I straightened up again, the house still looked like a squat.

'She doesn't live here.' There was no way my mother lived in that house.

'Emma, you can't have preconceptions like that. She might. We're fairly sure an Ann Paramor lives here. What we don't know is if it's *the* Ann Paramor.'

The video camera was fixed on my disappointed face, and I wanted to punch its unfeeling glass eye.

Mack gestured up the street. 'Look. It's not a bad little road. Most of the houses are well kept.'

'Except number seven,' I wailed.

'You never know, Emma. Maybe she's renting it out, or has sold it, or is getting it done up tomorrow. That could be her skip. And don't forget, this is the reason we're here, so you can find out for yourself. She might well not even be the one.'

I exhaled so deeply that the windscreen steamed up. I hoped his camera lens had too. 'So what do we do now?'

Mack reclined back his seat and grinned. 'It's a stakeout, baby. I've always wanted to do this.' He pulled a pair of shades from the pocket of his denim jacket and handed them to me. 'Binoculars would be better, but these'll have to do. We sit here for a few hours, right. Nothing happens, then one of us goes to buy coffee and doughnuts, and the second we tuck in and stop surveillance, the subject comes and goes and we don't even notice. That's how it usually works in the films.'

'Yeah, right. Grow up, can't you?' I meant it as a joke, kind of, only it came out more harshly than I'd intended, and Mack looked hurt.

'I'm really sorry, Mack. I didn't mean it. I'm just a bit ... tense.' I handed back his sunglasses, and he put them in his pocket again.

'Don't worry about it,' he said lightly, and I felt like a heel.

The house really did not look promising. Surely my birth mother couldn't live in a place like that? It wasn't the size or the modesty of the house, just the complete dilapidation. It was ... *slovenly*.

I remembered our immaculate Victorian detached house in Acton, with the tiled front path and the stained glass panels in the door. When the sun shone through them, light danced a crimson welcome all around the hallway. I felt a deep pang of sadness at the memory of our lost home, and then an uneasy guilt. No, I wasn't being a snob. It was only natural to hope that this Ann Paramor couldn't be the one. Why would anyone want to admit to a relative who lived in a place like this?

'Sew, who laves in a playce like thi-is?' Mack joked, in a terrible Loyd Grossman accent, and I rewarded him with a faint smile and rolled eyes.

After an hour, our eyes ached from staring and our legs were cramped. There had been no movement from number seven, and even Mack had given up filming. I convinced myself that it was either the wrong house, or the wrong mother, and felt as much relief as disappointment. I still had absolutely no idea what I'd say to her, even if she were suddenly to appear.

The Indian ladies were long gone, and only one man had passed by since, a large Rasta whose dreadlocks hung in a long straight tube down his back, secured in three places so that they resembled some kind of plumbing arrangement. He half walked, half skanked into the butcher's, and came out clutching a softly bulging package in a paper bag.

Bored with staring at number seven's blank face, I studied the butcher's shop instead. Four weeks before Christmas, and the interior was already festooned with paperchains and crappy plastic trees; snowflakes and deformed-looking snowmen stuck to the edges of the windows. Lurid baubles littered the sawdust, lying with the fake parsley where disembowelled loins and ribs and shiny dead organs jostled for space with one another. Across the middle of the plate glass was a foot-high cardboard Father Christmas with a blood-stained striped apron tied over the top of his red uniform. 'Ho, ho, ho, and a Merry Christmas from Winthrop the Butcher' said the cartoon Santa, a meat cleaver in one hand and a string of sausages in the other. I thought it would have been funny to have Donner and Blitzen lurking petrified in the background, but there were no reindeer in sight.

I tried to imagine myself growing up in this street; riding my bicycle along its uneven pavements; maybe playing Knock Down Ginger with other local kids – although I'd never played it at our house in Acton. It just seemed fitting, like the thought of me as a latchkey child, letting myself into the cold, dank little house opposite every day after school, making my own tea and watching television while Ann – my mother – was out at work as a cleaner, maybe, or a factory worker. Oh, the crassness of my preconceptions, I thought. Just because she lived in a run-down house? I'd never realized what a snob I secretly was; I, who always tried to be liberal, egalitarian. I felt ashamed of myself.

'Come on, Emma. We've been here for an hour and nothing's happened. I really think you should knock on the door – she might not come out all day.'

I took out my mobile phone and rang the number again. Still no answer. 'That's because she's not *in*,' I said. 'We're waiting for her to come back, not go out.'

'She's probably at work.'

'Yes.'

'So knock on the neighbours' doors. You don't have to tell them why you're looking for her. At least they should be able to tell you if she even does still live there. They might know where she works, and we could go there instead.'

He had a point.

'Come on, then.' I climbed out of the car and jogged reluctantly across the road, feeling like Anneka Rice, my trusty cameraman by my side. 'Let's try this one,' I said, opening the gate to number five.

I rang the doorbell and a small child with a dirty face opened the door, a thick plug of green creeping from her nostril inexorably towards her top lip, like lava flow. She wore a pair of Bob the Builder pyjama trousers on her head, the empty legs draped over her shoulders. As soon as she saw Mack and his video camera, her mouth dropped open in a gormless stare of bewildered suspicion.

I crouched down in front of her, although the snot was making me feel sick. 'What's your name?' I asked. She was about four or five.

Still staring at the camera, she wiped her nose on her sleeve, dashing the slime across her cheek in a splatter effect. 'My name is Mrs Pringle,' she said. 'Do you like my hair?' She tossed her head, and the pyjama trouser legs swung from side to side.

'Yes, it's lovely and . . . long,' I said. 'Is your mummy there, Mrs Pringle?'

'*Mu-um!*' she suddenly screamed into my ear, so

loudly that my eye twitched involuntarily.

A tired-looking blonde woman about my age appeared in the doorframe. The roots of her hair were black and strong, as if responsible for the energy drain in the rest of her body. 'Yeah?' she said, unsmiling, staring at the camera as suspiciously as her daughter had. I felt the old, discomforting shyness flit across my skin like a shadow across the sun.

'Oh, um, hello. Please take no notice of the camera; my friend's just filming me for a documentary he's making. If it's a problem just say and we'll stop. I'm really sorry to bother you, but I'm actually trying to get in touch with the lady next door, Ann Paramor. Do you know if she's out at work?'

The woman rubbed a finger across her front teeth as if checking that she didn't have lipstick on them. Since she wasn't even wearing lipstick, it seemed like an unnecessary precaution.

'This gonna be on telly then?'

'Possibly,' said Mack, ostentatiously zooming in on her. The little girl tried to push her way past her mother's legs to get in the frame, but her mother blocked the doorway and wouldn't let her through. A discreet but unseemly tussle ensued.

'I wanna be on teeveeeee!' came a muffled voice from behind the mother's thighs.

The woman folded her arms across her chest, pursed her lips, and spoke directly to the camera, ignoring me. 'Her next door works down the Post Office, on the counter.'

'She's a weeeeirdo an' she eats bats,' added the little girl, forcing her head out in the gap between her mother's skinny thigh and the doorframe.

'Shut up, Charlotte,' said the mother, reaching back to slap Mrs Pringle lightly on the pyjama-clad head. They both had severely adenoidal voices, and breathed noisily through their mouths when not talking.

'Is it far?' I felt sick again, this time with nerves.

'Nah. Round the corner, second right, can't miss it.'

'Thank you very much. Um – can you tell me, roughly, how old she is?'

The woman looked at me as if I'd asked if she knew how many sexual partners Ann Paramor had had.

'Late forties?' she said, shrugging.

Shit. The right sort of age. And we knew where she worked.

'Right. Thanks. One more question – is there a Mr Paramor?'

'Telly or no telly, if you're from the police, I wanna see your badge,' said the woman, moving to close the door in my face.

A blush branded my face, and I could feel sweat on my palms. It wouldn't be nearly so awful if Mack and his bloody camera weren't recording every painful exchange. I considered asking him to stop.

'No, no, I'm not from the police at all, it's just . . . personal. She, um, used to know somebody that I know.'

'No, there ain't no Mr Paramor. Not that I ever saw. Divorced, maybe.'

Shit, shit. With every new piece of information, I realized with a sinking heart exactly how much I didn't want this to be the right Ann Paramor, and how much she really could be.

I thanked the woman and her daughter, and trailed back to the car, trembling. Mack bounded gleefully in beside me, still filming.

'Right! Post Office, here we come!' he said, making ignition-key-turning motions with his free hand. 'It's perfect. You can check her out by buying a couple of stamps; she's bound to have a name tag on.'

I made a decision.

'No,' I said, folding my sheet of Paramors into a fan as wobbly as my lower lip. 'I'm not going to the Post Office.'

'Why?'

'Because I'm a snob and a terrible person, but I don't want it to be her because of where she lives,' I said, and burst into tears.

Mack turned off the camera at once. He hugged me awkwardly, leaning across the handbrake. 'You're not a snob or a terrible person. I'm sorry, Emma. God knows I should have been more sensitive, after my own experiences. I just got carried away with finally getting somewhere.'

'I know. But I keep thinking about you and your birth mother. What if Ann's like that?'

'Emma, I keep telling you: what if she *isn't*? Of course it's natural to be apprehensive, but you've got to be prepared for anything. She might be an alcoholic, or a criminal, or mentally ill – you just have no way of knowing until you find her. At least this Ann is responsible enough to hold down a job at the Post Office, so she can't be a complete loser.'

'You're right. Maybe if I draw a blank with all the others, I'll come back here and try again another time,' I sniffed, taking off my glasses and drying my eyes.

'Well, up to you, of course. Although I do think that it would be best to rule her out altogether, otherwise you'll always be wondering.'

'I know. Just . . . not today, OK? I feel like such a failure, running away like this when we're potentially so close, but I can't face it.'

'Emma, you aren't a failure. Don't be daft. It's a very traumatic thing you're doing – take all the time you need. We'll try the others first, and then take a view on coming back here later, OK?'

I nodded miserably. As I pulled away, I looked back at number seven in my rear-view mirror, hoping against hope that I'd never have to see it again. A small canary-coloured fledgling was standing disconsolately in the road, gazing after my retreating car.

'Damn,' said Mack. 'I should've filmed all that.'

'Too late,' I replied. Too late.

21

I felt depressed after the abortive trip to Harlesden. Despite Mack's reassurances that my concerns were completely natural, I couldn't stop feeling ashamed of my negative feelings about the house and its putative occupant. Every time I tried to think positively, I saw the muscular weeds forcing their way up between the paving stones on Ann Paramor's front path, and the scabrous moulting once-white pebbledash on the house's exterior, grey and baggy like elderly underwear, and it made me feel sick. Perhaps it was a mistake. Perhaps it was better never to know. There would be no shame in giving up. I could stop the filming, and Stella would never find out.

Stella wasn't helping, tripping around the flat in huge clunky wedges and a skintight dress, preparing for another Saturday night out. She was sitting at the kitchen table, peering into a compact, putting on make-up with the painstaking application of Michelangelo painting the Sistine Chapel.

'Are you OK, Em?' she said, plucking a rogue hair out of her eyebrow. 'You're biting your fingers.'

I looked down at my hands. I was literally tearing at the skin around my cuticles, shredding it with my teeth even as I was aware of the white pain which would follow later, after the blood had stopped flowing.

'No. I'm fed up. I want to see Gav.'

I was missing Gavin even more than ever, too. I wondered what he was doing tonight. There were four probable options: beer 'n' takeaway in front of the telly; night out with the lads; unidentified dodgy dealings with unnamed contacts in out-of-the-way places, probably underneath railway arches or round the back of empty shopping precincts. Or there was a worse possibility: out with new girlfriend. I didn't even want to *think* about that one.

It occurred to me that none of the first three options made him sound like a particularly good catch, and then found myself leaping to his defence. Ridiculous – defending him against my own charges . . .

'So do you?'

I hadn't even noticed that Stella was talking to me. 'Do I what?'

'Want to come to this party with me and Suzanne?'

Here we go again, I thought. Younger sister takes pity on sad, Bridget-Jonesesque spinster. I couldn't think why she was asking me, after our last fiasco at the pub.

'I don't think so, thanks. I fancy a night in watching TV.'

Stella cackled like Cruella de Vil. 'What, another one? There's nothing worth watching tonight.'

'Yes there is, actually. There's a really interesting documentary on about the rise of Nazism.'

Stella laughed again, thinking I was being sarcastic. I was annoyed.

'I'm serious, Stella. I'm sick of watching these stupid vacuous reality TV things or unfunny sitcoms. We should both watch more educational television. I mean, what do we ever talk about, except blokes, pop music, last night's crap TV, or what shopping we need to get?'

Stella rolled her sparkly eyes at me. 'Emma, I'm

nineteen. I don't care about politics or history. I just want to have a good time.'

'Well, I'm twenty-nine, and I do care,' I said. 'I want to be someone who has *opinions*. I want to be able to make informed decisions about things other than how many boob jobs Scary Spice has had.'

'OK then, you should definitely come to this party. It's at Yehudi's house, you know, my art tutor, so there'll be lots of mature people there. Probably masses of single, intelligent men who can talk to you about Nazism until they're blue in the face.'

'I don't know,' I said, relenting slightly. It did sound better than the usual brain-dead student gatherings Stella attended.

'It's entirely up to you, Em. I'm not going to beg.'

'Where is it, and how are you getting there?'

'Barnes. We were going to cab it, but if you're coming, then it would make sense for you to drive, wouldn't it?'

'What if I want to drink?'

'Oh go on, Emma, please? It'll cost us a fortune in cab fares otherwise.'

'I thought you said you weren't going to beg.'

I took them to the party. I suddenly couldn't bear the thought of staying in, yet again waiting for the phone not to ring. And to be honest, I hadn't really fancied the documentary. Plus, I had a new dress that I hadn't yet had the opportunity to wear, and my cosmetics were in danger of drying up and fossilizing if I didn't give them an outing soon. Even putting on lipstick *and* lip-liner felt like an adventure.

After some very militant navigation from Stella in the passenger seat, I found a parking place at the end of the road and briefly scrutinized my appearance in the rear-view mirror. Next to Suzanne, with her beautiful glossy brown skin and doe eyes, and Stella's gorgeous face and cool hair, I felt distinctly old-haggish, despite them both sitting up and whistling

194

when I emerged from my bedroom in my new Jigsaw dress. It was the element of surprise to the whistle which I didn't like: sort of, Wow, for an ancient person, you scrub up quite well . . . But I supposed that Suzanne *had* deigned to ask me where I got my eyeshadow from, and had looked impressed when I told her it was Urban Decay. So maybe I was over-blowing this OAP trip. I wasn't even thirty yet, for God's sake.

They were both still grumbling in anticipation, with the blithe confidence of teenagers: '*And* it's creepy old Yankee Yehudi, too – not even someone sexy like Collin or Scott. Oh well, let's make the most of it. Free booze and maybe some spliff, and he might even give us a better mark in our life class.'

'Yeah, but we'll probably have to listen to him banging on about California all night. If he loves it so much, why doesn't he just go home? It's not like he needs the money, teaching life drawing. He's loaded already.'

'Come on, let's get it over with.'

The three of us marched into the house through the open front door, me trailing marginally behind, and out the other side onto a large patio in the garden, where the party was in full swing.

'Oh my God,' whispered Stella in my ear, 'it's even worse than I knew it would be.'

'What do you mean? You just spent half an hour convincing me it was going to be a fantastic party!'

'Well, you wouldn't have come otherwise, would you? Look, he's got a vodka luge, and people are queuing up for it – in this weather! They'll freeze.'

She pointed towards the far corner of the garden, where a specially built wooden frame supported an enormous block of ice. Behind the frame was a stepladder, on which Yehudi was perilously perched, pouring something, presumably vodka, down a chute carved in the ice. At the end stood a woman, scantily dressed in a worn T-shirt and a hippy skirt with bells hanging off it, straggly blue streaks in her hair, her head tilted back and her mouth wide open to receive the flow of interestingly-chilled alcohol.

Three or four small children stood around, fascinated at the proceedings. One little boy was clutching a toy car, his fingers almost visibly itching to put it at the top of the luge and let it go skidding down his very own mini bobsleigh run.

'Blimey, it must have cost him a fortune to get that ice delivered. What a poser. It might be quite a cool thing to have – *if* the temperature was eighty degrees. That woman'll catch her death.' Suzanne disgustedly helped herself to a cup of wine from a bottle open on the table, and poured one for Stella and me too.

Stella tittered. 'Yehudi's got confused, he thinks he's in Venice Beach, not Barnes. Is this really what Americans do at Thanksgiving parties?'

The woman who had just drunk from the luge went around to the stepladder, patted Yehudi's bottom, and called out something to her friends, an assortment of female hippies. They all laughed as they whirled and shook their hair to a James Brown CD which blared from a boombox on the patio. I was immoderately relieved to see that there were indeed plenty of people there older than me.

'Do you think that's Yehudi's girlfriend?' Stella asked Suzanne.

'I doubt it. I thought he liked his women young and fresh, not old and wrinkly like that one. Look at her, she's got to be the wrong side of forty.'

They shuddered with horror at the mere idea of someone that old having a sex life. Then Yehudi spotted us from his vantage point atop the stepladder and, gesturing to someone else to take his place, he jumped down and rushed across to greet us.

'Suzanne! Stella! Great to see you, girls, so glad you could make it!' He turned to me: 'And you must be? Hmm? . . . Oh, right, *Emma*. Lovely to meet you,' and leaned over and kissed my hand ostentatiously. I had a simultaneous urge to slap away his shiny bald head and to wipe my hand on my dress, but I managed instead to smile, gamely.

'Not many of you young folk here, but hey, early days yet. We got turkey burgers and corn on the barbecue over there, and pecan pie for dessert, so go help yourselves. I see you found the wine – sodas in the kitchen if you want them. What do you think of the luge – isn't it just the coolest thing you ever saw? I want you kids to see that us Americans really know how to throw a party!'

Oh well, I thought. At least someone believed I still fell into the category of 'kid'.

He hared off again to put a new tape in the ghetto-blaster, and presently the intro to Parliament's *Up For The Down Stroke* rang out around the yard. Suzanne and Stella looked at one another and made faces.

'Did you see what he was wearing? That hideous tanktop, and light tan Timberlands? *So* ninety-five, darling . . . For someone who teaches on a fashion course, you'd think he'd have better taste. Not to *mention* his hippy friends.'

They spent a happy ten minutes doing such a good impersonation of the Fashion Police that I could practically see the blue lights flashing around them. I identified more with the way that Yehudi and the hippies were dressed than with Stella and Suzanne's outrageous garb, so kept quiet. Thankfully, they were eventually interrupted by a knock on the kitchen window.

'Oh look, there's Kevin and Elias. Thank God, some-one else made it. Come on, Emma, we'll introduce you.'

We traipsed into the kitchen, where huge bottles of generic-brand supermarket pop in lurid fizzy hues jostled for every available inch of counter space with forty-packs of cheap toilet paper, its dull scratchy off-whiteness providing a welcome break from the hectic sodas. Kevin and Elias were standing staring out the window in abject queeny horror at the proceedings. A man and a woman sat at the kitchen table, both rolling joints, and with a sinking heart I recognized the man as Charlie the Creep.

'Hi! What a relief to see you. Happy Thanksgiving – as if we care. And what the hell is going on in the garden? Why is Yehudi up a ladder? Is he making an ice sculpture?'

Stella and Suzanne kissed their classmates. 'Vodka luge, dude,' said Suzanne. 'You mean you've never seen one before? Rumour has it that they were all the rage in ninety-three on the Beach. We're supposed to be witnessing how the Californians throw a party.' She made a pouting face, and swigged the rest of her plastic cup of wine.

I cleared my throat conspicuously, making a face at Stella. Normally I'd have lurked shyly until introduced, but with this teenage rabble I was more or less beyond caring.

'Oh, sorry, Em. Everyone, this is my sister Emma.'

Elias and Kevin rushed over and shook hands with me. 'Oh my God, Kev,' said Elias. 'Just *look* at those eyelashes!'

'Aren't they to die for?' Kevin agreed, and I annoyed myself by blushing.

Charlie raised his head and nodded at me. 'We met before, didn't we,' he said, a comment, not a question, looking as uninterested as he had on the first occasion.

'So where're Lawrence and Dan tonight? Are they coming?' Stella peered out of the window, trying to spot them in the garden, and I could see Suzanne holding her breath in anticipation at the mention of Dan's name.

'No, I heard they were going to see Limp Bizkit in concert, ' said Elias.

Suzanne looked bereft, and helped herself to another drink. 'I *love* Limp Bizkit,' she said, sadly.

I leaned my back against the kitchen counter and watched Charlie at work on his joint. He was enormous, bigger than I remembered, perched gingerly on the small kitchen chair as though it were made of matchsticks. He had very short cropped black hair and a charcoal five o'clock shadow. When he opened his mouth to speak, his voice was so low that it almost made the floorboards vibrate. I supposed he was actually pretty handsome, if you liked that kind of thing. But he gave me the creeps, without a doubt.

Charlie twisted the end of the joint, lit it, and inhaled with a brief fierce crackle of flame and paper. He took a couple more drags then passed it to the dark-haired girl next to him, who so far had not spoken.

I sat down at the table next to her. 'Hi, I'm Emma. Are you Charlie's girlfriend?'

Shaking her head and laughing, the girl took several hefty sucks of the joint, having to choke back a coughing fit which made her shoulders quake. When she could breathe once more, she said, 'Ugh, no! He's my brother.'

I wasn't surprised that she wasn't his girlfriend; not with the way he stared at Stella. The girl neither volunteered her own name, nor passed me the joint. Instead I saw it head around in Stella's direction. Stella took a couple of drags, challenging me from beneath her sparkly eyelids. Of course I knew she partook, but I didn't particularly like to witness it.

'What's Yehudi doing with all these bottles of fizzy drink?' asked Suzanne. 'Grape, lemon-lime, cherry – who drinks this stuff?'

Charlie looked behind him at the regimented stacks of white toilet paper.

'I shouldn't think we'll get through that lot, either, not unless the turkey burgers are off.'

His pronunciation of 'off' sounded like 'orf'. Prat, I thought. But Stella was laughing like he'd said something incredibly funny. She already looked stoned.

I decided I'd better leave them alone, before I said

something I regretted. It was Stella's life. She was on her own path, I reminded myself. It was nothing to do with me.

22

I stepped back out into the garden and headed straight for the bonfire, to keep the cold November chill out of my bones. It felt strange, to have a hot front and cold back, but I was enjoying the feeling of my cheeks reddening and my outspread hands toasting in the heat.

Charlie's sister had also come into the garden, where I spotted her in earnest conversation with the women hippies, looking like an anthropologist trying to communicate with a hitherto undiscovered tribe. Shifting from foot to foot, I surreptitiously checked out the talent.

There was none. Apart from the students in the kitchen, all the men were like Yehudi – over forty-five and 'loosely woven', as Mum would have said. They all seemed to have too much facial hair, smoked roll-ups, and were indeed talking about earnest subjects: devolution, solar energy, Wittgenstein. Despite what I'd said to Stella earlier, I felt an overwhelming desire to instigate a conversation about whether Tom Cruise was gay or not. Perhaps I just didn't have it in me to become an intellectual.

I felt another pang for Gavin, who had two modes of conversation: vacuous ramblings on topics about which he actually knew very little, or lengthy diatribes about people who'd ripped him off. Both modes were always entertaining, even if often extremely light on fact.

I wondered if I *should* give him a call after all, just to say hi, see how he was. Surely, after a six-year relationship, he wouldn't think this was out of order? There was no rule saying we couldn't be friends . . . But then the thought of Gavin with another woman, as was probably the case by now, made me realize that I didn't want to be friends with Gavin. I wanted to be Gavin's lover, or nothing at all. Sex was the glue which had sealed our relationship, like a broken handle stuck on a teapot; if the glue dried up and peeled off, there was no hope of the teapot ever functioning again.

'Hello. I'm Hugo.' I nearly jumped out of my skin. A man had materialized next to me, and was sticking his hand out for me to shake. His wrists poked endlessly out of an unravelling bottle-green jumper, and I just knew his handshake would be limp.

'Oh, hi. I'm Emma. Sorry, I was miles away.'

'Have you had any food yet? I know Yehudi's laid on some burgers and things. I brought a nice bean dish, too, for all the veggies amongst us. What about yourself? Do you partake of the flesh?'

I thought about Gavin, lying naked on a bed with a big smile and an even bigger erection. 'Oh, most definitely,' I replied, although I hardly ever ate meat. 'The rarer the better. In fact, I just like the cow to walk over to my plate and lie down.' God, if only I could be that confident with good-looking men instead of with middle-aged untrendy no-hopers like Hugo.

Hugo laughed uneasily, and I felt sorry for him. In the firelight I noticed his bristly red hair and scaly skin. I could see him wondering if I was serious about the beef remarks. 'Are you, um, here with anyone, Emma?'

'Just my little sister and her friend. Yehudi teaches them life drawing at Ealing – they're in the kitchen with their mates.'

He brightened. 'And what do you do?'

'I'm an aromatherapist.'

'*Really?*' Now he looked positively gleeful. 'Do you know, I've been looking for a good aromatherapist for ages. I suffer from psoriasis, and I was wondering if a good massage might help.'

I smiled sympathetically at him. 'Probably. Although you might be better off with reflexology – sometimes the aromatherapy oils can exacerbate the condition. It varies from person to person.'

'I think I'd like to give it a try, though,' he said with barely disguised lust. I had to blink away a mental image of Hugo lying on my massage table, his white flesh spread out before me. I bet he had tufts of red hair on his buttocks.

I never used to think like that. In fact, I hadn't cared about what anyone's body was like since Nigel and his mole, spread out before me at my very first massage class. Old, young, pock-marked, smooth, scaly, cellulitey – I just registered them all with a detached professional awareness of the sort of pressure I should exert on them, or the blends of oils I should use. It was ironic, considering how utterly self-conscious I'd been when it had been my turn to strip off for a massage in class.

Massage was the only thing in my life that I'd ever truly excelled at. I did OK at school, but I never got a 'A' for anything until I did my aromatherapy diploma. Then I wiped the floor with the lot of them. It wasn't done to be openly competitive, but everyone commented on how I sailed through the course. I couldn't have anticipated that I would be so good at the actual massage – although I still suspected that Betsey's influence was, somehow, something to do with it – and I was so determined to pass the other, more technical parts of the course that I just swotted like I'd never swotted before. I even got top marks in the horrendous tests on the properties of all forty-nine of the essential oils.

It was an unexpected gift, really; the one positive thing which had emerged out of the chaos of Mum and Dad's death, considering that my original plan had been to study teacher training at Exeter University. I'd have made a lousy teacher. I only chose massage because it was a local, and short, course, qualifying me for a job which I could do from home, enabling me to be available to Stella after school. Those endless, endless, school afternoons: Stella dishevelled and obnoxious in her school uniform, over-tired and crotchety, ketchup on her tie and sometimes the smell of cigarette smoke in her hair, resenting me making her do her homework . . .

Hugo was still rambling on about something – what? Oh, rambling. He was rambling about rambling; so I tuned out again and tried to see if I could remember the physiological properties of *Lavandula angustifolia*: anticonvulsive; cicatrisant; immune stimulant; cytophylactic; anti-venomous. Ugh, that exam had been horrific. Lavender might be good for Hugo's psoriasis, though.

'Hi, Em, are you having fun? Just thought I'd come out and say hellooooo. Charlie's getting the drinks in.'

Stella came up behind me and put her arms around my waist, fitting her sharp little chin into the groove of my shoulder blade. She was stoned, giggling. Her pupils were huge and she had an undefined look about her, like a cartoon ghost with black holes for eyes. The flickering bonfire light made her seem even more ethereal.

'I'm in love,' she said dreamily, ignoring Hugo, who was still standing awkwardly next to us. 'Isn't it funny, when you've known someone so long and you suddenly start to fancy them?' She laughed again. 'Y'know, if I keep laughing, it feels like I might just float away.'

I gripped her arm, understanding perfectly how she felt, wanting to secure her ghostly weightlessness. Charlie loomed next to us, carrying two plastic cups

204

full of wine. He gave one to Stella and kept the other, not even including me in his gaze, let alone his drinks round.

Stella turned away from me and nuzzled up to Charlie instead. 'Why are you so big?' she asked him, touching his rugby-toned bull neck with two fingers as though taking his pulse.

'Why are your fingers so cold?' he replied, grabbing her hand and squeezing it.

'Cos I'm a ghost, left over from Halloween.' It made me half proud, half sad, somehow, that we'd shared the same thought. Stella giggled, and Charlie pulled her to him, one arm loosely draped in front of her chest and up the side of her neck, in what was obviously meant to be an affectionate manner, but which looked as if he was trying to strangle her.

'It's OK, Em, I needed an anchor,' Stella called across in my direction.

'Anchor' was not quite the word I'd use for that man, I thought. I felt faintly nauseous.

'I'm going back inside,' I said abruptly. 'I'm cold. Nice to meet you, Hugo,' and I strode back into the cold blue-black chill of the air away from the bonfire, trying to take my mind off the uneasiness caused by Charlie's presence by thinking of the first time I'd ever massaged another person.

On the third day of my aromatherapy course, the tutor had showed twenty of us into a large room containing a line of massage couches down each side, like a makeshift hospital ward in a village hall, except for the one additional couch standing alone in the middle of the room, forming a large letter H. The tutor was called Shelley, and she was extremely softly spoken, with lots of fluffy blonde hair, big Deirdre Barlow glasses, and a large crystal pendant around her neck. She stationed herself next to the lone couch.

'Right, everybody,' she whispered in a drizzled-lavender oil voice, as we all strained to hear. 'Today I'm going to teach you some essential towel techniques, and we'll start learning the basic massage strokes for the back and shoulders. Please choose a partner, go and stand beside a bed, and decide between yourselves who's going to massage first. I'll need a volunteer for me to work on here, too.'

I nearly began to hyperventilate on the spot. I'm expected to strip off in front of all these people? You must be *joking*, I thought. There weren't even any curtains or anything around the beds! Why, oh why, hadn't I gone into some sensible profession, like hairdressing or journalism, where you didn't have to take your clothes off in front of strangers? It wasn't that I was ashamed of my body, particularly – although it has to be said that I didn't exactly love it. If I'd only been six inches taller, I'd be fine, because everything would stretch to fit; my thighs and calves and hips would all look much more in proportion. *Stella* was almost as tall as me, and at the time she was only eleven . . .

As I fretted and gazed frantically around the group, wondering why I hadn't thought of earmarking any possible partners sooner, I felt a tap on my shoulder. Horror of horrors – it was the token male in the group, Nigel.

'Hi,' he said. 'Want to be my partner?' It was the first time I'd seen him close up, and I noticed how his plump, dry lower lip stuck out in a permanent chapped pout. For some reason I thought of kissing it, of how its dry rasp would feel against my own lips. Oh *no*. Please no. Why did I have to get the man? I closed my eyes.

'I – um – didn't realize we'd have to practise on *each other*. I thought there'd be, you know, members of the public, like when you can get your hair cut free by students.' I had no idea why I said that. Of course I'd known we'd be working on each other – Shelley had said so from the beginning. I'd even gone to Marks &

Spencer and purchased an entire new selection of chaste white underwear to replace the greying shreds which had previously lain limply in my knicker drawer. But now the dreaded moment had come, I was panicking.

Nigel smiled again, which made his lip stick out even further. He was very tall, with long, tanned bony shanks in cotton football shorts. Far too old and hippy-looking for my taste, and unmistakably male. For some reason I'd never even thought about massaging men. What if he, you know, got a bit excited? Men couldn't help that kind of thing, could they? Apart from Dad getting out of the bath or dressing in the mornings, I'd never seen a naked man before. I hadn't even managed to lose my virginity yet, at the shamefully late age of twenty-one.

'Don't worry,' said Nigel. 'I promise you, you'll get used to it really soon. My wife's an aromatherapist too, and I remember when she trained, she found it a bit weird to begin with. Tell you what, why don't you do me first?'

He was already sliding his feet out of his sandals and pulling off his T-shirt to reveal a chest populated with scrubby pale hairs. I shuddered, although the mention of his wife had put me slightly more at ease. All around me, the massagees were tentatively sliding out of their clothes, casting shifty glances from side to side to check that nobody else was peeking. There was a considerable amount of very unprofessional self-conscious tittering going on, which also put me at ease, as did the fact that everybody, with the exception of Nigel, was wearing pristine new underwear like my own. The place briefly sparkled with dazzling white pants before nine self-conscious women and one utterly blithe man wriggled onto the massage couches and lay face down. I felt much better, although I still wished I didn't have Nigel as a partner.

After Shelley had taught us how to tuck the towels in firmly, and how to uncover only the pertinent part of the anatomy at any one time, we were ready to proceed with the massage. I uncovered Nigel's stringy back, staring at the huge ragged mole which was leeching onto the skin just below his right shoulderblade. I felt sick. In a few minutes that would be me, lying there, and him staring at my wobbly tummy and cellulite. Actually, I didn't have any cellulite, but the mere thought of such close scrutiny made me feel as if it was blossoming on my legs just standing there, busting out all over like a speeded-up film of mould growing in a petri dish.

'We're not going to talk about the different oils today,' said Shelley. 'I'm just going to show you the basic massage strokes. You'll find under your tables a small bowl containing the base oil, a sweet almond oil. Pour a small amount into the palm of your hand, rub your hands together, and we'll start with effleurage . . .'

A strange thing happened as soon as I touched Nigel's flesh. I stopped worrying about getting undressed, or my own body, or even snagging my fingers on Nigel's fierce mole. My hands just seemed to take over. Shelley's whispered instructions flowed into my ears, apparently bypassing my brain and coming straight out again through my hands. It was wonderful, although my hands were really aching when I'd finished.

'Wow,' said Nigel when he sat up. 'That's not the first time you've done that, is it? My wife's been giving me massages for five years, and you seemed as confident as she is.'

I glowed with delight, a feeling that helped me through the awkwardness of having to climb onto a massage bed, naked except for a pair of pants and a towel, in a room full of strangers. When my turn came, I managed to manoeuvre myself onto my stomach by shutting my eyes and pretending there was nobody else in the room.

Unfortunately, when I opened them again, I noticed

two men in boiler suits jostling with each other to peer through the glass of the classroom door, their eyes on stalks, fingertips clutching the bottom of the little window. They reminded me of the cartoon we used to draw all over our schoolbooks: 'Kilroy Woz 'Ere', a wall with a huge nose, eyes and fingers sticking over the top of it. I never did know who Kilroy was.

I yelped, and pointed at them, whereupon they immediately sank out of sight, leaving only a guilty square of empty air.

'Is everything OK, Emma?' whispered Shelley, coming over to see what the matter was.

'Um – sorry – there were two men looking in just now,' I muttered, my cheeks flaming. I could feel my rash spreading across my chest and neck, and when I closed my eyes again it was there behind my eyelids.

Shelley tsked, a small tender sound. 'There are some workmen here sorting out the plumbing in the downstairs cloakroom,' she said. 'They were under strict instructions not to come near this room.'

Yeah, right, I thought. How stupid was that: telling workmen to keep away from a roomful of naked women? By now my heart was pounding, and I remained rigid with tension throughout Nigel's massage, feeling as if a million ballbearings were rolling around underneath my skin, wondering if Nigel, or worse, the workmen, could see my breasts sticking out on either side of my body. It was unlikely, given their resemblance to two fried eggs, but none the less I worried about it. Nigel's hands were cold, and I could smell last night's garlic on his breath, even though I was lying face down.

'Relax,' said Nigel, leaning his face down close to mine, bathing me in a hot garlic wind.

I closed my eyes and pretended that Nigel's long fingers belonged to Betsey instead, and that helped a little; but I couldn't fully relax until it was my turn to do the massage again. Only then did I feel as if the ballbearings had dissolved, taking my bones with them. My body ceased to be flesh and blood and became pure distilled movement, a spiritual connection. It was the first time I'd felt anything spiritual for a long time; certainly the first time since Mum and Dad were killed. I breathed a sigh of relief. I had finally found something I was good at.

Back in the kitchen at the party I saw, through a very unfashionable hatch in the wall, that Suzanne and her two gay friends had adjourned to the dining room. Trails of watery-nosed, wrapped-up people kept coming in and out of the house, ignoring the tangerine soda and the toilet paper, but calling out things like, 'Nippy out there now,' or 'Where's the bathroom?' or 'Any more beer in that fridge?' so I supposed that the students had eventually got tired of the interruptions and moved en masse next door in search of some uninterrupted smoking time. As if I was watching her on television, Suzanne waved at me through the hatch, beckoning me in. 'In a minute,' I mouthed, as I stood at the kitchen sink, running my cold purple hands under the hot tap until they began to thaw out and redden even more. They reminded me of Nigel's hands, on that first massage day.

Just as I was drying them on a damp tea-towel, Stella and Charlie came bumping back into the house, still giggling, and headed straight for the dining room, so I changed my mind and went back outside again. I'd rather take my chances with Hugo and Yehudi than sit and watch those two pawing each other all over, I thought crossly. It was only eleven o'clock, too early to insist on going home.

In the garden, Yehudi had worked up to his grand finale: the fireworks display. He tried to set them off, but only a couple exploded; the rest writhed weakly on the grass out of boredom before fizzling out in disgust. The party outside talked loudly to cover Yehudi's embarrassment, and someone turned the music up. The blue-haired hippy chivvied everyone into dancing around the bonfire, and I lurked out of sight in case Hugo tried to chat me up again.

I noticed that Charlie's sister had found a hippy she really seemed to like, and was admiring her alpaca poncho. Everyone except the little boys had got bored of the liquor luge by now, which was indeed beginning to melt from the heat of the bonfire. The children were whizzing all kinds of objects down the chute: matchbox cars, sticks, bonfire-baked potatoes. It was dripping so much that it was more like white-water rafting than a bobsleigh course.

I found the food, and ate as much of a baked potato as I could manage before its tough hide defeated the flimsy plastic fork with which I was attempting to tackle it. I threw the skin underneath a handy hydrangea bush, and entered into a bit of desultory chit-chat about holistic practices with a couple of the hippies, which ended up being pretty interesting. It passed another hour, anyway, and I managed to avoid Hugo's lovestruck glances from across the bonfire.

When I next went in to see what Stella was doing, she and the others were still sitting solemnly around the huge polished mahogany dining table, as if they were at a funeral and not a party. Charlie had brought in a guitar, which he had apparently found in Yehudi's bedroom on his way back from the toilet, and which he was playing exquisitely, further enthralling Stella. His big sausagey fingers formed complicated bar chords, sending them skittering so effortlessly up and down the frets that the strings squeaked like a kitten with each change of key. The untrimmed ends of the strings waved around the guitar's neck like whiskers.

I stayed with them for a while, gradually lulled by the room's tranquil haze, even relenting enough to accept several tokes of the next joint being passed around. It was ages since I'd last smoked – with Gavin, of course. We used to like to smoke before having sex. Mmmn, I thought longingly, wishing that he wasn't so on my mind.

Charlie's gentle chords played over a myriad of muttered secrets and one or two lies. The accumulation of cigarette ends and flimsy smoked joints floating in the dregs of beer cups were the only indications of the hours passing. I put my elbows on the table and eavesdropped shamelessly on all the stoner conversations.

Charlie told Stella that his sister Lucy was a lesbian, and that 'Mummy was furious' when she found out. So that was her name. Good for Lucy, I thought, feeling faintly affronted that she hadn't tried to chat me up.

Suzanne told Stella that she had gone off men and was thinking about becoming a lesbian. Dan hadn't rung her in five days.

Stella told Charlie that our parents had both been killed in a car crash ten years ago, which made me wince. But Charlie didn't even look over at me. I felt invisible; that encroaching older-woman invisibility which descends like a fog on all but the most stunning thirty-somethings. Heads no longer turn, builders no longer whistle, eyes no longer open wide with startled pleasure at your approach. I didn't count Hugo.

Kevin told Elias that he wanted to marry him when they graduated; then Elias told Kevin that he wanted to marry him too. I could tell he was lying.

Stella told Suzanne that I had led a raving flasher off the tube train, but Suzanne didn't seem very interested. She replied by telling Stella that her hairdresser's mother worked on the Graham Norton show, and I wondered if this was a complete non sequitur, or if there was some connection of which I wasn't aware.

Then Charlie asked Stella if she'd like to come on a date with him. Dinner or something. Stella instantly forgot about Suzanne's hairdresser's mum and Graham Norton, and said she would. Charlie celebrated by putting down the guitar and stroking Stella's breast, and I felt like picking up Suzanne's lighter and setting fire to the hairs in his nose.

'Let's go for a walk,' I heard him whisper in her ear.

Stella's face lit up, in the guilty, furtive way it always did when she was plotting something evil. Again, I feared for her. As they stood, unsteadily, I pulled her aside.

'Please be careful, Stell,' I said in a low voice, willing her to take in what I was saying. 'Talk to the hand cos the face ain't listening' was a college catchphrase of hers and Suzanne's; the traffic policeman's palm pushed out in a stop sign, the head flashily turned away. As I spoke to her, I caught both her hands in my own so that her face *had* to listen to me. 'It's important, Stella. Please. Don't be long. I'm going to have a coffee then I think we should go home, OK?'

Stella rolled her eyes at me. 'I'll be fine. Chill out. We're just going for a walk, that's all.'

I looked to Suzanne for support, but she had fallen asleep, her breath misting up the mahogany table surface, making its shiny depths shallow again. When I turned back, Stella and Charlie had gone.

I drank three cups of black coffee and succeeded in chasing almost all the webby remnants of the smoke from my head; out from behind my eyes, out of my fillings, sluiced from underneath my tongue, even the wisps which had stuck in the crevices of my brain were dislodged. With each fresh cup I looked at my watch. Eventually my head was clear, but fifty-five minutes had passed and there was still no sign of Stella or Charlie.

Suzanne was still asleep. Elias and Kevin were kissing in a corner of the room, perched uncomfortably on one of Yehudi's dining chairs. I identified Kevin's shoulder from the mêlée of tangled limbs, and tapped him on it.

'Whose car did you come in?' I demanded.

Kevin raised his head about an inch, a delicate strand of spit running from his mouth to Elias's.

'Charlie's.' The strand popped and vanished, and he looked away from me.

I tapped him again, more of a poke this time. 'It's important. Stella's not back. What does the car look like, and where did you park?'

'It's a red GTi. End of the road. Want us to come and help you find her?'

'No, don't worry. I'll just go and have a wander. They're probably snogging on the back seat. Thanks.'

I came down the front steps into the cold November night, flattened party sounds rising above the roof behind me. It felt good to be out in the crisp frosty air after the cloying warmth of the smoky dining room. Yehudi's house was in the middle of the street, but I couldn't see a red GTi in either direction. Tutting, I strolled down to one end of the road, then back to the other. No red cars at all; no Stella. I decided that Charlie must have taken her off for a drive, and hoped fervently he hadn't taken her home without telling anyone. I was by now really ready to leave, and didn't want to be stuck at Yehudi's after everyone else had gone, waiting for Stella perhaps not to reappear at all.

As I turned back towards the party, I made out a dark shape by the rear wheel of my own car. It moved, and I stopped. I squinted through the darkness, trying to work out what it was – a large dog, perhaps. Then it moved again, and I heard a muffled moan. I ran forward as Stella lifted her head very slowly and painfully from between her knees, a vast heavy bowling-ball head, swaying and out of proportion with her body like a baby who couldn't yet sit up. There was blood coming out of her mouth, and one eye was beginning to squeeze shut, blackening in its socket, like the ghost Stella and I had both suspected she already was.

214

23

I woke early the next morning with an awful pressing feeling of doom hanging over me as soon as I struggled into consciousness; the sort of feeling when you know something horrible has happened, but can't immediately think what.

Then I remembered Stella, and the way her swollen eyes had looked as blank as a switched-off television when I'd helped her into bed the previous night. She hadn't spoken a word all the way home, to me or to Suzanne, just mutely and stubbornly shaking her head whenever I said she should go to the police. I still didn't know exactly what Charlie had done to her.

Suzanne had stayed for a drink with me, crying, saying how she had never trusted him, he had a really bad reputation, he'd been in trouble with college before; until eventually I had to bundle her home in a mini-cab, her eyes as raccoon-black as Stella's but with smudged mascara, not violence. It was all I could do to prevent myself shouting at her, 'How could you let her go off with him if you knew that?'

Going back to sleep was out of the question, even at seven a.m. on a Sunday. I got up, dressed, and pottered around the flat, which was infused with a leaden, uncomfortable silence, not the usual easy peace of early morning. I dismissed it as my own stress from the trauma of Stella's injuries, and started to make myself some toast, deciding not to try and wake her. But then I began to worry that she wasn't asleep at all, but lying in a coma with head injuries, or worse. I should've insisted on taking her to Casualty last night, I fretted.

I peered around her bedroom door, squinting through the gloom at the faint bump in the bedclothes. Her breathing, thankfully, was regular, but even with her hair covering her face, I could see that her cheek wasn't the shape it was supposed to be. It was too dark to make out the bruises.

'Stell?' I whispered tentatively, kneeling down beside her. 'Are you OK?'

She groaned and shrugged my hand off her shoulder. 'Leave me alone,' she muttered.

'It's OK. It's early. Go back to sleep. I just wanted to check on you.'

Stella made another sound, an exasperated sort of sigh, and pulled the bedclothes over her head.

The hours until she woke again seemed to last for ever. I couldn't even face playing the recorder – in fact, I didn't know what to do with myself. So I closed the kitchen door behind me and began to clean: surfaces, floor, hob, extractor, even the oven. I put yellow rubber gloves on my hands and Lou Reed's *Transformer* on the boombox, and got down to work. But I had to skip over track three, 'Perfect Day', because it was so far from being a perfect day that bile rose in my throat and tears to my eyes as I scrubbed and squirted and wiped and polished. I knew I'd never again be able to think of the song's simple piano introduction without feeling the same frustrated pain and the harsh scent of cleaning fluid; not just in my nostrils and my throat but also, synaesthetically, yellow and abrasive under my skin, like hate. Like fury.

I emerged from a gleaming kitchen two hours later, panting and exhausted, my lower back aching, but intending to start on the living room next. Stella's door was still closed, and I was just tiptoeing past when I heard a small sound from my own bedroom. It sounded suspiciously like a mouse, and I was terrified of mice.

Perhaps it would leave quietly and a confrontation would never be necessary. There had been a mouse in the health centre's waiting room once; it ate through a stack of envelopes and some herbal cough sweets in Joanne's desk drawer, and left little black turds all over the headed paper. My eyes suddenly filled with tears at the thought that Charlie had hurt Stella, and all I was worrying about was a stupid *mouse*. But then I heard it again, a shuffly, quiet noise, not, in fact, like the sound any type of small vermin would make.

I gulped, and wondered if I should phone Mack, or the police, but the thought of a policeman turning up to rescue us from what was potentially a mouse was too humiliating. Still, maybe if a policeman were actually there I could persuade Stella to file a complaint against Charlie. I crept down the hall. Again I thought that there was something odd about the silence in the flat. Something seemed to be missing.

Still with my rubber gloves on, and armed with a bottle of antibacterial spray which I held out in front of me like a weapon, I tiptoed cautiously into my room. It was empty, and momentarily silent until suddenly, from my walk-in wardrobe, came the unmistakable sound of floodgate-opening, gasping sobs. For a second I didn't even think it *was* Stella, because Stella hardly ever cried. Even under the current circumstances, it was more likely that a stranger had broken into the flat for the sole purpose of having a good cry in my bedroom than Stella. I put it down to the amount of tears she'd shed when our parents died – it was as if she'd approached adulthood like something dessicated and hollow, a plant needing hydration. I hadn't seen her cry, properly, since 1998 when she fell halfway down the escalator in

217

Shepherd's Bush station, hungover, and tore a ligament in her ankle so badly that it took a chunk of bone with it.

I ran over to the cupboard and wrenched open the door. That cupboard always used to be our repository of junk, until I decided that I'd really like a place of my own to meditate in. I'd commandeered the vegetable rack from the kitchen, and installed a small brass Buddha on one of its onion-flaky shelves. The cupboard was huge, and so with an old rug on the floor, and candles and incense perched on either side of the Buddha, it made a great meditation space – although I'd only actually meditated in there twice. Stella used it more often, with 'meditation' being a euphemism for the smoking of a surreptitious joint. She thought I didn't know.

Gradually, due to a general lack of storage space, the erstwhile occupants of the wardrobe – namely the ironing board, iron, a suitcase full of winter clothes and some tacky framed posters left by the flat's previous owner – had crept back in again, one by one, jostling for space with the spiritual paraphernalia. Contemplative it wasn't.

Stella was crouched on the rug, squeezed in between the vegetable rack and the suitcase, howling like a baby. I dropped the cleaning stuff, yanked off my gloves with a rubbery plop, and pulled her out, sending the ironing board crashing down on both of us. I threw it aside as though it was made of balsawood in my haste to get to her.

'Oh Stell, my baby. Tell me what he did to you . . . I'm calling the police. We should've gone to the police last night. Oh my God . . .'

Stella crawled into my arms and bawled without restraint, eyes and nose running, leaving wet stigmata of grief on my shoulder. I was speechless with horror at the daytime sight of her face and arms, now that the cuts and scratches had swollen and the bruises purpled. She looked far worse than she had the night before.

'Emma, it really hurts,' she sobbed. 'My face is throbbing. I've got such a headache.'

I swallowed, wondering what else hurt her. 'Stell, you have to tell me. Did he . . .'

She looked away, but answered. 'No. He didn't . . . quite . . . rape me.'

I exhaled with both relief and renewed terror at what that might mean.

'OK. You don't have to tell me anything else yet, if you don't want to. Come on, I'll run you a bath, make you a cup of tea and get you some Nurofen. I think I should call the doctor.'

'No! It's just a headache. Please don't, Emma. Just get me some painkillers.'

I led her by the hand, compliant as a child, into the bathroom where she stood vacantly on the bathmat, waiting as I ran her a huge bubbly bath. She looked so forlorn and small, still in the old T-shirt of Dad's which she wore in bed, her shoulders shaking with sobs.

'Hop in, and I'll get the tea.'

'And the Nurofen,' she said, weakly stripping off the T-shirt and climbing into the bath.

I ran into the kitchen, put on the kettle, and ransacked the drawer where we usually kept the painkillers. But there was nothing in there except the usual miscellany which ended up in kitchen drawers: books of matches, odd clothes pegs, plastic ice-lolly moulds, guarantees from various kitchen appliances. No Nurofen; not even an aspirin. I raced back to the bathroom.

'We're out of Nuros. Shall I nip down to the shop for you?'

Stella nodded once, her chin dipping in and out of the deep water as she lay motionless. I retreated, grabbed my bag and keys, flicked the kettle on, and left the flat.

It was on the stairs that I realized what was different about the silence that morning. It wasn't only a manifestation of the dark moods and pain inside the flat, something was actually, physically missing: the persistent warble of Percy's television.

Percy *always* had his TV on. He was an early bird, and he switched it on as soon as he woke up, usually at six or seven in the morning, and always at window-rattling volume. At first Stella and I used to complain, shoving large-lettered but polite notes underneath his door, but after a while we just got used to Richard and Judy bellowing at one another as our morning wake-up calls. Percy did turn the sound down a bit when he received the notes, but after a few minutes he'd forget, and crank it back up again.

I stood outside his door, concerned and dithering. This was serious enough to warrant further investigation, but Stella was up there, in pain, in the bath. I decided not to do anything until I'd been to the shop for the painkillers. After all, I might spot Percy on the way out, in his habitual position, scratching and mumbling on the doorstep downstairs, or on his daily ramble along the terrace and back again. Although, that said, he usually left his door open when he went out, and it was firmly closed.

I went down to the main front door and checked around, but there was no sign of him, and his two milk bottles were sitting unclaimed on the doorstep. Now I was seriously worried.

'Bugger you, Percy,' I muttered. 'Don't do this to me, not today.'

He definitely wasn't away or anything – as if he ever went on holiday! – because I'd been aware of him the previous night, thumping around, slamming doors. When I'd gone to the loo after putting Stella to bed and seeing Suzanne off, I'd heard a muffled chuntering through the floorboards as Percy went into his own bathroom, directly underneath. Straining my ears to hear better, I'd identified the clunk of a heavy cistern lid being lifted and propped against the wall. An echoey old voice had floated up, and I'd overheard the words, ''Ello, ballcock! How're you doing then?' The lid had crashed back down and Percy had stomped out of the bathroom, evidently satisfied by his small talk with the plumbing. Even in the midst of the horror of that night, it had almost made me smile.

I dashed to the Narayan Grocery, purchased a packet of Nurofen and some fresh orange juice, and hurried back to the house. On the way up, I listened again at Percy's door, and again there was nothing but hollow silence. I knocked, loudly and fruitlessly, for a long time, bearing in mind Percy's deafness. Still nothing. We had a key to his flat, which his Age Concern lady had asked if we could keep for when Percy locked himself out or lost his own key – a regular occurrence – and so, with a sinking heart, I realized I was going to have to go in.

I traipsed back up to our own flat, made Stella a cup of tea, and took it in to her with the pills and a glass of water. She was lying completely still in the bath, her eyes shut, furrows of pain corrugating her usually smooth forehead. Her hair snaked across the surface of the water, and she looked like the Lady of the Lake – if said Lady had been in a nasty scrap.

'Take these,' I said, popping three Nurofens out for her. 'Your tea's down here on the floor. Will you be all right for five minutes? Percy's TV isn't on and he didn't answer the door. I'm worried about him.'

Stella dipped her chin in the water again, in a martyred sort of way, which I took as an affirmation.

'Sorry, Stell. I won't be long.'

But just as I was about to go out of the door, she said, in the faintest of ghost voices, 'Wait, please. Just a minute. I want to tell you what happened first.'

I sat down on the floor, pressing my palm against the unfeeling smooth white pedestal of the basin for support while Stella began to speak, the low flat monotone of her voice rendered even more eerie by the bathroom's acoustics. I hoped Percy was OK, that

221

he could hang on, but I couldn't walk out on Stella until she was finished.

She told me how Charlie had kissed her and touched her and it was lovely.

How they'd walked out to his car and got in the back and kissed more; and then he had put his hand up her dress and pulled her knickers across to one side so he could touch her with his fingers.

I twitched my own fingers involuntarily against the white porcelain, forcing them to mime the notes for 'Creep' by Radiohead, hearing it in my head as a tinny descant, wishing that I could make it drown out what Stella was saying.

She told me that they'd got close to having sex, but that neither of them had any condoms. It hadn't bothered Charlie at all, but she'd said that she couldn't, unprotected. She wasn't on the pill, and besides, in this day and age . . .

She told me how he hadn't listened, just yanked the thin waistband of her lacy pants so it snapped clean through, and how the last barrier was gone, and she had felt the first sublime sensation of heat and solidity as he began to enter her. How at that point it had felt too good to protest.

And then how it had all gone really wrong, when, three seconds later, she'd come to her senses and sat up in the car – quite happily – and said, 'Oh well, next time, eh?' and tried to pull her dress down again.

'He called me a fucking pricktease. He grabbed my arms and tried to force it back inside me. I wriggled away, but I couldn't get to the door. He got hold of my hair and pulled my head down and stuck his dick in my mouth . . .'

I couldn't bear to listen to it. I jumped up and ran over to the bath, to give Stella a hug, I suppose. But she was under the water, hiding beneath its inviolable smooth surface, and I couldn't reach her. So I sat down again, drawing my knees up to my chin, feeling utterly helpless.

'I bit it.'

'You did *what*?'

'I bit his dick. Really hard. I think I drew blood.'

I sighed, a very distant long-lost cousin of a laugh. 'Oh Stella. Then what?'

She trembled and the water rippled slightly, tiny vibrations of pain.

'He kneed me in the face, and hit me a few times, really punched me. I don't think it sunk in at first, what I'd done to him, until it started to hurt, because he suddenly grabbed his dick and screamed, and that's when I got out the car and ran off. I hid until I heard him drive away, and then I went and waited by your car. I couldn't go back into the party. I couldn't bear all your "I told you so" faces.'

She sloshed back in the bathwater, out of sight.

'As if we'd ever say "I told you so".'

We were silent for a few more long minutes, and then I remembered Percy. I reached across and turned on the hot tap. 'I'd better go, Stell. I won't be long, I promise.'

Feeling sick to my stomach at what I'd just heard, and at the thought of what I might find, I tentatively let myself into Percy's flat. The usual sour smell engulfed me, and I had to put my sleeve over my nose before stepping into the hallway, still calling Percy's name over and over: 'Mr Weston? Are you there? Are you OK? Mr Weston?'

Percy's cat, a starved-looking tabby with a perpetual expression of desperation on its face, shot down the hall and began hurling itself at my legs, mewing tonelessly. 'Go away, cat,' I whispered, trying to walk further into the flat but hindered by the weaving feline. I imagined I could actually see the fleas leaping out of its fur and onto my ankles, making new homes in the turn-ups of my jeans. 'Where's Percy then, eh?'

Then I saw him – his feet, at least, sticking out of the living room and into the hall. As I ran up to where he

223

lay, I became aware of a dark puddle surrounding him, and couldn't prevent myself screaming: an inadvertent but ineffectual girly sort of yelp, which I felt briefly glad that nobody but the cat had heard. When I realized that the liquid wasn't blood, but stout – a can of it had fallen with Percy to the floor and saturated his limp body – I had to lean against the dank, dark walls of the hallway, hyperventilating with relief and panic in tandem. He seemed to have tripped over the lead to his television, as there was a socket in the hall nearby, and a plug tangled loosely around his ankles. It looked as if someone had unplugged Percy.

My first thought was, Oh God, I wish Mum was here. She'd know what to do; and my second thought, Why on earth was he plugging in his TV in the hall anyway? I dithered for a second, wondering if I should try and resuscitate the old man. His eyes were half open, milky and coated, but I was certain he wasn't breathing. To my utter shame, I couldn't even bring myself to crouch down next to him and hold my ear to his fragile chest to make sure, let alone think of administering mouth-to-mouth. Instead I ran back down the sticky-linoed floor, almost falling over the frantic cat, out of his flat and up to our own, where I lunged for the telephone and dialled 999.

'Stella,' I said on my way out again, barely believing that this was happening. 'Percy's collapsed. I have to go and let the police and the ambulance in. Are you OK?'

That nod again. She had turned off the hot tap, but otherwise hadn't moved. Even from a distance I could see how pale and shrivelled her fingers and toes were.

I sat waiting on the front doorstep downstairs, hugging Percy's milk bottles, gazing with eyes as unseeing as Percy's out into the street. I tried to think whom to tell the police to contact about Percy – for I was sure that he was dead – but as far as I knew, he had nobody. No friends, no children, no relatives at all that I'd ever been aware of. Susan, the child he sometimes accused me of being, had been drowned in an accident on holiday, mown down by a speedboat; the Age Concern lady told me that. The Age Concern lady was the only person I had ever seen go into Percy's flat, apart from the GP, and I couldn't remember what her name was.

Poor Percy, I thought. What a way to go. Completely alone. Nobody even to grieve for him. Then it occurred to me that I wasn't in that different a situation. Apart from Stella, there was nobody who would miss me, not really, if I died. People would be sorry; Gavin, and Mack, and all the friends I was out of touch with. They'd say nice things about me, probably shed a few tears, but my death wouldn't change their lives.

I looked down at the bottles I held, and the words of a Jam song flitted through my mind: the one about the lonely housewives clutching empty milk bottles to their hearts. Funny how I still knew every single lyric of that song, even though I hadn't heard it for years.

The police arrived first. They asked me to show them where Percy's body was, but I couldn't move, transfixed by depression and self-pity, and could only point back and up to the first floor, towards Percy's open door. They loped up the stairs with their long black-clad policemen's legs, like two tall dark shadows. Like Death, coming to take Percy away.

Within a minute, one of them was back. He hovered awkwardly above me, until I realized that he was waiting for me to stand up. I slowly hauled my cold body off the step, feeling very old and stiff.

'The ambulance will be here shortly,' said one of them, 'but I'm afraid you're right, he is dead. We'll need to call a doctor to certify it. Do you know who his GP was?'

I shook my head, and leaned against the doorframe. This was all like a terrible dream. 'Age Concern lady – don't remember her name,' I muttered.

'Are you all right, miss?' I shook my head again, and took off my glasses to clean them on the hem of my shirt, hoping that the act of giving my hands something to do would distract my brain from the fizzing, burning urge to cry.

Everything was horrible. Everything was wrong: Stella, Charlie, Percy, Gavin, Harlesden Ann, and I knew that crying wouldn't make me feel better, about any of it. I just felt so cold. My backside was numb from the iron chill of the step, and my hands equally frozen from the cold glass of the milk bottles. But even that cold misery was more appealing than what I had to do next; go upstairs and deal with what a drunk six-foot-six rugby-playing Neanderthal had done to my beautiful eight-stone sister. Every fibre in my body begged me to walk away, to not have to face it . . . but I couldn't.

I pulled myself together, and took a decision for which I hoped Stella wouldn't hate me for ever.

'There's something else,' I said. 'I need you to come and take a statement from my sister. She was attacked last night. Sexually attacked.'

'I see,' said the leggy copper, shifting from one big foot to the other. He was young, inexperienced looking, with bumfluff and traces of acne, and his uniform seemed somehow loose on him, as if he was trying desperately hard to grow into it. I instantly cursed myself. As if Stella would tell *him* anything.

'Would it be better for us to come down to the station? I think she might, um, want to talk to a woman about it.'

He looked relieved. 'Yes. I'll radio through and get someone to look after her when she comes in. We do have specially trained personnel to, ah, deal with this kind of thing.'

'Right then,' I said despondently. My limbs felt like lead weights; pendulums swinging relentlessly off an old, faceless clock. I wanted it all to stop, but it wouldn't. 'I'll go and get her ready.'

'And I'll need to take some details from you, too, about your neighbour. If you'll be at the station with your sister I can do it then.'

I nodded, and trudged back upstairs to break the news to Stella.

'He's dead,' I told her.

'Poor Percy,' she whispered. I could see the gooseflesh breaking out all over her body through the bathwater, a slow graceful sweep of a response. It reminded me of a field of corn disturbed by the wind.

We were silent for a moment, but the clamouring inside both our heads sounded loud in the quiet bathroom, and I knew we were both remembering the last time I'd told her about a death. Two deaths. One ripped-up patchwork quilt. The sound of screaming. The mixed-up memories of loss and pain and unhappiness which were our shared legacy.

I yanked a towel off the towel rail, an old bald beach towel with pulled loops of threads, in colours which didn't match anything else in our bathroom, and held it out for her. Why couldn't we at least have matching towels? I ought to have been able to wrap her in huge fluffy pre-warmed bath sheets; one to swallow up her body, another to gently rub her wet, injured head.

She rose slowly, stiffly out of the tepid water and I wrapped the inadequate towel around her.

'Your hands are freezing,' she said, as my fingers made contact with her shoulder.

'It's really cold out there. Is the Nurofen working yet?'

She shrugged. 'A bit. I think.'

I let her dry herself, and then handed her her bathrobe. I shouldn't have let her have a bath at all, I thought. It might have got rid of the evidence. 'Stella, you have to get dressed now. We have to go to the police station.'

'About Percy?'

'No. Well, yes, they want to talk to me about him. But more about what Charlie did to you.'

I waited for the scene: the rage, the fear, the refusal. But it never came.

'I know,' she said simply. I had to turn away as tears flooded my eyes at her unexpected maturity.

At that moment I decided that, in all likelihood, I was never going to have children. I never wanted to go through this again, ever. It was hard enough to bear from my little sister. It would have been impossible to bear from my *own* child. It would have broken my heart.

24

Mid-December. Christmas trees were appearing in front windows in a rash of blinking lights as I walked back from the tube after baby massage. Four o'clock, and already it was cloudy-dark, feeble prongs of street light trying and failing to compensate for the truncated daytime. Since the attack on Stella, and Percy's death, I had not regained any of my enthusiasm for the Ann Paramor Project, as Mack called it.

'Sounds like a seventies concept band,' I said, trying to be jolly. 'Sorry, Mack, we'll go to the next Ann soon, honest; it's just that I've been really busy with everything lately.'

It was true that a lot seemed to be going on. Stella was jittery and hyped, waiting to hear if she'd have to go to court for Charlie's assault trial. The swabs that the police doctor took from her mouth had been sent away for analysis, and apparently it would be a while before the results came back. Because Charlie had denied the assault – denied everything except going for a walk with Stella, and then going home – the police could not charge him until they proved that his DNA had been present in Stella's mouth.

Stella and I were both raging that he hadn't been examined on his arrest, since the damage to his penis inflicted by Stella's teeth would have proved where it had been that night, and we would already have had a date for a jury to decide which of them was telling the truth regarding consent. This way was far more tortuous. But apparently he had refused to allow an intimate examination, and according to our solicitor, for some reason this had been within his rights.

'Still,' I told her. 'Better to have the actual evidence.'

'If there is any,' she said glumly. 'I might have got rid of it when I cleaned my teeth the next morning.'

The police had told us that even though Charlie hadn't actually ejaculated, and Stella had cleaned her teeth, it was still possible for traces of his DNA to be there. I imagined those traces, lurking like infinitesimally small shadowy minnows in the secretive dark cave of Stella's mouth, trying to disguise themselves, waiting to be found out. I felt so sorry for her – if it were me, knowing that bits of him, however small, were still inside me, I'd have been throwing up for days.

We too just had to wait and see.

Charlie turned out to have a criminal record already, for an assault on another woman five years before, so the police had instantly been able to identify him and arrest him after the attack. They'd had to contact the college to check his address, and in doing so had let it slip as to why they were enquiring. To Stella's great relief, Charlie had been promptly expelled. He had also spent twenty-four hours in a cell at the police station, in between vigorous sessions of questioning, before being released on bail; so Stella and I revelled – miserably – in the knowledge that he was probably not a very happy bunny.

But however bad things were looking for him, Stella was in a worse state; volatile as a volcano, as unpredictable as lava; alternately terrified that there wouldn't be a court case, and then terrified that there would. She was hard to be around, but I couldn't blame her.

Thankfully, work was busier, and it took my mind off Stella's problems, at least during the day. I'd landed a new on-site corporate account, and a couple of my old, lapsed, aromatherapy clients had begun coming over for regular massages again.

All in all, then, despite Mack's chivvying, I felt that I had neither the time nor the emotional resources for the search. After Christmas, I told myself. A new year.

'Just don't leave it too long, please,' Mack pleaded. 'My film's got to be finished by March.'

If I had been carrying the Bastard with me on that particular day, I'd have been bent over from the weight of it, and probably wouldn't have noticed Gavin close our front door, lope down the path, swing his leg over the seat of his bike, and drive away in the opposite direction. In a subconscious part of my mind, I might have recognized the throaty sound of the engine as belonging to a Harley, but probably wouldn't have bothered to look up and identify it as Gavin's.

But because it was baby-massage day I was unburdened by anything heavier than my backpack. I was just greeting the Blind Shop ladies at the end of the road, who were closing up for the day, when I stopped, mid-sentence. Gavin was hurrying out of our house, practically running, and leaping onto his bike. My heart pole-vaulted into my throat at the welcome familiarity of the sight.

'Gav!' I yelled, just as he turned the key in the ignition and threw his weight forward on the bike to release the kick-stand. The ensuing meaty roar drowned me out. 'Wait!

'Sorry, I've got to go,' I said over my shoulder to the yellow-haired old ladies, dashing towards the house, my backpack bumping against my shoulder blades and my coat flapping open at the sides as I ran.

But it was too late. Gavin's bike had vanished around the now empty corner, and I slowed to a despairing walk.

Before I even got in through the door of the flat, I heard Stella's voice on the telephone, shouting at someone. She turned her back on me as I walked in.

'Anyhow, I've got to go now,' she said sulkily down the phone. 'I just can't believe you did that – you've only made things worse. He wouldn't have rung me if you hadn't got him all mad.'

There was an enraged female squeaking from the receiver.

'But it's none of your business!' Stella slammed down the phone, and turned to me, fists clenched by her sides. 'Oh, that bloody Suzanne. She does my *head* in. You won't believe what she went and did in the pub last night.'

'What's the matter, Stell? You're all red in the face.' I badly wanted to ask what Gavin had been doing there just now, and why Stella hadn't called me on the mobile to let me know, but I could see by Stella's puffy eyes that this conversation with Suzanne wasn't just a falling out over whether Eminem was any good or not. I swallowed down my questions like medicine.

'Listen to this.' Stella pressed PLAY on the answer machine and I heard a spiteful Sloaney voice, slightly slurring and indistinct in places, pompous in others. The same feeling of desolate frustration I'd experienced before, when I found Stella sobbing in the cupboard, flooded over me.

'. . . *Charlie Simmonds here. It's the final straw when some little bimbo throws her drink at me in a pub and calls me all kinds of names. Innocent until proven guilty, I think you'll find. And you don't have a hope in hell of getting me found guilty, because you know, and I know, that I'm not fucking guilty. I never touched you – more's the pity. I suppose you think you're so clever, spinning that story to the police. Well, this is to let you know that you don't stand a chance. If you take it any further, I'll sue you for damages. You'll be hearing from my solicitors. See you in court. Goodbye.'*

'He's off his head,' I said as I hugged Stella in panic.

'All we have to do is play that to the police and it'll count against him in court. He's threatening you, and he's out on bail. They could nick him.'

Stella said softly into my shoulder, 'I don't think I want it to come to court.'

'What?'

'I can't face it, Em. Having to tell a load of strangers all that intimate stuff. Having them judge me. Having the defence make out that I'm a tart who deserved it . . . I can't do it.'

'But what about Charlie? He can't get away with it!'

She shrugged, a small flutter which felt almost like it came from inside me. 'He hates me now. If he goes to prison it won't be for very long, and he'll hate me even more. I'll always be afraid that he'd . . . you know . . .'

'Oh, Stella.' How could I protect her? I felt like a failure, because I wouldn't always be there for her when she needed me. 'Don't make any decisions yet. Let's wait until the lab results come back, OK? Then you can decide. If there's no evidence, they won't be able to charge him anyway.'

'OK,' she said painfully, and I breathed in her scent, the pure, familiar scent of my family.

As she broke away from my arms, I thought I smelled something else: a whiff of a different sort of familiarity, a delicious, musky note of something from my past . . . aftershave? *Gavin's* aftershave. I couldn't stop myself.

'Stell, what was Gavin doing here?'

Stella's eyes filled with tears again. 'Is that all that matters to you? I've just had this really traumatic message from Charlie to deal with, and then a row with Suzanne, and all you want to know about is your *ex*? I bumped into him outside the gym and he gave me a lift back on his bike; said he wanted to see you. I played the message and was upset, and he gave me a hug, that's all. You just missed him.'

Stella was staring hard at me as I spoke, holding me

with her eyes as if challenging me to disbelieve her. I thought that we resembled two tigers circling around one another, testing each other's nerve; and then I thought, No, that's ridiculous. Stella had had a new shock, that was all. It was a good thing Gavin had been there to help her through it. He was the closest thing she had to a father.

'Sorry, Stell. Please don't think I'm accusing you of anything, because of course I'm not. I'm glad he was there for you. Let me just hang up my coat and we'll have a cup of tea and talk more about Charlie's message, if you want to.'

I walked over to the hooks in the hall, sliding the shoulders of my coat carefully onto a hanger. Overcome with all this new emotional turmoil, I buried my face into its soft afghan-furry collar, allowing myself just one tiny thrill of excitement at the thought that Gavin had come over especially to see me. It skittered briefly up and down my ribs, before vanishing back into the morass of rage at Charlie's message.

I let her rant. I let her whinge about Suzanne; spit vitriol about Charlie; speculate as to what she'd do to him if she could – it involved his testicles, naturally enough, two large spikes and a barbeque – and tried to calm her down as she paced the room and fretted. Then I made her phone Suzanne and apologize, since it was obvious that Suzanne had only acted in what she believed was a sisterly fashion.

Finally, once she'd got it all out of her system, I said as casually as I could, 'So do you know why Gavin wanted to see me? Did he say?'

Stella looked cagey. 'Not really. He just asked how you were, and said it would be nice to see you and would I like a lift home.'

'What was he doing at the gym?'

'He joined recently. His new – I mean, someone – said he was putting on weight.'

234

'His new girlfriend? He's got a new girlfriend?'

Stella turned to face me, her mouth in a rueful wavy line. She bit the inside of her cheek, chewing on it as if she actually wanted to eat herself up.

'Sorry, Em,' she said uncomfortably. 'I've been putting off telling you. But he seemed genuinely keen to know how you were. Told me to tell you to call him, and maybe you could meet for coffee or something. He wants to stay friends with you.'

I snorted. 'That's big of him.'

'Don't be bitter about it, Em. You'll meet someone else. He's not worth it. You're better than him.'

'I hate men.'

'So do I.'

I did call Gavin, though. I left a message on his mobile, a stilted um-er type of message, but permeated with so much artificially injected jollity that it nearly choked me. He didn't ring me back again.

25

'Em.'

Stella's voice was muffled in the rough towel covering her pillow. I was straddled across her giving her a massage, working my thumbs into the small hollows surrounding each of her vertebrae. 'You know Suzanne's family moved out of London last year, down to Wiltshire. She's invited me to their house for Christmas.'

I stopped at the seventh vertebrae and sat back on Stella's bottom. 'Oh great. So what am I supposed to do then? Hang about here on my own all day?'

Stella twisted her head around and sat up as far as she could. She was naked except for a very small pair of pants, and her long, hard body was beautiful, flawless, just like our mother's had been. For some reason, an image of Gavin racing away on his Harley jumped into my head, and I shook it out again, puzzled.

'No, listen, Em. Of course I wouldn't leave you on your own at Christmastime. I said I'd only go if you could come too. What do you think? It'll be fun. Please come. You know how much you moaned last year, that all we ever do is lie around and watch telly all day. It's a lovely village, apparently, near Salisbury. Just think: country air, a change of scene. Someone else cooking a yummy dinner for us. We haven't had a family Christmas since Mum and Dad died. Oh go on . . .'

'But the Hiscocks aren't *our* family. And Salisbury's down the M3.' Even as I said it, my throat constricted. Teffont, where Ann Paramor had once lived, was also near Salisbury. Why did this place seem to be the epicentre of all my emotional dramas? I'd never even been there.

'Well, beggars can't be choosers,' said Stella, flopping morosely back down on the bed. 'Could you just do my right shoulder, please? I've got so many knots that I could – *Ow!* Yes, that's them.'

'I can't drive down the M3.'

'You can. It's just another road; I don't know why it upsets you so much. We don't even know exactly where the accident happened. I get far more upset at the thought of going to their graves.'

I worked my way around both of Stella's shoulder blades, worrying at them with my thumbs until the kinks in her muscles gradually straightened out.

'Not that we do that very often, either.'

'Yeah. I know.'

We were silent for a moment. I poured a little well of oil into one of my palms, rubbed them together, and began to push in great long sweeps along Stella's downy golden back. Five years ago neither of us would have been able to have this conversation without crying.

'So who's going to be there?'

'Um . . . Suzanne, obviously. You remember her mum, don't you? And you've probably never met her stepdad, Greg, but he's really nice too. And she's got a kid stepbrother, Ben. That's it, I suppose. Oh, and two guinea pigs, Scratch and Sniff. Suze told me a very funny story about those guinea pigs. Her mum had to take them to the vet's for some booster shots, right, and she was sitting in the waiting room, which was packed, and when it's her turn, the vet's assistant shouts out in front of everyone: "Scratch and Sniff Hiscock!" Geddit?'

I laughed, grateful to Stella for lifting the sombre mood. I did remember Denise Hiscock well, actually, and had always really liked her. We had chatted on several occasions when dropping off or collecting Stella and Suzanne from each other's houses when they were much younger. Naturally, since they started making their own social arrangements, our paths no longer crossed.

'Yeah, that is pretty embarrassing. Are you sure they don't mind us coming?'

'Well, apparently it was Denise's suggestion to invite us.'

'Oh, all right then. It's got to be better than hanging around here, drinking too much and feeling guilty that we didn't go to midnight mass.'

Stella pushed me off, gave me a slippery hug, and then dragged on Dad's old holey fishing jumper. 'Brilliant! I'll go and ring Suzanne to tell her.'

I sighed, replaced the cap on my bottle of sweet almond oil, and threw the towel Stella had been lying on into the laundry basket.

I survived the car journey. In fact, I was feeling some-what foolish for having made such a fuss about it. Ten years was a long time, and since I didn't know the site of the crash, only that it was somewhere just past the Fleet Service Station, it was thankfully difficult to visualize. During the three-mile stretch of road after Fleet, though, I had an unpleasant sick feeling in my stomach, and the conversation in the car petered out into a tense silence. I scanned the motorway verge, as if there might still be skidmarks or broken glass to mark the spot, but no scars betrayed the loss of life which had occurred there. It was as if a new grass tide swept in each year and cleared away more memories; rain washing out the bloodstains many times over until nothing was left. I didn't know whether this made me more sad or relieved.

'Maybe we should have put a cross there, so we

could leave flowers and stuff,' I said, after we were safely past the danger zone.

Stella lit a cigarette. 'It's not exactly the most accessible place to make into a shrine,' she said through a mouthful of smoke.

I wound down the window a few inches to let the smoke out, and the noise of the wind screaming around the car rendered further conversation futile.

Suzanne's family lived in the quaintly named village of Tidpit, a few miles west of Salisbury. When Stella and I drove through it on Christmas morning it appeared completely deserted, only the green and red lights twinkling on Christmas trees in the windows of a few of the cottages lending any sort of festive air to the place. It was a still and cloudy day, leaden and unchristmassy, no movement anywhere except for a pile of horse dung in the road which was still steaming, even though no living creature was in sight.

'There's her mum's Merc. That must be Chestnut Cottage then. We're here.'

The house was the building equivalent of Suzanne's mother's car. It sounded smart in theory: a thatched eighteenth-century rose-covered cottage, but the reality was not quite as glamorous. Like the Mercedes, it was shabby and clapped out; the thatch looked as if it needed a leave-in conditioner, and one of the gateposts had crumbled into a ruin.

I parked the Golf, badly, and we gathered up our overnight bags, armfuls of gifts, and bottle of dessert wine for our hosts. A small face pressed itself briefly up against the front window of the cottage before vanishing again, and then the door opened.

'Hi, Merry Christmas!' Suzanne ran down the path to meet us, followed by the owner of the small face, a skinny red-haired little boy of three or four.

'Oh, Ben, for God's sake, where are your shoes? Your socks will get filthy; go back inside.' As Suzanne hugged Stella she said gaily, 'Thank God you're here. Family Christmases are *such* a drag.' Stella and I exchanged rueful glances, and I felt a pang of loss.

No, I told myself firmly. You are *not* to get all mopey at the sight of parents and children and presents under trees from aunties and uncles. Just don't.

'Come in, come in. Hi, Emma, how are you? Did you have a good journey down? Lunch isn't going to be ready for ages, so let's go and have a drink and open some presents. Ben's gagging to get stuck in.'

Inside, the cottage was a low-beamed jumble of warm chaos. An indolent cat lay in front of an open fire, and there were chintzy sofas and armchairs scattered haphazardly about, as if dropped from a great height. Everything had the appearance of being covered with dog hair, although I later discovered that the Hiscocks did not own a dog, only the two afore-mentioned guinea pigs. The tree was magnificent, crammed into the low-ceiled room so that the angel on top had to be squashed against the beams in order to fit. It took my breath away. Stella and I never bothered getting a real fir tree; we just got out our tiny silver fake one every year. It had one sorry strand of red tinsel draped over it, and nothing else.

Denise rushed out and kissed me on the cheek. I'd forgotten how pretty she was, with blonde straggly hair and a soft Welsh accent, as different as she possibly could have been from her beautiful olive-skinned dreadlocked daughter. She had split up with Suzanne's father years ago and, until meeting Greg, had brought up Suzanne single-handedly.

I should have made more of an effort to be friends with her, I realized with the benefit of hindsight. We'd had a lot in common, and plenty of opportunities to spend time together. She'd seemed to like me, even though I was so much younger than her. But back then I'd been far more readily poleaxed with shyness, and I remembered how in control she always appeared; how I'd been intimidated by her composure, next to my own haphazard attempts at parenting. Plus Stella and Suzanne would probably have had fifty fits at the thought of their two sole guardians in cahoots.

'It's really lovely to see you again, Emma, I've thought of you often,' Denise said, squeezing my arm. 'What can I get you to drink? Greg makes a mean G&T, and there's champagne, or wine, or a soft drink if you prefer?'

'Champagne, please. Thanks for inviting me. I was looking forward to seeing you again too.'

Ben came back into the room holding a doll in his hand, to which he was, somewhat indiscreetly, trying to draw my attention by tapping it insistently on my leg. I crouched down so that I was at eye-level with him.

'Who's this, then?'

'It's Jessie, from *Toy Story*. She guards rooms when nobody's not in them.'

'Really? Can I have a look?' I took the doll and scrutinized it carefully. Jessie had a big surprised face and such enormously round staring eyes that it looked as if she was still suffering the effects of a particularly unpleasant encounter with some PCP. 'Ooh, she's lovely, isn't she?'

'Yeah, but Buzz is better, 'cos he's a boy. I want Buzz for Christmas. *To Imfinity am Eyonne!*' he suddenly shrieked, swooping Jessie through the air and rushing off into the kitchen, whacking Stella in the shins with Jessie's hard little cowboy boots on the way.

Stella turned to Suzanne for a translation, rubbing her leg. 'What did he say?'

'"*To Infinity and Beyond*", obviously. It's what Buzz Lightyear says. Don't you know anything?'

'Not about small children, no.'

It was true, I reflected. Stella probably hadn't encountered anyone that age since her own kindergarten classmates, and she was gazing after Ben now with a bemused expression. Bemused, and with faint but definite overtones of horror and disgust. Uh oh, I thought. This could be where we discover that Stella and kids do not mix.

A short, squat man with a shock of auburn hair and a bright red friendly face appeared, wearing a white chef's apron and a tartan paper crown from a Christmas cracker. He was holding four flutes of champagne, which he distributed, keeping one for himself. 'Hi, Stella, how are you? Hello, you must be Emma. I'm Greg. Sorry I didn't come out earlier, I was at a crucial stage with my gravy. Anyway, cheers, all.' Denise and Ben joined us; Denise with a glass of wine and Ben with an orange plastic beaker. 'Glad you could come. Merry Christmas.'

We all raised our glasses, including Ben. 'Merry Christmas!' As the first pale amber bubbles fizzed down my throat, I began to relax.

'So,' Greg said at lunch as he carved the turkey and everyone grappled with serving spoons and bouncing Brussels sprouts, 'do either of you know this part of the world at all?'

I couldn't help a guilty blush spreading over my face, which I was sure clashed nastily with my red paper hat. 'No – well, no, I've never been here before. I used to know someone who lived in Teffont though. Is that near here?' For one mad minute I fantasized that Teffont turned out to be down the road, and I could go and quiz Ann Paramor's old neighbours, in the middle of the Queen's Speech or as they opened their presents, as to her whereabouts. I wondered if Rose Cottage had been like this one: warm and festive and welcoming.

'Who was that, then?' asked Stella, pouring so much gravy over her roast potatoes that I felt like throwing them a life raft. Gravy was not a substance which featured much in post-parental Victor cuisine, and Stella was making up for it now.

'Oh, um, just a girl who was on my aromatherapy course,' I lied.

'Teffont's on the other side of Salisbury. About, what, fifteen or so miles from here?' Greg looked at his wife for confirmation and she nodded. 'Nice little place.'

'Urrrgh! This is *'gusting*!' Ben had taken a forkful of his turkey and had mistakenly ingested some stuffing as well. He began spluttering and making faces like Tom Hanks in *Big*. Denise reached over and slid the offending stuffing off his plate and onto her own.

'Gone now, Bence. Here, you love potatoes and turkey and sausages, don't you?'

'No. I hate them. I want Shreddies instead.' Ben stared belligerently at his plate, and Suzanne narrowed her eyes.

'Oh, just eat it, you little snot. It's Christmas.'

'Suzanne! That's not very constructive, or polite.' Denise began to cut up a chipolata, which she put on a clean side plate for her son.

Trying to defuse the momentary tension, I turned to Suzanne. 'So, remind me what the age gap between you and Ben is? There's nearly ten years between me and Stella. It's weird remembering that it used to be like that, Stella spitting out her food and having tantrums; and now look at us . . . nothing's changed!'

Stella reached over and pretended to slap me. She seemed happy: pink-cheeked and pretty, with her paper hat listing lopsidedly over her face.

Suzanne looked at her little brother with a mixture of irritation and affection. 'Well, there's fifteen years between us. I can't quite visualize you and me ever sharing a flat together, Bence, can you?'

'No, I can't,' said Ben with dignity. 'Can I have some ketchup with my sausages?'

'No,' chorused Greg, Denise and Suzanne. Ben stuck out his lower lip but kept eating.

'Are you two real sisters then, or do you only have one parent in common? You look about as alike as Suzanne and Ben.' Greg was scrutinizing us in turn.

'We're real sisters,' said Stella.

Suzanne, who already knew that I was adopted – and that my best friend used, allegedly, to be a gorilla

– kept her mouth shut, but raised her eyebrows at Stella when she thought nobody else was looking. Stella took a forkful of gravy-sodden roast potato, and made a face back at her. I just grinned into my turkey and didn't disagree.

After lunch and a walk, Ben conked out on the sofa, exhausted. 'He's been up since five o'clock,' said Denise. Suzanne spirited Stella away upstairs, ostensibly to get her advice on whether to use chiffon or silk for next term's college project, and Greg and Denise, refusing all offers of help clearing up, vanished into the kitchen.

I was left on my own in an armchair in front of the fire, contented, tipsy and very, very full. None the less, my hand kept snaking its way automatically into the colossal tin of Quality Street next to me. I lay back, savouring the mingled tastes of toffee and chocolate melting on my tongue, and watched Ben sleep. His small face was lit up warm by the flickering orange flames, his mouth open and his lashes spiky on his cheeks. The sound of his steady breathing was so peculiarly hypnotic that, within just a few minutes, my own eyelids had closed, and I joined him in a melted-chocolate, holly-decorated sleep.

26

For a split second, when I jerked awake again, I had the strangest sensation of having been whirled back in time. There was the sound of a child singing 'Baa Baa Black Sheep', off-key; adults chatting in the background; a giggle and a clink of glasses. Christmas carols swelled from the television set, soft choral melodies clashing with the tuneless nursery rhyme; and a blur of lights and ornaments twinkled from the tree in the corner. Delicious smells of pine, burning firewood and roast turkey were wafting around the room, and it was already dark outside. The fire was dying down, and the lights were on low.

'Oh God,' I thought with a start. 'This is not my family.' I sat up hastily, scattering the Quality Street wrappers which I had left shamefully strewn on my lap, and wiped away the seepage of dribble which was running down my chin. I had the uncomfortable feeling that I'd probably been snoring too.

Ben popped up next to me. 'Hello, Emma. It's me, Benjamin Louis Hiscock. Will you read to me?'

'Sure, Ben. Why don't you go and get a book?'

Denise appeared. 'Ah, Sleeping Beauty awakes. Did you have a nice nap?'

'I did, actually. But sorry, it was so rude of me to

crash out like that—'

'Oh, not at all. I'm delighted that you feel comfortable enough here to fall asleep. Besides, we've had a bit of a kip too. Would you like a cup of tea and some Christmas cake? The girls are still upstairs. They're allegedly working, but they think I don't know that they're smoking out of the window and listening to rap CDs.'

I laughed. 'I'd love some tea, thanks.' It was so wonderful to be looked after, waited on like this. To be brought cups of tea and cake, and fed nice meals. I hoped fervently that this was what it would be like when I found Ann Paramor: a chance to catch up on all the mothering arrears. The idea of somebody else, for example, doing my washing for me, was as tempting as a free weekend at a health spa.

Ben returned, climbed onto my lap, and plonked down a Spot the Dog book. I instinctively put one arm around him and began to read it aloud, not taking in the words at all, just relishing the long-dormant sensation of warm attentive child. Now that I thought about it, it was odd, I mused: whenever I started to yearn for the sensation of being mothered, I always seemed to do something which put me in the role of a mother myself. When I thought about Ann Paramor, for example, I would then, more often than not, find myself going through Stella's sock drawer and matching up her odd socks; or baking a cake; or having a sudden strong urge to ring her and check that she was dressed warmly enough. How sad was that?

I desperately hoped that finding Ann Paramor – whatever the result – would nip that particular behavioural tic in the bud. Or rather, deadhead it altogether. No wonder I cramped Stella's style at times.

'More,' demanded Ben when I'd finished, sliding off my lap and over to a low bookshelf. 'I get anozzer one.'

Almost before his sticky hand landed on the book's spine, I knew what it was. That sky-blue and red cover, the familiar little bird sitting on the lugubrious dog's head. 'Oh!' I exclaimed, leaping up and practically grabbing it out of his hands. '*Are You My Mother?* I *love* this book!'

Denise came in with a mug of tea and a slice of rich, black Christmas cake, which she set down on the floor next to my armchair. 'Yes, it's a fabulous book, isn't it? Bence loves it – and it's one of only a few that I actually still enjoy reading to him.'

'I used to read it to Stella when she was younger than Ben.' I felt excited, like being reunited with a long-lost friend. 'Come on, Ben, let's get stuck in.'

Ben obligingly climbed back up again, and I turned to the first page, smiling with glee as I saw all the little details of the story I'd forgotten: the mother bird's red-and-white-checked headscarf, the way she straddled her skinny bird legs over the enormous egg, the look of immense self-satisfaction on her face as she waited for it to hatch.

I read on, almost forgetting that Denise, not Mum, had brought me tea and cake; almost forgetting that Ben wasn't Stella aged three. By the time the baby bird had asked the kitten, the hen, the dog and cow if any of them were his mother, the pathos of the story had reached down the years and twined a noose of nostalgic sadness around my throat, threatening to choke me. He was so lost and alone, and I already knew he was so desperate to find out who his mother was, that he would soon start asking rusty old cars, boats and aeroplanes. I looked around the room, half expecting to see him sitting on top of the Christmas tree or hopping over the hearth, but the room was the same as before.

I had to stop for a minute.

'Go on,' said Ben.

But I'd come to the most touching part so far, where the baby bird had a moment's doubt as to whether he even had a mother. Then he collected himself, frowned, rested his wings on his hips and, with an expression of bravado covering up his mingled confusion and fear, he declared that he was *sure* he had a mother; and that he just *had* to find her; and that he *would* find her. Tears welled in my eyes, making the words blur and dance on the page. Even though I knew the book had a happy ending, when I got to the bit where the bird looked up into the sky, saw an enormous jumbo jet and called out, '"'Here I am, Mother,'"' my voice was wobbling so much that I could barely continue. By the final page, I was all but sobbing out each word, and tears were rolling unrestrained down my face and onto the top of Ben's silky head.

When I looked up, Stella, Suzanne, Denise and Greg were standing staring at me, concerned and embarrassed. Stella leaped forward, kneeling down and putting both her hands on the fatly upholstered arm of the chair. 'Em! What's the matter?'

I took off my glasses and wiped my eyes. Then I replaced them, and gently slid Ben off my lap. Ben's eyes were as big and saucery as Jessie the doll's.

'Can I talk to you outside please, Stella?'

The temperature had dropped dramatically since darkness fell. Frost already glittered on the tree branches and the droopy nylon strings of a lopsided rotary washing line. Beyond the garden fence was nothing but a black expanse of fields, which the moon was still too low in the sky to illuminate. The clouds had dispersed, though, and stars already dotted the blackness above their heads. It was eerily silent.

Denise opened the back door and came out, carrying our coats, two cups of tea, and a tissue for me, which she distributed wordlessly before patting my arm and going back inside again.

'She's lovely, isn't she?' said Stella wistfully, zipping up her coat and lighting a cigarette, almost simultaneously.

I nodded and sniffed and blew my nose. 'Stell,' I began, sitting down on a step which led to the lawn.

'I've got something to tell you, and please, please believe me when I say that I will never, ever let it jeopardize our relationship.'

I told Stella everything: from finding Ann's original letter and getting her surname from the tweedy-voiced librarian, to Mack printing off the list for me, and my intention of checking out each Ann Paramor individually, starting with our unsuccessful 'stakeout' in Harlesden. Stella listened and smoked, her breath showing in thick nicotiney plumes contrasting with my chaotic cloudy breath, which spilled out like my words into the frosty air. Our tea got cold, and our gloveless fingers colder, but neither of us really noticed.

'You've no idea how much I really wanted to tell you, but I was afraid it would upset you too much, especially after all that Charlie stuff. I'm so sorry, Stell. I can't stand it when we have secrets from each other.'

Stella stared at the sky, exhaling a final drag of the cigarette before stubbing it out on the step and flicking the dog end into the bushes. I bit my lip and managed not to upbraid her for it. She plunged her hands into the pockets of her puffy jacket and sank her chin deep into its collar.

'So why now?'

I wriggled over on the cold concrete step and slid my arm around her. 'You're grown up now. You've got your own life, and you're starting a career. You don't need me so much any more. It was meeting that homeless guy on the tube which suddenly got me thinking about it, how at some point people have to take decisions which change their lives one way or another. I just want to do something for myself for once, and I suppose I want some answers, really. I've been a bit, well, *down*, I suppose, especially after Gavin dumped me . . . I don't for a minute think that Ann Paramor could be a substitute for Mum, though,' I added hastily.

But even as I said it, I realized that it wasn't entirely true. Whilst I didn't think that Ann Paramor *would* turn out to be another Barbara, or maybe (and I hesitated even to think it) *better* than Barbara, I couldn't – despite all the literature I'd read and all Mack's advice – suppress a deep-seated yearning that she might. It would be so completely wonderful to have a real mother again. I imagined being hugged by plump, perfumed, mummyish arms, and felt my heart constrict with guilty longing.

The back door opened and Suzanne came out. 'Mum says she's made mulled wine and why don't you two come in and have some before you die of hypothermia?'

'Two minutes, Suze,' said Stella. 'We'll be right in.'

Suzanne retreated back into the cottage, and all was quiet again. An owl hooted in the distance and Stella gripped my forearm. 'Was that an owl? I've never heard one before.'

I nodded. 'Yeah, I suppose it must be. I'm not sure I've ever heard one, either.' I looked at Stella, who was staring straight ahead again. 'Are you OK about this, then? It's really important to me.'

Stella looked at the sky, and I wondered what she was thinking. Was she, like me, remembering the blank unfeeling swell of that motorway verge? Her shredded patchwork quilt? Thinking of how I'd comforted her at night, listened to her problems, always been there for her? If our positions were reversed, I knew without a doubt that the idea of Stella finding a whole new family would have sent a spear of jealousy stabbing through me, so deep that blood would have oozed across the front of my jacket. It was intolerable, unthinkable. But that's what I was asking her to understand.

'You know when Charlie . . . you know,' she began. I nodded, holding my breath. 'I missed Mum then, more than I ever have done since she died. I missed her so much that I woke up crying for a week after. I haven't thought about her so much for years. It's just not fucking fair, is it? Most people have parents who stick around for decades, become grandparents, get old, and even if they get irritating and incontinent and moaned about, at least they're still on the scene. Ours didn't even live to see me pass my eleven plus, let alone see me get into college. Even Linda McCartney saw Stella do her first Chloë show. Mum will never know what I'm going to achieve, or what you'll achieve. It's not fair!'

I listened in silence, too choked to speak, tears dripping down my cheeks again, cold on my face. Stella's eyes were dry, but her breathing was ragged and every muscle in her body tense with sorrow. My first thought was that I obviously hadn't been good enough for her after the attack. I had let her down.

'I'm sorry,' I said.

'What for?'

'It feels like my fault that you were crying for Mum after Charlie attacked you.'

Stella turned, astonished. '*Why?*'

I was sobbing now. 'Because . . . because I've tried to be your mother, ever since Mum died. I've tried to be Mum and Dad to you, to make it up to you because they were taken away from you so young. I feel like I've failed you.'

She turned to me, pulling her hands out of her pockets and clasping my frozen ones. 'Emma, you idiot. I don't want you to be my bloody mother! I never have done! God, did you really think that? It drives me mad when you cluck over me. That was why I was so over the moon when you started taking me to parties with you. I thought, finally, you were beginning to treat me like a sister at last, a mate, and not some little baby to fuss over. In fact, I've been feeling guilty for years too, that you didn't take your university place because of me. I feel like *I've* fucked up *your* life. So of course you should look for your real mother – I've always wondered why you didn't do it sooner. You deserve all the happiness you can get, Em. Of *course* I'm OK about it – as long as you promise not to vanish off the face of the earth and never speak to me again.'

'As *if*,' I blubbed.

'I'll help you look for her too, if you like.'

'Sure,' I said thickly, blowing my nose and taking a slurp of tepid tea. 'Well, you've always wanted to be on TV, haven't you? This could be your chance. Mack's filming me for a documentary he's been commissioned to make for the BBC. You can be in it too.'

'Really? I can't believe you didn't tell me *that*,' she said, instantly perking up. 'Bagsy be the stylist, though. We'll both have to wear my designs. It could be my big break!'

I laughed, and we hugged, pressing our cold cheeks together, instinctively slotting our arms and heads into the right places, from years of practice.

PART TWO

PART TWO

27

An icy February wind blasted down the steps of
Olympia tube station as Mack, Katrina, Stella and I
emerged. Katrina was the girl Mack sometimes used as
his sound recordist, and she trailed behind us carrying
a boom microphone and wearing headphones. It was
making Stella feel extremely self-important and, I had
to admit, it did give the whole outfit a lot more of a
professional appearance than when Mack did it all
himself with radio mikes. Katrina's ears must have
been lovely and warm, I thought enviously. My own
were numb.

Mack hung back to film some small, artily-swirling
pieces of charred paper as they blew in a teasing spiral
towards our faces and made us jump.

'Check out old Roman Polanski back there,' said
Stella, nudging me.

'Guy Ritchie, if you don't mind,' replied Mack,
panning slowly up the steps after us.

'I don't *think* so,' Stella said scornfully. 'Does Emma
hang out with many gangsters?'

'Not since she split up with Gavin, anyway,' Mack
ventured, fiddling with the zoom on his camera, probably reframing from a long shot to a tight close-up to
capture my reaction to his jibe. I was learning more

than I thought I ever wanted to know about crash zooms, medium close-ups and logging rushes.

'Bastard,' I shot at him. Hardly sparkling repartee, but at least if I swore he'd have to edit out the entire exchange.

As undeniably terrified as I felt at the thought that I might be about to meet my mother, there were elements to the filming process I was really beginning to enjoy: the creativity of it, and the feeling that we were all in it as a team. It was great, having Stella involved too. I couldn't remember the last time we'd done anything together like this.

'How're you doing, Em?' Stella asked, sensing my mingled trepidation and excitement. She linked arms with me, briefly leaning her head on my shoulder as we walked up the stairs, the boom mike wobbling over our heads like a small furry angel.

'Nervous. But I'll be fine. Look out for signs, the map says it's right next to the tube.'

'It is – look.' Stella pointed at a sign indicating that the entrance of the Exhibition Centre was around the corner. '*Ten* pounds?' she screeched as we came in sight of the main doors, noticing the admission fee prominently displayed. 'Daylight robbery, if you ask me. And that's before you've bought any of their crap crystals or paid to have your chakras fondled, or whatever the hell it is they do in there. Pay for me, Em, would you? I won't be able to afford lunch otherwise.'

I rolled my eyes, but was about to pull out my wallet anyway when Mack stopped me.

'Don't, Emma, the BBC can get this. I'll expense it.'

'Are you sure? Still, compared to what I might have paid for a private detective, it's not all that much.'

Mack handed me four ten-pound notes. One was crisp and fresh, but the others were old and softly wrinkled, reminding me of the scene in the tube station, with the tramp's horny fingernails under the ten pounds I gave him. It seemed like years ago, although it was only a few months. I wondered how he

256

was doing, and if the money had gone on alcohol and fags, or sustenance and shelter. I felt newly grateful to him for spurring me into changing my life.

I handed over the forty pounds and the wide-eyed cashier let us all through the turnstile.

'BBC film crew,' said Stella smugly.

It was incredible and frankly ridiculous how many people gawped at Stella and me, just because we were being followed by a camera and a boom mike. The crowds parted to let us through at every turn – which was, admittedly, quite handy in the hippy crush.

Stella was basking in the attention, hamming it up to the maximum and swanning about like a true luvvie. I was glad she was there, since it meant that less of the attention was focused on me, although I was attracting a lot of stares too, in the outrageous electric-blue fake-fur jacket she'd designed. I felt like a Furby. Stella herself was resplendent in a very eighties tartan blouson affair, so, on reflection, perhaps the reason people were staring at us wasn't so much to do with the film crew at all . . .

A barrage of sound and activity greeted us when we entered the hall, a sort of spiritual indoor marketplace. There was something almost biblical about the hubbub and strange smells in the air, perhaps because of the baggy hessian shirts many of the men were wearing, and the sound of a whiny snake-charming instrument floating above the heads of the nirvana-seeking punters. A middle-aged half-naked belly-dancer wobbled her way past us through the crowds, accompanied by a dark skinny man who was the source of the whingeing trumpet.

The belly-dancer's stomach fat jiggled and undulated, swirling softly like kneaded pizza dough. The bottoms of her heavy breasts were escaping from underneath her spangly bra-top, and a couple of wiry pubic hairs were clearly visible above the silk loon pants which cinched her hips, cutting hard into the fleshy love-handles.

Stella stared, blinking with horror. 'That', she said, too loudly, to camera, 'is unacceptable.'

I had a sudden irrational flash of panic that this woman, cavorting in pyjama bottoms with her tummy doing impressions of jelly on a trampoline, might be Ann Paramor. Shaking my head to dispel the notion, I consulted the floor plan and exhibitors' guide to try and figure out where Ann might be. But the stands were listed by company only, and I couldn't see any mention of her name.

'Come on,' I said to Mack, a lot more bravely than I felt. 'We're just going to have to take it stand by stand.' My knees were shaking.

We plunged into the mêlée and began walking up and down each aisle, staring at and then dismissing the occupants of each stand, despite their breezy sales pitches and welcoming New Age smiles. None of them resembled me in any way.

After forty minutes, my head was reeling with new and strange words, and images of bizarre holistic gadgets and therapies that no well-informed twenty-first-century dweller should live without. We could, had we so wished, have had a mineral analysis of our hands, our toes read, our auras photographed, our Third Eyes opened, our irises diagnosed, or our PMT Ayurvedically cured.

'I'm knackered,' whined Stella. 'Look, there's a Yogurt Shoppe, can we go and sit down please?'

We adjourned to a plastic table and chairs in the Holistic Vegetarian Food court, and Stella and I slumped down over some reassuringly normal frozen yogurt, while Mack continued to film. I was beginning to have a niggling sensation in my chest that perhaps Ann Paramor wasn't exhibiting after all, but I wasn't sure if this possibility made me feel worse or better.

'Stella, I'm sorry, but I have to take off this jacket,' I said, sliding out of it. 'I'm absolutely boiling. Do you think there's a cloakroom here?' I hung it on the back of my chair and fanned my hot face with a paper napkin.

'Well, all right then, if you must,' she said reluctantly. 'Hey, what's Hawaiian Tuna Massage, do you suppose?' She squinted at a sign above a nearby stand. 'Apparently it creates profound states of transformation and self-love.'

Mack panned the camera across to the sign, and back to us again.

'What do you reckon, Em? Maybe women in grass skirts rub you down with tuna steaks while chanting Om. God, we've only been here an hour, and I'm already fed up with all these extravagant claims to the Path of True Consciousness or Knowledge or Enlightenment or whatever. You're an aromatherapist, you know all about all this hippy shit, but it doesn't do anything for me.'

I looked more closely at the sign. 'It's not tuna, it's huna. That curly writing is confusing. And anyway, even I think half this stuff is rubbish. Don't diss it all, though, Stella. A lot of these therapies have been around for thousands of years . . . Look, can we get on with the business in hand, please? The suspense is killing me. I don't think she's here – surely we'd have seen her by now.'

'OK. Don't worry, we'll find her. We haven't looked at all the stands yet. And even if her name's not on her stand, there's bound to be someone we can ask.'

I managed a smile at Stella's laboured sympathy, and we set off again, me with an armful of synthetic blue fur jacket, Mack and Katrina following silently along behind. I noticed that Mack seemed to be filming rather more shots of Stella's bottom than I felt was strictly relevant to the project, but I was at least grateful that he'd stopped banging on about how gorgeous she was, and if she might possibly be interested in him.

We trawled down two more aisles, and Stella had to be restrained from buying – with my money – a pair of 'Chi-Pants' solely because of their advertising pitch: 'Chi-Pants replace the cross-seam crotch with a gusset.

They give room to move and room to . . . be.' I, in the meantime, was seriously tempted to sign up for a UFO Abductee Probability Measurement Test – a confidential 388-question test revealing High or Low Probability with personal recovery package. I thought that it might explain a lot.

Eventually we had zigzagged up and down all the aisles except the final one, nearest the big stage at the end of the room.

'She's got to be down here somewhere. I'll meet you back at her stand if you find her, or by the stage if you don't, OK? I'm dying for the loo. Don't want to be meeting your mum with a full bladder, now do I?' Stella disappeared towards a sign saying 'Toilets'.

Typical, I thought. Deserting me when I need her most. I took a deep breath and headed down the final aisle.

Halfway along on the left, I spotted the name Ann Paramor on a banner above a stall. A plump red-haired woman stood with her back to me. Unable to continue, I paused by a stand displaying Real Mirrors. 'See yourself as others see you!' said the blurb on the banner above the table. 'Our mirrors don't reverse your image, so you see your true reflection.' I looked first at the three mirrors hanging in front of me, before peering at myself in them. They acted as a useful screen between me and Holistic Mother. I generally disliked my reflection, and had a sudden stab of hope that a Real Mirror would show me that, in fact, I was a lot more beautiful than all the other normal mirrors in the world had always led me to believe.

I slowly raised my eyes to meet myself as I really was. But hope faded, to be replaced by a sludgy disappointment. If anything, I thought I looked far less attractive than I'd always assumed myself to be. How could I ever have thought I was pretty? Lank dark hair, pale skin, too many wrinkles . . . I stared again, this time trying to look less critically at myself, focusing on my nice curvy lips and large brown eyes behind my oblong glasses. Better. Not great, but better.

'You look gorgeous, me darlin,' said Mack in an appalling Irish accent. I was mortified. I'd got so used to him following me around with a camera that I had actually forgotten he was there.

'Oh, shut up,' I said, blushing puce. 'You won't put that in the film, will you?'

He laughed and shook his head. 'Do you think it's her?' he whispered, pointing at Ann.

'Don't know. Haven't managed to see her properly yet.'

Taking a deep breath, I peeped around the mirror's frame to see what Ann – assuming that it was indeed her – was doing. She was deep in conversation with a man with a ridiculous beard, plaited into a skinny grey braid secured at the end by a bead. I couldn't hear what they were saying, but Mack and I watched as Ann placed a small cardboard pyramid, painted purple, on the customer's outstretched palm. A look of wonder spread over the man's face as Ann gestured to him to pass his free hand over the top of the model and back.

All over the stand were stacks of other pyramids, in different colours and sizes, most of them just flimsy-looking frames. Only one was completely three-dimensional, the largest of them all. This took pride of place on the table, and was a multi-tiered green affair, about two feet in diameter, faintly Mayan in appearance. On each of its corners and tiers sat crystals, different colours for each layer. The whole thing appealed to my innate sense of order.

More crystals were spread out over all the remaining available space, scattered loose or sitting colour-coded in trays. The banner over the top of the table read 'Love Lines Inc. (Ann Paramor, specialist in Pyramid Energy and Crystal Layouts)'.

How on earth did I feel about having a birth mother who made pyramids? I gazed spellbound at Holistic Mother's back. At least we had alternative pursuits in common, after a fashion. That might explain how I'd ended up as an aromatherapist. It would be cool, actually, to have a mother who was, roughly, in the same sort of professional field. Perhaps we could even go into business together.

The implausibly bearded man fished in his jeans pocket and handed Ann a crumpled note in exchange for the purple pyramid, which he placed gingerly in his rucksack, and wandered off with a big smile. Ann began to tidy up the stack of pyramids she had disturbed to show the man, and I seized my opportunity.

Sidling round to the front of the stand, I picked up a blue pyramid frame, examining it with trembling hands as Mack lurked behind, surreptitiously filming through the gap between two of the 'real' mirrors.

As I slowly looked up, the woman turned and smiled at me. She looked nothing like me at all, although she was the right sort of age: late forties, early fifties. She had pale blue eyes, fleshy foundation-covered cheeks, and her nose was dotted with a smattering of splodgy freckles. Her lips, coated with a generously sticky layer of orangey lipstick, were thin, and her long auburn hair needed a good brushing.

'Hello there. Can I help you with anything?' I immediately recognized her deep voice and thick Yorkshire accent from her answerphone message.

Yes, I thought. Are you my mother? 'Um,' I said instead, tearing my gaze back to the pyramid. 'Could you tell me what pyramid energy is, please?'

Ann's face lit up and she launched into her set piece, a condensed lecture on 'pyramid power for beginners'. As she had with the last customer, she selected a pyramid and rested it gently on my palm. I tried to stop my hands from shaking.

'Now,' she said, somewhat smugly, 'wave your other hand slowly across the top, palm down. What do you feel?'

I rotated my free hand in the air above the pyramid, feeling like a mystic about to peer into a crystal ball.

I felt nothing, but was finding it very hard to concentrate.

'Take your time,' Ann said.

Suddenly I felt a warmth in the hand holding the pyramid. As I tried to concentrate on the sensation to make sure I wasn't imagining it, a light upwards breeze tickled my other palm.

'Wow!' It was a relief to have something else to focus on. 'I can feel cool air on my hand!' It was a disconcerting feeling, and I couldn't help shoving the pyramid back onto the table as if it were red hot. 'How come? It's made of cardboard.'

Ann looked at me indulgently, like a physics teacher who had just shown her class how to make iron filings dance to a magnet's tune.

'Polyboard, actually. But that's what I'm saying: pyramid energy. The basic structure of the pyramid changes positive ions into negative: it's the shape that matters, not what it's constructed from. Some people feel it as heat given off, others feel a rush of air.'

'Yeah, I felt heat in my other hand. So what can you do with them?'

'What *can't* you do with them, love, is more the question. In the kitchen, keep your fruit under a pyramid and it will stay fresh for twice as long. Milk will keep, without needing refrigeration. Cut flowers don't wither nearly as quickly. I had a mouse in my flat; I put one of these outside his mouse hole, and he grew to twice his size in a few weeks! Sleep under a big pyramid and your health will improve dramatically.'

'Wow,' I said again, my armpits prickling with nervous sweat. I made a private note never to sleep under a pyramid, in case it made *me* grow to twice my size in a few weeks.

The more I scrutinized her, the more convinced I was that she was the wrong Ann Paramor. Even if I took after my natural father, surely there would be a *slight* resemblance? Still, this time I really would have to find out for sure.

'The Egyptians really knew what they were doing. Haven't you ever seen pictures of the mummies? Preserved far better than would ever be expected from bodies five thousand years old – it's not the embalming, it's because they were buried in a pyramid. If you're dead it keeps you fresh, if you're alive it keeps you young and healthy. In an ideal world we'd all live in pyramid-shaped houses, and hospitals and government buildings would be pyramids too.' Ann had a dreamy distant look in her eyes as she rambled on. 'Of course, what I really want to do is . . .'

At that point a group of Hare Krishnas took the stage and a loud chanting and tinny clashing of tiny cymbals commenced, drowning out her next words. I hadn't been paying all that much attention, but I just caught the words: '. . . build a giant Kermit at Saopaul.'

I stared at Ann, confused and embarrassed. This was getting more surreal by the minute. Why on earth did she want to build a giant Kermit? Perhaps she was quite simply off her rocker.

'Oh really?' I shouted gamely back over the noise, trying to sound interested. 'Where is Saopaul, exactly?'

Ann looked at me. 'Surely you know where Saopaul is!' she yelled back.

Never heard of it, I thought, not wanting to admit ignorance. 'Southall?' I hazarded, wishing Stella would come back and help me out. I wondered if Mack was getting all this on film. Southall wouldn't, I'd have thought, be an obvious choice of location for a fifty-foot Muppet, unless maybe it was an ironic post-modern statement, or had some cultural significance of which I wasn't aware.

'No, *Saopaul*.' A hint of irritation had crept into Ann's voice. By now I was really hoping that I hadn't reached the end of my search.

'I'm sorry, but my geography isn't great,' I said, my cheeks hot enough to defrost frozen peas. 'I've never heard of Saopaul.'

A sound engineer must have returned to the stage and lowered the volume on the speakers, because the Hare Krishnas suddenly became much more muted.

'You must have heard of it, love. You know, North Pole and Saopaul. I want to build a giant pyramid at t'South Pole.'

The South Pole! A giant *pyramid*! I stifled a laugh. Lucky I hadn't started asking what Ann Paramor was going to make the Kermit out of, or if she needed permission from Jim Henson. I didn't dare look around to see what Mack and Katrina were making of this exchange.

'Oh, of course. I'm so sorry, it was the noise from the stage, it drowned you out.'

With relief, I saw Stella sauntering towards us, weaving elegantly around a small ashy-bearded man carrying a didgeridoo, white lines and dots painted all over his face and torso. 'Excuse me, I'll be back in a minute,' I said to Ann, and rushed off to intercept Stella, followed discreetly by Mack and Katrina.

'I'm sure it's not her. She doesn't look anything like me.'

Stella glanced over. 'No, you're right, she doesn't. But I don't look much like Mum either, do I? You've got to be sure.'

'What do you mean? You're the spitting image of Mum. Oh, but I hope it's not her. You know, I actually thought she said she wanted to build a giant Kermit in Southall.'

They all stared at me, their eyes popping. Emma's finally flipped, their expressions said.

'I just *misheard*, all right?' I wished I hadn't mentioned it now. 'It's just that there's no – you know – *connection* there.'

'Don't be silly, why would there be?' Stella was brisk and matter-of-fact.

'So how do we find out then? I can't just go up and ask her, can I?'

Stella thought for a moment. 'Leave this to me.

265

We're at a spiritual convention, aren't we?' Dragging me by the arm, she marched us both back up to Holistic Mother. 'Ann Paramor?' Mack hung behind, whizzing out the zoom on his camera.

Ann tilted her head to one side, nodding enthusiastically, her eyebrows asking questions.

'My name is Stella . . . Chambers, and I'm learning how to become a psychic. This is my sister Emma, who's an aromatherapist. We were just passing your stand earlier and something drew me to you. This is a bit delicate . . . I hope you don't mind me asking you this but . . .' Stella dropped her voice and looked around surreptitiously, '*did you by any chance have a baby girl who you gave up for adoption?*'

Ann's eyes opened wide with shock, and I felt dizzy. I couldn't believe that Stella had just come right out with it like that. Oh Lord, I thought. This Ann Paramor really is my mother; the first one I've actually met. I tried hard to ignore the feeling of my heart sinking. At least it hadn't been Harlesden Ann.

But then the shock on Ann's face turned into puzzlement, and a moué of displeasure flitted across her lips. 'Well actually, love, no, I've never had any children. Which college are you studying at?'

Taken by surprise, Stella began to say, 'The Ealing Fash—', but I stepped hard on her toe, and she managed just in time to change it to: '*Faculty* of, er, Psychic Training.'

Ann Paramor – now safely no longer Holistic Mother – looked distinctly schoolmarmish. 'Listen, love, I've never heard of that school. Is it endorsed by the National Federation of Spiritual Healers? If they're teaching you to just come up to strangers and blurt out that kind of personal information – whether it's correct or not – well, that's not good practice, even in a place like this. What if I *had* given up a child for adoption? Do you think I'd want the likes of you coming up and reminding me of it?'

Despite my irritation at Stella's lack of tact, I came to

her rescue. Now that Mother No. 2 had been eliminated from our enquiries, I was beginning to feel more together again.

'Listen, I'm terribly sorry. It was very rude of us. Stella isn't really a psychic student at all, she's a fashion-design student. That was just an excuse to ask you the question about adoption. The thing is that I'm adopted, and I've recently discovered that my birth mother's name is Ann Paramor. I've found several Ann Paramors, but you're the first one I've actually met. So please forgive our technique, it needs a bit of honing.'

Ann Paramor's orange face relaxed into a smile, making her look quite pretty. 'I could tell you're searching, pet,' she said, peering into my eyes. 'It's written all over you.' She hesitated. 'Do you mind if I tell you something you may not be aware of yet?'

'Um, yeah, sure.'

'You're not really looking for another mother. What you're actually looking for is answers, am I right? You've had a great deal of loss in your life already, haven't you? No wonder you're a bit afraid. But you will find your answers, eventually. It'll be all right, as long as you keep your expectations under control.'

I laughed, a little nervously, and exchanged looks with Stella. 'That's amazing. How do you know that?'

'*I* don't, love. There's someone else, up there, who tells me.' Ann gestured matter-of-factly with her thumb towards the large polystyrene ceiling tiles.

'What, *God* tells you?' gasped Stella in amazement. She had a look on her face which made me think she was about to fall to the floor and wash Ann's M&S Footglove-clad feet.

Ann laughed. 'I can tell you're not a real psychic student. No, not that high up. I have a spirit guide. He tells me all kinds of things.'

I suddenly experienced a wave of envy. It would be pretty handy to be in touch with a spirit guide. He could tell me if I was on the right track or not, without me having to trail around these bloody stupid Holistic Fayres.

'You have one too,' Ann was telling Stella. 'Everyone does. You just have to know how to get in touch with them.' She looked intently into Stella's eyes. 'Ooh, love, you've not had it easy lately either. In fact, you've taken a bit of a knock, haven't you?'

She picked up a stone from the tray behind her and pressed it into Stella's hand. 'This will help you feel better. It's rose quartz. It helps clear stored anger, fear, guilt, and resentment or jealousy. And you're feeling quite guilty at the moment, aren't you?'

She wrapped Stella's hand around the pink stone, which looked soft and inviting, as if it might squish between her fingers like a warm marshmallow. Stella's ears had reddened and she looked away from the camera.

'It's really good for creativity and self-confidence, too. It cools hot temper, and can help sort out emotional or sexual imbalances. Carry it with you all the time, and sleep with it near your head. You'll feel better soon; less afraid.'

'Thank you. And I'm sorry I lied to you,' muttered Stella, turning her back on Mack and Katrina so they wouldn't be able to film her apology. Somewhat to my surprise, she slipped the stone into the pocket of her jacket without denying the charges of fear and guilt.

'Well, we'd better get going,' I said, finally warming to this strange Northern lady with her ill-advised lipstick and cardboard pyramids. 'I'm really sorry we bothered you, but at least I can cross you off my list. Thank you for being so understanding.' I winced, thinking how much this expressed my relief at Holistic Mother not being the one, but Ann Paramor didn't take offence.

'Don't mention it, love. You haven't bothered me at all. In fact, even though you're looking for a different woman, meeting me will prove to be the catalyst in your search. *I* will be the one who makes it all fall into place, you mark my words. And if you need any more

268

help of a spiritual nature, I assume you know where to find me.'

'Thanks,' we chorused.

'Crikey,' whispered Stella as we walked away. 'Who does she think she is, the flippin' Messiah?' But she looked more at peace as she fingered the smooth stone in her pocket.

28

The postman didn't exactly fire cupid's arrow through our letterbox alongside the gas bills that year – two cards for Stella, and nothing for me, except a confirmation from the Nottingham B. & B. where Mack and I were booked to stay that weekend, in the next instalment of the Ann Paramor Project.

'I'm losing my touch,' Stella said, screwing the two different shades of pink envelope into a tight twist and lobbing them with deadly accuracy into the swingbin. 'They aren't even nice cards; they're both tacky and disgusting. I bet neither of them cost over two quid. That one with the perverted-looking bear on is probably from Mack. And Lawrence already told me he was sending me one.' She seemed edgy, joking with misery in her eyes. Something more than cheap Valentines was up, and I wondered if I dared ask.

'So? You've got two more cards than I have. In fact, I can't even remember the last time I got one.'

I decided that this was not the time to tell her that the cross-eyed teddy bear almost certainly wasn't from Mack at all, since he and Katrina had just started going out together officially. All those hours in the edit suite had bred a close friendship, which had travelled slowly up through familiarity, respect, and eventually arrived at desire. He was in love, and I was happy for him. I had a feeling that Mack would decide that it was imperative to have a sound recordist accompany us to Nottingham – no prizes for guessing who *that* might be. Still, I didn't mind. I liked Katrina. Although not exactly attractive – her jaw was so square that it looked like she had marbles stuffed down her cheeks – she was as petite as a newsreader, with a forceful, funny personality that suited Mack down to the ground.

I examined Stella's cards. Under the halogen spot-lights of the kitchen they glittered with promiscuity and cheap red propositions. She was right, they weren't exactly an inspiring sight.

'Yeah, but *Gavin* always used to send you roses instead, didn't he?' Stella asked.

'What do you mean, *Gavin*? You're saying it like he's a bad smell. You and Gavin always got on so well, and now you seem more down on him than you were when he dumped me.'

Stella turned away and started loading our breakfast things into the dishwasher, which was already almost full. Neither of us had put it on for about three days. 'Sorry. I'm just pissed off about my rubbish Valentines. Do you remember that year I got nine?'

'Yes, but weren't they all from the same boy, that one with the Dracula teeth and the squint? And, let's face it, I don't recall that selection being particularly good quality either.'

The telephone rang, and I was relieved to get off the subject, shuddering at the thought of a schoolboy's optimism: that nine Hallmark cards might just equal one sweaty hand down my sister's knickers. I picked it up.

'Hello?'

'Emma, it's Mack. Listen, about this weekend. I'm really sorry but . . .'

'You're not blowing me out, are you?'

'Well, I was just wondering if we could go another

271

time? Katrina's at a crucial stage with an edit she's doing on her own project, and I'd really like to stay and help her with it. Emma? You've gone all quiet.'

'I'm still here. No, of course, it's fine. But I think I'll go anyway. I've booked the B. & B. now, and I'm all psyched up for it.'

'But what if it's her, and I'm not there to film it?'

Tough. Mack, you're making that classic mistake: freshly in love and all your friends get demoted to the status of chopped liver. We've all done it. You think you and Katrina will be together for ever, but what if she gets fed up with your fibre-optic hair and your red All Stars? Or dumps you after a Who concert? *Then* you'll see where all your old friends are and, let me tell you, it might come as a bit of a shock . . .

But I didn't say any of that. 'We'll have to risk it. It's probably not her, anyway.'

'Why don't I get you a camera for the weekend, so you can film it yourself. You know, like a video diary?'

I laughed hollowly. 'No chance. I'm not carrying around two grand's worth of digital video equipment that doesn't belong to me. Besides, I'm hopeless with technology – you know that. I can't even get a photo in focus in an automatic camera. If it is her, you'll just have to interview us afterwards, if she's willing.'

'Maybe you could re-enact your reunion for the camera,' Mack suggested vaguely. He seemed distracted, and I wondered what, exactly, Katrina might be doing south of his telephone receiver.

'*Mack!*' I squawked, incensed. 'That was the one thing I said there was no way I'd do, not in a million years. You'll just have to take a chance on it. I'll ring you when I get back and tell you how I get on.'

'Why isn't Mack coming with you?' asked Stella after I'd hung up.

'Oh, too much work,' I said. 'And he's in love.'

Her freckles drooped. 'Great. Even Mack doesn't fancy me any more. God, I'm nineteen, I'm over the hill, and I'm getting fat. ' She pinched a non-existent love-handle above where the waistband of her jeans should have been, had she not removed it to make a pair of DIY hipsters.

'Fat? You must be joking. You're practically anorexic. And since you didn't even remotely fancy Mack, you should be happy that he's met someone he really likes.'

Stella still had a face like a wet dishrag, so I tried again.

'Look at it in a positive way, if Mack didn't send you that teddy bear card, then it means you've got at least one secret admirer.'

Still nothing. I made one last attempt.

'Why don't you come to Nottingham with me? I could do with the company.'

She looked up vacantly, her skin as dull as the unpolished chrome inside the dishwasher. I wanted to stuff her so full of echinacea and vitamin C tablets that she rattled.

'Oh, um, no, sorry, I'd love to, but I've got to finish my project on Decorative Techniques, otherwise I'm in deep shit. Suzanne's going to help me. In fact, I'm going to stay at her place from tonight till Sunday to get it done. And then we're going to The Cross on Saturday.'

'Oh. OK, then. Although I don't see how much work you'll do out clubbing with Suzanne.'

'Don't nag me, Em, I'm not in the mood.'

I took the bull by the horns. 'I'm just worried about you, that's all. You seem run down, and you haven't been on good form for ages, not since . . .'

We stared wordlessly at the two Valentine cards.

'Apparently Charlie's still really mad.' Stella started to rearrange the dirty cutlery in the basket of the dishwasher, turning her back on me again. 'Suzanne saw his sister and she was really nasty to her about me, saying that I was a lying slag, and I'd ruined his life. Now his parents have kicked him out of the house. His sister doesn't even know where he's living.'

I wasn't sure what to say. I went over and touched her back, but she shrugged me away.

'Please try to take no notice, Stell. His sister was nearly as weird as he was. You did the right thing. He'd attacked someone before, and if you hadn't told the police, he might have done it again.'

'He still might,' said Stella, trying to force one cereal bowl too many into the already full dishwasher rack. 'Oh, *get in*, you *bastard* bowl!'

'What do you mean? Of course he won't – he wouldn't dare; not with the court case and all. They'd throw the book at him if he tried anything else.'

She straightened up abruptly and stared out of the kitchen window at a magpie pounding flat-footed and grumpily along a tree branch. Her voice was strained and miserable.

'Then how come I thought I saw him the other day in the street? Coming out of the Blind Shop? It might not have been, but it really looked like him. And twice when I've been here on my own, the phone's rung but no one's been there, and 1471 hasn't worked.'

I shut my eyes in horror, seeing Stella's body once more slumped by the wheel of my car. Fury and protectiveness swelled up in a spiral inside me, squeezing the air from my lungs until I could barely breathe. She seemed so vulnerable, standing there by the window, her back to me. I rushed over and hugged her tightly, feeling her bony ribcage frail against my chest. She had yet to sculpt her hair into its harsh snakey waves that morning, and it was soft and scented with my Aveda shampoo, resting fluffily on her shoulders in a way she detested, but which I preferred. She thought it was boring, unwaxed and unmoulded. I thought it was safer, less . . . available. I hated myself for thinking it.

'Oh *Stell*. I can't bear it. Why didn't you tell me? We'll ring the police. He'd be mad to come near you.'

She shrugged and looked away, a childish, wordless

gesture. 'They won't do anything. Not unless I could prove it was him, or if he did . . . try anything.'

I realized that she was right. 'That's it,' I said decisively. 'I'm not going to Nottingham. If you can't come with me, I'm not having you here on your own all weekend.'

'Don't be stupid. That's why I didn't say anything; I knew you'd panic. Besides, I've already told you I'm staying at Suzanne's until Sunday. Go. I want you to go.'

Panic? What did she mean, panic? I didn't bloody panic. I was the voice of reason around here. 'Are you sure?'

'Yeah. Anyway, listen, I'd better get a move on. I've got a Millinery class in forty minutes, and I haven't even done my hair yet.'

'Want me to give you a lift?'

Stella laughed, a brittle, humourless sound which made me feel like crying. 'Oh, give it a rest, Emma, I'm not a kid. I wish I hadn't mentioned it now.'

'OK. Well, make me a nice hat then. See you on Sunday night, I suppose. Ring me if you need me. I'll be on the mobile. And take cabs everywhere if you're out late, won't you?'

Stella retrieved a small pot from her bag, dipped her fingers in the sticky white gel and began moulding her hair, twisting it, tamping it down and coating it until the waves began to take shape, like twirls of pasta. 'Can you give me some money, then? I'm a bit short at the moment.'

Another sore point. We weren't hard up, thanks to my extreme financial prudence – or, as Stella called it, 'tightarsedness' – but she passionately resented the control I kept on our bank accounts, via our account-ant. If I were ever to let her loose, she'd spend all her tuition fees on holidays in Ibiza and outrageous designer clothes, probably in the time it took me to decide whether to splash out the extra two pounds for mineral water in a restaurant. I gave us both identical allowances, only somehow Stella's never seemed to go as far as mine did.

It wasn't worth a disagreement, though, not at the moment. I gave her my last forty pounds, and waved her off down the stairs as if we were parting for weeks, not just a few nights. Less than five minutes later, the doorbell rang. Clutching a handful of silver coins, I plodded down to the front door, assuming it was someone collecting for charity.

A single, long-stemmed red rose lay on the doorstep, a small splash of colour against the grey granite. I instantly thought of Charlie, although I wasn't sure why. After his behaviour, and the threatening message, he was hardly likely to be sending Stella flowers, but you never knew. If he really had been lurking around here, perhaps he was schizophrenic, or obsessed by Stella, despite the damage she'd inflicted on him. Had I not had bare feet, I'd have stamped on it then and there, pulping its petals into a watery perfume to try and dissolve the fear I felt for Stella.

I made a mental note to get her to ring the police and find out why it was taking so long to get the swab analyses back. They'd said the lab was busy, but it had been nearly three months already.

Then I heard a sheepish-sounding and very familiar voice from the direction of the privet hedge.

'It won't bite you, it's only a rose. Happy Valentine's Day, sweetheart.'

Gavin stepped out from behind the hedge, wearing his old leather jacket and his twisty-seamed Levi's, his bike helmet looped over one forearm like a shield of honour. He was grinning at me, his arms opened wide in my direction. Before I'd even moved a muscle I felt the familiar sensation of being hugged against his warm chest, and the smell of his aftershave, and my cheek itched with longing to be pressed against his shirt buttons.

'What are you doing here? Where's the bike?'

'Oh cheers, Emma, is that all the welcome I get? A

cuddle and a cup of tea wouldn't go amiss. It's not one of your massage days, is it?' He picked up the rose and twirled it coquettishly in my direction. 'The bike's just down there, I didn't want you to see it and ruin the surprise.'

I shook my head, unable to think what to say. I wanted to take a running jump into his arms, strangle him with hugs, inhale the motorbike oil and CK One smell of his stubbly chin, smack his face with kisses. But I didn't. I couldn't.

'Gavin, you dumped me. You can't come swanning round here, months later, when you fancy it, expecting me to fall into your arms. I've only just got used to you not being around. It's not fair. And Stella told me you've got a new girlfriend. So what are you doing bringing *me* a rose?'

Gavin scratched the side of his thigh with the stem of the rose. 'Ah, yes, well, I haven't any more. Got a girlfriend, that is. She dumped me. Said I was too fat, can you believe it?'

He patted the soft mound of his little beer belly, an outraged expression on his face. Come to think of it, the belly wasn't as small as it used to be. It looked like something was in the process of melting down the front of his shirt, pooling above his belt in his own private reservoir of fat. And was that half an inch more forehead exposed, in only four months? He'd be as bald as a coot in a year if he continued at this rate.

But he was still Gavin, smiling his wicked smile on my doorstep. Nobody was perfect, I told myself. We were both getting older, and there were plenty of reasons for Gavin to criticize my own body, if he chose to. All in all, he looked pretty good for his age.

Predictably, I relented. 'I suppose you'd better come in, then.'

To no one's great surprise, the one cup of tea turned into a lengthy lunch at the River Café – Gavin claimed to be flush from a deal he'd just managed to pull off. I didn't want to know the details. It was like that with

Gavin. Too much knowledge was a bad thing; you just enjoyed the experience. And, half an hour earlier, flying through the streets of Hammersmith on his Harley, my arms wrapped around his waist, the wind whipping my hair in a mad maypole dance across the visor of his spare helmet, I sensed that I was already enjoying an experience of which there might well be more to come.

We had a great lunch. I marvelled at how comfortable I felt with Gavin; how I never felt shy with him, and I talked more than I'd talked to anybody, including Stella, in months. I told him about the man on the tube, all the Ann Paramors, my planned trip to Nottingham that weekend, the Holistic Fayre, the house in Harlesden. For once, he couldn't jump in and outdo me with one of his own stories, because this was something outside even his realm of experience. He just listened, and nodded, and said 'Wow' occasionally. I revelled in the telling, and in the unspoken implication that even though he'd dumped me, I had not fallen to pieces. Instead I was finally doing something for myself – not him, nor Stella, nor my various aromatherapy clients with their low blood pressure, their dicky backs, their PMT; but me, Emma.

'So you heard about the business with Stella then, and that bloke?' I asked casually over sticky toffee pudding.

Gavin made himself an expertly rolled cigarette, a tiny, perfect cylinder, put together as delicately as if he were constructing a banister for a doll's house. He sealed it shut with a cat-lick of his tongue, and flicked his lighter open. Then, obviously remembering how much I hated him lighting his smokes while I was still eating, he put the roll-up on his side plate.

'What bloke?'

'Charlie, his name is, the one from her college who attacked her. Weren't you there that day, when she got a message from him on the answerphone?'

Gavin looked out of the window, and although his voice was calm, his fingers fiddled with the cigarette.

'Oh yeah, poor Stella. I've never seen her so gutted.'

You comforted her, didn't you, I wanted to say. Suddenly there was a pall cast over the conversation. I was afraid to say it, in case I asked him what I'd been wondering about for weeks now, on and off, what Stella's shifty expressions and Gavin's studied casualness seemed to be confirming: *how* much, exactly, did you comfort her?

'She all right now, then?'

'Well. She seemed to be getting better, but this morning she told me someone's been ringing the flat and hanging up when she answers – I'm assuming it wasn't you.'

Gavin gave me a 'don't flatter yourself, darling' look.

'He's really bitter about being arrested and kicked out of college, and now she says that she's been seeing him hanging around in our street.'

'I'll sort him out for you, if you like. I told her that, and I meant it. I could get Heavy Eddie onto him. Just get a photo and—'

'Oh, for God's sake, Gav, you're not in the bloody mafia,' I snapped, more harshly than I'd intended, and then bit my lip. Getting cross with Gavin never got me anywhere, however tempting it was. 'Sorry. I'm just so worried about her.'

He reached out his long dry hand, chapped and sandpapery from riding a motorbike gloveless in winter, and put it on top of mine. 'Seriously, babes, if he comes anywhere near either of you, you let me know immediately, and I'll be there, I promise.'

I snorted. 'This, from the man who takes six weeks to return a phone call? Fat lot of help you'd be in an emergency. I rang you after you came round to see me that time, you know, when I was out and Stella was upset. Why didn't you ring me back?'

Gavin lit the cigarette and poured me another glass of Chablis. 'Oh. Yeah. Sorry about that. I meant to ring you but, to be honest, I'd just met Julia and was, well, a bit distracted.'

Taking too big a swig of the wine, I clenched my teeth to avoid showing pain at the mental image of my Gavin being distracted by another woman.

'So if you were all that busy in the first flush of love, why did you come over to the flat in the first place?'

Gavin shrugged. 'Just being sociable. Bumped into Stella, offered her a lift home, came in for a chat, hoping to see how you were. That's all.'

'Oh. Right. Is Julia the one who said you were too fat?'

'Yup. Nice bird, did PR for BT Cellnet. Hey, if you don't want that, I'll finish it.' He dragged my dessert plate across to his side of the table and enthusiastically spooned up the remainder of my pudding – which I'd been fully intending to eat myself. I was just having a rest.

'Good. I'm glad she's ditched you. Now maybe there's a chance you might return my calls again.' I grinned at him, suddenly relaxing back into the old familiar banter I'd missed so much. I decided to forget my paranoid suspicions about him and a weeping Stella alone in the flat together.

He made a soppy face, and licked the last drips of syrupy sauce off my spoon. I saw my own tiny face reflected convex and inverted on the silver back of it.

'I can never remember why reflections are upside-down in the backs of spoons,' I said, feeling a little tipsy. 'My dad was always really good at explaining that sort of thing; you know, why planes don't fall out of the sky, how microwaves work, where the whirlpool of bathwater down the plughole comes from, how waiters do that origami thing on napkins in posh restaurants.'

Too bad he was killed before he could solve the tea-spoon conundrum for me, I thought. I didn't even consider asking Gavin if he knew, since there wasn't a snowflake's chance in hell that he would. Gav was the most unscientific, un-practical male I'd ever met. He couldn't even wire a plug. Rolling a cigarette was the pinnacle of his dexterity, and that was only because he'd been practising for twenty years.

'Tell you what,' Gavin said. 'Why don't you stand on your head, right now, and we'll see if your face appears the right way up in the spoon. Plus, I get to see what colour knickers you're wearing.'

'Ha, ha, very funny. I knew I could count on you for some truly scientific experimentation.'

Gavin grinned. 'And in answer to your question, yes, I might.'

'Might what?'

'Return your calls. I've missed you, actually.'

'*Have* you?'

Had he? Was he saying that we should get back together again? Did he really think that he could just decide to pick up where we left off, after all my heartache and soul-searching? This smacked more of mid-life crisis than true love.

And what effect would it have on me if we did? I'd gradually been coming to realize that my lethargy and despondency, the rows with Stella, my obsessive reminiscing over the past few months weren't just manifestations of newly dumped emotions. I'd been depressed, in a rut, feeling that I had no future, no motivation. Even the aromatherapy, the one thing in my life I had succeeded at, was becoming old and stale. Only the search for Ann Paramor, however protracted and tortuous I was making it, had been a distraction.

Could I really risk letting Gavin hurt me again? I needed to be as strong as possible, now that I felt I was getting closer to finding my birth mother. Suddenly I was glad I was going to Nottingham on my own that weekend. It was proof that I was finally putting myself and my goals first, at last. Before, I would without a doubt have rescheduled the trip to fit in with Mack's schedule.

As all these thoughts were stirring around in my head like cake-mix, Gavin was looking at me with an unmistakably suggestive expression. He stuck out his tongue and slowly, deliberately, licked all around the rim of the spoon, not for a minute taking his eyes away from mine. I hesitated, and then, under cover of the long white tablecloth, I slipped my foot out of my shoe and slid it up his shin, my toes creeping along his inner thigh until they reached what I knew would be waiting for me in his crotch. As always, he did not disappoint me. Mmmm. My very own horn of plenty, my cornucopia of carnality, I thought with tipsy pomposity. My old friend. I stroked my big toe along the column of muscle, mentally greeting it, wishing it weren't so unfairly sheathed in indigo denim. The contents of his trousers had always comprised the most important part of our relationship, I realized. Even if Gavin wasn't exactly the most considerate of lovers, he was certainly enthusiastic and appreciative. I could always forgive him an awful lot after we'd been to bed.

I drained my wine glass, and picked Gavin's spare bike helmet off the floor. 'Back to mine, then, I think. Don't you?' I said, putting my shoe back on again. Being assertive was almost as liberating as the sexual energy flowing between us.

Gavin paid the bill and dragged me out of there so fast that if I hadn't just seen him laying down the cash, I'd have sworn we'd done a runner.

29

I did it. With a still-sexy faint throbbing between my legs, I successfully navigated my way up the motorway to Nottingham. I drove into the outskirts of the city on an adrenalin high, singing along with the Hallelujah Chorus on Classic FM, screeching the high soprano in my alto voice until I began to feel dizzy. I didn't even remotely care that people in adjoining vehicles were giving me funny looks, because now, yes, I was finally feeling that this was an adventure. Anything could happen, and I was the one to make it happen. Even just getting myself to Nottingham on my own, without once freaking out on the motorway, had to be one of the most empowering things I'd ever done.

And Gavin had been *magnificent.* We'd spent three days together, and my cup had runneth over. Many times. He had been passionate, repentant, and when he climaxed – for the first time – he called out my name as if nothing had ever meant more to him. I wish he hadn't left so abruptly, though. At about four o'clock on Friday afternoon, he'd hauled himself out of bed, fished his Calvin Kleins off my bedside light, and got dressed.

'See you soon, sweetheart.' He'd kissed my forehead, my nose, and then my mouth, in one of those gorgeously luxuriant and sloppy post-coital kisses. 'Let's give it another go, shall we?'

Driving through Nottingham, I agreed to myself again, out loud. 'Yes, let's,' I said to an old lady dragging her shopping trolley over a zebra crossing in front of me. I felt ludicrously happy.

I consulted the hand-drawn map posted to me by Janet and Gil Hawkins, the proprietors of the bed and breakfast, and, without one single wrong turning or hesitation, got myself to 'Treetops' within ten minutes. As the line drawing on their headed stationery had indicated, the house was a lovely Victorian detached villa, whose tiled porch and creeper-clad walls reminded me of a bigger version of my childhood home.

Hauling my overnight bag from the back seat of the car, I was just approaching the front door when it opened and a very tall, very beautiful light-skinned black man wearing cream chinos came out, whistling. He wasn't wearing a cricketing tanktop, but somehow I felt he should have been – although this would have been a minus; I hate cricket. I glanced at his face, and then stared. His eyes were a magnificent tawny amber, flecked with gold specks, crinkling at the corners with what looked like good humour. Best of all, they were fringed with carpet-sweeper lashes just like mine, and I got a sudden image of us, kissing, accidentally weaving our eyelashes together, like teenagers getting their braces ensnared.

I looked away again, hastily.

''Lo,' he said cheerfully to me, before striding away down the drive.

'Hi,' I called after him too quietly, shaking my head. Typical – hadn't seen a decent bloke for months and then, with the feeling of Gavin still inside me, I bumped into one at a B. & B. Still, he's not my type, I thought. I could never go out with a cricketer.

I rang the doorbell. A dumpy, sixty-something woman in a crimson Jaeger two-piece and with a rather gummy smile eventually answered, introducing herself as Janet. Unable to stop myself judging every new female I clapped eyes on as potential Mummy material, I instantly thought, Yes, you could be a mummy.

Following Janet's impressive rump down the hall and up the stairs, I called out answers to the questions which were being dropped around my ears like bouncing bombs.

'Up here on business, are you?' She had a strange, unplaceable accent, not British, not Australian or South African.

'No, not really. I'm . . . in search of an old friend.'

'Lovely. I got the message that you only need the one room now. On your own, are you?'

'Yes.'

'Well, here we are then. The bathroom's just next door. Will you be late in tonight? Only Gil locks up at eleven on weeknights – we do have such an early start in the mornings.'

'Oh, I'm sure I won't be late. Do you have many guests at the moment?' I couldn't help visualizing an entire cricket team being put up in the house. Perhaps I could *learn* to like cricket.

'Just one other gentleman tonight, a Mr Tilt from Birmingham. He's in titanium, so he says. He's just gone out, but you'll probably see him at breakfast.'

Guiltily pushing aside the memory of Gavin spread-eagled on my bed, I hoped that I would. At least it would liven up the cornflakes. I had no idea what being 'in titanium' was – some kind of scientific or industrial field perhaps, but all the same it seemed rather at odds with the tall, sporty-looking man who'd smiled at me.

Eventually Janet left me alone. I flopped down on my back on the double bed and surveyed the room: reasonably subtle flock wallpaper, Laura Ashley rather than Indian restaurant; antique pine wardrobe. A faint, sickly-sweet smell of roasted meat wafted around the room, and a distant sound of clanging pots indicated that the kitchen must be below.

There was something very bizarre about the concept of a bed and breakfast, I thought. Within moments of setting foot in a stranger's house, you were lying on their beds, smelling their cooking and reading their books. I couldn't understand how anybody would want to subject themselves and their homes to such a gross intrusion, even for £39.50 per night.

I sat up and examined the three paperbacks on the bedside table: Jilly Cooper's *Riders*, a Wilbur Smith and a dog-eared Anne Rice. Resisting the temptation to curl up under the cool slippery eiderdown and start reading the Jilly Cooper, I got my phone out of my handbag and rang Stella's mobile. No reply, and I hadn't taken Suzanne's number with me, so I tried Gavin instead. No answer there, either, but I left him a very lovey-dovey message, underlined with kisses.

'Right,' I said, out loud. 'Ann Paramor Number Three.' I looked at my watch: two-thirty. Plenty of time . . . for what? With a small shock, I realized that, subconsciously, I'd planned out the day to include not only the possibility of Ann Paramor being my birth mother, but that she would invite me to dinner that evening too. 'Ridiculous,' I muttered, a leap of hope in my chest none the less.

Clutching my washbag, I slipped out of the room and into the chilly salmon-pink bathroom next door, where I washed my face and hands, brushed my hair, and reapplied my lipstick. The mirror over the basin was faintly but disgustingly flecked with what could only be the detritus of past lodgers' teeth-flossing endeavours, which seemed like a bad lapse, or, as Dad used to say, paraphrasing Reggie Perrin's military brother-in-law, 'Bit of a cock-up on the old hygiene front.'

I examined myself critically, nervously. If this was the right Ann Paramor, what would she think of me? What would I say to her? Would her eyes be like these brown ones? Would her nose be shiny like mine; would her lips have a tendency to chap? More than almost anything else, I desperately wanted to resemble her. I wanted to know from whom I inherited my eyelashes, the intermittent patch of eczema on my wrist, or the way my hair frizzed so hopelessly in a humid climate. Whether Ann Paramor also had clicky knees, or if she could fold her tongue into a V-shape like I could.

I'd always been fascinated by the different ways that children inherited their parents' characteristics. At every possible opportunity I studied families: parents and children, siblings. Not just for the obvious physical resemblances – matching flame hair or fat ankles – but gestures, facial tics, toe-shapes, cuticle growth patterns. When a new mother in one of my post-natal massage classes had pointed out that her baby son had inherited her double-jointed thumbs, holding up one of his weeny curved-back digits by way of example, I was overcome with envy and admiration.

'That is *so cool*,' I'd said, in tones of such utter awe that the mother thought I was taking the piss, and gave me a dark look.

Stella was like Dad in so many, mostly non-physical, ways: they were both hardly ever ill, and if they were, it was practically life-threatening for one day, and then they'd both make a miraculous recovery the next. My own bugs and coughs and colds used to drag on for weeks and weeks.

Stella used to come home from playgroup every day and rush to the bathroom, clutching her bottom and squealing 'I need poo!' because she didn't like to go in a strange toilet. Dad was exactly the same – without the accompanying explanations, of course. He'd come back from his photographic assignments and it was always the first thing he did: grab the sports section of the newspaper and head off upstairs for twenty minutes. I remember his homecomings more clearly as him coming *down* the stairs, not in through the front door.

287

I shot back the bolt on the bathroom door and returned to my room to assemble map, bag, coat, phone and key before leaving the house. As I took the left, first right, and right again, which I'd learned off by heart from the spidery legs of the road map, my hands were beginning to shake just enough so that I had to ram them into my coat pockets,

Three minutes later I was standing outside another large Victorian house, albeit a very different one to Treetops. Several small and elderly cars were parked haphazardly in the crazy-paved drive, and there was a faintly neglected mien to the building. A neat vertical row of bells to the left of the front door indicated that the house was split into several flats. Taking such a deep breath that I felt dizzy, I examined the little cardboard labels next to each bell. There it was: *Flat 3, Paramor/Jenkins*.

So who was Jenkins then, I wondered, feeling almost jealous. Partner, husband, lesbian lover, flatmate?

There was only one way to find out. I made myself push the innocuous white button of Flat 3's doorbell. There was no corresponding sound from inside, but it was a big house, so I waited, my heart in my mouth.

Eventually I heard distant footsteps, clattering fast down at least three flights of stairs. It took all my will-power not to bend down and peer through the letterbox. A shape loomed behind the frosted glass panels of the door and the door was flung open with an unpleasant grinding squeak as it scraped across the stone hall floor. I thought my heart would stop.

'Yes?' A man in grey stained jogging pants stood on the doorstep, brandishing a paintbrush and looking faintly irritated. He was middle-aged, slightly out of breath, and very hairy with too many teeth, like a DIY Bee Gee, or Kenny Rogers on a bad day. There was a splodge of apple white paint caught in one side of his beard, and my first reaction was to wonder if I should point it out to him.

'Hi,' I said, swallowing so hard that I actually gulped, ridiculously and audibly. 'Sorry to bother you but I'm, um, looking for Ann Paramor.'

I'd decided that straightforwardness was the only way to do this. I didn't have to tell him *why* I was looking for her. But to my relief, he didn't ask. 'She's not here. She's working today.'

'Do you know when she'll be home?'

'Sorry.' He peered past me into the road. 'I'm expecting a delivery.' He looked suddenly hopeful, as if his delivery might just be arriving after all, and he wouldn't have had a wasted trip down the stairs.

'Sorry,' I said back to him, just like in the supermarket, when you and the checkout person say 'thank you' to one another about twenty-five times in the space of one brief transaction.

I took another deep breath. 'Are you Mr Jenkins?' I gesticulated vaguely towards the name beneath the doorbell as if to underline my question, and his gaze followed my hand.

'Oh,' he said, rubbing his forehead with the back of his wrist. 'No. I'm just doing a decorating job. I don't live here. Anyway, I'd better get on. Do you want to leave a message for her?'

Are *you* my mother? I thought. 'No. Thanks. I suppose I'll just come back again later, see if she'll be in this evening.' Part of me wanted to bombard him with questions: how old is she? Does she look like me? OK, so you're only the painter, but might you know, perchance, if her middle toe is longer than her big toe or if she suffers from stress-related nosebleeds?

'Right,' he said absently, and began to close the door, grinding it back over the floor. Then he stopped. 'Oh, actually, I don't think she's in tonight, not till late. She said something about teaching at the pool this evening.'

I could. Why not? If Ann Paramor was teaching in a public pool, there was no reason why I shouldn't go and *see* her, at least. In all my mother-meeting scenarios, I had never envisaged the possibility of me in five feet of water when I first clapped eyes on her – but this was all so surreal anyway. I had nothing to lose. And at least Mack and his camera wouldn't be able to record it.

I went back to the guesthouse and asked Janet if she had a Yellow Pages. Keeping a weather eye out for the delectable Mr Tilt, I carried the phone book back to my bedroom, but the upstairs of the house was silent and still, with not a cricketer in sight. My room was hot and centrally-heated dry, so I heaved up the old sash window with a rattle and a thump before flopping open the big yellow book, grateful for the cold February air ruffling my hair along with the flimsy printed pages.

There were no less than eight swimming pools in the Nottingham area. Thank God for mobile phones, I thought as I rang the first one on the list.

Five pools later, I hit pay dirt.

'Could you tell me if Ann Paramor is teaching a class with you tonight?'

'Just a moment, please . . .' I heard a rustling of paper and a distant ringing telephone, but no swimming pool sounds: no echoey squeals or splashes of dive-bombing children. 'Yes, the six-thirty Aquafit, in the small pool.'

I shivered, as if I already had one toe in cold water. 'Is it open to the public?'

'Yes, of course. Three pounds fifty. It gets busy so it's best to put your name down for it.'

'Right . . . um, Emma Victor, then.'

'Thank you.' The woman hung up, sealing me off from her turquoise-tiled and chlorinated world. Even if her office wasn't right next to the pool, I wondered if her eyes smarted when she went home at night.

Aquafit. Was I completely mad? I rang Stella again, and this time she answered.

'Stell, you'll never guess what.'

'*You found her!* Oh my God, what's she like?'

'No, wait, I still don't know if it's her or not.'

'Oh. What then?'

'I went to her house, and her decorator told me she was teaching an aqua aerobics class at the pool tonight, so I've rung round all the pools and—'

Gales of crackly laughter interrupted me. 'You're never going!'

'I might. What do you think?'

'*Go* for it. God, I wish I was coming too, if only for the spectacle of you jiggling around in the water. You hate swimming!'

'I know. Shut up. Anyway, it's not swimming. I'll probably just go and check it out, then join the class if it looks any good. How else am I going to get a proper look at her?'

Stella laughed again. She sounded much happier, and I felt a tiny pang of jealousy that Suzanne could cheer her up in a way I couldn't.

'Excellent. I think it's a great idea. You wanted some different experiences, and you're certainly getting them . . .'

I giggled too. 'You only live once, as they say. Hey, Stell, you'll never guess what else – Gavin and I are back together. Isn't it great? He turned up on Wednesday and took me to lunch, then one thing led to another and . . . I think I'm in love again.'

There was such a profound silence that I thought I'd been cut off. 'Stell?'

'Yeah? Oh right, that's . . . great. If it's what you really want. Anyhow, listen, I've got to run. I'm late for meeting Suzanne. We're going to the library. Let me know how you get on at the aerobics, OK? Talk to you soon.'

Before I had the chance to check that she hadn't seen or heard from Charlie again, she hung up on me – or whatever the correct expression was when you terminated a conversation on a mobile telephone. Switched off, perhaps.

'But I thought *you* liked Gavin?' I said into the ether, worried and momentarily hurt.

Still, at that moment I had more pressing concerns – where was I going to get a swimsuit from in time for the class? I hadn't brought mine of course. It was about time I purchased a new one, anyway: because I didn't swim very often, I still had the same costume I'd had since school, and it had deteriorated with age, to the point that at sites of stress – bottom, breasts, stomach – it had become almost transparent, and bobbly like a badly pilled sweater. I always worried whether my nipples and pubic hair were on display. No wonder I never went swimming.

In a flash of inspiration, I rang back the lady at the pool, asking if they by any chance sold swimwear, and, if so, did they have any size twelve women's Speedos. After another lengthy pause, she confirmed that they did indeed.

By six-ten I was standing in the reception area of the pool, after triumphantly parking in the municipal car park outside: another successful navigation experience. I'd even had the correct change for the Pay & Display meters. Superstitiously, I convinced myself that the omens were good; that this Ann Paramor would be the one.

I bought a nice keyhole racing-back blue and yellow swimsuit, pristine in its cellophane wrapper and smelling of petroleum by-products and, after hiring a towel, wandered cautiously into the changing rooms. In a cubicle with the approximate square footage of a coffin, I managed to wriggle into the new costume, deciding that it did fit, if a little snugly.

I can't believe I'm doing this, I thought as I emerged self-consciously, pulling the back of the swimsuit down lower over my backside. I shut my clothes, watch and – reluctantly – my glasses, into a locker, and snapped the thick elastic band holding the locker key onto my ankle. Then, my entire body speckled with goosebumps of fear, I ventured forth to meet Ann Paramor.

Even without my glasses on, I could see an alarmingly high incidence of huge bellies amongst the seven or so women sitting on a chilly-looking tiled seat which ran alongside the baby pool, plus a couple of babies in carseats being rocked by their mothers' bare feet. The receptionist hadn't mentioned anything about it being ante- or post-natal! I looked wildly around for any other potential classes waiting by either of the two pools, but there were none. I'd made a terrible mistake.

I swallowed hard and picked my way carefully over the wet tiles, wishing that I'd thought to put my towel around my waist before the meaty-looking blokes thrashing up and down lanes in the big pool got an eyeful of my ass. Pay and display, indeed. They should put the meters inside the building, not out in the car park.

It seemed a very long walk to the baby pool, and when I got there, all the women ignored me. I sat down gingerly a little way apart from them, feeling that, as with the baby-massage classes, I'd once again stumbled into a members-only club for which I didn't fit the admission criteria. Shyness washed over me, bathing my chest and neck in a raspberry rash of discomfort. Think what Gavin would do, I told myself, and then almost laughed aloud at the thought of Gavin sitting in his trunks amid this display of female fecundity. Panic, that's what Gavin would do, without a shadow of a doubt.

It didn't matter what these women thought of me. I was in a strange town, taking a gamble, being a detective. None of them would ever see me again. So what if I wasn't pregnant?

'How far along are you, then?' I jumped. The woman next to me had slid along until our hips almost touched.

My hand shot to my throat, trying to cover up its

redness. 'Actually, I'm here under false pretences. I didn't realize this was an ante-natal class. I feel a bit stupid – I'm not pregnant at all.'

The woman waved her hand in front of her face dismissively, then rested it on the balloon of her belly. Apart from the dark puffy circles under her eyes, she was very pretty, with blonde wavy hair and neat features. She reminded me of Jenny Seagrove, or one of those other delicate little bird-boned actresses.

'Oh, it doesn't matter. There's another woman who comes every week – look, her over there, and she's not pregnant or post-natal either. Don't worry about it.'

I relaxed a little. 'Phew. That's a relief. I bought a new costume and everything – I'd be mortified if I got chucked out before it even started.' Particularly by my own mother, I thought.

'It's a nice costume,' said the woman wistfully. 'God, I wish I could wear a flimsy little Speedo again – I hate these disgusting Mothercare efforts.'

'When are you due?'

'Not for another month. But I tell you, it won't be a moment too soon. I bloody hate being pregnant. Have you got kids?'

We cast surreptitious glances at each other's ring fingers. She didn't wear one either. I shook my head. 'Is this your first?'

'And last. My name's Ruth, by the way. Do you live around here?'

'Emma. No, I don't, actually, I—'

'Oh *no*,' Ruth interrupted, nodding towards a hugely fat man waddling towards them, improbably clad in skin-tight black lycra. 'Ann's not here – Marty's standing in for her. Nightmare! He's rubbish.'

My face fell so far that Ruth looked askance at me. 'Don't worry, he's not *that* bad. I was exaggerating. Ann's much better, that's all. Hey, you think Marty's fat now, apparently he's already lost six stone.'

The news of Ann's absence hit me hard, and tears of frustration welled momentarily in my eyes. I told myself not to be so ridiculous; I'd just have to make the most of it for now, and go and visit Ann's flat again tomorrow. I'd psyched myself up this far.

The women stood up and headed for the wide submerged steps into the shallow pool, and I followed, embarrassment preventing me from simply turning around and leaving. Ruth waded into the pool in front of me, knelt down and threw her head back in the water, shaking out her long hair in slow seaweedy slithers underneath the surface. I approved – Stella and I, on the few occasions we'd been swimming together, always laughed privately about the women who kept their heads out of water at all costs, paddling around, long of neck and strained of throat. I followed her, leaning my own head back, feeling the kiss of the blue unthreatening water wash over my scalp.

Marty put a tape into the boombox and then, when the B-52s' 'Love Shack' began ricocheting across the water's surface, knelt down on the edge of the pool so he was closer to us, waving his arms and exhorting us to jog around in a clockwise direction. Nobody took any notice of him at first, so I stayed floating on my back for a moment more. Underwater, the music sounded different, more menacing, distorted and dominated by the thud of the drumbeats.

Ruth hauled herself upright again, and yanked her head towards Marty.

'Come on then,' she mouthed to me, stroking her belly. I watched her begin to wade towards the raggedy circle of women, her familiarity endearing her to me hugely. Despite her complaints about her appearance, she looked sleek and elegant in her spotted maternity swimsuit, still fetchingly baggy around the middle. Even eight months into the pregnancy, she only had a medium-sized bump, halfway along the spectrum of roundness on display. I wondered what sort of bump I'd have. Then I wondered how I had carried myself in Ann Paramor's womb. Perkily high and proud, like Ruth's baby? Or low-slung and thrashing about?

I caught up with Ruth. 'All right?' she said. 'Wait till we change direction – then it gets hard.' I tried to talk back to her, but it was difficult to make myself heard over the tinny pop and all the other women's voices, echoing in the chlorine-heavy air. A fluke of the pool's acoustics occasionally permitted a comment from someone down the other end to be distinctly heard: '. . . my boobs have got so saggy I might as well just *roll* the buggers up,' said a weary-looking post-natal mother.

'Well, I've got varicose veins like an ordnance survey map,' replied her friend, one of the biggest bellies. I thought that if she got any bigger she'd need scaffolding to support her stomach. Ruth saw me looking at her and nudged me. 'That's Charlotte. She's two weeks overdue. I really don't think she ought to be here. She looks as if she's going to spawn an entire litter of babies instead of just the one, doesn't she?'

Under Marty's orders we all began to jog backwards, the pull from the swirl of forward-flowing water making us work much harder, as Ruth had warned. My leg muscles were already beginning to ache, and I could feel an unpleasant rippling sensation around my bottom as the water tugged unforgivingly at my untoned thighs.

'I – must – do – more – exercise,' I puffed at Ruth over my shoulder. She grimaced back at me, as if we were old friends. It felt great. I toyed with the idea of quizzing her about Ann: what age was she? What did she look like? But then I decided against it. I wanted to find out for myself, even if it meant waiting until the next day.

Words and music mingled with the echoey shouts and slap of wet feet on tiles as children took running dives into the adjacent big pool, and I wondered if one day I would be carrying a new life inside my very own maternity swimsuit as I jogged around a magic circle of sisterhood. I felt suddenly sad that I was only passing through, and would never see Ruth again. Unless of course my intuitions were sound, and this did turn out to be the right Ann Paramor . . . No, I told myself firmly. I must not project.

More jogging and jiggling ensued, with some stretches and vaguely co-ordinated limb-waving thrown in for good measure. Marty distributed webbed gloves to us all, to create maximum resistance against the water. He looked slightly nervous, as if worried that he would suddenly be required to assist at an emergency water birth. The women seemed to sense his unease, and for the most part ignored him completely, continuing to splash sedately along and talk amongst themselves.

By this time I, as one of the more conscientious participants, was purple in the face and gasping. 'These gloves are a killer,' I managed to say to Ruth, surreptitiously peeling them off and leaving them in a wedged-up ball on the side of the pool. Ruth had been right behind me, but when she didn't answer, I turned to look at her, noticing that her face suddenly seemed very tired and greyish.

'Are you feeling all right?' I asked, but she just half nodded, half shook her head and carried on.

The two tiny babies at the side of the pool, strapped into their car seats, were looking bemused next to a giant basket full of orange armbands. They were spellbound by Marty prancing up and down in front of them and, indeed, appeared to comprise his most attentive audience. He eventually got so fed up with being ignored that he jumped into the pool himself, trainers and all, causing a mini tidal wave which splashed one of the babies and made it cry.

Our attention attracted, the class reluctantly conceded to perform an underwater rendition of the Macarena, followed by a half-hearted Twist. The women, myself included, all made cringing faces at each other behind Marty's back. I realized that I was beginning to enjoy myself, and vowed to find a similar class in Ealing on my return. I could ask Stella to pick me up a class timetable next time she went swimming.

Meanwhile, a small crowd of young boys, skinny and shiny-wet in their minuscule swimming trunks, had assembled, sniggering, at a safe distance, fascinated by these fat ladies with webbed hands.

'Now jump up and down!' commanded Marty. I tried hard to do so with dignity, but failed. The rest of the women obliged, some giggling, some grumbling; the big ones all clasping their gloved hands underneath their bulges as though afraid the baby might just fall out. The post-natal ones jumped much higher than their pregnant friends. There was a thwacking sound of buttocks colliding with the water's surface, and the water got quite choppy; waves slapping over the sides and rolling around us as we jumped. It was an incongruous sight in such a shallow pool.

Well, this is certainly a novel way to meet people, I thought. Suddenly all the stress and uncertainty and anxiety of the whole Ann Paramor undertaking faded away to be replaced by a strong sense of the absurdity of the situation. For the first time in months I felt my depression being shaken out of me, each jump dislodging a little more of the old miserable Emma until I felt so light and free I could have pogoed right out of the pool and into a new life. I thought of my adventure, of getting myself here, and doing this, and meeting Ruth. And then I thought of going home to Gavin the next day, of us starting again, and it made me so happy that I laughed out loud. Things were finally, finally, looking up; and at that moment I didn't care whether I found Ann Paramor or not.

With a last burst of energy, I jumped up and down as vigorously as I could, and Ruth, next to me, jumped enthusiastically too. Suddenly she cried out in pain and doubled over.

'Ruth? Are you OK?'

Ruth gasped and scrunched up her face, her hair sticking in wet streaks to her cheeks. She grabbed my arm. 'I need to get out. Please could you get my stuff from the locker?'

I took one look at Marty's horrified face, and the way the rest of the group seemed to wade backwards away from Ruth and, feeling as if someone more assertive had suddenly inhabited my body, took charge. Grabbing the thick rubber band from Ruth's wrist, and snapping mine from my ankle, I handed both keys to Marty, who was white with panic.

'Get a lifeguard or someone to bring our things from the lockers.'

Ruth moaned and wrapped her arms around her stomach. A yellowish cloud appeared in the water between her legs, eddying gently around her, and the other women moved even further away, sympathy and disgust flitting in tandem across their faces.

'Her waters have broken. Call an ambulance! Come on, Ruth, you'll be fine.'

Ruth clung on to my elbow. 'It's too early! It can't happen yet! Help, someone do something, please.' She was panting with pain.

Marty was clinging to the side of the pool like a big shiny barnacle. I shoved my finger into the spongy black rubber flesh on his chest and shouted at him, 'An ambulance – now! Move it! You two, give me a hand getting her out the water.'

I beckoned to the non-pregnant woman and the one with the saggy boobs. They waded hastily over, and between us, supported and propelled Ruth forward and up the steps to where the towels were. I wrapped one around Ruth's shoulders and one around where her waist used to be, and then someone else volunteered their bath robe, into which I manoeuvred Ruth with difficulty.

Marty had hauled himself out of the pool, where he lay for a second like a beached whale, before gathering the strength to straighten up and pad over to the nearest lifeguard. His waterlogged trainers squelched at every step.

'Don't worry, you'll be fine . . . Can I call anyone for you?'

299

'Noooo,' she wailed. 'I'm on my own. Please don't leave me.'

I grabbed her hand and held it, tightly. 'I won't, I promise.'

Two more lifeguards came rushing over and ushered us both in a little wet huddle towards reception. 'Hi Ho Silver Lining' still blared incongruously from the boombox in the background, but the class had ground to a halt. Ruth refused to let go of my hand.

Just as the blue lights of an ambulance swirled up to the swimming pool's main doors, bathing the surrounding cars and wet tarmac in ghoulish shadows, Marty came panting up to us trailing Ruth's and my bags and clothes. He practically threw them at Ruth and shot off again, embarrassedly muttering, 'Get well soon . . . Ah, no, I mean, good luck, hope it all goes well . . .'

She looked at me through her pain, and shook her head. 'Bloody useless,' we said in tandem.

The lifeguards gathered up the strewn possessions as two burly ambulance men strapped Ruth into a stretcher on wheels, whose pillow-end was propped at a forty-five-degree angle.

'What's your name, love?' asked one of the ambulance men.

'Ruth Jackson. I'm not due for another month!'

'Righty-ho. Don't you worry, love, we'll look after you. I'm Gerry, by the way, and this is Matt.'

Our odd-looking posse of uniformed men and undressed women swept outside and into the waiting ambulance. I winced as the cold night air hit my wet body – I hadn't even had a chance to dry myself or put on any shoes. I shivered, and legions of gooseflesh presented arms from my face to my cold, bare feet. A small crowd of curious onlookers stared at my back view as I climbed into the ambulance, still clad only in my Speedo, but I didn't give it a second thought.

'For God's sake, get dressed. Don't want to be called out to see to your pneumonia tomorrow, do we?' Matt, the younger ambulance man, threw me a small towel and a blanket while Gerry attended to Ruth, timing her contractions and offering her gas and air through a mask held to her mouth.

I had no idea where exactly my clothes were, and no intention of stripping off inside a moving ambulance, so I rubbed myself perfunctorily with the towel, and wrapped myself in the prickly hospital blanket.

'I'm fine,' I said. 'I'll sort out my clothes when we get there.'

Ruth looked up at the sound of my voice, her eyes huge above the mask.

'Thank you so much for coming. I'm scared. There's nobody else . . . This shouldn't be happening, it's too early and . . .*ohhhhh*.'

She screamed and panted with pain. I stroked her forehead and gently dried the ends of her hair in the towel, as it occurred to me that I'd left my car in the car park. Oh well, I thought, hoping it would still be there when I eventually got back to it. The worst that could happen would be a parking ticket, if I was at the hospital all night. Or vandalism. Or theft . . .

'Ruth,' I said, 'I'm an aromatherapist. Can I massage you? Just your feet? I could give you a little bit of reflexology.'

Ruth nodded, sticking her damp white-pruny foot out from underneath the blanket covering her. I moved down to the other end of her, still wrapped in my own blanket, and took her foot in my lap. 'I'm not in the way, am I?' I asked Gerry.

'You're all right just for a minute. I'll need to check her once I've got these contractions timed, though.'

I struggled to remember the right acupressure points. It had been a long time since I'd massaged a pregnant woman, and I'd never done one in labour before. 'Kidney 3, or "Bigger Stream",' I muttered to myself, finding the right place inside Ruth's ankle. 'Midway between high point of ankle bone and Achilles tendon, yes, there we are.'

I pushed firmly on the spot for a minute or two. 'This is to help ease labour pain, or fatigue,' I told her, although, frankly, it didn't seem to be making any discernible difference. Ruth was gripped with another contraction, and I had to clamp her ankle with my other hand to stop her kicking me away. I wondered if I should go for Bladder 67, or 'Reaching Inside', which was located on the bottom corner of the nail of the fifth toe, the pressure preferably to be applied with the point of a key, or other such object. But that was for difficult labour, or turning a breech, and I wasn't sure if it might be overkill in Ruth's case . . .

'Sorry, miss, but you'll have to move out of the way for a bit. I need to take a quick look.' Gerry manoeuvred me gently out of the way so he could attend to Ruth. I felt frustrated that I couldn't be more helpful.

'A month early, is he? Well, he might be on the small side, but I'm sure there won't be anything to worry about. Let's have a little check, shall we?' Gerry kept reassuring Ruth as he deftly unfastened the borrowed bathrobe, pulled away the towels, and peeled her wet costume off to examine her. Matt whipped two more blankets over her torso as Gerry rummaged around between her legs. He had an absent, unfocused look in his eyes, as though he was trying to locate, by feel alone, the satsuma at the toe of his Christmas stocking.

'Six centimetres dilated already! He's trying to take you by surprise, the cheeky little bugger.'

We reached the hospital, sirens blaring, before I could do any more acupressure. 'Good luck. I'll wait for you outside,' I said, disengaging Ruth's clamped fingers from my own with difficulty, and wondering if I should offer to come in with her.

'Thank yoooooo,' Ruth wailed as she was lowered out of the ambulance and whisked off through the swing doors. I was disappointed. I'd always wanted to massage a woman through labour, but, I supposed, she might still ask for me. I wouldn't have been surprised if she hadn't wanted me there. I was a stranger, after all.

I gathered up the pile of our possessions, shoved my feet halfway into my trainers without undoing the laces, and threw my coat on over the blanket. Feeling like a bag lady, or Tom's mistress from *Tom and Jerry*, I flip-flopped my way down the metal steps of the ambulance and into the maternity unit, where I went to the reception desk, waiting to ask directions to the nearest bathroom. A tired-looking balding man clutching an equally weary potted chrysanthemum walked past me, in a wide arc as though I were armed and dangerous. Now I knew just how that man on the tube train had felt.

30

Nobody appeared, so I took matters in my own hands and wandered around until I saw a ladies' loo. Thank God, I thought, bolting in and stripping off my wet swimsuit. My breasts and belly were icy cold to the touch, and clammy, like dead flesh. I was shivering so hard by then that my hands had a hard time obeying commands, but eventually I managed to separate my own clothes from the jumble of Ruth's, noting with admiration her Agnès B hooded cardigan and smart black Hennes maternity trousers.

Once dressed, I dried my hair by holding my head underneath the hand drier, the feel of the hot air blasting into my ears and through my brain making red stars dance before my eyes. Then I wrapped everything – Ruth's clothes, my wet costume, the borrowed bathrobe, towels, bags and coats – into the ambulance blanket, and wearily plodded back out into the corridor in search of a vending machine and somewhere to sit down.

I found coffee, and a seat; but even though my body temperature had returned to normal, I still couldn't relax. My heart went out to Ruth, alone and in pain, and the pathos with which she'd said 'there's nobody else'. Was that how Ann Paramor had felt when she'd had me? I didn't know what to do. I didn't really want to stay sitting on this awful black slippery leatherette bench, drinking plastic coffee – she could be in labour for twelve or fourteen hours. No, it wouldn't be that long. She was already six centimetres dilated, I reminded myself. I wished I had my massage oils with me: then I'd definitely have offered to come into the delivery room with her.

But this thought dissolved into more worrying issues of whether or not I had enough money to get a cab back to my car; and what if Janet locked the door of the guesthouse and I couldn't wake anybody up? Plus, I couldn't just leave – I had all Ruth's belongings with me.

I decided to wait for a bit and ask a midwife what was happening. They should know roughly how long it would take. But every person in uniform I saw seemed to be rushing around manically, as if I was watching them on speeded-up film, and I didn't get the chance. Well, I'll just close my eyes for a few minutes, I thought. They felt pink and tense from all the chlorine and panic, and it was good to rest them. Draining the dregs of my disgusting coffee, I swivelled my legs around on the leatherette bench, put my coat under my head, and drifted off into an uneasy damp sleep.

I awoke with a gasp from a dream in which Mum and Dad were adrift on a stormy sea, waves lashing and slapping against the side of their tiny, vulnerable boat. I was standing on the shore, one hand crooked over my eyes to try and see them better, unable to help. Mum was in labour with Stella, screaming and crying, ranting almost incoherently, the way she had after Stella was born, when she didn't know that I was listening.

In my dream, the sea was chlorinated.

I sat up, feeling woozy and upset. I must have been asleep for quite some time. Usually I loved dreaming about Mum and Dad; it was a small gift of their presence which stayed with me for days afterwards. But they'd been so far away, and in trouble.

The vertebrae in my neck cracked and crunched as I rolled my head around, trying to shake off the memory of the dream. Miraculously, a midwife walked past me slowly enough for me to stop her, and I jumped up off the bench. 'Excuse me. Can you tell me how Ruth . . . um . . . Jackson is getting on? I came in with her.' I tried to run my hand through my squiffy hair, but my fingers got stuck in a tangle, which made me accidentally yank my head to one side in a demented-looking fashion.

The midwife smiled at me. She was an Indian lady, large and soft with arms like hams, flabby with love and determinedly forgiving. Just how a midwife should be, I thought. 'I think she's had it already – was she the one who came in from the swimming pool? Yes? No, she has. A little girl, fifteen minutes ago. Very quick labour.'

'Oh! Are they both all right?'

'Baby's quite premature, and she has a touch of jaundice. We're going to incubate her for a while, keep an eye on her. Would you like to see Mum?'

'Sure, if she's up to visitors. I've got some stuff of hers here. What time is it, anyway?' I realized I'd left my watch in my bag, and began vaguely to fish about for it amidst the damp costume and towel.

'It's ten o'clock.'

Blimey, I thought, feeling like Cinderella. Better hie me back to my guesthouse pronto, before I'm locked out all night. I decided to stay just long enough to congratulate Ruth, and leave her stuff, and then I'd get a taxi back to the pool and pick up the car.

Ruth was just tottering gingerly, bandy-legged, back from the shower as I was being shown into her room. The air around us smelled earthy, viscous, and it seemed terribly sad that the baby wasn't there in person, the live trophy from Ruth's elemental struggle.

I loved babies. It would be such a disappointment to leave without seeing it first.

'Hi. Me again,' I said, helping Ruth into bed. She smiled at me, her lips trembling with weariness.

'I can't believe you're still here. It's so good of you, really, I—' Her eyes suddenly flooded with tears, which trickled exhaustedly down the sides of her face and onto her pillow.

'Hey, don't, please. It's all going to be fine. Congratulations, by the way. I hear you've got a daughter.'

'Thanks.' Ruth sniffed. 'I'm sorry. I'm not a crier, normally. I'm just so . . . *knackered*.'

'Was it awful?' I couldn't help asking.

'Hideous. I am never, never going to have sex again. Ever. The pain was unbelievable. I'd have had an epidural only there wasn't time.'

I made a face. 'Well, I won't keep you. You look like you need a sleep. I just wanted to make sure you were OK, and that you got your stuff back.' I gestured towards her clothes and bag, which I'd left by the door.

'Stay for a bit, please. I don't want to be on my own.' Ruth's lips were quivering again, but this time I could see that it was born of the humiliation of having to admit weakness, of the need to ask for company. My heart went out to her.

I sat down on the end of the bed, feeling the texture of the white cotton blankets rough under the palms of my hands.

'So what are you going to call your baby?'

'I don't know. What's your name? Oh, I remember, it's Emma, isn't it – oh, sorry, no. I can't call her Emma. I had a great-aunt called Emma; I hated her. She had a moustache and she smelled of wee.'

I laughed. 'Don't worry. I'm flattered at the thought, though.'

'What's your middle name?'

'Imogen, but I hate that name. Besides, don't feel that you—'

'Imogen. Do you know, I like that. Maybe I'll call her Imogen.'

I looked away, embarrassed and flattered. The conversation petered out.

'She's really gorgeous, though. I thought babies came out all squashed and purple, but she didn't. She looks beautiful already.'

'I wish I could see her.'

'Yeah. Well, leave me your address, and, if you fancy it, maybe we could meet up for a coffee or something, once I'm back on my feet?'

I sighed a sigh, which turned into a jaw-splitting yawn. 'I'd love that. But I don't live in Nottingham. I live in London.'

'Don't tell me you came all this way to go to Marty's aqua aerobics class.'

'Actually . . . no. But I did come all this way to see Ann Paramor.'

'Who?'

'Ann, you know, Ann Paramor who normally takes the class.'

'Oh, right. I didn't know that was her surname. Why? If you don't mind me being nosy, of course.'

I hesitated, then thought, Sod it, why not.

'This might sound kind of weird, but there are five Ann Paramors in the country, and one of them is probably my mother. I was adopted. I found out her name a while ago, and now I'm trying to track her down. I'm staying at a B. & B. in Lenton Sands, and since she wasn't at the pool tonight, I'm planning to go to her flat tomorrow. I've got her address.'

Ruth looked at me with sympathetic awe. She bit her lip, as if wanting to tell me something, and I immediately knew that I'd hit another brick wall. This wasn't going to be the right Ann after all.

'It's not her, is it?'

Ruth shook her head. 'I very much doubt it. She looks about twenty-two, and she's black. Jamaica, I think she's from. I'm sorry.'

I suddenly felt very, very tired, not least at the thought of how much I still had to do that night before I could collapse into a warm bed with a Jilly Cooper novel. I half felt like asking Ruth if I could kip on the daybed in the corner of her delivery room.

'Oh well. That's why I'm doing this – I can rule out another one now.'

Ruth's eyes were beginning to drift and flutter shut, so I slid off her bed.

'I really think I'd better go, though. They lock the door of my B. & B. at eleven. Can I take your address? Even if I don't live up here, I'd love to keep in touch, and maybe see your baby at some point.'

She nodded. 'Yeah . . . me too. Are you on email? We could email each other . . .'

I rooted around in my bag to find a biro and an old dry-cleaning receipt, on which I wrote down the details Ruth wearily dictated, as well as my own addresses, email and postal, which I tore off the bottom of the receipt and tucked into Ruth's handbag.

'So,' I said, smiling shyly at her. 'It was a real pleasure to meet you. I'm sorry we didn't meet sooner.'

'Selfishly, I'm not,' she said. 'I don't know what I'd have done without you tonight, honestly. I can't thank you enough for looking after me.'

I made self-effacing blustery noises, and flapped my hand dismissively, feeling ridiculously over-emotional. 'Bye, then. I hope you'll be OK. I'm sure you will. If you're ever in London, look me up, won't you?'

'Definitely. Bye, Emma. Thanks again.'

'Bye.'

I turned at the door to look back, but Ruth was already asleep, cut off from me and her new baby and, mercifully, all the fatigue and stress and anxieties that she still had ahead of her.

31

The weirdnesses of the day were far from over. After an uneventful journey by minicab back to my car – which was, thankfully, untampered with – and then another easy drive back to the B. & B., I was crunching the Golf's wheels on the gravel driveway towards the front door with precisely four minutes to spare.

Another car, a smart silver Audi, swept in immediately behind me, but I was too tired to worry about whether I was taking someone else's parking space. I just switched off the engine and the lights, pulled on the handbrake, and hauled myself and my bag of wet things – including the towel I'd rented from the swimming pool and forgotten to return – out of the car.

'Hello again,' said a man's voice by my right ear as I fumbled with the door.

Oh bugger, I thought. It's the gorgeous Mr Tilt. And I probably look as if I've been dragged through a bush backwards.

'Hello.' I turned and looked up at him properly. He was devastatingly sexy, with skin like melting milk chocolate, and those big calf's eyes.

'Been out on the town?'

I laughed self-consciously. If only he knew. 'No, not exactly. In fact, not at all. It's been a very – strange –

night.' I wasn't sure if it was fatigue or attraction making my words staccato.

He opened the door for me and suddenly we were standing in the hall, close together, in a soft pool of light from a small table lamp nearby. The dark and quiet of the rest of the house made our presence far too intimate, and I felt nervous energy zing around my stomach.

'So Mr Thingy – Gil – presumably hasn't locked up, then,' I said, looking around me in an exaggerated movement, as if to say, Don't try anything, buster. The guvnor'll be along in a minute.

'Oh, Mr Thingy's usually late.' The man grinned, as if I'd said something funny. 'I'll lock up. There isn't anybody else coming in tonight. I'm Robert, by the way.'

'Emma,' I said, thinking, He's got a nerve. Locking up someone else's guesthouse. And how did he know there were no more guests coming?

'So, Emma, I was going to make some hot chocolate and toast. Would you like to join me and tell me about your weird evening?'

I was about to say no and head for the stairs at a crawl, but what I'd mistaken for nervous energy in my stomach gave a long, low, growl, and I realized that I was absolutely ravenous.

'Yes, please. I'm starving.'

Robert moved down the hallway, casually switching on lights as if he owned the place, before ushering me into a large, pristine kitchen and pointing at a ladder-back chair by a big pine table. 'Have a seat.'

Salivating at the thought of hot buttered toast, I watched him bustling about, pulling out saucepans and cartons of milk, peeling slices of bread off a loaf in the breadbin, clicking the gas into purple-blue life to heat the milk.

'You stay here a lot, then.'

'I'm living here at the moment, until my flat's ready to move into.'

I almost said, 'Wow, that must be expensive,' but stopped myself. It was so rude to comment on other people's financial arrangements. Instead, I watched with admiration as he strode around the kitchen, unloading the dishwasher and setting out plates and knives. His body looked as if it was constructed of pure muscle, and it made me shiver. Then I thought of Gavin's lanky, puny frame, and that made me shiver too.

'So I understand you're in titanium. What does that mean?'

Spooning hot chocolate into two mugs, Robert stopped mid-scoop. 'Titanium? As in, the metal titanium? I don't know what you're talking about. I'm an agent, for TV presenters mostly.'

'Oh. Right.' Janet must have been mistaken. Cool job, though. 'In television' sounded much more glamorous than 'in titanium'.

'What do you do, Emma?'

'I'm an aromatherapist.'

'Really? How interesting. Do you know, I've always wanted to learn massage. It seems like it would be so rewarding. I had regular acupuncture when I had a dodgy back, and that was brilliant too.'

No jokes about massage parlours or Miss Whiplash outfits. No snickers or lewd expressions. Just interest and admiration in his voice. Robert handed me a plate of toast, warm, brown and delicious-smelling, a personification of himself.

'Jam or Marmite?'

'Marmite, thanks.'

The Marmite and butter marbled together in an intoxicating swirl of oil and brown, and the toast became slightly damp to the touch. I bit into it, and a drip of melted butter slid sensuously down my chin. Robert saw, and I had an overwhelming urge to beckon him over to lick it off me. I was shocked at how attracted to him I was, but decided it was probably to do with having had sex so recently. Amid long arid spells of celibacy, I hardly gave sex a thought, but the more I had, the more I wanted. I wondered what Gavin was up to tonight.

'This,' I said, chewing and wiping the drip off with my finger instead, 'is absolutely, completely delicious.'

Robert poured milk into the two mugs and stirred it round, releasing chocolatey vapours into the air of the cold night kitchen, twining us together with its warmth and scent.

He came and sat opposite me, pushing a mug in my direction, and began to butter his own toast. I noticed his hands, brown, strong, with bitten nails and exaggerated wrinkles at the joints of his fingers. A cricketer's hands.

'Do you play cricket?' I blurted.

'Well, no, not any more. Not since school, anyway. Footie's my game, and squash. Why do you ask?'

I was mortified. 'You, um, I mean, when I first saw you this morning, I thought you looked like a cricketer.' How racist did that sound? *You're slightly dark-skinned so I assumed you batted for the West Indies* . . . oh God.

But Robert just laughed. 'Yes, I thought that chinos and a cream jumper looked a bit stupid in the middle of winter, too, but by then I was out the door and it was too late to change.'

'Oh no, I didn't think you looked stupid, just, you know . . .' I was floundering badly, but worse was to come. I took too big a mouthful of hot chocolate, and hiccuped, at top volume.

'Sorry,' I said, hiccuping again. 'Hot drinks often do this to – *hic* – me.' I covered my mouth with my hand in embarrassment.

Just then, the kitchen door opened and Janet came in, with her hair in rollers, wearing a dazzlingly white towelling bathrobe and matching slippers, as if she was at a health farm.

'Ah, it's you two. Good, you're both in. I can lock up, then.'

'All done already,' said Robert. 'You can go to bed now. Don't worry, I'll clean up in here first.' To my astonishment he stood up, walked over to Janet, and put his arms around her waist, kissing her lavishly on the side of the neck. She giggled girlishly and pushed him away. 'Oh, Robbie, you daft ha'porth,' she said.

I shut my mouth hastily, aware that I was gaping like a moomintroll, and then hiccuped again. Oh please, I thought, don't tell me I've stumbled into some kind of upmarket wife-swapping set-up. He's her toy-boy. Did Gil know? What if Gil wanted me to . . . The prospect of a tryst with Robert was, frankly, very appealing, but I'd never met Gil, and he was, presumably, Janet's age. I was so busy panicking at the possibility of being propositioned by a sixty-year old B. & B. proprietor, and hiccuping, that I nearly didn't hear Robert's reply as Janet kissed him goodnight.

'Night then, Mum. Sleep well.' He looked at me, my dripping toast suspended halfway to my mouth. 'You thought that I was just a lodger here, didn't you?'

I nodded, mutely, before we both burst out laughing. 'I thought you were Mr Tilt from Birmingham. He's – *hic* – in titanium, apparently.'

'Oh, him! He's about forty-five, buck teeth, bald as a coot. You wouldn't fancy him.'

I raised my eyebrows so far that they felt they would slide over the back of my head. The implication was unmistakably 'but you fancy me, though, don't you?' and I didn't quite know how to take it.

Then I thought, who cared if it was obvious? Yes, I did fancy him. He was utterly gorgeous, and the fact that he seemed to be interested in me too was hugely flattering, even with my chlorine-stringy hair, the ghosts of day-old mascara lurking shadowy beneath my tired eyes, and the involuntary explosions coming from my mouth at regular intervals. Despite all that, I saluted my return to life as a sexual, sensuous being . . . well, in a manner of speaking.

Robert evidently realized what he'd said too, and

314

took a long slurp of his hot chocolate to cover his confusion. I stared shamelessly at him, hiccuping. Despite recent events, it was the first time in years that Gavin hadn't come into the equation.

'Right,' said Robert assertively. 'Time to get rid of those hiccups. I'll get you a glass of water and then you have to follow my instructions.'

'Oh good – *hic*. I'm really bored of them now. But drinking out of the wrong side of the glass has never done it for me before.'

'No, it's not that. This is a much better hiccup cure.' He handed me a glass of tap water. 'I'm going to ask you three questions, and no matter what the questions are, you have to reply "Yes, Daddy," and then take a sip of water. OK?'

I frowned at him. 'Yes, *Daddy*? Well, OK, if you say so. *Hic*.'

'Ready? First question. Let's see . . . Am I the short leg for the West Indian cricket team?'

'Yes, Daddy,' I said, taking a sip of water. No hiccup.

'Did you think, for a minute there, that there was something very fishy going on between me and the proprietress of this guesthouse?'

I gave him a hard stare. 'Yes, Daddy,' I said reluctantly. Another sip. I could feel an absence in my throat which signified that my hiccups had gone already, but I kept quiet in case I was imagining it.

There was something very odd about addressing somebody as Daddy again after so many years. I closed my eyes briefly and imagined that it really was Dad sitting there trying to cure my hiccups, and the feeling took my breath away.

'Last question. Are you really sorry that you ever set foot in this guesthouse and do you wish that you were staying in that lovely hotel down the road instead?'

I laughed. 'Oh yes, Daddy. You have no idea how sorry.' A third sip of water.

'Well?' said Robert, raising his eyebrows. 'Are they gone?'

315

I swallowed tentatively, to make sure. 'Yes. I think they went after the first question. That's amazing! Does it work every time?'

'Ninety per cent of the time, yes. I think it's something to do with having to concentrate on answering "yes" to "no" questions, and then taking the sips of water.'

I smiled at him. 'Thanks, anyway.'

'Don't mention it.'

We sat in warm silence for a few minutes, until something occurred to me.

'I hope you don't mind me asking, but . . . are you adopted? Being a different colour to your mum, and all.' I winced, thinking that just bringing it up had made me sound even more of a racist.

'No, I'm not adopted. You obviously haven't met my dad yet, then?'

I shook my head.

'He's Trinidadian. So's mum, but as you can see, she's white. I was born there, but we all moved to England when I was seven.'

'Oh, right. Sorry, that sounded so nosy, didn't it? I only asked because I am – adopted, as well as nosy – and other people's families kind of intrigue me. That's why I'm here, actually. I'm looking for my birth mother, and I thought she might live around the corner. But it turns out it's not her after all.'

It was funny how it got easier to tell the story with each telling. Soon I'd be accosting complete strangers on the street and filling them in on the details of my family life. I told him about the search, and the Ann Paramors, and then moved on to my day: the decorator at Ann's place, the pool, Ruth, the baby. The words flowed out of me so easily, lubricated by lust and identification, attraction and emotion. It wasn't like talking to a stranger at all – I had never felt so comfortable with anyone new. Perhaps if Gavin and I hadn't been a couple again I'd have felt more threatened. Or perhaps not. I just knew that I really liked this man.

After that, we fell into an easy conversation, back and forwards, more like badminton than squash – a gentle exchange, on equal terms. He told me about his childhood in Trinidad, his early years as a struggling actor, the move into agenting. His failed marriage, two years ago, and his four-year-old daughter. How he was now, finally, on good terms with his ex-wife and her new husband.

I listened and sympathized. I told him about Dad and Mum, and Betsey – he didn't even smirk – and Stella, of course. The only person I omitted to mention was Gavin.

'Well, I don't know about you,' he said, after we'd talked for two hours straight. 'But I'm still hungry. I was playing football earlier, and we went to the pub afterwards. I wasn't drinking, because I had the car, but unfortunately I wasn't eating either. Fancy a plate of bacon and eggs?'

'You bet,' I replied. Anything to prolong this magical, unexpected, charged meeting.

As Robert heated up oil in a big frying pan, he said, 'Do you think we could keep in touch? I'm often down in London on business. We could have dinner, or something.'

For the second time in one day, someone I really liked had asked to keep in touch with me. It was a heady pleasure, and I felt I could float away on it.

'Sure. That would be lovely.' I tried not to sound too twee, but couldn't prevent myself coyly rubbing a pattern in the tabletop with my fingertip.

'Great. One egg or two?' He peered into the frying pan. 'Do you think this oil is hot enough yet?'

I joined him at the hob and gazed in too, as if the black shiny surface of the pan held the secrets of our future. 'One, please.' As Robert moved across to the fridge to take the eggs off their little eggy thrones, I remembered something Mum had once taught me: how to tell if oil was ready for frying or not.

I spat into the pan. I'd meant to spit a tiny little fleck

317

of saliva, just enough to evaporate in a brief flurry of boiling bubbles, but, of course, in true embarrassing-first-meeting style, far more spit that I'd intended splatted into the pan. It wasn't a dirty great gob or anything, but it was enough that it clumped itself into a small sort of spit fritter, taunting me with its impression of a fried kiss. I watched it cook with grim horror and a toe-curling embarrassment.

Robert returned with his eggs and bacon and glanced into the pan. Thankfully he was too much of a gentleman to comment on the phlegm which was merrily frying away, but I knew that he knew. Fortunately, however, it did eventually disperse, and Robert laid four rashers into the now-smoking pan. I turned away, puce, wondering if I should make a run for it, but then I felt a gentle hand on my shoulder.

'I'll be down for a meeting in a couple of weeks' time, if you're free.'

I nodded, too terrified to look round. The hand moved around to the scruff of my neck, and I felt his thumb gently caress the knobbly top of my spine. Shivers concertinaed down my back, and gooseflesh broke out on my arms. The hand was gone again. I heard the hiss and crackle of bacon being turned in the pan, and then it was back.

Robert turned me around to face him, and I stared up into his gorgeous, kind face, praying that my intuition wasn't misleading me, that this beautiful man was as good inside as he looked from the outside.

'This is weird,' I said, awkwardly.

'Yeah,' he replied, even more inarticulately.

He moved closer to me, and I smelled hot chocolate and Marmite, aftershave and a faint, sweet sweat. I wanted to touch him so badly that longing pinged in my ovaries.

'Emma . . .'

He touched my face with his finger, and rubbed his forehead against mine. I wanted him to rub himself against me all over. I wanted to capture his smell, the feeling of his skin. I wanted to wrap my arms and legs around his back, just as I had with . . .

Gavin. Shit! I jerked backwards as if Robert had stood on my toe.

'I think the bacon's burning,' I said abruptly, and shot back over to sit at the table again. Robert dashed across to the pan and turned off the gas, extinguishing only one of the three flames which were presently heating up the kitchen. The other two were still burning strong, despite me pulling away.

'What's the matter, Emma?' Instead of corny movie lines – 'This is bigger than both of us', or 'Let's not fight it' – he placed before me a fragrant plate of egg and bacon. 'Eat up,' he said, handing me a knife and fork and sliding onto a chair opposite me at the table.

'It's just a bit . . . complicated,' I said, thinking of Gavin. My stomach, already full enough with toast and hot chocolate, constricted a little, and I pushed the plate away again after only a couple of bites. I had never been faced with a choice like this before: to go with what was familiar, even if it might not be perfect; or to take a running jump into the unknown. It wasn't dissimilar to the Ann Paramor situation. But Ann Paramor – one of them, out there somewhere – gave birth to me. This man, Robert, was ten times more of a stranger.

'You're already involved with somebody, aren't you?'

It was almost a relief, that I didn't have to actually tell him myself. 'Yes. Sort of.'

'What does "sort of" mean?'

'Well. We were together a long time, then we split up a few months ago, and he's just come back on the scene.' And how, I thought sadly. Gavin, back on the scene in a womb-exploring, hanging-from-the-chandeliers kind of way. Oh, hell, what was I going to do?

'Is it serious?'

I looked across the table at this lovely person, with

whom I was eating what could have been a post-coital breakfast, except that we'd never even kissed. Just leave it, Emma, I told myself. He's coming on too strong. You know nothing about him – he might even turn out to be another Charlie. Your life is complicated enough. This time last night you couldn't think of anything you wanted more than to be with Gavin, and now you're considering telling him that Gavin means nothing?

'Yeah. I suppose it is kind of serious. I'm sorry.'

And boy, was I ever sorry. I was so sorry that I wanted to bang my head rhythmically on the pine tabletop. Robert looked pretty sorry, too. He put his hand in his pocket and fished out a business card.

'Here,' he said. 'If it ever stops being serious, or better still, just stops being a relationship at all, give me a call, would you?'

I pulled the card slowly from between his out-stretched fingers.

'Thank you,' I said. 'For everything, not just the card. It's been so nice to meet you.'

'Sure you wouldn't like to have lunch with me some time?'

I hesitated for a nano-second. Gavin needn't know. Nothing need happen. I just couldn't bear the thought of all that mutual attraction shrivelling up and turning black.

'OK then. I don't see why not,' I said, adjusting my mental blindfold, astonished at myself. I glanced up at the big clock on the wall, momentarily hypnotized by the slow sweep of its second hand as it ticked away my second chance of romance in twenty-four hours. Funny how it felt about a million times more romantic than it had with Gavin. But it was two a.m., my eyes were gritty with exhaustion, and my heart believed that I belonged to someone whose idea of romance was 'get your kit off, girl'. Even if my mind was telling me different.

'Robert, I've got to go to bed now. I'm so worn out I

can hardly think straight.' I yawned so hugely that I felt my jaw was hinged, and my face about to tip over my head backwards.

'It doesn't matter,' he said. 'I'm sure we'll see each other again. Not in the morning, though. I've got to leave early. I promised to take my daughter to Alton Towers. Enjoy your breakfast with Mr Tilt.'

I mustered the last of my energy for a tired laugh, wondering if he was aware how appealing the thought of breakfast with Mr Tilt had been, back in the old hours when I thought Mr Tilt was a six-foot half-caste cricketing sex god.

We both stood up, scraping our chairs across the tiled floor with an abrasive honk, at which we both winced. Now what? The feel of his warm thumb against my neck already seemed like a distant memory. We hovered on either side of the table, as if it was an electric fence separating us.

'Well, thanks for all the food,' I said.

'Thanks for keeping me company. And good luck finding your mother. Keep me posted.'

'I will, definitely. Night, then.'

'Night. Can I take your number, to get in touch about lunch?'

'Oh . . . sure.' I dictated my home and mobile numbers to him, watching the two faint vertical furrows on his brow crease as he tapped them straight into the phonebook of his own mobile, before tucking it back into his pocket.

'Night then,' I repeated. I couldn't quite bring myself to move, but was unsure whether it was from desire or just plain exhaustion.

A toilet flushed, faintly, somewhere upstairs and rain pattered lightly at the window. I found myself wondering if Robert kissed differently to Gavin, if his tongue felt different; what he liked in bed. It was so long since I'd been attracted to anyone other than Gavin that I was having trouble even quite imagining it. It was as if Gavin had imprinted himself on my own

321

DNA code; I was Gavin-compatible, and no one else.

Although it certainly hadn't felt that way tonight.

We stood opposite one another for so long, immobile, that I began to feel embarrassed. Robert was looking at me with the kind of amused tenderness I had previously only associated with movies starring Clark Gable. Eventually I waved, a small and self-conscious wave across the pine divide, turned, and crept upstairs, the joint weights of fatigue and anti-climax pressing on my shoulders. Up to my chilly eiderdown and Jilly Cooper, whose words I already knew my tired eyes would merely skim before sailing away into sleep. Satisfied by one man whilst craving another, like too much chocolate. Still, I thought wearily, at least it took my mind off the disappointment of another wrong Ann Paramor. This meant that it was likely to be either the one in Devon, or the post-office employee from Harlesden.

It was all too exhausting to contemplate, so I closed my eyes and allowed myself to drift away, trying to reserve my final waking thought for Ruth and her baby, exploring each other's skin and scents and emotions like new lovers. I remembered that vanilla was the closest instinctive smell to breast milk, and hoped that Ruth's child would grow up with the scent of it always warm in her heart.

Then I thought, in a semi-conscious *non sequitur*, thank God for Katrina, because if Mack and his camera *had* come with me, I'd never have got to meet Robert.

32

By the following lunchtime I'd returned to Shepherd's Bush, which looked even more grimy than usual, and browbeaten by the curses of the traffic-jammed drivers. There were major roadworks on the Askew Road and consequently, it seemed, every single vehicle in London had been diverted along our street. 'Sorry for the inconvenience', a very unapologetic yellow board announced gaily. 'We will be doing essential roadworks for the next 10–12 weeks.' I toyed with the idea of moving to Nottingham.

I hadn't seen Robert again in the morning, despite entertaining a faint hope that the outing with his daughter would be cancelled, or that he'd invite me along too.

As I shoehorned the Golf into a space outside the charity shop, causing a further hold-up to the impatient traffic, I wondered who Robert's TV clients were. I hadn't thought to ask him at the time, since it seemed a little indiscreet, but my interest was piqued. I was by no means a star-struck person – imagine Stella's delight at nabbing a boyfriend who was a television agent! – but I thought a little bit of hobnobbing with celebs might cheer me up a bit. It seemed to be a generally approved method of boosting one's

323

self-esteem, at least in the eyes of Stella and her friends.

Then I remembered that I didn't need cheering up any more. I was back with Gavin. I was getting closer to tracking down Ann Paramor. Everything was fine.

Getting out of the car, I glimpsed a sudden, unnaturally fast movement on the opposite side of the road. A sort of ducking-down-behind a car movement. I stood stock-still for a moment, hackles prickling, and waited. My first thought was that it must be Gavin, acting shiftily as per usual, for reasons best known to himself. Then, as I walked towards my flat, lugging my overnight bag, the crown of a dark head and two mean eyes appeared momentarily, peeping through both side windows of a parked BMW. The eyes glanced towards our front path, and then slid back to me. Oh Jesus, no. I was sure it was Charlie.

Whipping out my mobile, I rang Stella. 'Stell, where are you?'

'Hi, Em, I'm in Camden market. So how did it go?'

'Fine, it went fine. She's not the right Ann, but it went fine.'

'Is everything all right? You sound distracted.'

'Yeah. I was just checking . . . When will you be home?'

'Five-ish. I'm meeting up with some people, and we thought we might go to the cinema this afternoon.'

'And then you're coming straight home?'

'Yes. Are you sure everything's all right?'

'Yes, honestly. I'll see you then, OK?'

The dark head had disappeared beneath the bodywork of the BMW, and I hadn't seen anyone scuttle out from either side of the car, so I knew he must still be there. I was about to charge across the road and confront him, when I was momentarily distracted by a beep-beep, signifying an instant message, on the telephone I still held in my hand.

Even though I had no intention of reading the message until I'd sorted Charlie out – for I was, by

324

now, pretty sure it was him – I couldn't help glancing down at the screen of my phone, to see the tantalizing envelope icon seducing me with its square promises of mystery. Knowing my luck, it was probably some boring message from BT Cellnet advising me of fantastic consumer offers I'd be mad to refuse.

By the time I looked up again, I caught sight of a tall, heavy-thighed figure loping furtively away. It was almost definitely Charlie, but I hadn't seen his face.

'Damn!' I kicked the nearest lamp-post out of frustration. What could I do? Stella would freak out if she knew Charlie was sniffing around again. I thought about calling the police, but knew there was nothing they could do, not unless Charlie was actually trespassing, or threatening Stella. He'd be long gone by the time they got here.

Once the flash of anxiety had subsided enough for me to refocus my driving-weary eyes, I looked down at the display on my phone: nothing exciting, after all, just a notification of a new voicemail message. I walked up the path, lugging my overnight bag in one hand and cradling the phone between ear and shoulder as I unlocked the front door, even though I hadn't yet dialled in for the message.

Two men were clumping down the stairs in dusty boots and overalls, carrying bulging binliners, and I had to flatten myself against the hall wall to let them pass. They nodded at me.

'Excuse me,' I said, just in case they were burglars and the bags were full of Stella's and my worldly possessions, 'I live in this building. Do you mind me asking what you're doing here?' My finger was surreptitiously poised over the nine digit of the phone, ready to press three times if they attacked.

'In-vironmentaw 'elf,' said the taller one. He had such a ludicrously bushy moustache dominating his narrow, lugubrious face that I considered making a complaint to his boss about it, on the grounds that it was surely a health hazard itself.

'Oh, right. You're clearing out Percy's flat.' I peered up the staircase and could see Percy's door was indeed open.

'Yup, if Percy is Mr Weston,' said the smaller one cheerfully. ''Orrible state, it is. 'E had 'undreds and 'undreds of—'

'Plates. Yes, I know. So is it going on the market, then?'

'Yup. It'll be a probate sale – flog it off cheap and the poor bugger wot buys it will 'ave to redecorate, an' that.'

'Right,' I said, heading up the stairs, not knowing what else to say. I felt a pang of sadness for poor old lonely Percy, with his plates and his serried rows of geraniums in the back garden. Still, it might be nice to get new neighbours . . .

I dialled my message retrieval service – disappointingly, it was only a message from a client ringing to cancel an appointment. Then I rang Gavin, but his mobile was switched off, and there was no answer from his flat. I hadn't been expecting the red carpet treatment, but I'd have thought he could at least have phoned to see how I got on.

I felt miserable again. Too much had happened in the past few days, good and bad. Gavin, Nottingham Ann, Ruth and the baby, Robert, and now Charlie. My head felt overloaded, and once more back in that slightly unhinged reality where even the task of peeling a sticker off an apple seemed so onerous that it threatened to make me cry. I still had to tell Mack that the mission had failed, and give Stella a post-mortem of the trip's events whilst not letting on that I'd seen Charlie outside. I felt that I simply didn't have the energy for any of it.

I went into my bedroom and climbed into bed, fully clad, relishing the sensation of lying down flat after hours of sitting tense in the driver's seat. I just wanted to shut it all out, to forget about everything.

I fell asleep immediately, plunging into a dream

where I was still driving on the M1 and singing, as lamp-posts whizzed past me. The yellow baby bird was huddled in a cage on the back seat of my car, reproachfully asking me over and over again where its mother was; but I turned up my Robbie Williams CD and drowned him out. 'Why do I bloody well have to do everything for you?' I demanded crossly of it. 'Find your own sodding mother; I've got enough problems of my own.'

Next time I turned around, the cage was empty.

I was woken by the sound of someone crashing into the flat, and the door slamming. I sat up, wide-eyed with befuddlement and momentary fear.

'Emma, are you there? It's me.' Stella stomped into the bedroom. 'God, the day I've had. It pissed with rain in Camden, and then the film we saw was rubbish. What a waste of money. So, how are you? Are you disappointed that you didn't find your mother?'

I rubbed my eyes, reached for my glasses on the bed-side table, and slid them on so I could see Stella better. She looked pale and cross and I wondered, if she too had seen Charlie hanging around outside the flat, would she tell me? Was I going to tell her that I had? Something was on her mind.

'Well, yes and no, I suppose.' I yawned, switching on the bedside lamp, feeling the strange fuzzy dis-location of waking from daylight sleep. 'It was a really great trip; you know, like an adventure. You wouldn't believe what happened when I went to the aqua class – I got talking to this really nice woman called Ruth who was pregnant, and she went into labour in the middle of the class! I went to hospital with her because she didn't have anybody else. It was all so dramatic that it kind of put looking for Ann into the shade somewhat. And then —'

I was about to tell her about meeting Robert when she reached out her hand and squeezed my wrist, hard enough that underneath her grasp the links of my silver bracelet left angry red indentations on my skin. Her face was so pale that even her freckles seemed to have disappeared.

'Ow. What's the matter?'

'I need to tell you something,' she said.

My heart jumped. 'Oh God, not about Charlie – what's he done? What's happened?'

'No. Nothing. Well, actually, not nothing. But that wasn't what I was going to say.'

'Not nothing? What do you mean? Tell me that first, then the other thing.'

'Well . . . OK.' She bit her lip and looked away, as if she'd had a brief stay of execution. 'The lab results came back. I got a call this morning.'

I sat up, fast. '*Well?*'

'They found his DNA in my mouth.'

I couldn't understand why she looked so miserable. 'But, Stella, that's great! We've got him now – that proves he was lying! When's the trial going to be set for?'

She twirled her tongue stud for a moment before answering. 'It's not.'

'What do you mean?'

'I've dropped the charges.'

I gaped at her. 'You WHAT?'

She stood up, marched over to my full-length mirror and examined herself, posing defensively, pulling at the hem of her skirt, flicking a tiny dot of eyeliner out of the corner of her eye.

'I don't want to hear it, Emma, OK? So just don't say it. It's my decision. I don't need my private life, or my dirty knickers, on display for an entire courtroom to see, and that's the end of it. Yes, I know he shouldn't be allowed to get away with it, blah blah; but I don't see why I should suffer any more for what he did, by having to rake it all up again. If it had been an actual . . . rape, then yes of course I'd do it. But we were both drunk and stoned, and while I'm not for a second condoning what he did, what if the jury believed him and not me? It's not a risk I'm willing to take. I just want to get on with my college work, and my life. That's it. It's over. The DNA results prove him a liar, and that's good enough for me.'

I sank back into my pillows, exhausted as an invalid. 'What did the police say when you told them?'

'They weren't happy. In fact that PC McClement was pretty cross with me. But I don't care.' She sounded like a sullen child.

'And does Charlie know that he's off the hook?'

I had a momentary and very appealing mental picture of Charlie hanging helplessly from a large meathook, but it was swiftly followed by the more realistic, and less attractive, memory of him hiding behind the car outside.

'Probably not yet. I only just got off the phone with the police.'

An idea came to me on delicate little trotters. Perhaps I could ring him, tell him that the charges were dropped, but if he even showed his face round here again, Stella wouldn't hesitate to haul his ass into court? But no. It probably didn't work like that, did it? Once you dropped the charges, there was no going back. I thought of charges like eggs on a stone floor: fragile things which you could drop but never pick up again. Stella's butterfingered fears meant that Charlie had got away with it.

I tried to look on the bright side. At least there would be no reason for Charlie to lurk around here any more. Surely the only reason he had been was to try and persuade Stella not to go to court? I decided not to tell her I'd seen him that day, and prayed that this would be the end of it.

I looked at her, still posing miserably in front of the mirror, sweeping up her hair with her hands and pouting. Her own reflection was her biggest comfort in times of stress, I thought, uncharitably.

'Well. I can't say that I think you've done the right thing, but I do understand why you don't want to go through with it.'

329

'And you won't give me a hard time about it?'

I sighed. 'No. I won't. Like you said, it's your life. So what was the other thing you were going to tell me?'

Stella gazed even harder at herself, and I thought I could see the panic reflected in her eyes. What now? I wondered.

'Gavin tried it on with me.'

A pigeon chose that moment to bump awkwardly onto the windowsill in a flap of wings and a crunching headbutt into the glass.

My first reaction was confusion. Part of me, in a bad sitcom kind of way, wanted to say, 'Sorry, Stella, I must have misheard. I thought you said Gavin *tried it on* with you.'

'Well, say something, then.' She had finally stopped looking at herself, and was staring at the pigeon so intently that I knew I hadn't misunderstood her.

'When?'

Stella wiggled her tongue stud around until it poked out of her mouth. I felt so enraged that I wanted to grab it, to yank it out myself. My voice was shaking with the effort of keeping it low, and I felt furious with her that I was in bed when she told me. I swung my legs over the side of the bed and stood up. Stella blinked at the sight of me emerging, fully dressed and crumpled.

'That day when you saw him leave the flat.'

I slapped the palm of my hand, hard, against the window frame, and the poor pigeon fell off the sill. I saw the brief panic in its eyes before it righted itself and flew away, and then I turned to face Stella, coming closer and closer to her. She shrank away slightly, but I advanced on her and hissed furiously in her ear, as if we were two soap-opera characters in the same shot. My palm smarted from the sting of the glossy window frame.

'I knew it! I *knew* something had gone on. I waited for you to say something – naturally I didn't expect Gavin to – but no, God forbid that you should be honest for once! You let me go through all that at

Suzanne's at Christmas, plucking up the courage to tell you about Ann Paramor, and all the while you omitted to tell me your own little secret? And now, right at the moment when things are starting to come right for me – Gavin and I are back together, I'm getting out and about a bit more, looking for my mother – *now* you tell me? Are you *trying* to ruin my life?'

Rare tears rolled silently down Stella's cheeks and she looked out of the window at the darkening cloudy sky. At five o'clock on a wet February evening, the pigeon should have been tucking its head under its wing and settling down for the night, not being scared away to find somewhere else to sleep. I felt bad for it.

'I'm sorry,' she whispered, finally turning to look at me. 'I know I was wrong not to tell you before, but I just couldn't. I know how much he meant – means – to you. I just hoped that we wouldn't see him again and you'd meet someone else, and I'd never have to tell you. Then you said on the phone yesterday that you were back together. It was nothing to do with me, though, Em, I swear I didn't come on to him. I was in a state about Charlie's message; Gavin was there. He cuddled me and then . . . it was like he just got carried away and kissed me. I told him to get lost. But that's twice now a man's got the wrong idea from me . . . What's *wrong* with me?'

However much sympathy I felt for her, I was not prepared to let Stella turn the conversation around to her own problems. Not this time.

'So how far, exactly, did you go?'

Stella sighed and bit her lip. 'I swear, Emma, on Mum and Dad's lives, I didn't lead him on.'

'Mum and Dad are already dead. Did you kiss him back?'

Stella blushed scarlet, fiddled with her hair.

'You did!'

She turned and looked at me, pleading with her eyes, clutching my arm with both hands so hard that she left more red marks on my skin.

'Only for two seconds, Em, I promise. I was just so taken aback, and so upset about the message, it was like this weird sort of dream. But as soon as I realized what was going on, I kicked him out.'

She hesitated. 'And if it's any consolation, Gavin immediately realized it was a mistake too. He jumped away from me like I was on fire. He was mortified – I honestly think he just got carried away. Mid-life crisis, that sort of thing.'

I snorted. 'Bloody great. The *asshole*! I can't believe he had the gall to show his face around me ever again. How dare he come crawling back and . . . Well, anyway, wait till I get hold of him!'

'What are you going to do?'

'Ditch him, of course. I should never have got carried away with him sniffing round again, being all lovey-dovey. He was obviously only after a quick shag. I'm such a moron. Why did I let myself do it?'

'I'm really sorry, Emma. I've wanted to tell you for weeks. I've been sick with the worry of it. Please forgive me?'

I thought about it. I *was* angry with her, but I was also only too aware of how persuasive Gavin could be, and how much else Stella had been through recently. Plus, as rekindled romances went, this one really had the makings of a damp squib. Gavin hadn't been in touch with me at all since Friday, not even to ask how things had gone in Nottingham.

'As it happens,' I said, dragging my trainers out of the bottom of the wardrobe and putting them on. 'You're somewhat off the hook. I met someone else in Nottingham.'

Stella gaped at me. I laced up my shoes, ferociously, letting my hair swing over my face so I didn't have to meet her eyes. It was a measure of conciliation to Stella that I was mentioning Robert, and suddenly I wished I hadn't. Superstitiously, I worried that telling her about him would somehow jeopardize our future – if we even had one.

'I don't expect anything will come of it. I'll probably never hear from him again. He did take my number though.'

'How did you find the time to meet somebody? I thought you spent the whole time doing aqua aerobics and delivering babies? What was he, a doctor?'

'No. His parents owned the guesthouse I stayed in.'

'What's he like, then?' Stella was so desperate to get off the subject of Gavin that she almost tripped over her words.

'Gorgeous. Great-looking, sensitive, smart, and he didn't even smirk when I told him that I play the recorder; he just said, "I love people who are musical." '

Stella was impressed. She knew that it had taken me two years to admit my recorder habit to Gavin, and that he'd teased me mercilessly about it from then on.

'But I'm still pissed off with you,' I continued severely. 'I'm going round to Mack's now, to tell him that I didn't find Ann, and if, by the time I come back, you have organized us some dinner, I might find it in me to forgive you. And if Gavin rings, tell him to go take a flying fuck. From me.'

I brushed my hair and twisted it up, securing it with a big flowery butterfly grip, before spotting my jacket lying on the floor where I'd discarded it when climbing into bed. Stella's foot was on the sleeve.

'You're standing on my jacket,' I said, tugging it out from underneath her sole. It reminded me of that trick when people pull tablecloths off fully laid tea-tables leaving all the crockery intact. Dad had tried it, once, for Stella's amusement, having set the table specially with her Winnie-the-Pooh tea service. It backfired on him when, predictably, the featherlight plastic cups and saucers flew all around the room, and the edge of the tablecloth caught Stella a glancing lash on the side of her face. Mum and I had laughed like drains about it for weeks afterwards. I almost told the story to Stella, just to make her smile, and then thought, No, I don't always have to think of ways to cheer Stella up. It actually isn't my job.

Instead, I pulled on the jacket, gathered up my keys, and left Stella sitting on my bed, looking somewhat shell-shocked.

'Bye,' I added, sticking my head back around the door.

'Bye,' she said faintly.

As I ran down the stairs, I felt strangely light-hearted.

33

Five days passed. Then seven, nine, eleven days: laborious clunking cogs of days, because Robert didn't ring me. Nor did Gavin, for that matter – but then, I was used to Gavin not ringing, and I didn't want to hear from him anyway. I was spending an awful lot of time on my own, too much of it checking that my mobile phone was fully charged and the phone at home properly on the hook. Stella claimed to be working 'all hours' on a term paper with Suzanne, but I suspected that her absence had more to do with her confession and subsequent reluctance to face me.

There was nothing I could do but carry on as usual: on-site, clients at home, baby massage, shopping, cleaning, watching television, playing the recorder. Luckily, I was very busy, and the jigsaw chunks of time which slotted into my days left few spaces in which to brood. To my fury, I couldn't find Robert's business card anywhere, and I vacillated between searching frenziedly for it, and feeling grateful that it was lost, so I could spare myself the potential humiliation of ringing and getting knocked back. I could have called the B. & B., I suppose, but it seemed too . . . desperate.

About the only out-of-the-ordinary event was going

round to Mack's to record a voiceover, describing what had occurred in Nottingham. Naturally I omitted the story of what happened when I went back to the guest-house; but when Mack finally allowed me to go home again, I continued the narration in my head, pretending that Mack's microphone was still held out in front of me: 'And then I met this cricketer, only he wasn't a cricketer at all, and he was so gorgeous, and I really felt that there was a spark between us – at least until I hiccuped the house down and gobbed into his frying pan, but we won't go into that – and he asked if I had a boyfriend and I said yes . . . Oh God, I said yes! How stupid *am* I, exactly? But nothing happened, not even a goodnight kiss, it was just sort of an atmosphere.'

At first, I'd been so sure Robert would call. But as time passed, gossamer threads of doubt as to what had actually gone on that night began to weave a web in my head, befuddling me, causing sudden hot flashes of embarrassment to wash over me when I least expected it. I had obviously misread the situation catastrophically. Perhaps he was only being hospitable – he was, after all, the son of the hosts. Perhaps – horrors – he just felt sorry for me when he saw me turn up in such a bedraggled state. Perhaps he was one of those people who were super-good listeners. It was easy to feel that you were interesting and fanciable with a gorgeous man gazing into your (chlorine-bloodshot) eyes.

I tried not to let the disappointment get to me, but I couldn't keep Robert out of my mind. As I stretched clingfilm over a bowl of cold boiled potatoes, I tortured myself with the thought that I'd told him I was already involved with somebody. As I played along to Squeeze's Greatest Hits on the recorder, I decided that whoever said that honesty was the best policy should be shot. As I demonstrated how to rub almond oil into tiny baggy baby backs, I succumbed to a growing conviction that I had made a huge fool of myself.

But I swallowed the sadness like medicine and

carried on, taking solace from my continuing ability to function. After everything I'd been through, I wasn't going to let another man ruin my life, however nice his eyes were. We hadn't even kissed. It was no real loss. I repeated this like a mantra, leaping inches into the air whenever the telephone rang, feeling the inside of my mouth turn to ashes whenever the message button blinked on the answer machine. At least it was a relief not to be pining for Gavin any more.

After eleven days, and some urging from an increasingly impatient Mack, I decided to do something practical. I was going to write to the final Ann Paramor. I perched on the funny K-shaped chair at the computer, one of those which was meant to be good for posture and spines, but which always gave me terrible backache after more than ten minutes, and gingerly found my way into Wordperfect, terrified that I'd accidentally delete all Stella's college projects in the process.

'Dear Ann,' I typed with two fingers.

You'd be so proud of me. I really think that I'm beginning to get my life together at last. Six months ago I was in such a rut, but you know how one little thing can trigger a change? Well, I met this homeless man on a tube, and it made me decide that I wanted to try and find you. It's been pretty scary, and loads of other stuff has happened too. My boyfriend Gavin dumped me. My sister Stella's been going through the wringer. I met a gorgeous man, but he hasn't phoned – probably because I told him I already had a boyfriend. But the point is that, even with all this crap going on, I'm OK. I just feel different, somehow . . .

I stopped, and backspace-deleted everything except the 'Dear Ann' bit. Then I backspaced a little further, and replaced 'Ann' with 'Mrs Paramor', which I then amended to 'Ms'. Trying to find the right words for the real letter was so much harder than my stream of consciousness ramble, but after a few drafts I settled on:

Ann Paramor
8 Back Lane
Tiverton
Devon

Dear Ms Paramor,

My name is Emma Victor. If you are my birth mother, you'll know why I'm writing. If not, then I'm terribly sorry to bother you, but I was adopted in 1971 and have been trying to track down my biological mother, who shares your name. I would really appreciate it if you could contact me to let me know either way, although if I haven't heard from you in six weeks then I'll assume this is either another blind alley, or that you do not wish to be in contact with me. It would be really good to know which, though. If you are my mother, and you would like to be in further contact with me, I would love to hear from you.

I toyed with the idea of enclosing a stamped addressed postcard with two boxes on the back: 'YES – I am your birth mother, or NO – quack quack oops, wrong again. Please tick as applicable.' I'd been caught out by Ann Paramor not answering my letters before. The typed sentences looked strange, disjointed, words jumping out at me randomly, like 'biological', and 'blind alley', none of which seemed to make sense. Perhaps it was all the hormones stirred up by the events of the previous week – Gavin, Robert, Ruth's baby – but I suddenly felt desperately emotional about it all. If this Devonshire woman wasn't my mother, then I'd pretty much run out of options. She might be dead, or abroad, and I'd never know. Also, if it wasn't her, I knew I'd have to go back to Harlesden again, and even the memory of that unloved, dirty house made my throat constrict. I wasn't sure I could face it. But I'd have to, if I wanted to know either way.

I printed out the letter, and was about to log off, when I suddenly thought of Ruth, and decided to send her an email to see how she was getting on. When I opened Outlook Express, I found to my surprise and pleasure that there was an email from her in there already.

Dear Emma, They let me out last week. Thank goodness. We were in that place far too long! I'm typing this with Evie Imogen asleep next to me in her Moses basket (the 'Imogen' is for you). She's adorable, and is already feeding up a storm and doing all the things which she's meant to be doing – admittedly not a lot, but it's early days. I'm very tired, obviously, but otherwise fine. My mum came over from Wales to help out, as soon as she heard.

Anyway, I meant it when I said I'd like us to keep in touch. I feel hugely grateful to you for 'rescuing' me like you did – God knows what would have happened if you hadn't been there. Well, actually, I do know. I'd have been on my own. Marty wouldn't have come with me in the ambulance (not that I'd have wanted him to!!) and nor would the others, I'm sure. We didn't get much of a chance to talk, but I really identified with you.

I'm coming down to London in a couple of weeks for an interview – did I tell you that I'm a graphic designer? I applied for the job ages ago, and just heard last week that I've got the interview. I'd thought Evie would still be on the inside if and when I made the journey, but it's not a problem, as long as the company don't mind me bringing her. I've been thinking of moving to London for ages, you see, since I split up with Evie's father (he's married, and doesn't want to know about her. Did I tell you that?). Maybe we could meet for a coffee or something. I don't know many people in London, but Evie and I need a fresh start.

Anyway, hope you got home OK, and aren't too upset

about not finding your real mother in Nottingham. I'd
love to hear from you if you have a chance. All the best,
Ruth xx

I was insanely chuffed; by the fact that she wanted
to see me again, and even more excitingly that she'd
really called her baby Imogen after me. I wrote back
immediately, saying I'd love to meet up, and if she
wanted a place to stay that night, she was welcome
here, and I'd happily look after Evie for her while she
went to the interview.

I sent the message off, instantly slightly regretting
the offer of accommodation – perhaps I was being a
little over-enthusiastic. But within ten minutes the
reply came back:

*Thanks for all this. Evie's breastfeeding too regularly for
me to leave her with anybody just yet; and I think I'll
drive home again this time, after we've met. But if I get
the job, I would love to take you up on the offer of your
spare room later – I'd need to be here for a couple of
days to sort out a flat to rent. Email me your phone
number and I'll ring you nearer the time so we can
arrange where to meet. Look forward to it!*

There must have been a particularly propititous
alignment of the planets going on in the heavens at
this time, at least in terms of beneficial new friend-
ships; Ruth's message wasn't the only pleasant
surprise I had that day. Just as I was leaving for baby
massage, the telephone rang. My heart jumped, but I
made myself leave it, since I was already late. When
the machine clicked on, I heard an unfamiliar
woman's voice, and my disappointment that it wasn't
Robert was immediately swept away by a split
second's conviction that it was Ann Paramor, *the* Ann
Paramor, having somehow tracked me down. I
clutched hard onto the edge of the open front door,
frozen like a tongue on icy metal.

'Hello, this is a message for Emma Victor. It's Denise Hiscock here. I got your number from Suzanne. I – well, Greg and I – have been wondering how you're getting on, if you had any luck looking for your birth mother. Anyway, we're having a bit of a dinner party in two weeks' time, Saturday the seventeenth, down at the cottage. We were wondering if you'd like to come? Bring a chap, if you've got one. And do stay the night, there's plenty of room. Our number is . . .'

I defrosted rapidly, closing and locking the door behind me, delighted by the invitation, already mentally planning what I would wear. I permitted myself a small fantasy: me, all dressed up, hooking on my slingbacks and combing my hair as my 'chap' waited, checking his watch and gently chiding me to hurry up. The chap had dark skin, sensitive cricketer's hands, just the right amount of aftershave, and a full-beam smile which scrambled my stomach . . .

Funny how I didn't once imagine that he was Gavin, I thought as I slotted the letter to Devon Ann into the postbox at the end of the road. Oh well. Date or no date, I was surviving on my own. I'd be OK. And perhaps I'd soon be hearing from my birth mother.

But all the same, I did hope that I wouldn't be the only single woman at the party.

34

The buzzer sounded at ten a.m. promptly the following day. I was expecting it to. I had a new client coming; one who'd been booked in by his secretary the previous week. As I pressed the button on the intercom, I found myself hoping that he was a nice clean businessman, and not one of the horrible hairy-backed sweaty ones.

'Hello?'

'It's, ahem, Mr Hawkins, come to see Ms Victor,' came a crackly voice.

'Come on up,' I said. 'Second floor; the door will be open.'

Footsteps echoed solidly along the tiled hall, and I felt the quick squeeze of nerves in the pit of my stomach at the thought of being alone in my flat with a strange man. A strange, soon to be semi-naked man. I didn't usually see new male clients without Stella in the flat, just in case, but I couldn't really afford to turn down the business, and this was when his secretary had said he wanted to come. I'd heard her flicking over the pages of a desk diary, and the office buzz of other phones ringing in the background – surely a businessman with a bona fide job and secretary wouldn't try any funny stuff. But as a precaution, I made sure my pepper spray was in my pocket, and fully intended to litter any conversation with references to my extremely large live-in boyfriend.

The footsteps were now heavy on the stairs. Oh God, what if it was Charlie? No, I told myself, it couldn't be. I was sure no woman would pretend to be that schmuck's PA just to aid him gain access to our flat. I peered over the banisters to see a dark, cropped head and broad shoulders in a suit. Not Charlie, definitely, I thought with relief. I looked again at the nubbly shorn curls and thought, How funny, it looks just like—

'Hello, Emma,' said the man, lifting his head and grinning at me. 'Ten o'clock massage?'

It was Robert.

The red blotches on my chest flared up my neck and throat as if controlled by a dimmer switch. It was the weirdest feeling: delight and terror, outrage and amusement, all swirling together with cold sweet surprise.

'I hope you don't mind. My shoulder's really playing me up, so I thought, Hmm, lucky I know the number of a good aromatherapist, isn't it?'

I was still speechless, but I managed the sort of inane giggle a twelve-year-old would produce, whilst simultaneously hoping that he didn't turn out to be an axe-murderer. By now we were face to face, and he looked even more delicious than he had at our last meeting, in a very angular good wool suit and a shiny tie. I didn't know any men who wore suits.

Robert kissed me gently on the cheek. 'Please don't look so flabbergasted. Didn't you recognize the name when my secretary booked the appointment?'

So that was why I hadn't heard from him. I shook my head, feeling the imprint of his lips soft on my cheek. How on earth was I going to control myself enough to massage this man? My hands were shaking and my palms already sweaty enough to steam wall-paper off the walls.

'I don't think you ever told me your surname,' I managed eventually.

'Well, it's the same as my parents', and I presumed you knew theirs.'

Hawkins. Of course. 'Oh yes. No, it never occurred to me. Do you come to London a lot?' I burbled, cringing.

'Yes. And when my flat's ready, I'll be here even more often. I really wanted to call you sooner, but I thought I'd surprise you instead. And I do genuinely need a massage, by the way. I think I strained something at football that day I met you – the next morning, I woke up *extremely* stiff.'

He said this with a poker face, and I didn't dare call him on it. I had to retain some vestiges of professionalism. Instead, I returned his blank face, and ushered him into the flat, while a jubilant symphony crashed cymbals in my head. 'Well, I'm definitely surprised. This way please, Mr Hawkins. We'll see what we can do.'

We had our preliminary consultation, and I wrote down as much of his medical history as necessary, my pen quivering as I asked him about his eating and sleeping patterns, his sore shoulder and any past injuries; just about managing not to slip in a few questions about past girlfriends or preferred sexual positions while I was at it. Then I wafted the mingled smell from the bottles of my suggested oils under Robert's nose for his approval: rosemary, nutmeg and lemongrass.

'Mmmm, gorgeous,' he said, closing his eyes.

'You don't, um, have an enlarged prostate, or damaged skin, do you? Because if so, I won't use the lemongrass. It's not advisable. It's quite a strong stimulant, you see.' Oh God, why did everything feel like it had another meaning? This was too weird.

'No. Not to my knowledge,' he replied, without an ounce of embarrassment, suddenly taking off his jacket and tie. My head spun.

'I'll let you get undressed then, while I go and mix up these oils and put some relaxing music on, if you don't object. If you could lie face down on the couch when you're ready.'

I had to lean on the back of the door after I'd gently closed it behind him. *Robert is getting undressed in my flat.* This was awful. What if he had this all planned, was treating me like some kind of a prostitute? What if he lunged at me, and said 'you know you want it'? But I did want it, I argued. Stop it, I argued back at myself. He's a client with a bad shoulder. You're a fully qualified aromatherapist – what are you going to do, refuse to massage him on the grounds that he might want to sleep with you? Besides, for all I knew, I was only feeling this intensely about him in the light of Gavin's treachery. It might be a rebound thing. But couldn't he have called me sooner, just for a chat, instead of keeping me hanging on for twelve days? Maybe he wasn't interested in me sexually, but just as a friend . . .

Ten minutes later, the most beautiful man I'd ever seen was lying on my massage couch, naked except for a pair of crisp cotton boxers. I was relieved that he'd kept them on, although the knowledge that I'd have to pull them down over his hips a little, to get access to the base of his spine, somehow felt even more erotic.

Stop it, Emma, I told myself again, horrified. I absolutely must not think of this in anything other than clinical terms. It's not erotic. It's not erotic. It's – oh my God, look at those muscles. Wrapped up like a gift in that satiny brown skin. Before I'd even touched him, I was imagining myself whispering the sensuous poetry of massage strokes in his ear: effleurage, petrissage, frictions, tapotement . . . It was a fantasy come true.

With the gentle strains of an ambient CD playing in the background, I tucked Robert up like a baby in fluffy white towels, which looked even whiter next to his brown skin. I began by pressing down gently and firmly with my forearms along his back, leaning my weight on either side of his spine to ground him and establish our connection, and then I peeled away the towel to expose his back again. I couldn't help sucking in my breath at the close-up sight of him as I began to work the oils into his shoulders.

I felt like an oversexed schoolboy with an erection in assembly, and found myself employing similar techniques to get rid of it: trying to visualize buckets of vomit, or imagining that Robert was William Hague or somebody equally repugnant. It wasn't working. Right from the first touch of his skin, I felt a tingling between my legs, and as he groaned with languid pleasure when I kneaded my thumbs underneath his shoulderblades, I realized I was damp with arousal. How on earth was I going to get through a whole hour of this?

I decided to talk. Not something I normally did during a massage, unless asked a question, but this wasn't a normal massage.

'So,' I said, rearranging the towels and starting work on his (wonderful, smooth) right leg, 'Nutmeg's an analgesic. Very good for muscular aches and pains, and so should really help your shoulder. It's also a very good mood lifter . . .'

'I don't think my mood could be lifted any further,' came the muted response through the face hole in the couch. 'This is fantastic.'

'Did you know,' I gabbled, cradling Robert's right foot in my arm and squeezing each of his toes in turn, 'that nutmeg has a similar action to MDMA? If you grated a whole nutmeg and ate it, you'd get high?'

'Mmmm,' said Robert, non-committally, his chunky square toes wiggling in my face. I wanted to bite them.

'And rosemary is analgesic too. Lynford Christie allegedly had a rosemary sports massage before every race. I wouldn't use this oil on you if it was night-time, because you should never take it before you go to sleep. It's a massive stimulant, mental and, um, physical.'

Oh no, I thought, what possessed me to give him such stimulating oils? It was asking for trouble. I was sweating now, feeling the damp patches under the arms of my T-shirt. The sharp but musky tang of the combined oils pervaded the small room, connecting us as we both inhaled it.

'So what are you going to do next about finding your mother?' he mumbled suddenly.

I paused, bending down to pick up my little bowl of oil, keeping one hand on Robert's leg the whole time so as not to break the connection. I suddenly could no longer picture what he looked like, and had to stifle an urge to peer under the table and up into his face, framed in the face hole.

'I'm not sure,' I said cautiously, replacing his right leg and picking up his left. 'The only other Ann Paramor on my list lives in Devon, and I wrote to her yesterday. Originally I wanted to just turn up and check them all out, but seeing as she's most likely to be the one, it seemed more fair somehow to warn her. Plus I don't really want to traipse all the way down there in case it's a wild goose chase and she turns out to be the wrong Ann too.'

'And what if she *is* the wrong one?'

I didn't mention the other possibility: Harlesden Ann. I was still too ashamed of myself for not following it through. 'Well. I'd always told myself that if I didn't find her straight away, I wasn't going to spend years and years wondering and spending more money on searching. I don't need to know *that* badly, but . . . I don't know, really. My friend Mack is making a documentary about the search for a BBC series, so maybe when it gets shown, there's a chance that someone who knows the right Ann might see it. Or even Ann herself. Although that would be a bit of a shock for her – if she saw me on TV looking for her. And, obviously, a very long shot for me.'

'So you're going to be on TV. Perhaps I'll have to start representing you. Is Mack your boyfriend?' I felt a distinct tightening of Robert's quadriceps muscle as I kneaded it, and the jealousy which slipped unmistakably into the flirtatious tone of his voice was a secret thrill which reverberated down my spine.

'No. He's just a mate. He's a freelance producer for the BBC, but this is his first full-length film.'

I momentarily forgot whether I'd done both his legs, or just the right one, even though the sequence usually came as second nature to me. Oh, this was impossible. I'd initiated the conversation because his flesh was distracting me, but now I wasn't focusing on the job in hand at all.

'I'm sorry to be bossy, Robert, but please would you shut up? I can't concentrate.'

I saw the side of Robert's cheek curve upwards in a smile. 'Yes, boss. Sorry, boss.'

I gently untucked the towel covering his back and bottom, deciding that I'd probably finished on both his legs. 'If you'd like to turn over now, please,' I said, holding my breath.

Robert rolled over, and I was horrified to realize that I was almost disappointed when the towel I replaced on his torso lay flat on him, as still as a becalmed sea. Perhaps it was all in my imagination, this attraction.

His chest was gorgeous, as I'd expected: taut and smooth, with just one patch of hair between his nipples – not enough to be a proper gross hairy chest, but just enough to make a macho sort of point. Gavin only had two hairs on *his* puny little chest. 'Quick, tie a knot in them before they slip back in again,' he used to joke.

Robert and I didn't speak for the next fifteen minutes or so. He lay there with his eyes closed, which afforded me an ideal opportunity to study him, every inch of his exposed skin, the way his lashes lay spiky on his cheeks, the memory of curls at his slightly – but only very slightly – receding hairline. I really got into the massage, and almost succeeded in forgetting about how much I fancied him.

Until I came to his stomach. By now his whole torso was uncovered, exposing a soft brown belly, endearing in its very faint podginess. It was a relief, actually, that he wasn't as completely godlike as he'd initially appeared – a sixpack would have been far too intimidating. I wanted to push my face in it, inhale its soft warmth, but instead I poured more oil into my hands and began to rub gentle circles, up to the bottom of his ribcage and down to where a line of dark hair was thickening as it headed south. His stomach rumbled musically, drowning out the CD, and he shifted a little on the couch.

'Sorry,' he muttered.

'Don't worry,' I said. 'It's just a sign that you're relaxing, that's all.'

As I worked, my right elbow suddenly knocked against something which hadn't been there before. Surprised, I glanced down – and there it was. He hadn't been apologizing for his stomach at all.

Talk about a tent pole. The entire towel was practically airborne and flapping. On an emotional level, it was nearly too much for me. I felt unprofessional and guilty – subconsciously I must have wanted this to happen. I never normally touched men's abdomens, for that very reason. On a practical level, I wasn't sure what to do. We'd been taught at college, as part of 'towel technique', that the correct procedure for dealing with men's frequent and usually minor tumescences was to tuck a thickly folded towel firmly over the offending area and then ignore it. But ignoring this one would have been like trying to work around a massive Christmas tree, flashing lights and all, which had appeared from nowhere on my massage couch. It was so mighty looking that I thought a breezeblock placed on top of it would have been ineffectual, let alone a folded towel. We both groaned involuntarily.

349

'I'm really sorry,' said Robert again, flinging his arm over his eyes as if dazzled by the sun. 'I can't believe it. I've been willing this not to happen since you started, and I thought I'd cracked it. I feel like a sixteen-year-old.'

'Sorry to disappoint you,' I said, beginning to work on his chest again. 'I'm nearly thirty.'

But Robert didn't laugh. He was so mortified that he had actually broken out in a sweat, and all the muscles I'd worked so hard to relax were visibly tensing up before me. His erection subsided of its own accord, but rigor mortis appeared to have set into the rest of his body. He fidgeted uncomfortably again on the couch, and then suddenly sat up, not meeting my eyes.

'I'm really sorry,' he muttered. 'I can't do this. I'm too embarrassed. I think I should leave.'

'Oh *no*,' I said frantically, clasping his shoulders, trying not to sound too desperate. 'Please. It's fine, I promise you. No big deal, it happens all the time.' Just not with men I really, really fancy, I thought.

He shook his head and swung his legs over the side of the couch. 'No. I can't. It feels all wrong – like I came here to take advantage of you or something.'

'Well,' I said. 'Of course, it's up to you. I'm not going to force you to let me continue the massage. But please don't just go. It's been so nice to see you.' We both laughed, sheepishly, at the implication. 'Why don't you stay for a cup of tea – herb tea would be best, after a massage – and then see how you feel?'

Robert hesitated.

'Oh, go on,' I said, nudging him shyly. 'It's like falling off a horse. You really should get straight back on again otherwise you get a phobia about riding.'

I winced, thinking again how suggestive that sounded. 'No, seriously,' I ploughed on. 'I'll leave you to get dressed while I put the kettle on. Then if you want me to finish the massage later, just give me the nod and I will. But please, please don't be embarrassed. What sort of tea would you like?'

'Camomile, if you've got it, please,' Robert said, reaching for his trousers. I left the room, torn between confusion and an empathic embarrassment at the turn of events, whilst simultaneously being deeply impressed at Robert's preference in herb teas. You'd have had to put a gun to Gavin's head to make him voluntarily request a cup of camomile tea.

By the time Robert marched into the kitchen, the kettle was already boiling, and his composure seemed to have returned, buttoned up around him like his pristine white shirt. I was glad that he hadn't put his jacket and tie back on – perhaps there was a chance we might be able to carry on where we left off.

I admired the way he'd stopped apologizing, too – if it had been me, I know I would have continued to do so, *ad nauseam* – and managed to sprawl himself loosely into a chair at the kitchen table as if he had been there a thousand times before.

The tea did us good; it restored a further sense of normality. We chatted as easily as we had in Nottingham, and I felt that the massage had somehow increased our sense of intimacy. I would never normally feel that with a client – seeing them naked made absolutely no difference to how I felt, or didn't feel, about them – but Robert was another matter. I felt a creepingly compelling sensation of ownership of him, and prayed silently that he'd change his mind about finishing the massage, so I could get my hands on that lovely body again. It felt like some kind of test – that I could massage him into belonging to me.

But eventually Robert stood up and emptied the rest of his mug down the sink.

'I'd better be off,' he said. 'How much do I owe you for the massage?'

He turned, saw my hurt face, and relented. 'You know, you probably won't believe this, but for a while there I almost forgot you had a boyfriend.'

The words splurged out of me. 'If I didn't have, would you be interested in the position?'

He came closer and crouched down by my chair, so I was staring into his amber eyes. They were so clear that I half expected small insects to be suspended inside them.

'Emma. Any position. Any time. I think you're absolutely gorgeous and I hate the thought that you're with someone else.' He smiled ruefully. 'Are you *sure* it's serious between you and him?'

I reached up and ran my fingers through his short hair. The gesture may have been tentative, but my reply was uttered with total conviction:

'Actually,' I said. 'I've done a lot of thinking since we met, about what – who – I want. I know it sounds, well, convenient, to say this now, but Gavin and I were a habit. He doesn't want me, and hasn't for ages. He said we were a habit when we finished, and I never really believed him.' I hesitated. 'Not until I met you. It was just bad timing that he and I had had one more fling, right before I came to Nottingham. And now I feel differently.'

'How differently?' He bent forward and whispered the words in my ear, so softly that they felt like kisses.

'Enough to promise you, on my life, that if I ever hear from him again – which I haven't, since Nottingham – I'll tell him he's history.'

'Excellent. Do you know what?'

'What?'

'That was without question the most fantastic massage I've ever had.' Robert tucked a loose strand of my hair behind my right ear, and moved even closer.

'I hope you're not just after me for my massage techniques,' I replied, feeling bolder by the second, digging my thumbs into pressure points on his skull until he shivered with pleasure.

'No,' he said. 'Not at all. But I must say, it's very nice that you're so talented.'

352

I stood up. 'Right then. Do I take it that you're ready to continue?'

Robert smiled sheepishly. 'Yes, but I can't guarantee that I won't have the same problem as before.'

'Good,' I said, as seductively as I could, marvelling that I was being neither shy, nor blushing and blotchy, nor depressed and anxious. But in charge, aroused, comfortable.

Before I could think too much about it, I took my glasses off, leaned forward and kissed him, my pony-tail falling around the side of my neck and tickling his nose and cheek. His arms shot out and wrapped them-selves around me, and he kissed me back, deep and hungry and scented with camomile, like being kissed in the countryside. His skin smelled of lemongrass.

'I could probably get struck off for this,' I said, after a few minutes. 'We should stop. At least let me finish the massage. I'm being so unprofessional.' I tried half-heartedly to pull away but he wouldn't let me.

'Kiss me again.'

I obliged. I felt close to orgasm already, although at the back of my head my old cautious-Emma voice was ranting at me, albeit with the volume turned down: OK, so you kissed him, but he could still be taking advantage because he knows you fancy him. He was aroused because of the massage, not because of you, despite what he's just said.

But somehow I knew, I just knew that he wasn't going to use me. That this wasn't a roll in the hay. After all the months of moping, and then Stella's revelation, I realized that without a doubt I didn't want Gavin any more. Really, honestly, hand on heart.

Actually, hand on something else. The Christmas tree had reappeared, and I couldn't help myself. I just wanted to touch it . . .

'Will you continue the massage?' Robert was already peeling off his clothes again, dragging me down the hall to the massage room, where he climbed back onto the couch, on his back.

I tried to reclaim some semblance of professionalism, and did the old towel trick across his torso – which, as I'd predicted, had absolutely no effect. I poured a well of oil into my hands and began to move around towards his head to work on his chest, but he reached up and caught my slippery hands and pulled me back towards him.

'Lie on top of me,' he whispered, not at all embarrassed any more.

Without giving it a second thought, I did. I scrambled awkwardly up on to my massage couch and straddled him, whipping away his towel in a movement akin to the men from Buck's Fizz ripping off Cheryl and Jay's skirts during 'Making Your Mind Up' – which I, conclusively, was. Robert's penis was poking out of his boxers, unveiled and looking as magnificent as I'd expected. I manoeuvred myself down on him so that I was rubbing it against me, and the pleasure was almost painful in its intensity as we kissed and kissed.

'This is awful, but – could we? Do you think we could? I really want you.' The sound of my voice, hoarse with lust, almost surprised me.

Robert sat up a little, on his elbows, lifting me with him. 'I've got a condom in my wallet,' he said, and I'd vaulted off the couch and over to his jacket before he changed his mind. I couldn't believe my wantonness.

'Do you want to go into my bedroom?' I said, handing him his wallet.

'No. I want to stay here.' He stripped off his boxers and sat up to roll on the condom before sinking back onto the couch. As his wallet fell to the floor, I saw a photograph of a little coffee-skinned girl, hair in bunches, beaming gap-toothed from a clear plastic display next to his credit cards, and my heart constricted. He was a dad, as well as a divinely attractive man.

Stopping myself before I began to picture us having our own babies, I whipped all my clothes off, far too turned on to feel more than a brief shiver of self-consciousness at exposing my body. In about half a minute flat I had climbed back on top of him, rubbing my hard nipples into his oily chest, feeling him between my legs probing to get into position. He pushed into me in one smooth movement as I swelled around him with pleasure and gratitude; he filled me up so tenderly that tears came to my eyes, and the couch began to rock gently, carrying us as if we were making love on a boat.

Within minutes, I couldn't bear it any more. 'Stop, or I'll come,' I said, gripping the sides of the massage couch. 'Me too,' Robert replied, running his hands frantically up and down my body as he thrust into me again and again. The couch began to rock harder.

'Steady,' I squawked, 'It won't collapse, but it might—'

CRASH! The couch's legs held firm, but the whole thing tipped over sideways and it fell, depositing us both in a very undignified manner onto the floor where we lay, still joined, laughing and coming simultaneously.

'—fall over,' I panted, before losing myself in the waves of orgasm which temporarily distracted me from the pain in my knee, which I'd banged when we toppled over.

'Are you all right?' Robert said afterwards. He kissed me again and I felt as if I'd known him for ever; there was none of that awful first-time awkwardness or embarrassment – fairly amazingly, under the some-what unconventional circumstances.

'Fine, except for the bruise I'm going to have on my knee,' I replied, light-headed and shaky. I stroked his bottom, noticing that it had broken out in oddly endearing post-climax goose-pimples, and snuggled into his arms as we lay shipwrecked on the carpeted floor, the white towels like torn sails around us. 'Although I'm never going to be able to look at my massage room in the same light.'

'I can imagine. Sorry about that. I'll buy you a new massage bed if it's broken.'

'No, it just overbalanced. These things are built to be pretty sturdy, if not perhaps to withstand quite such vigorous activity . . . Come into the bedroom, and we can chill out in bed for a bit.'

As I spoke, the telephone rang in the hall, and after four rings, the answer-machine picked up. It was Gavin, with his usual impeccable sense of timing.

'Hiya, babes, sorry I didn't get back to you before. Something's come up. Actually, what it is, right, Customs and Excise have raided my flat and impounded all my furniture. Everything. Even my bloody mobile phone. Luckily I wasn't there at the time – Jim saw them go in and came down the pub to warn me – but apparently they want to interview me about my last little trip to Holland. So it's best if I lie low for a while; get out of London altogether. I'm really sorry. It might be a few weeks. This is all a real fuckin' headache, and I promise I'll be in touch as soon as I can, OK? Take care, darling, lots of love.'

I pulled away from Robert, propping my head up with my elbow so I could look into his face. 'That,' I said, 'in case you hadn't guessed, was my so-called boyfriend.'

'He sounds like a lovely boy,' said Robert, in a mock-jovial camp accent. 'Very reliable and trustworthy. *What* exactly was he doing in Holland?'

'You don't want to know. Well, I certainly didn't, anyhow. With Gavin it's always better not to ask . . . Come on.' I stood up, holding out my hand to lead him down the hall into my bedroom; me limping, both of us naked.

On the way past, I pressed the REWIND button on the answering machine to erase Gavin's message.

PART THREE

35

'Did you know that there's a message on the machine?' Stella asked me, coming into the room with a fresh jug of margaritas and a bowl of pistachios.

'No, I didn't even hear the phone ring. Go and see who it was, would you? I'll sort everyone out with drinks.'

As I poured a new round of frothy margaritas for everyone present, I had a sudden flashback to the last message Gavin left me, almost six months ago. It would have been recorded over so many times now; his voice buried beneath new greetings from new friends, or the endearing little messages Robert recorded for me whenever he couldn't stay over.

'It was Suzanne, ringing to wish you and Mack luck,' said Stella, stretching out her hand for her drink. 'She said she'd try to come over after work, although she's sure we'll be taping it, and besides, she has serious qualms about attending any party that her parents have also been invited to. It's just not cool.'

We all laughed, particularly Denise and Greg, the parents in question. Robert and I had had such a good time at the Hiscocks' dinner party, back in March, that we'd made every effort to keep in touch. We'd been out to dinner to celebrate my thirtieth birthday a couple of weeks later, and were now planning to rent a villa in Portugal for a winter holiday.

I caught Mack surreptitiously checking – for the tenth time – that there was a videotape in the machine, and that it was set to record BBC2.

'Why are you taping it, Mack? Aren't you awash with VHSs of it already?' asked Greg, who'd obviously noticed him checking too.

Katrina answered on Mack's behalf – something she often did. 'Yes, of course we are, but it's not the same as having it on tape with the programme announcer's comments and everything, is it?'

She and Mack were holding hands so tightly that Mack's knuckles were white bumps through his skin, even though the documentary didn't start for another hour. I wasn't surprised at how nervous he was – Robert had told me how much would be riding on how well received Mack's first full-length commissioned film was. It could make or break his career, so I was glad that he had Katrina there for him. He adored her, and I knew that if the reviews weren't good, she'd get him through it.

With adoration on my mind, I turned to look at Robert, struck by the sexy curve of his throat and quick movements of his hands as he shucked pistachio nuts and tossed them into his mouth, head back, in between chatting with Stella's boyfriend of four months, Zubin.

Zubin was a lanky, laidback Zoroastrian Indian, who had the sweetest nature imaginable, and even let Stella dress him up like an oversized dolly in her outlandish designs. He was sitting there now, completely complacently, in a ludicrous orange frilly shirt done up to the top button on a hot August night, and I felt a pang of affection for him. I half waited for Stella to berate him for producing the huge moons of sweat which blossomed out from his armpits, but she didn't comment, just sat on his knee and snuggled up to his neck. She was so much more mellow that she glowed

– even her freckles appeared to radiate a kind of milk-maid contentment. I wondered if Zubin would ever be my brother-in-law. It was a nice thought, and not beyond the realms of possibility. Since Stella and he had met at the clothes shop he managed in Putney, they'd been as inseparable as Robert and me.

We hadn't seen hair nor hide of Charlie since Stella agreed to drop the charges on condition that he stayed away. Rumour at Stella's college had it that he was living in Spain, very disgruntled, teaching English to Spanish students, God help them. I had a horrible image of a roomful of innocent teenage Spaniards learning to say in perfect Sloaney brays: 'You fucking pricktease.'

As for Gavin, there hadn't been a peep out of him, either. I suspected he had absconded to somewhere remote enough to escape the long arm of Customs and Excise – or else he was in jail – and while I was concerned for him, I wasn't losing any sleep over it. Robert was the only one who could make me lose sleep these days. Most nights I begged him to.

The other invited guest was Ruth, who sat on the floor with a cordless baby listener beside her, at which she looked anxiously every ten seconds, checking that the single red light didn't suddenly multiply into a semi-circular howl. But Evie appeared to be sleeping peacefully in her cot downstairs.

They had moved into Percy's old flat the previous month after a builder had bought it, done it up, and screwed a 'FOR RENT' board into the wall, directly below my bedroom window. It was fantastic having them there. Evie had grown into a cherubic baby with huge wide-apart blue eyes, rubberband wrists, podgy thighs and a constantly surprised expression. But most notable of all, she had a great soft swathe of thin blonde hair on her head which made her look exactly like Mack.

'Are you sure there isn't something you want to tell me about Evie's father?' I'd teased Ruth, privately, the first time we'd seen Mack and Evie together.

'Well, it's not Mack, if that's what you're getting at, because Mack's a good bloke and not an asshole. Oops, don't listen, Eves.' She had covered Evie's tiny ears with her hands, to which Evie responded by releasing a volley of farts into her nappy like ack-ack fire, which made us laugh even more.

I worshipped Evie; taught Ruth to massage her; collected her from the childminder's, babysat her, and read my brand new copy of *Are You My Mother?* to her. And the best thing of all was that she wasn't even remotely my responsibility. I wished that I could have materialized my baby bird for her entertainment, to see her wave her fists and crow with delight, but he hadn't been around, not since Robert came on the scene.

We'd decided to make a bit of a party for the occasion of Mack's full-length directorial début. I'd declined the invitation to go to a preliminary screening of it for that reason – I wanted to have my friends and family with me when I watched it. Besides, Stella and I had never, in eleven years of living together, had a party before. I'd never known enough people that I liked enough to provide hospitality for.

'I don't know why Suzanne's wishing you luck,' Stella said to Mack. 'It's going ahead regardless, isn't it? I mean, you've got your slot.'

Mack looked a little sick. 'But what if the critics slate it? Then I'm finished. And you haven't seen it yet either, Emma. I wish you'd come to that screening . . .'

'What, and spoil the surprise?' I tried to make my tone flippant, but it was a struggle. Mack's nerves were rubbing off on me. 'I told you, I didn't want to see it in advance. I'd have been too tempted to try and make you edit out any unflattering shots of me, and then you'd have been left with no documentary at all.'

Robert pointed at me. '*You*, don't be so self-deprecating.' Then he pointed at Mack. 'And *you*, stop being so pessimistic! They won't hate it – it's not a controversial enough subject. And even if they did hate it, of course you wouldn't be *finished*.'

'But maybe they'll hate it for not being controversial . . . Oh God, maybe I should've gone with the idea about ratcatchers on heroin in the sewers of São Paulo . . .'

'Shut up, Mack,' Robert, Stella, and I chorused.

'It'll be *fine*,' I added. 'I'm sure I'll like it, honestly. Even if I do cringe a bit at the sight of myself on TV . . . Here, let's have a toast. To Mack, and his wonderful documentary.'

Katrina nudged Mack. 'Wasn't there something you wanted to say too – before you're swallowed up by your own nervous gloom?'

'Oh yeah. I wanted to thank Emma – and Stella – for this little party, but more importantly, Emma, thanks for letting me film you. I know how hard it was for you to talk about yourself and your feelings, but I'm so glad you stuck with it. Despite my whingeing, I do actually think we've got a great film, thanks to you. I just hope the critics feel the same. And that you've got something out of it too.'

He leaned over and kissed my cheek, and Robert squeezed my arm.

'Don't thank me,' I said. 'You should thank that homeless man I met on the tube. He's the one who really began all this.'

Watching Mack's documentary for the first time was the strangest experience of my life. I'd thought it would be a straightforward story about the search for Ann Paramor, but Mack had gone much deeper. He had me pinned out like a butterfly: my powdery emotions on display, my history raw. Everything I'd said over the months he interviewed me was somehow in there, condensed, distilled into a need so naked that at times it made me squirm. It wasn't at all comfortable to watch, but even I could see that it made compulsive television.

We sat perfectly still throughout, apart from Stella giving the odd yelp when she saw herself in the Olympia scene, or me burying my head in Robert's lap with embarrassment at some of the inane things I came out with on film. It was all there, though: the list; the telephone calls; the inconclusive visit to Harlesden and the little girl with pyjamas on her head; the more conclusive trips to the Holistic Fayre and Nottingham. When I talked about things which Mack hadn't actually filmed, such as the man on the tube, and the scene in the swimming pool in Nottingham, he used voiceovers: him asking gentle questions, my replies, hesitant at first and then more confident, over a collage of images – homeless people, shots of such desolate loneliness and abandonment that we were all silent and choked. The isolation of crowded tube trains. Zoos, orang-utans, coachloads of wriggling schoolchildren. He'd even gone and found another, local, ante-natal aqua exercise class and filmed that, which made Ruth bark with laughter into her margarita.

'Thank God you weren't there for the actual event. If anyone had filmed me going into labour, I'd have killed them,' she said before we all shushed her.

The penultimate scene had been shot in Mack's flat, on the day the letter had arrived from the last Ann Paramor, in its thick cream envelope stamped with a Devon postmark as wavy as my stomach at the thought of what it might contain.

Robert had been up in Manchester for a meeting that day, so I'd rushed straight over to Mack's flat, where he and Katrina were having breakfast. He had instantly got his PD100 out of the case and begun to rig up some sort of complicated arrangement by which he strapped the camera to his skateboard, so he could pull it down the hall in what he told me was a 'tracking shot', to capture my expression as I came into the kitchen. Katrina started to set up the radio mikes, and I had waited at the kitchen table, glumly watching the activity around me as their half-finished cornflakes began to congeal around the sides of their bowls. Pat Sharp on Heart FM was playing songs from 'this week in 1981': Randy Crawford, 'Rainy Night in Georgia' and Smokey Robinson's 'Being With You'. 'What were you doing in that year?' Pat asked, rhetorically, and I'd thought back: it was the year of Stella's birth. That was the year when everything had changed, although not in the bad way I'd feared. I'd been dreading the prospect of no longer being number one; but what I actually became was a big sister. Number ones and number twos stopped existing as terms of competition, and merely became euphemisms for what Stella did in her nappy.

The shot in Mack's flat seemed to take for ever to set up, and I was ready to punch him for all that assing about with skateboards, pretending to be a creative wunderkind, when all I wanted to do was to rip open the envelope.

'Hurry *up*,' I'd called out, snappily. 'This is torture!'

But finally it was ready, and I had to admit, when I saw it on TV, it was very atmospheric. Mack had filmed me in slow motion as I walked down the hall, like a condemned prisoner on Death Row, reframing for a tight close-up of my white face when I sat at the kitchen table – the cereal bowls had been cleared away and the radio switched off – and began to tear open the envelope.

Then my voice, heavy with disappointment, reading out the letter from Devonshire Ann, the perfectly nice, perfectly apologetic letter saying that there was absolutely no way that she could be my mother since she was eight in the year I was born, but that she did hope I found her and it all worked out for the best in the end.

'So that's that,' my disembodied voice said flatly over the top of a close-up of another wrong Ann Paramor's handwriting. 'That only leaves the Harlesden one, and I'm sure it's not her. I just feel it. It feels right to stop here. To finish. I just want to move on with my life. We tried.' My words oozed, dripping with a defeatism I hadn't really even realized I felt until I heard them.

Back in our sitting room, Robert reached over and hugged me tightly. On TV, my voiceover faded out, replaced by the swelling introduction to 'Everybody Hurts' by R.E.M.

There was one final piece of footage, before Mack's closing credits. Just as I was thinking to myself, Well, hope springing eternal and all, maybe I was a bit hasty about Harlesden Ann; maybe I should go back, just to make sure. I'd always wonder, otherwise – Mack said to me, anxiously, from across the room, 'I hope you don't mind that I did this, Emma.'

As Michael Stipe's plaintive voice filled our ears, the shot changed to a street I recognized – back to Harlesden Ann's street, as if Mack's film had read my thoughts. My heart leaped into my mouth. He's found her, I thought. A close-up of the house, still deserted, ugly, unkempt.

Then, oh God, cutting to the exterior of a post office. Mack shooting hand-held as he walked slowly inside and through the roped-off queuing lines, towards the counters, a close-up of a name badge reading 'Ann Paramor', then a slow pan over an enormous chest, up three chins to a pasty, sullen face, zooming outwards to film sparse eyebrow hairs raised in enquiry, but not surprise at the sight of the camera and microphone – Mack had obviously gone in first and asked her if he could film – then another close-up of her looking down at a photograph of me as a baby and then—

I held my breath, pressure building and building inside my head until I felt sure I'd start hissing like a pressure cooker and nobody in the room would be able to hear my voiceover on screen; at least not the 's's anyhow—

—she was shaking her head, blankly. Shrugging her shoulders. Shaking her head again. Arranging her tight lips into a wavy rueful expression. Looking smug that she was going to be on television.

It wasn't her.

'It wasn't her,' said Mack, looking at me worriedly as the screen went blank and words scrolled up, over the final verse and chorus of 'Everybody Hurts':

None of the Ann Paramors on the list turned out to be Emma's birth mother. She has decided not to take her search any further, although she entertains a faint hope that if the right woman is out there, she might still come forward and contact the makers of this film.

The final words were mine, spoken over a photograph of Mum, Dad, Stella and me, taken on a beach in Cornwall, Stella and I squinting into the unknown, but never suspecting that the unknown would turn out to be a place without the two adults hugging us from behind. My words made me want to scream; brave, made-for-TV words forming trite, pat sentiments: 'I consider myself to be one of the lucky ones. I had wonderful adoptive parents for nineteen years. Of course I'll always wonder, and I'll always want answers about myself, but I can survive without them. I've survived for this long. As long as I can keep it all in perspective, and concentrate on the people I have in my life now whom I love and who love me – well, that's all that is important, at the end of the day.'

I got up and stormed out of the room, suddenly furious. There was a momentary silence behind me, and then I was aware of a buzz of concerned voices as Stella, Mack, Ruth and Robert all got up and debated which of them should go after me.

Ruth, who was nearest the door, took an executive decision. 'Give us a minute, will you?' I heard her say as she followed me out into my bedroom.

She found me leaning my forehead against the cool glass of the window, watching the roofs of cars passing below in a blur of metallic colours still just about discernible in the dusk.

'Are you all right?'

'No,' I said morosely.

'I don't blame you.' I heard a creak as Ruth sat down on my bed, and then a faint lip-smacking, snuffly sound which was Evie through the baby monitor Ruth still held, stirring in her sleep. 'It's hard enough, what you've been through. It must be doubly hard seeing Mack making such a big, suspenseful drama out of it.'

I gulped. 'I thought . . . I thought that the Ann in the post office must be her. I thought he'd found her and she didn't want to know me. That's why he didn't tell me beforehand.'

'Mack would never do that to you. He'd never set you up like that.'

'But he did set me up! He used me. OK, it would have been worse if she *had* turned out to be my mother, but still, he manipulated me. I can't believe he did that; I'm so angry with him, Ruth. And tired. This whole thing has been such a series of huge hopes and then even bigger anti-climaxes – my emotions are up and down like a . . . like a . . . *whore's drawers.*'

'Perhaps that's part of the reason you're so angry with Mack now too: because he didn't manage to help you find your mother?'

I turned slowly and went to sit on the bed next to Ruth. My hands were shaking. I flopped back, looking at the way my beaded lampshade sent globules of shadow dappling across the ceiling.

'Yeah. You're right. It's the scene in his film which wasn't there that upsets me most,' I said slowly. 'I've tried and tried not to have any expectations, not to fantasize about it, but I just can't help it. I so wanted there to be a scene at the end where I walk up a garden path somewhere, and there's a small, dark-haired, friendly woman who looks just like me, only twenty years older. She's framed in the doorway. Her arms are open wide. We're both crying, and we hug and laugh. Mack's panning slowly around us . . .' My voice was thick with tears, which started to drip self-pityingly out of the sides of my eyes and into my ears.

Ruth sighed sympathetically. 'Poor you,' she said, making me cry even harder.

'I didn't want it to end with a picture of Mum and Dad. I didn't want to be reminded of what I've already lost,' I sobbed, flinging my arm across my face to hide my eyes. 'I miss them so much.'

As if in sympathy, a tinny wail suddenly emanated from the baby listener. I sat up, sniffling, and we both watched the arc of tomato-red lights flaring angrily into a howl of action.

'She's so restless tonight,' said Ruth, pulling a key out of her pocket. 'Must be the heat. Will you go? I guarantee that a cuddle of a sleepy baby will make you feel better. Go on. I promise I'll turn off the listener, so if you want to talk to her, or have more of a cry, you can. She'll probably go straight back to sleep, and if she doesn't, just bring her up here.'

I took the key. It did seem like a nice idea. 'OK then, just for a bit. Will you tell Mack I think his documentary was brilliant, even if the ending did upset me. And tell Robert I'll be back soon?'

Ruth nodded, putting her arm around my shoulders and squeezing.

'Thanks, pal,' I said, leaning my head against hers.

I wanted to go in and see Robert, but I couldn't face everyone else's sympathetic noises, so instead I sneaked straight past the now muted party in the living room and down to Ruth's flat.

Evie's door was ajar, and I could see wavery pink shadows being thrown around the room from the magic lantern on the bookcase: little cartoonish angels with triangles for bodies blowing heavenly trumpets and playing celestial tambourines, dancing round in an eternal circle of soft red light.

Evie, however, was not impressed. She was kneeling up, clad in a baggy nappy and nothing else, rattling the bars of her cot like a wrongfully arrested political prisoner. Her tear-stained face was puce with heat and fury and, as she reached out her arms to be lifted up, she gave me a look which very obviously said, 'What the hell kept you?'

I scooped her out over the side of the cot and held her close. She instantly stopped crying and, sticking her forefinger into her mouth, nuzzled her head into the space between my neck and my shoulder. Her earlobe against my cheek felt strangely cool in contrast to her hot face.

I eased myself as carefully as possible down in the deep white rocking chair by the window, and we sat and rocked, in silence apart from the sound of a small finger being sucked. I thought how, only a few months ago, Percy had lived here. This probably hadn't been where he slept, being the smallest of the three potential bedrooms, but I had no doubts that it had been as brown and dingy as the rest of the flat.

It was so strange, how quickly everything could change. Percy was gone, but Ruth and Evie were here. Mack may have laid me bare for the nation's entertainment, but look what else had come out of it. Maybe not a new mother, but a lover, and several new friends.

Evie muttered and briefly complained, so, fervently hoping that Ruth had stuck to her promise of switching off the monitor, I began to sing to her. But I couldn't find the right song. 'Hotel California', which for some reason sprung to mind first, turned out to be very tricky, a cappella, and I couldn't remember the words to 'One Man Went to Mow', when I tried to start that one. I seemed to have forgotten all the lullabies I used to know. I wished I'd had the foresight to bring my recorder down – it was funny how playing it was so much easier than singing, a more tuneful conduit for the notes in my brain.

Then suddenly it came to me. The song that Mum used to sing Stella as a baby: 'Goodbye Yellow Brick Road'. Not particularly soothing, or somnolent – especially when sung flat by me – but it flooded out of me, even though I hadn't heard it for years: all the words of the chorus and most of the verses, too. I closed my eyes and saw my mother, my *real* mother, rocking Stella and singing, smiling at me over Stella's baby shoulder when I appeared in another doorway, in another age. It was Mum and Dad I missed, I thought as the tears began to drop again into Evie's fine hair. Not the stranger who'd given birth to me. I was wrong even to try and replace them, for that was what I had hoped, even if I wouldn't admit to anybody.

Evie gradually fell quiet, and the room seemed full of the energies of innocence and safety, a place of transformation; a room where needs were always met and loved ones always close. I felt sad that it hadn't been that way for Percy – at least, not towards the end of his life. Who knew what had gone before that. Maybe he too had once sat and rocked a child in this room. The magic lantern continued to throw coloured angels around the walls and golden-pink spirals spinning onto the ceiling, illuminating the shelf full of stuffed animals, the white fluffy rug on the floor, and the clumsily done painting of Humpty Dumpty.

Humpty was still perched on his wall, but he had a lopsided look about him which suggested that all the King's men – four of them, rosy-cheeked and musketed – may have already had an unsuccessful stab at putting him back together again after some previous unrecorded tumble. Ruth later told me that her mother had painted it.

After ten more minutes, I did feel much better, and Evie was asleep again. As I stood up and crept gingerly back over to the cot, a tall silhouette appeared in the doorway.

'Hi,' Robert whispered.

I smiled at him, and lowered Evie back into bed. She wailed briefly, but was asleep again before she made contact with the mattress. I tucked a sheet around her, and arranged a platoon of soft pigs and small teddies above her head to keep her company. 'Good night, sleep tight, don't let the bedbugs bite,' I whispered, stroking down the haze of fine hair sprouting vertically from her soft head. The feel of it made my solar plexus hurt with love – for Evie, and for Robert, standing so protectively near me.

As I turned to leave the room, a sudden impulse made me stop and look in the chest of drawers where Evie's clothes were kept. I beckoned Robert in, and together we peered at a multitude of neat pairs of tiny white socks, and heart-stoppingly cute dresses and embroidered cardigans. Evie's whole wardrobe fitted into three small drawers. Robert made an 'aah' face at me, and then at Evie, and we crept out of the bedroom, escorted protectively by the translucent angels whirling around our heads.

For the first time, I realized that I'd stopped feeling so fearful at the very idea of procreation, and was day-dreaming that one day Robert and I would be cooing over our own baby; that maybe becoming a parent for real – instead of struggling to be a substitute – might lay to rest the ghosts of parents past and missing; that maybe I'd be brave enough to risk the emotional pain of having children.

One day, though. Not yet. I had some freedom to enjoy first, now that Stella was grown up and settled, and now that I had someone with whom to do all the things I'd never had the chance to do before – at least not without feeling guilty: travel, play tennis, go to gigs and clubs and museums . . .

'I think the others are leaving in a minute,' Robert said when we were back in the hall. 'Are you going to come up and say goodbye?'

'Yeah, of course,' I said, hugging him. 'I'm sorry I ran off like that. I just felt a bit – overwhelmed by it all. I hope I haven't upset Mack.'

Robert's arms felt so good, tightly around me. 'Well, he's concerned for you. All your friends are.'

36

The week after Mack's documentary was shown, Robert drove Zubin up to Milton Keynes for a Bon Jovi concert, much to Stella's and my derision.

'That's a chuckable offence,' I told Robert, sternly. 'And you're corrupting poor Zubin.'

'I'm not corrupting anybody. Zubin likes Bon Jovi, don't you, Zub?'

Zubin nodded enthusiastically and mimed a frenzied guitar solo. 'Hell, yeah. There's still time for you both to come with us – I'm sure we could pick up a couple of extra tickets from touts.'

Stella and I exchanged long-suffering looks. 'I'd rather saw off my own leg with a rusty breadknife than go to an American hair band gig, thanks,' I said haughtily. 'Even if Jon Bon Jovi is pretty damn cute. For a midget.'

Robert had kissed me goodbye. 'Oh, well, I suppose it's a boy thing,' he said sadly. 'You just don't understand.'

Since Robert had moved into his flat in Hammersmith, I hadn't seen an awful lot of Stella – I'd only really been coming home when I had massage appointments booked. It was the first evening in weeks that Stella and I hadn't had our men with us, so we decided to do something we hadn't done for a long time – to go and play tennis.

But Stella wasn't on good form at all, and I could tell it wasn't just because she was missing Zub. I thought a bit of running around might shake her out of it. Now that term had finished and her end-of-year exams were over, she'd been spending far too many nights out drinking with Zub.

We walked down to Ravenscourt Park and found a free court next to two teenaged boys who were playing appallingly badly – hitting the ball straight up in the air or over the wire fence onto the grass outside the court. I turned to comment to Stella on how crap they were, and saw her face, glum and closed-down, staring at the bumpy tarmac of the court.

'What's up, Stell? Don't you want to play?'

'Oh . . . sure,' she said vaguely. 'I'm just a bit tired, that's all. I'll be OK when we get going.' She unzipped her racket and opened the can of balls, dropping them one by one onto the ground where they bounced away from her like eager puppies.

'Is everything all right between you and Zubin?' I persisted, taking off my sweatshirt and stretching forwards, then up, enjoying the feeling of my muscles tensing and elongating and the warm night air soft against the skin of my arms and legs. The clouds were changing colour as the sun began to set; their pearly whiteness was edged with peach tinges, and the sky between them had turned an exquisitely rich but pale summer blue.

'Yeah. Everything's fine with Zub. It's not that. It's—'

'What?' I stopped mid-stretch, held my breath, and hoped she wasn't going to announce that she was pregnant.

She pulled a hat from her bag and rammed it onto her head. It was her 'festival hat', an old floppy blue denim hat, so called because it kept off rain and sun alike at outdoor music events, and she used it for tennis to keep the hair out of her eyes. She looked away from me, over at the boy who was trying to serve. He hit the ball hard, but it shot straight down the court and into the fence at the opposite end, without bouncing, narrowly missing his opponent.

'Long,' called the opponent unnecessarily, rolling his eyes and sticking his tongue down into the space beneath his lower lip to indicate his friend's extreme ineptitude.

'There's been a couple more phone calls when you've been over at Robert's for the night – you know, hang-ups. And I've had this weird feeling that I'm being . . . followed. I'm worried that Charlie's back.'

I felt a cold, scared shiver in my shoulder blades, remembering the sight of Charlie's eyes peering through the window of a parked car outside our flat back in February. 'Oh no. Are you sure?'

Stella walked over to the baseline and threw the ball into the air, slamming it with her racket. It flew into the net, and rolled back towards her feet again.

'No, I'm not *sure*,' she said crossly, picking it up and trying her serve again, more slowly. I unzipped the cover from my own racket.

'Have you told Zub?'

Stella shook her head miserably. Her hair was currently in dozens of tiny little braids which swung about like a bead curtain under the hat, reminding me of when she was a short-haired kid and she used to clip large clothes pegs to the ends of her hair to try and achieve the same effect.

'I don't want to freak him out, or make him feel that he has to do anything about it. He'd hardly be a match for that great ugly shit-for-brains.'

I agreed, quelling a mental image of poor little Zubin, brave but puny, getting sand kicked in his face on the beach by a musclebound bully boy like Charlie.

'If it happens again when I'm not there, ring Ruth and ask if you can go down and stay with her for the night. Why's he doing this? You must tell the police, the second you see him.'

I walked around to the other side of the net and we began to knock the ball back and forth, hitting it to one another, playing in the service boxes without moving more than a couple of feet in either direction, so that we could still talk out of earshot of the boys on the next court.

'It won't do any good, unless we've got proof that he wants to hurt me in some way. And I'm probably the Met's biggest timewaster right now.'

'It was your prerogative. They couldn't *make* you take him to court, though God knows I wish you had.'

Suddenly furious, I lobbed a ball past Stella, hard, down to the other end of the court where it jangled against the fence and rolled to a stop, a small spent missile.

Stella stopped, leaning on the handle of her racket. She had gone white.

'When is it ever going to *fucking* end?' she asked slowly. 'I really did think that if I dropped the charges, he'd leave me alone. I can't go to the police again. They'll think I'm crying wolf.'

I ran up to the net. 'Oh Stella, I know, it must be horrendous. You were so brave to report him in the first place, and I'm sure the police would take you seriously again. I wish I could do something about it, though. About him. I'd kill him, if I could.'

Stella laughed, mirthlessly but with affection. 'Emma, how many times do I have to tell you: stop trying to fight my battles for me. I'm an adult. It's enough to know that you're there for me – I don't expect you to come up with solutions as well.'

I walked miserably back towards the baseline, and we began to play a more strenuous rally. We had only just got going when I heard the muffled sound of my mobile phone coming from my bag. Robert had recently, in a bored five minutes, fiddled with the ring-tones and changed my existing innocuous one into a speeded-up, tinny rendition of 'The Flight of the Bumblebee'.

'Sorry, Stella, it's probably Robert, to say they've just got there . . .'

I ran over, cringing at the sound, and just managed to pull it out and answer it before it switched over to the messaging service. It was a relief to cut off the obnoxious travesty of a piece of classical music. 'Hello?'

It took a couple of seconds to place the voice on the other end of the line.

'Hello, sweetheart. Bet you thought I'd forgotten all about you. How've you been, angel?'

Stella looked over the net at me with surprise, and I realized it was because I was brandishing my racket in my fist like a weapon. I mouthed 'It's Gavin' at her but she didn't manage to lipread what I'd said, and pantomimed an expression of incomprehension.

'It's Gavin!' I hissed again, burying the phone in my shoulder so he wouldn't hear. Her eyes opened wide.

'Emma? Are you there? Where are you, anyway?'

'Oh, I'm – um, playing tennis in the park with Stella. What do—' But Gavin was already talking over the top of me.

'Ravenscourt? Great! I'll pop over. Can't wait to see you, babes!'

And before I could object, the line went dead. I slumped against the side fence as Stella jogged across to me.

'The bloody *nerve* of that man. After six months, he assumes I'm still here, gagging to see him. What kind of a sad person does he think I *am*?'

'The kind of sad person you were when you went out with him, probably. Always at his beck and call,' said Stella, picking up a stray ball and bouncing it with her racket. 'What did he say? Has he been in prison?'

I shrugged, deciding to let her first comment pass. It was true, after all. 'I don't know. But I think we're about to find out – he said he's coming over here now.' I noticed dispassionately that I didn't remotely care that my face was bright red, my nose shiny, and I hadn't shaved my legs.

'Oh, right. Well, in Gavin time that probably means he'll be here in two hours, if at all, so I wouldn't hold your breath.' Stella looked at her watch scornfully, but I detected a flicker of nerves across her face.

'Well, I hope he does come, so I can tell him that I'm madly in love with someone else, and that I know he tried it on with you, that I think he's a total wanker, and I have less than no interest in ever having anything else to do with him.'

Stella grimaced. 'Oh please don't, if I'm here. It'll be too embarrassing. I don't want to get involved.'

'You are involved,' I said darkly, and she blushed.

We continued playing, but with an air of tension in every stroke from both of us. By the time we finished the two sets we'd agreed we'd play it was getting dark but there was still, predictably, no sign of Gavin. I won, 6–2, 6–1; Stella was as good a player as I was, but her serve let her down, and she always got so annoyed when she started to lose. I gave her the benefit of the doubt on numerous points, and even fluffed several of my own serves, but I still kept winning. I'd forgotten that that was the reason we didn't play very often.

We packed up our things, mopped our sweating foreheads, and finished the last of the water in the one small plastic bottle I'd brought. It tasted warm and brackish. Stella looked even more distant than she had before the game.

'What are you thinking?' I asked, screwing the top back on and throwing the empty bottle into my backpack. 'About Charlie? Because, like I said—'

'No,' she said as we closed the heavy iron gate of the court behind us and began to walk through the dusk towards the park exit. 'In fact, I don't want to think about Charlie at all any more. Can we not talk about him please? Actually, I was thinking about all that business at Sainsbury's.'

I knew instantly what she was talking about, but let

her continue. When she was fifteen, she'd had an evening job at Sainsbury's, which she'd loved, until her till began to be mysteriously 'out' or 'under' at the end of the evening. She had been convinced she wasn't screwing it up, because she only worked two three-hour shifts a week after school.

'I keep thinking about how I used to come home really stressed, after evil Daphne had cashed up my till. She'd slime over to me and fold her arms and say, "Fifteen pounds out tonight, Stella. You need to be more careful." It was hideous.'

I nodded, but wasn't really listening. I'd heard it all before, and besides, I was still wondering what I could do about Charlie. The trees loomed over us, seeming to draw all the moisture out of the air, and I felt an odd sense of foreboding as we walked beneath them. I turned sharply, to check we weren't being followed, but the path behind was empty.

'The first few times I thought I must just be giving people the wrong change, so I kept checking and double-checking every single transaction. But it just seemed so weird that the more careful I got, the more often my till would be out: five, ten, fifteen pounds – it was always a round figure, wasn't it? Never ninety-six p or fifty-eight p or anything. I felt like a failure – I so badly wanted to put something towards the house-keeping as well. That was why I got so angry about it. My first job, a poxy little checkout job, and I couldn't keep it for more than five minutes. '

The notion of Stella wanting to contribute to the household finances caught my attention. 'You never told me that, about wanting to contribute money.'

'Well, I did want to. I felt awful that you were working so hard and I was doing nothing except eat and spend and go to school.'

'But you were a kid. That's what you were meant to be doing. And besides, most of what we were living off then was Mum and Dad's life-insurance money. What's making you think of it now?'

'You are. Your reaction to Charlie. The way you always leap to my defence. I just remember you back then, massaging my shoulders and head when I got home every night. I know it drives me mad sometimes, how protective you are, but, you know . . .'

'You remember that I did that?' I was touched. Stella had never mentioned it before, or thanked me for all those nights when I soothed the anger and frustration out of her with love and oils, so that she could sleep peacefully, even though it usually meant that I was awake for hours afterwards worrying about her; believing her when she repeatedly wailed, 'I'm not doing it wrong!' Terrified that she'd get branded a thief.

Stella echoed my thoughts. 'You never patronized me or told me that I was probably making a mistake; you just kept agreeing with me: "I know you aren't. It's not you. Don't worry," with such conviction that it gave me the strength to go back in the next time, and sit like a zombie in that little bleeping cage, swiping and handing out Reward vouchers, bagging up people's sanitary towels and cereals, getting headaches from all the screaming fractious children and official warnings from the manager, all the time knowing that they thought I was probably robbing them . . .'

She broke off for a moment as we reached the gate, away from the silent somnolent trees, back into the roar of traffic and the grey poison of exhaust.

'I suppose I just wanted to say, Em, that you kept me going then. You always have. And even though I was pissed off with you for threatening to storm down there and ram a till-roll up Daphne's bum after they finally fired me – well, I suppose I did appreciate that you were angry on my behalf.'

I grinned. 'Have you still got that newspaper cutting?'

Stella smiled back at me. 'You bet. I keep meaning to frame it and put it on the wall as a reminder to keep the faith: "Daphne McVicar, 49, convicted for stealing over £11,000 from the tills at Sainsbury's, where she was a supervisor . . ." Fantastic.'

I stopped to rub the handle of my racket down my left leg, scratching an itch where I appeared to have been bitten by a mosquito.

'See?' I said, straightening up again. 'It all turns out OK in the end, if you just hang in there long enough.'

'But what about you? It didn't turn out OK for you finding your mother, did it?'

'Yes it did. I met Ruth and Evie. You could argue that it was the search which brought me closer to Denise and Greg too – if you and I hadn't had that scene in their garden at Christmas, I wouldn't have stayed up talking to them for so long. Then I helped Mack with his documentary. And, best of all, I met Robert, and all because I got off my ass and went to look for Ann Paramor.' Stella stopped, and I faced her.

'Just because I didn't find her doesn't mean I'm any worse off than I was before. I was depressed before. I'm not now. Ann Paramor gave me a life – literally, gave birth to me; and now it's like she has again.'

'But don't you *mind* that you didn't find her?'

I sighed. 'Well, of course I'm disappointed. Gutted, if I let myself think about it too hard. But I've got to tell myself that maybe it's better never to know – and maybe that's true. I mean, it could quite easily have turned out badly, and she could have been someone like Mack's birth mother. I always vowed that if I didn't find her within a few months then I wasn't going to keep trying, and that's what's happened. I can live with that.'

We walked on, turning the corner past the shops at the end of our road, which was when I heard the familiar throaty chug of the Harley slowing to a stop behind us. I turned to see Gavin taking off his helmet, revealing a broad grin on his disgustingly brown and healthy-looking face. Less hair than the last time I'd seen him, though.

'Anyone for tennis?' he said, glancing at my and

381

Stella's bare legs in shorts as he climbed off the bike and kicked the stand forwards. He advanced towards me but I remained still, my arms at my sides. What a weasel he looked in comparison to Robert, I thought coldly.

'Have you missed me?'

I shot a look at Stella, who was intently tracing a whorl of lichen on top of a low garden wall. 'Actually, no, I haven't.'

Gavin was a little taken aback. 'All right, Stell?' he said in her direction.

She ignored him. 'Well, I think I'll go on home and let you two talk,' she said to me.

'You're not walking home on your own!'

'Don't be ridiculous, Emma, you can see the house from here. I'll be fine.' She marched away, and I saw Gavin's eyes slide surreptitiously across her bottom as she walked. Curiosity got the better of me.

'Where have you been for the last six months, Gavin? Obviously not in prison, by the looks of that tan.'

Gavin hooked his helmet over his forearm – like Little Red Riding Hood's basket appropriated by the big bad wolf – put his hands on either side of my waist and tried to look into my eyes, but I shook him off.

'I've been in Goa. I just had to get away for a while, lie low. There was some deep shit going down. I'm really sorry. But I'm back now, and I was kind of hoping we could carry on where we left off. What do you think? You knew I was away, right? You got my message?'

I snorted, looking away to watch Stella walk towards the house, swinging her racket between her thumb and middle finger with each stride. She was walking slightly oddly, as if she were drunk; her feet in their big trainers seemed to be doing a small subtle dance on the pavement. I knew that she was probably just trying to avoid the cracks. She used to do that, often, when under stress.

I didn't even feel the old, tired urge to ask Gavin if they had a postal system in Goa, and if so, why he hadn't taken advantage of it. 'A lot's changed since then, Gav. More than you could imagine.'

He raised his eyebrows. 'Really? Did you find your mother then, or what?'

Stella turned right into our front garden, out of sight, and I opened my mouth to blurt out my rehearsed speech.

'Gavin—' I began. But I was interrupted by a truncated scream coming from outside our house.

37

'Shit! *Stella!*' I screamed back, ripping myself into a flat-out run, pounding the pavement, skidding round the corner and onto our front path. Stella was there, by the bamboo plant we'd given up for dead but which had finally started sprouting tiny new bright green leaves, but she wasn't alone.

She was clamped against Charlie's broad chest, face outwards, very similar to the way he'd held her at Yehudi's party, except that now there was an empty wine bottle held tightly against her throat, and her terrified face was the sickly greyish-white of a prawn cracker.

I stopped at the gate, barely able to breathe. 'What are you *doing*?'

I was trying to make my voice sound schoolmistressy and in control – this had once worked in a similar situation when Stella and I, walking alone in a dodgy part of East London, had been accosted by a hollow-eyed thirteen-year-old wielding a knife. He'd said, 'Give me your money,' and I had somehow managed to give him a withering look and say, pompously, 'Don't be so ridiculous. Come along, Stella,' as we brushed past him and on our way, unscathed.

But this time it didn't work, and my words came out in a mangled kind of shriek. I accidentally bit my tongue with panic, too. It tasted metallic: the taste of blood and fear. Charlie was a lot more intimidating than a skinny adolescent in a mangy parka with a flick knife. I gripped my racket, wondering if I could bash him over the head with the handle.

'This little slut has ruined my life,' Charlie said, almost conversationally, his words thick and slurred in Stella's ear. I could smell the alcohol coming from him, pumping like toxic emissions into the air with his mingled rage and adrenalin. He pulled the bottle harder and Stella gagged and whimpered against the thick green glass. She was trying to say something, but at first I could not work out what. I couldn't help thinking how *typical* that it was a wine bottle and not Scotch or vodka – what was worse than a psycho but an upper-class psycho? I couldn't see the label, but it was probably vintage.

Charlie, I thought, had probably gone to some minor public school where, being such a creep, he'd been ritually humiliated, bullied and beaten, leading to a lifelong inferiority complex and a desire to subjugate what he thought of as the weaker sex, nevertheless, at that moment I hated him in a way that I'd never hated anybody in my entire life. It was a strange and unpleasant emotion, but one which was quickly submerged again beneath the great stormy waves of my fear. I finally realized what Stella was repeating, like an invocation: '*But I dropped the charges; I dropped the charges; I dropped the charges.*'

She was trying to scream it, but she wasn't able to raise her voice above a strangled mantra.

I glanced to my right, but there was no sign of Gavin. Oh God, please don't let Gavin desert us now, I prayed, regretting the times I'd denounced him as a feckless flake, just in case it would somehow psychically count against us when we needed him most.

I was just deciding that it would be better to try and

aim the racket handle into Charlie's already (hopefully permanently) impaired groin, when there was a blur of movement behind him, and Gavin appeared, in flight, leaping dramatically off the low wall dividing our building from next door. He was shouting fearsomely, and landed an impressive punch to the side of Charlie's head which knocked him sideways and made him drop the bottle, releasing Stella. When I relived that moment later, it occurred to me that Gavin had probably really enjoyed it – it was the sort of Jackie Chan movement that Mack would have spent ages setting up, rehearsing and then shooting.

Charlie yelped with pain, and the bottle smashed on the ground. I dashed forwards and grabbed Stella, fumbling with trembling hands in my pockets for my keys, as Gavin and Charlie grappled one another on our narrow front path, locked together. With a small glimmer of satisfaction, I noticed that they were both rolling over the ornamental triangles of tile tips which formed the edge of the path.

They weren't far away from the broken glass, either, and satisfaction rapidly turned to anxiety at the thought of Gavin's back being ripped to shreds. However antipathetic I felt towards him, I didn't want to see him really hurt, especially not when he was leaping – literally – to Stella's rescue.

Gavin managed to roll on top and struggled to his feet, first pushing Charlie's chin backwards with the heel of his hand, and then kicking him as hard as he could in the ribs and chest and back. His formative years as a Bristol bootboy had obviously not gone to waste. It made a horrible dull thumping sound.

'Quick, get inside,' I said to Stella, pulling her sleeve and trying to make her look away, but she was transfixed with horror. As my unsteady right hand jiggled to try and get the key into the lock, I pressed Ruth's door buzzer with my left, praying that it wouldn't choose this opportunity to be temperamental. But she answered immediately and I howled into the intercom, 'Call the police, Ruth, now, there's a fight!'

I just couldn't get the damn key in. Gavin was still attacking Charlie, but Charlie had at least a two-stone advantage and, although very drunk, was much fitter. With a growl of pain he pushed Gavin away and lunged for the broken bottle neck.

I wanted to scream at them both, terrified that one of them would get killed, but it was as if all my energy had been used up. I opened my mouth, but nothing happened.

Squealing as if she were stamping on a large predatory spider, Stella rushed forwards before I could prevent her and jumped hard on Charlie's hand, making him release the bottle, before scuttling back to join me on the front door step.

'Hurry *up*,' she moaned, fidgeting and pressing herself against the door just as Ruth opened it, so she almost knocked Ruth over. I threw myself inside after her.

'I heard all the noise. What the hell's going on?' said Ruth aghast, taking in the grunting and rolling around of the two men outside, and then the sight of us, like a couple of facsimiles of Edvard Munch's *The Scream*. She was in her white towelling dressing gown, and her hair had a freshly washed wave and sheen to it. I felt unutterably hot and grubby in contrast.

'Gavin, Emma's ex,' Stella croaked as Ruth shut the door on them. Stella and I both slid down the wall and sat on the hall floor, hugging each other and quivering with adrenalin and a sort of sickened astonishment as the sound of a siren wailed in the distance.

Immediately afterwards we heard Gavin shout, 'And if you EVER come near her AGAIN, you're a DEAD MAN, do you UNDERSTAND?' There was a loud crack, a thud, and then a frenzied hammering on the door. The letterbox creaked open and I saw Gavin's eye peering frantically through, looking as wild as a bullock about to be slaughtered.

'It's me, Gav. Let me in, Emma, quick.' His voice

sounded disembodied, like he was all eye and voice and violence.

I hauled myself up, renewed terror giving me back my own voice. 'I don't want Charlie in here!' I screeched at him through the slot.

'He's out for the count. I nutted him. Please, Em, before the Old Bill gets here!'

Cautiously, I began to open the door and, as soon as I did, Gavin hurled himself inside and slammed the door behind us. He had a cut on his forehead, grazes on his knuckles, his eye was already beginning to swell, and he was breathing heavily. He bent down, palms on knees, to try and recover himself. We all stared at him as if he'd just beamed down from another planet.

'I don't want to talk to the police. Let me out the back door, baby, OK? I'll call you tomorrow and we'll have dinner.'

On cue, an eerie blue light swept around the hallway through the skylight above the door, and we heard the sound of car doors slamming.

I ushered Gavin down the hall and began unbolting the back door, pausing to look him full in the face. It seemed a bizarre way to formally end a long-dead relationship but, really, considering that it was Gavin, not very surprising.

'Thanks, Gav, I really appreciate your help. Thank God you were there,' I gabbled, aware that I didn't have the luxury of time on my side. 'But the truth is . . . I've met someone else. We've been together since you left, and we're really happy. I wish you all the best, but I don't ever want to see you again.'

For a moment he looked utterly flabbergasted, and I felt offended that he appeared to be so amazed that anyone else might fancy me. Then he shrugged. 'So I've blown it, then. Well, can't say I blame you, after all this time. I haven't exactly been Boyfriend of the Year. Be happy, sweetheart.'

As I opened the door, he leaned forward and kissed

me, briefly but very tenderly, on the lips. He smelled of sweat and the gristle of a fight, but none the less I caught a glimpse of the old, irresistible Gavin.

There was a heavy knock at the front door and the sound of a distant doorbell, and Gavin hared out into the evening. My last sight of him was as he crashed across Percy's regimented rows of geraniums and over the back wall, like Peter Rabbit trying to escape from Mr McGregor's garden. I knew I was never likely to see him again.

I hastily shut and bolted the back door, ran back up the hallway and hissed to Ruth and Stella, '*Don't let on we knew who Gavin was,*' before nodding at Ruth to open the front door.

There were the inevitable two officers in peak caps, a young and slightly nervous-looking woman police constable, and her partner, a lanky, skinny male one. I had a sudden feeling that the male one might have been the same as the one who turned up after Percy died, but then I wondered if policemen's faces had all just blended together for me into one shiny brass and dark serge amalgam of bad news. He was bending over the unconscious Charlie, pressing his ear against Charlie's chest, which was claret-coloured from the stream of blood swirling slowly out of his nose and down his face and neck. Ruth, Stella and I all goggled out, horrified, at his prone form.

When the PC straightened up, he had blood on the side of his own cheek. The WPC silently handed him a hankerchief, tapping a forefinger on the side of her face to indicate the problem, and the PC wiped himself down before stuffing the blood-speckled handkerchief back into his own pocket.

'I'll have that back when you've washed it,' the WPC muttered to him, flicking open her notebook and dropping her chin down to order an ambulance via the walkie-talkie at her shoulder.

'What do you know about this man?' The policeman finally addressed us, jerking a thumb back to the prone

Charlie. 'We'll need to take statements from whoever saw what happened. Who did this to him?' It couldn't be the same constable after all, for surely he'd have mentioned meeting us before.

'Why don't we all go up to my flat?' said Ruth. 'I think these two are a bit shocked, and I'd like to make them some tea or something. Plus my baby is upstairs on her own, and I want to get back to her to make sure she hasn't woken up.'

'Right you are. I'll wait for the ambulance, if you want to start on the statements upstairs,' said the WPC to her colleague.

Another ambulance, I thought wearily; more police statements. I felt like offering the Met our spare room, so we could have our very own PC as a lodger, to save them the cost of petrol and the little bulbs to swirl in their blue sirens.

I was beginning to feel more than a little unwell, actually, what with the gory sight of Charlie, and the discomfiting prospect of lying to the police about Gavin. The mere presence of the police still unnerved me. However friendly they were, I never seemed to get used to the strangeness of their uniforms or all the intimidating bits and bobs at their waists. Or the way they crackled constantly. They didn't seem like 'normal' people. I tried to imagine those two down the pub on a Friday night, in mufti, smoking fags and drinking bottled lager, but failed miserably. All I could see was a nine-year-old Stella, sewing and watching *Sleeping Beauty* with Ffyfield on her lap, still unaware that her life was ruined whilst PC whatever-his-name-had-been lurked in the hall outside.

We trudged upstairs with the constable, Stella and I on legs of jelly. In the mercifully calm sanctuary of Ruth's flat he took us, one by one, through the by-now familiar rigmarole of the statement. It felt like being called to the headmaster's study as he closed the living-room door behind us individually, and we in turn gabbled and stuttered, gesticulated and hesitated,

I hoping fervently Stella had managed not to drop Gavin's name into the proceedings.

When he had finally done both of us, Stella was white with the effort of not crying, and I was red with the same effort – but at least it was over. We all reconvened in the kitchen while the PC finished his notes.

I glanced at my sister, sitting at the table rubbing her throat with a spaced-out glassy wideness in her eyes. It hurt me to look at her, so I gazed around the room instead. Ruth's kitchen was identical to ours, except that at that moment hers felt, in my feverish imagination, haunted. Haunted by the memories of plates and a troubled cat. I wondered what had happened to Percy's cat. Had it run off, like Ffyfield? Unreliable beasts, I thought vaguely. Gavin was probably a cat in a former life. Then I remembered that the RSPCA had taken it away because we'd declined the offer to house it. It probably thought *we* were the unreliable beasts. I rested my forehead on the table, too weighed down to keep my head upright any more.

I wished that Robert and Zubin were there, and just about managed to summon up the energy to check my watch: it was only nine-thirty and they weren't expected back from Milton Keynes until late.

'I want Robert,' I said pathetically, my voice muffled. My muscles were beginning to ache now too, but I wasn't sure if it was from the tennis or the stress.

Ruth took over. 'Do you need any more details from us?' she asked the PC, who had reappeared in the doorway. He hesitated, and then pulled a business card out of his breast pocket, which he handed to Stella. It seemed odd to think of the police having business cards.

'I've got all I need for now, I think,' he said, consulting his scribbled notes. 'Obviously, as soon your assailant is fit to talk, we'll take a statement from him too. If you want to press further charges against him, then ring this number and we'll take it from there. He was lucky to escape a charge last time. You might want to reconsider the matter in the light of a second assault.'

Stella shook her head miserably.

Despite my exhaustion, I felt curious about Charlie's apparent lack of any sense of self-preservation, given his last close shave. 'Why *would* he risk it again? We think he's been hanging around here on and off for months. Surely he'd know it would make things worse for him if Stella changed her mind?'

The PC dipped his head knowledgeably, exposing a prematurely thinning patch of sandy hair on top of his head, which reminded me of Gavin. I hoped he'd got away all right.

'You'd be surprised', he said, 'how many of them take stupid risks. It's arrogance, usually, or alcoholism, making them think they can do whatever they like without redress. We see it all the time. Out on bail, under court order, whatever: they keep coming back regardless. I maybe shouldn't say it, but sometimes it takes a good kicking to get the message through in a language they understand. What I mean is,' he added hastily, lest we were about to level charges of police brutality at him, 'your have-a-go hero out there. We certainly don't condone that sort of behaviour, but if I were Charlie Simmonds with my face all smashed in, I might think twice about coming back again.'

'Let's hope so,' said Ruth. 'Have you got all you need from us now?'

The constable put away his notebook and replaced his peak cap, swivelling it briskly around to the correct position. 'Well, yes. Unless' – he jerked his thumb back in the direction of the window to indicate where Charlie had fallen – 'his story is significantly different from yours.'

'Which it probably will be, since he's a deranged liar and an alcoholic,' said Stella quietly. 'I wouldn't put it past him to say that *I* did this to him.'

'He can't,' I said, reaching down and squeezing her

shoulder. 'There's a witness this time. It's over, I'm sure of it.'

After the policeman left, we were all silent for a few minutes. Ruth put on the kettle, but then fetched a bottle of brandy from one of her kitchen cupboards, poured generous slugs into three glasses, and carried them in the fingers of one hand across to where Stella and I sat at the rickety Formica kitchen table. I envied Ruth her steady hands. Mine were still shaking so much that it was beginning to get on my nerves. We were all so inured to the *principle* of grown men punching and kicking the crap out of one another, because we saw it on television pretty much every day, but the reality of it – the bloody crunches and yelps of pain; the rage and the violence – that was an entirely different matter. I never wanted to witness anything like that ever again.

'Let's get this down us,' Ruth said eventually. We each tipped back our heads and drank, making versions of the same strange noise at the back of our throats as the brandy seared us.

The baby monitor was on one steady red light – indicating Ruth's extreme overprotectiveness, since Evie was only down the other end of the hall – and this somehow calmed me more than the alcohol flowing down my gullet. I had an overpowering urge to creep into Evie's room and watch her sleeping, but I felt too sullied by the evening's events. And surely, however bad I felt, Stella must have been feeling far worse.

'Are you sure you aren't injured, Stell? Did he hurt you?' I asked.

Stella put her hand to her throat again, exploring it, swallowing hard as if to see if she still could. There was a red mark against the white skin of her neck, but she shook her head. 'I think I'm OK,' she said croakily. 'The bottle hurt, but he only pressed hard when Gavin appeared, and that was only for a second. It's a bit painful to swallow, though.' She paused, staring at me with huge eyes. 'What's going to happen now, Emma? Will I have to go to court this time?'

I shook my head. 'I don't know. Probably not unless Charlie presses charges against Gavin, and then we'd have to be witnesses. But he can't press charges against Gavin unless he knows who he is. And frankly he'd be insane even to think about it.'

'Have they ever met before?' asked Stella, drilling her fingers into her temples and wincing. I moved round the table behind her and began to massage her head. Gradually she began to yield up some of her tension into my hands. It helped calm me too.

I racked my brains to try to remember if Gavin and Charlie's paths had ever crossed. 'Don't think so. God, I hope not. Otherwise Gav's really in trouble. But I don't think Charlie started hanging around here until after Gav and I split up, so Gavin should be in the clear.'

The kettle came to a noisy boil and Ruth stood up to make some tea.

'But won't *you* want to press charges this time, against whatshisname – Charlie?' she said as she threw teabags into mugs and poured boiling water on them.

'No. I couldn't face it,' Stella said dully. 'I just never want to see him again. I couldn't stand going over and over it, and then it would all come out about that night at the party again – and he'll probably end up suing *me*, like he said in that phone message . . .'

Her voice began to tremble, and I hugged her. 'You know, Stell, I really, really doubt that we will ever hear from him again, not after a hiding like that. Gavin was a totally unreliable boyfriend, but, like he boasted to me on many occasions, he was a good shit-kicker . . . And Charlie's too much of a coward. For all he knows, Gavin could be your new man.'

Ruth interrupted. 'Will someone please tell me where the infamous Gavin suddenly sprang from, like Superman, in your hour of need? I thought he was off the scene months ago?'

'He was,' I said, releasing Stella and pouring myself another small brandy. 'He just pitched up tonight after ringing me when we were playing tennis. He wanted us to get back together.' I laughed hollowly. 'Still, I'm glad he was there and not Robert or Zubin. I wouldn't have wanted to risk either of them getting injured fighting that schmuck.'

I pulled my phone out of my bag and dialled Robert's mobile. It was on voicemail. 'Robert, when you get this message, please can you and Zub come back? I'm really sorry to make you miss the rest of the gig, but something's happened. I'm fine but Stella needs to see Zub, and I need to see you. Don't worry, just please come back as soon as you can? Bye.'

We fell silent again as Ruth handed us each a mug of tea. I took a sip and my glasses instantly steamed up. Drifting down through the ceiling above came the faint sound of our telephone ringing, and then the click of our answering machine picking up.

'Wonder who that was?' I said, to no response from Stella.

A couple of minutes later, Ruth's door buzzer sounded. She picked up the entry phone in the hall and spoke into it, but it was dead. 'Nothing,' she said in disgust, shaking it. 'It was fine earlier, and now it's not working again. I can't even hear the traffic.'

The temperamental buzzer sounded again.

'At least yours makes a noise,' I said vacantly. 'I've lost clients because ours sometimes doesn't even buzz.'

'I don't want to let anyone in until I know who it is. It couldn't be the boys back already, could it?'

I shook my head. 'Doubt it, not unless they left an hour ago. They'd call our mobiles if they couldn't get in. And I didn't hear our doorbell ringing upstairs.'

Ruth tightened the belt of her dressing gown. There was a faint, rancid whiff coming from her right shoulder which marred her otherwise shining cleanliness: baby sick. 'I'd better go down and open the door. It might be the police again. Will you come with me, Emma, just in case it's . . .'

I nodded, feeling nauseous at the thought of an even more vengeful Charlie somehow struggling out of Casualty, like a zombie crawling out of a tomb, back for another go at Stella. No, that would be impossible. He was in no fit state to do anything except have his smashed nose X-rayed.

'Come on,' I said to Ruth over the noise of the buzzer being pressed a third time. 'Stella, you stay here.'

She nodded, looking catatonic again. 'What a day,' I heard her whisper as we left the room.

38

I followed Ruth down the stairs, grateful for the solid smooth roundness of the banister, feeling so tired that I could have just lain down then and there on the stairs and gone to sleep. After two brandies, I was also feeling fuzzy-headed and swimmy. I fervently hoped it wasn't the police again, come to arrest us for covering up for Gavin – I didn't think I'd be capable of stringing together a convincing sentence.

Ruth bent down, prising open the letterbox with her thumbnail and calling through it: 'Who's there?'

A man's voice answered, startlingly familiar yet oddly unplaceable. 'I'm looking for Emma Victor. Does she still live in this building? I rang but nobody's in, and as your light was on, I thought I'd ask if you knew her.'

Where did I recognize that voice from? My first thought was perhaps an old boyfriend of Stella's, or maybe someone like Greg Hiscock, someone that I didn't see a lot of but knew quite well. It was a comforting voice, and it gave me a warm feeling, welcome after the harsh events of the night.

Curious, I gently pushed Ruth aside and peered through the letterbox myself, shuddering at the recent memory of Gavin's fight-widened eyes framed in the same rectangular space. I was at waist level with a pair of jeans: clean, but respectably faded around the knees and pockets. At the bottom of my peripheral vision I could still see a dark bloodstain on the path.

'Who is it?' I called. There was the sound of leather shoes creaking and the person crouched down.

I saw two brown eyes regarding mine through the letterbox: calm eyes in tanned, slightly wrinkled skin. A beard, once dark brown, now salt-and-pepper, decorated the edges of a broad, square-jawed face that I knew – or, at least, used to know . . .

I looked slowly up again, back into the eyes, and saw they were full of tears. We were both silent.

With a colossal emotional *whump* in my solar plexus I thought how I knew this person, and wondered how I could ever have doubted that he was still alive . . . why on earth hadn't I kept the faith in those long, dark nights after the funeral, when I dreamed that it was all a mistake, and it would all be OK, it was all just a great big administrative blunder which, given time, would get sorted out?

I was torn, for a second, between running straight upstairs to grab Stella and bring her down, or flinging open the front door and jumping into his arms like I used to do when I was a kid, arms around his neck, legs around his waist, the blissful smell of him: pipe tobacco and wool, aftershave and mint . . .

It was the moment I'd longed for, dreamed of, fantasized about for a decade. But I did neither, because at that same moment the hall walls began to close in on me, squeezing the breath from me, and the tiled floor started to rock and undulate, spinning me around like a top until I felt too dizzy to do anything but blink and blink to try and refocus my blurred world . . .

'*Daddy?*' I whispered through the letterbox, right before it all went dark and I crashed backwards into oblivion.

* * *

When I came round on the cool tiles of the hall floor, he and Ruth were kneeling over me. My glasses had fallen off and my vision was blurred, but I could see that he was crying. Ruth's face had folded into creases of confusion, concern, anxiety.

I wanted to hear him laugh, not see him cry. That was how I remembered him: laughing. But then, with a pain in my heart more vicious than anything I'd experienced before, I realized that it wasn't Dad at all.

Just somebody who looked astonishingly like him.

Ruth handed me my glasses, and I began to struggle up to a sitting position, feeling utterly defeated and more than a little embarrassed. Fainting – for God's sake. Such a ludicrous, hysterical, Victorian thing to do.

'Emma,' the man said. 'I'm so sorry. I would never have sprung this on you. I didn't think you were in, which is why I rang your neighbour's doorbell, to check you really lived here. I looked you up in the phone book – you said you lived in Shepherd's Bush in that documentary. I'm his brother. I'm Tony. I'm Ted's brother.'

I took a deep, painful breath, unable to speak at all for a couple of minutes. 'Ruth,' I croaked eventually. 'Please can you go upstairs and warn Stella, if she's up to it, so that she doesn't get the same shock as I've just had? He looks just like our dad . . .'

'I'll get you a glass of water,' she said, standing up.

'No, don't, I'm fine.' I reached out for her hand. 'Don't tell Stella I passed out. In fact, don't tell Stella anything unless you think she can handle it. She's too freaked out already as it is. We'll come up in a few minutes.'

Ruth bent down again and hugged me, both her knees clicking like the snap of dead branches, and then she retreated down the hall and up the stairs to her flat.

Uncle Tony and I sat there in the hall, in silence. I couldn't bear to look at him; it hurt too much. The weight of disappointment pressed me to the floor and prevented me from moving at all. Plus, I had absolutely no idea what to say to him. I'd never even met him before.

'Did you know they were dead?' I asked eventually, still not meeting his eyes.

'No. I couldn't believe it. When? How?'

'Ten years ago. A car crash. In Wiltshire.'

Uncle Tony raked his top teeth over the beard beneath his lower lip, and dropped his head into his folded arms. 'What a mess,' he said, his voice muffled in the sleeve of his sweater. 'Oh Jesus, what a mess.' He sounded almost as if he was crying again.

I huffed through my nose. A mess it most certainly had been. 'I tried to get in touch with you, to let you know so you could come to the funeral, but nobody seemed to know where you were.'

'That was because I didn't want anybody to know.'

Finally, I lifted my chin and gazed at him. Now that the shock was receding, the experience was bitter-sweet. Close up, I could tell he wasn't Dad, for they weren't by any means identical. There was an un-mistakable similarity, though, as if Dad had dressed up as a hippy for a fancy-dress party, and never quite relinquished the feel of the costume. Once I started to look at him, I couldn't stop; he was a better reminder than a photograph ever could be. And even better, he was family. Stella and I had family again.

'You're so like him.'

'I know. At least, we always were as kids. I wonder what he'd look like now.'

You, I thought. He'd still look like you.

'I haven't – hadn't – seen him for thirty years. Twenty years *before* he died.'

'He never talked about you.' I traced a pattern around the diamonds of glazed putty holding the floor tiles in place. I felt I needed some putty to hold myself together after the shocks of the evening.

'We fell out.'

400

'What could be so bad that you don't speak for twenty years? Dad wasn't the sort to fall out with people. He hated arguments.'

Uncle Tony winced and looked away. Then he moved around so that he was sitting next to me, our backs against the wall, our shoulders almost touching.

'It's a long story. Can I tell you another time?'

I leaned away from him, feeling that I couldn't handle this unexpected proximity. Thirty years of nothing, and now here he was wanting to rub shoulders with me? Where had he been when we needed him?

He sensed that I was rolling myself up into a ball and, to his credit, he edged slightly away from me too.

'I didn't even know Stella existed until I saw her in the programme with you,' he said, fiddling with something in his jacket pocket which sounded like keys, a muffled heavy jingling. My uncle's fingers, fiddling with his car keys. It was amazing. We had a real uncle.

'She's lovely, isn't she?' he continued. He had a faint Scottish accent, and it sounded like a successful version of one of the impressions Dad used to try to do for us. *Donald, where's your trooosers?* 'You both are. But she looks so like Barbara. I couldn't believe it, that they ended up having a child of their own – another child, I mean . . .' He tailed off.

'It's OK,' I said. 'I know what you mean. Yes, it was a complete surprise to them. I was ten when Stella was born.'

My bottom was beginning to get numb on the hard tiled floor, and I shifted uncomfortably, relaxing enough to begin to slowly uncurl. I stretched my legs out in front of me, and then noticed how stubbly, bordering on hairy, they were. I hadn't cared if Gavin saw them, but now I felt self-conscious. Was it appropriate to mind if one's uncle observed one's hairy legs or not? Was it normal? I had no idea if uncles and nieces even hugged and kissed hello and goodbye, or if they shook hands. Still, I could ask Stella to ask Suzanne later. Or Mack might know.

Mack, I thought. He'd be delighted with this un-expected corollary to his documentary. As for Stella, she'd be over the moon.

'Why don't you come up and meet her? She's – well, we've all – had a bit of a shock tonight; something happened earlier. I won't bore you with the details now. But I'm sure she'll be ecstatic about meeting you.'

I began to push myself up to standing, still a little wobbly, but more optimistic.

'You know,' I said, 'I had this secret hope that my birth mother might see the documentary and get in touch, but this is almost as good. And who knows, she still might.'

'She won't,' said Uncle Tony, putting his hand on my arm.

I froze, palms flat, stuck like a barnacle halfway up. 'Pardon?' I felt stiff all over, not just from the tennis but from shock, like a pillar of salt. I wished Robert was there to lick me back into life.

'You'd better sit down again. I think I should tell you now, while we're alone.'

I felt myself turn pale, and the black spots on the hall tiles detached themselves and began to dance in front of my eyes again. Uncle Tony peeled my hands away from the wall and held them in his – oh his hands! They were Dad's hands, down to the half-moons on the fingernails and the fine black hairs between the knuckle and the first joint. I couldn't pull away from him this time.

'You *knew* my mother?'

'Yes. And I'm so, so sorry, Emma, but she died, some time ago.'

My lips trembled violently, cartoonishly, and I bit down hard on the lower one to stop it. I couldn't swallow the lump in my throat; it just seemed to be inflating itself, bigger and bigger, as I looked into the brown eyes in front of me. I thought of Dad comforting me in the larder over Pat Short with those same eyes, the same hands.

Finally I forced the lump down far enough that I could speak again. 'How ... did you know my mother?'

A tear sprang out of his eye and I watched it, with something approaching detached fascination, slide down his cheek until it disappeared into the undergrowth of his beard. I was a little embarrassed at his emotion. *Dad* had never cried, not to my knowledge. In fact, I'd never seen a grown man cry before. Why was he crying anyway? It was I who should be crying. He'd just told me that my birth mother was dead.

A big lorry thundered past outside with a rumble which shook the house very slightly. Tony gulped, and stared intently through the fanlight above the door, above my head.

'Emma, the reason that I knew your mother was because I'm your natural father.'

39

It turned out that the pyramid lady, holistic Ann – she of the orange lipstick and deep voice – had been kind of right when she'd announced that she would be the one to make it all fall into place for me. This thought occurred to me much later that night, as Tony – my father – and I sat alone at the kitchen table, drinking tea. He talked himself hoarse, and I mostly just listened, gazing at him with awe. My father. How had I managed to overlook the probability of his existence for all those years?

Of course, there had been a few scenarios involving him, which I'd concocted when I was younger: that he was a one-night stand from a party, whose name Ann had never asked; or a holiday romance conducted with love as an interpreter when the language barriers became too great. Perhaps he was a beautiful fading consumptive whose dying act was to create a baby as a lasting memorial to his love for my mother; or even a prisoner of conscience, languishing in a dank cell with rays of distant sun slanting through the bars onto the one tatty photograph he had of the girl he adored. (Well, I was *much* younger when I came up with the last two.)

But he'd always been a fictional character to me,

someone whose speech I read in mental inverted commas. Because I'd had Ann's name and not his, I'd always assumed that I wouldn't stand a chance of tracking him down unless I found her first.

Stella had gone to bed, some time earlier. She hadn't really taken it in, on top of everything else that had already happened. Ruth did go up to forewarn her, and Stella had come crashing down the stairs, two by two, to meet her uncle. But soon afterwards she lapsed into uncharacteristic silence, just staring from him to me and back again, pensively rolling her tongue stud. I knew it would take her a few days to get her head around it all.

'Ask Zub to come in to me when they get back, will you?' she said finally. 'It doesn't matter if I'm already asleep.' Then she paused, and kissed us both goodnight.

'You're my cousin now as well as my sister,' were her parting words to me. 'How weird is that? Two for the price of one.'

It was Tony's wife, Melissa, whose attention had been caught by what she believed to be a programme on television about pyramid energy. Since Melissa was herself a t'ai chi instructor, Tony told me, and very interested in holistic practices, she'd stopped channel-hopping and begun to watch.

After a short scene in which a gruff, freckly, middle-aged Yorkshire woman explained the principles of pyramid power to an anxious-looking dark-haired girl, the camera had panned back to show the banner above the pyramid stall: 'Love Lines Inc. (Ann Paramor, specialist in Pyramid Energy and Crystal Layouts)'.

'I was in the kitchen at the time,' said Tony, 'chopping a chilli.' He paused. 'I lived on a remote Hebridean commune during the seventies, where there wasn't much in the way of spicy food, and I've been fanatical about it ever since. She called out to me, something like, "Ann Paramor — wasn't that the name of your ex, the one who died?" So I said, "yes", and she said, "That's weird. There's an Ann Paramor on TV at the moment, that's all. It looks like a really interesting programme, actually. Pyramid energy – I've always wanted to know more about that. Check it out." '

And so Tony had tipped the chillis into a frying pan of sizzling onions and walked into the sitting room, barefoot, still holding a small sharp knife stained with hot red juice. He'd leaned on the back of the armchair in which his wife sat curled up, and looked at the television, not really noticing the woman with the same name as the woman whose life he'd ruined so long ago. Instead, he had been transfixed by the other person in the frame. A short but attractive bespectacled girl – his words – late twenties, perhaps, carrying a strange electric-blue furry garment bundled up under her arm like a small artificial dog, looking earnestly at the pyramids.

I laughed at him having noticed the Furby jacket, but my hands were still shaking, so I cupped them around my warm mug and clung on.

'There was something about the curve of your jaw, and that slight bump on your nose . . . It just seemed so familiar somehow.'

The camera had panned away and caught another girl in its wide gaze: a taller, younger, beautiful girl with mad blonde zigzags for hair and, oddly, an equally familiar face. The camera followed her intently as she approached the pyramid stand.

'I asked Melissa who the two actresses were. I thought I'd seen them – you – in other things on TV. She told me it was a documentary. She'd thought it was about pyramids, but now she wasn't so sure.'

Then the blonde girl had spoken to the woman with the orange lips: *'This is my sister Emma, who's an aromatherapist. We were just passing your stand earlier and something drew me to you. This is a bit delicate . . . I hope you don't mind me asking you this, but . . . did you, by any chance, have a baby girl who you gave up for adoption?'*

'My onions were sticking,' said Tony abruptly. 'I had to run back into the kitchen. I decided it was all just a figment of my guilty imagination. It still plays on my mind, Emma, all these years later. I've done so many hours of meditation, put so many miles between me and what had happened when I met Ann, but I—'

He broke off, struggling for composure but still holding my gaze. For a few moments he was unable to speak.

'Then I heard the voiceover from the television screen and it stopped me in my tracks . . .'

My voice had penetrated his brain; tiny innocuous words like the seeds inside the chilli, with a bite shocking enough to spring tears to his eyes and a burn to his heart. A voice, from out of the television, which he never thought he would hear: *'The thing is that I'm adopted, and I've recently discovered that my birth mother's name is Ann Paramor. I've found several Ann Paramors, but you're the first one I've actually met.'*

Tony spoke slowly and carefully, as if he was concentrating on his own words. 'Melissa ran straight into the kitchen – I'd told her about you already, of course. She hugged me, and I remember that she made this really strange sound, a cross between a gasp and a sort of . . . shocked moan, I suppose. But the weird thing was that it was just like the sound Ann Paramor made . . . when I told her I was leaving her.'

It was then that he finally dropped my gaze, and looked away from me, pulling his lower lip in underneath the top one so that a little brush of bristles from the front of his beard popped up horizontally. I studied it, so that I wouldn't have to see the shame in his eyes.

'What happened?' I asked, holding my breath.

Tony told me how he'd met my mother. How, in the space of six weeks in the early summer of 1970, he had

407

wooed her, charmed her into cheating on her much older husband, and, when she told him she was pregnant, persuaded her to run away with him so that they could bring up their baby together. But not long before I was born, the reckless adrenalin rush and forbidden thrill of the affair had palled. Ann's husband had written to Tony to inform him that he was welcome to Ann, that she was an unstable, hysterical bitch and they deserved one another; and Tony had realized that he was twenty-two years old and did not wish to be saddled with a manic-depressive – for so Ann was emerging to be – or a baby that neither of them really wanted nor could adequately take care of.

I stood up abruptly, scraping the chair legs back with a screech, and marched across to the sink; ran the cold tap at full strength; filled a glass; drank. My mother was a manic-depressive hysterical bitch, and neither of my real parents had wanted me, I thought with a dull throb of horror. It was the worst-case scenario I'd always feared. At the very least I had hoped that they'd given me away because they couldn't physically afford to raise a baby, not because they simply didn't want me . . .

'I'm sorry, Emma, that was a terrible thing for me to say. It was much more complicated than that. It wasn't that we didn't want you, personally, it was the circumstances. Please try and understand. I can't bear the thought that I've hurt you so much. And Ann. I hurt Ann so badly.'

I turned to face him again. He was still seated at the table, his lip trembling. I took a deep breath, refilled my glass with water, and sat down again. 'Go on,' I said.

Exercising his powers of persuasion, Tony had told Ann the sad story of how his older brother Ted, and Ted's wife Barbara, were desperate for a child of their own, but were unable to conceive. He explained how it would really be for the best for Ann and himself not to be tied down with a child after all, when they were so young – Ann was only twenty. They needed time for one another, to establish their own relationship. Then maybe they could think about starting a family.

So the deed was done. Tony was briefly delighted at the joy he'd brought to Ted and Barbara, and at the neat solution he believed had been wrought. But Ann, he said, had taken it badly. Instead of getting better, once the threatened burden of unexpected motherhood had been lifted, she went further downhill, until all traces of the high-spirited, outrageous, fun girl Tony had originally seduced were gone.

'When I first got that letter from her husband I assumed that he was just calling her names to vent his rage. It was only gradually that I realized that he'd been right. She was – oh God, Emma, I hate to say it – but she *was* unstable. She was lonely too, I suppose, and isolated. She blamed me for everything; badgered me day and night to let her go and see her baby girl. I couldn't handle it . . . Do you want me to stop now?'

He reached across the table and took my hand, icy cold in his warm grasp. I thought again of Dad – Ted – my uncle. Oh, this was too confusing. Did I have two fathers, or two uncles? I couldn't bear to think about poor Ann, frightened and confused, railing against Tony, about to discover that even he was leaving her. But I couldn't not hear it, either. 'No. I'm OK.'

He continued, not letting go of my hand but holding on to it until warmth gradually flowed back into it, softening the blow of his words.

By then, he said, Ted and Barbara had legally adopted me. It was too late for Ann to get me back – and, despite everything, Tony felt he had done the right thing. At least he knew that I would have a happy, secure future. It was the present he couldn't deal with. Eventually he announced to Ann that he'd had enough, and headed off to the remotest place he could think of: a commune he'd heard about in the Hebrides.

Ann's husband Doug Paramor declined to take her

back – he'd already settled down with a portly middle-aged widow he'd met at Bingo, with whom he felt far more content. Ann succumbed to bouts of manic depression and, via Doug, Tony heard that she'd spent several protracted spells in a mental hospital in Wiltshire.

After a few difficult years, however, Ann recovered enough to hold down a part-time job and live on her own, in a cottage near Salisbury. She'd looked up Dad's name in the phone book and begun a sporadic correspondence with him and Mum, enquiring after my welfare and progress at school, in which Mum cautiously participated, because she felt so sorry for Ann.

'I saw those letters after she died. Doug sent them to me. Your mother – Barbara – hadn't gone into too much detail, but she did admit that, however much it had benefited her and Ted, they'd been disgusted at my behaviour in arranging the adoption and then deserting Ann. The last time they saw me was just after I walked out on her.' Tony stopped again, and pulled at his beard.

'I called in to say goodbye to them both, on my way up to Scotland, and it all blew up into a colossal row. You were just a few months old, and were sitting wailing on Barbara's lap, with so many harsh words flying back and forth above your head. I remember looking at you and feeling that this was it, there was no going back now. You were my child and I'd never see you again . . .'

Tony was crying once more. I squeezed his hand. 'But you did see me again, eventually.'

He nodded and squeezed back. 'Thank God. I did. I'm so glad, Emma. I've thought of you so often, wondered how you turned out. It's so fantastic to know.'

So Mum had felt, at least indirectly, in some way responsible for Ann. That would account for the letters, I thought. I wondered what sort of things she'd written to her, how much she'd told Ann about me. Tony appeared to read my mind.

'I wish I'd kept her letters for you, but I threw them away. I was upset, I suppose, because Barbara wrote that she thought it better that no one heard from me. At the time I felt that I'd just been written out of your life, but I understand now why she said it. She was only thinking of you. She also told Ann that she hoped Ann would understand, but she did not want you to know that her mother and her birth mother were in communication, not until you were an adult.'

'But they didn't tell me anything about Ann, not even after I turned sixteen.'

'Did you ask?'

I thought back. 'Well, no, I suppose I didn't. I was desperate to know, but I was afraid it would upset Mum and Dad if I declared that I wanted to meet her. Besides, I believed that they didn't even know who she was.'

Tony leaned towards me and took my other hand in his too. 'Ann really did care about you, Emma. Whatever else she did or said, she loved you very much. But she got much iller again. You'd have been about nineteen by then.'

'Which I was when Mum and Dad died.'

'They must have all died in the same year.'

We were silent, thinking about it.

'She obviously wrote to Ted and Barbara again, begging to see you. The last letter from them was explaining why they didn't think it would be a good idea, not unless you were asking to meet her. The law then stated that a birth mother could not seek out her child; the impetus had to come from the child. I think this suited Barbara and Ted very well. Reading between the lines, they were probably afraid that Ann would put pressure on you to be a daughter to her; or worse, expect you to take care of her. I think they offered to visit her themselves, though, to check that she was OK and properly medicated. I don't know whether they ever did that.'

I had a horrible, horrible thought.

What if, on the day of the accident, Mum and Dad hadn't been going to a wedding in Wiltshire at all, but to see Ann? It was too awful to contemplate. But then I remembered Mum all dressed up with her sparkly clutch bag and good shoes on, and Dad brushing lint off the arm of his suit with a funny little sticky roller thing. They must have been going to a wedding. They wouldn't have pretended otherwise; they weren't duplicitous.

'What is it, Emma? You look pale again.'

I opened my mouth to voice my concerns. Then I closed it again, clamping my lips together. 'Nothing. I'm fine.'

Some things were best left alone.

Ann's suicide note had been found at the cottage, on top of a pile of all Mum's letters to her over the years, and a faded, creased photograph of me, aged seven, gap-toothed and innocent of all the heartache I was causing.

Tony had let go of my hands just long enough to pull that same photograph out of his wallet and lay it in front of me, when we heard two sets of feet pounding up the stairs, making us both jump.

Robert burst through the door, stopping short when he saw me sitting in the kitchen, holding hands with a strange man and crying. Zub piled comically into the back of him, and then peered over his shoulder.

'What's going on? What's the matter?' demanded Robert in a panicked voice, giving Tony an extremely dirty look.

I wiped my eyes and smiled at him. 'Hi, darling. Zub, Stella's gone to bed. She wants you to go and see her anyway, even if she's asleep.'

Zubin turned and vanished into Stella's room, kicking off his trainers on the way and leaving them sprawled in the hall. Even in the emotionally heightened circumstances, I felt a faint stab of annoyance.

'Well?' said Robert.

I stood up, my legs so shaky that I wondered where my kneecaps had got to, and walked over to him, sliding my arms around his waist and burying my face in his chest. When I looked around, I saw that Tony had got up too, and was holding out his hand towards Robert.

'Robert,' I said, my voice as wobbly as my legs. 'I'd like you to meet my . . . father.'

40

Tony and I saw each other every day over the next fort-
night. He stayed in a local B. & B. for a couple of
nights, and then in the spare room at Robert's flat,
spending every possible minute with me. Other
people drifted in and out, extras to our talking heads,
filling in details, providing colour: Stella, Robert,
Ruth, Mack, and then Tony's wife Melissa, who came
down from Scotland to join him after a few days. She
was gorgeous: calm and beautiful, with a mass of curly
brown hair and appealingly crooked Dracula teeth,
like David Bowie's before he got them capped. She
showed us how she could leave two puncture marks in
an apple, and taught me and Stella some Qi Gong. She
laughed an impulsive, delighted laugh whenever
Stella insisted on calling her Auntie Melissa. She was
my stepmother, kind of.

Mostly, however, Tony and I just talked. Talked and
cried and talked. After a few days, we tentatively
hugged. And then we cried again. He'd been terrified,
he said, that I would hate him for what he'd done.

But how could I hate him? After everything that had
happened over the past year, the one thing I'd learned
was that we had to make the choices which felt right
to us, and to live with the consequences, whatever

they were. It was our responsibility, and no one else's. Poor Ann, I thought, young and ill and easily swayed. But it wasn't Tony's fault that she hadn't been strong enough to do what she really wanted to do: keep me. And this, for me, made all the difference.

He and I were out on our own for a walk one day, along the river just past Hammersmith Bridge, when Tony pointed at a nearby bench. He looked anxious and edgy, as if he'd been wrestling with some kind of knotty internal problem and then come to a decision.

'Sit down for a minute, I want to show you something.'

I sat, noticing the dull brass plaque screwed to the back of the bench: 'In memory of Elizabeth Hannon. She loved this place'. Underneath, in green aerosol, someone had sprayed 'Shaz is a slut'. I turned my back on it and watched the thick swirling water flow past.

Tony reached in his trouser pocket and pulled out a crumpled envelope. Sitting down next to me, he extracted an old photograph and handed it to me, and I felt a physical swooping in my belly.

'Ann.' We both said it at the same time.

She was a small woman, except for her nose, which sat awkwardly on her face as if dropped on there from a great height. She looked dislocated, uncomfortable in her skin and whey-pale, with a large mole near her left eye. Her hair was the same colour as mine, but dull, with a stubborn sort of curl. She was leaning against a mantelpiece, raising a glass of red wine in a toast, but with an expression of abject misery on her face. She looked nothing like me.

'She wasn't very well then,' said Tony. 'She was so beautiful when I first met her, but it wasn't because she had a stunning face or anything. She just had so much – energy. Vitality, I suppose. It's so sad . . .'

His voice trailed off once more, and he rubbed his beard. The small scratchy sound it made sent a funny electric sort of shock down my legs; not sexual, just the realization that these two people, one real, one on photographic paper, had given birth to me. Their absence in my lives had made me into who I was.

The next afternoon I had a couple of massages to do, so Tony and Melissa took Stella out for lunch. They discovered a mutual love of explosive curries, and were gone for hours, returning with scalded tongues and garlic breath, tipsy with Cobra beer; and Tony announced himself fully up to speed on everything in Stella's life.

They had had a long chat about Charlie, in which Stella had finally made peace with her decision to drop the original charges, and not pursue this latest attack despite the obvious, and understandable, disapproval of the police. In her mind, Charlie had got what he deserved, without anybody else – i.e. herself, me, Zub, Charlie's family – having to suffer further.

'Karma,' Tony said, and Melissa agreed solemnly.

Stella had also told Tony that she and Zubin were going to get a flat together – which was news to me. I felt a momentary panic, until I remembered that I spent most days at Robert's anyway, and really it was as if she and I had stopped living together months ago. I wouldn't miss Zubin's trainers in the hall, either.

'I think we should sell the flat, then, and split the money,' I said recklessly. Robert had been badgering me for weeks to move in with him permanently, but I'd been reluctant to abandon Stella, in case things didn't work out between her and Zub. Old habits died hard . . .

But, in the long term, Robert wanted to be closer to his daughter Grace. Every time we came back from Nottingham he marvelled about what she'd learned in his absence: colouring inside the lines; understanding and following the 'dee-structions' for a new board game; singing 'Trinkle trinkle little star' in a round. I could have listened to him talk about her all day, just for the expression on his face. And Grace was such a lovely, funny little girl, with a fearsome comedy frown and a brilliant smile.

When we were with her, I surreptitiously studied the way she interacted with her mother and stepfather and realized that she ebbed and flowed between all the adults in her life, effortlessly adapting to the different personalities around her. It made me think that perhaps the circumstances of my childhood, or even Stella's, hadn't been all that remarkable after all. Families came in all shapes and sizes.

Mack begged me to let him make a follow-up documentary, a sort of 'what happened next', but I stood my ground and refused. I'd had enough of baring my soul on television. I wanted to put it all behind me and move on. Besides, the first documentary had been so well received that Mack had a constant stream of work offers.

But I did think about how different a programme it would have made this time. I could see why Mack wanted to do it. I could see it when I looked in the mirror, when I opened my mouth to speak, when I lay down to sleep curled up close to Robert at night. Everything was different. I felt that instead of my cells renewing themselves gradually over a seven-year period, it had all happened at once and I'd sloughed off my old body and suddenly become a new person. For the first time in my adult life, I felt the feathery wings of freedom take hold of me and lift me up, as if throwing me into the sky, confident in the knowledge that I'd fly. It was the most amazing feeling.

41

Towards the end of summer, when the late sun was getting weaker and the shadows on the pavement skinnier, Tony came down to London again, alone this time, announcing that Melissa had just found out that she was six weeks pregnant.

'My *second* child's due in early June,' he said when he arrived at the flat, a broad smile elongating the word 'early' even further than his acquired Scottish accent already had. He looked fantastic, I thought, much brighter-eyed, without the hovering anxiety of his last visit. Even his beard had been cropped into angular topiary on his chin – not quite George Michael, thankfully, but much smarter and far less hippyish. When he rubbed it, it no longer made such a rustling sound, more a brisk zipping.

I had some news of my own, which I'd been saving for when I saw Tony face to face. When I waggled my finger to show off the small sparkly diamond engagement ring Robert had given me just the week before, Tony smiled an even wider beam of delight. And, unless I was very much mistaken, pride.

'That's fantastic news,' he said joyfully. 'I want to hear all about it over lunch. Are we meeting Stella there?'

I hesitated. 'Yes. But, um, before we go . . . I wanted to ask you something.'

'Anything.'

'Would you . . . um, I mean, would it be OK if . . . Do you think . . .' I was beginning to hyperventilate, and I could feel my face getting damp and hot with fluster. I felt even more vulnerable than when I'd visited the Ann Paramors, and really began to understand why Robert had been so nervous when he proposed to me.

We had gone for what I thought was a normal day out to London Zoo, and I couldn't figure out why Robert was so jumpy and distracted – until we got to the orang-utan enclosure. There, with an audience more than likely comprised of Betsey's nieces and nephews, clustered on the bank on their side of the fence, all collapsed down into seated positions like a display of fold-up pushchairs in a baby shop, Robert got down on one knee and handed me the tiny ring box. The orang-utans looked solemnly across at us, as if appreciating the momentous occasion – apart from one baby one, who was loping cautiously around on the grass, showing off his smooth hairless inner arms as he swung around a tree-trunk, like Gene Kelly in *Singin' in the Rain*.

'Oh, yes please, definitely,' I'd said as I jumped tearfully into Robert's arms, half expecting a haphazard smattering of leathery applause to drift across to us.

Tony was looking at me with the same loving expression I'd seen in my other dad's eyes, long ago, when I'd been crying in the larder with prepubescent outrage and heartache.

'Come on then, spit it out,' he said as I dithered and bumbled and couldn't meet his gaze.

'I – er – wondered if you might consider . . . giving me away at my wedding,' I finally blurted out, the blood roaring in my ears.

My father held out his arms to me. 'I'd be honoured,' he said.

I burst into tears.

* * *

Stella met us at the Yellow River Café – she'd come straight from her and Zub's new flat in Putney – and when she heard Tony's news, she poked me in the ribs.

'There you go, Em, another little brother or sister for you to fuss over,' she said, and I gave her a hard stare.

'I'm so happy for you,' I told him. 'Specially because I won't have to take care of this one. It can come and stay with its big sister and her husband, and then we'll put it on the train back home to Scotland again afterwards.'

'Now you're getting married, do you and Robert think you'll start a family soon?' Tony asked, as we settled ourselves around a table and perused menus.

Stella laughed a loud barking laugh. 'Is the Pope Catholic?' she hooted. 'Of course Emma's going to have children. It's *obvious* that Emma is going to have children. You're *gagging* to have children, aren't you, Em?'

As it happened I had, by then, well and truly got over my earlier fear that I'd never be willing to put myself through the fearful protectiveness of parenthood. I'd watched Robert with Grace, and Ruth with Evie, and realized that the measure of instinctive adoration a parent felt for a child far outweighed the terror of that child being harmed in any way.

'Actually,' I said, lowering my menu and withering Stella with a glance before turning to my father, 'yes, I do, and I hope we will – but not for a few years yet. Robert and I see Grace, who's nearly five, every other weekend and that's lovely; but to be honest I'm sort of tired of looking after everybody else.'

I saw Stella's stunned face. Her tongue stud appeared slowly from between her lips before sinking back out of sight again as she took this in.

'I don't mean just you, Stell. I mean, generally, I want to stop caretaking. Looking for my birth mother was the start of it, but now I want to let go of everything else I've been clinging on to: even the baby massage and the aromatherapy business. I want to do something for myself. I want to travel.'

'*Travel?*' Stella was obviously remembering how I got galloping nervous diarrhoea just organizing the two of us on a charter flight, for a week at a hotel in Portugal on our last holiday, four years earlier.

'Yes, travel. I told Robert, and he said he's always wanted to do it too, so we're going to take an extended honeymoon. At least six months. It's going to be hard for him to be away from Grace for that long, but when we come back, we'll buy a house closer to where she lives. Listening to all Tony's stories of his travels made me realize how much I want to see some of the world before I think about having a family. There are so many things I know nothing about. I want to go and eat real Chinese food in China. I want to climb up mountains in Nepal, and do a Vipassana course in India and – and – oh, *everything*. Once we sell the flat, I'll be able to use my half of the money from that.'

'Wow,' said Stella.

'That's fantastic,' said Tony.

'Thanks,' I said, beaming at them both.

Two elderly ladies on the next table were peering at a large portrait on the restaurant wall. 'Don't you think it's a little blatantly political that a Chinese restaurant would have a portrait of Chairman *Mao* on the walls?' we all overheard one of the women say to her friend in hushed tones.

'Yes, my goodness, and look, they even have him on the menus,' her friend replied nervously, peering over half-moon glasses at the line drawings of a jovial bald Chinese man, and clearly wondering if they'd stumbled into a hotbed of anti-capitalism. Not at these prices, I thought, feeling wild with exhilaration.

Stella rolled her eyes, and I leaned in towards the centre of the table, beckoning them to join me so that our heads were almost touching. 'That,' I said, 'is why I want to go travelling. So I don't end up thinking that

Ken Hom is a Chinese leader and not a celebrity chef.'

We all laughed conspiratorially, and I felt comfortable. Happy. Like people did, with their families.

When we came out of the restaurant again two hours later, we set off for the flat in the dusty late summer heat, walking around the corner past Stamford Brook tube station. There was a *Big Issue* seller there, partially blocking our path, deep in conversation with the owner of the flower stall outside the station, leaning on the handle of an old tartan shopping trolley containing all his copies of the magazine.

'Excuse me,' said Tony politely, waiting for him to move aside.

The man turned and thrust a magazine, its pages flapping, towards us.

'*Bi-iiig* Iss*ue*?' It sounded like a sneeze.

We all stopped, awkwardly, and performed a small pocket-searching dance for change. I was the first to find a pound, and began to reach my hand out towards the seller's, a young man with tanned, weatherbeaten skin and bright, bright green eyes. I froze, the coin in my fist suspended in mid air.

It was him. The man from the tube. The man I'd led up the escalator. Something was sticking out of the front pocket of his jeans: the neck of a small brown pill bottle. Half the label was showing, and I tried unsuccessfully to see if I could make out his name from the writing on it. He must be on medication, I thought, feeling relieved and somewhat proprietorial. But I'd have known that, even if I hadn't seen the bottle. For a start, he could never have done that job if he was in the same state he'd been in last year; and besides, I could tell from his eyes. They were still striking and compelling, but the terrible wildness had gone from them. His jeans were clean, and he didn't smell bad.

I stared at the hand he had stretched towards me. No more thick yellow claws; just slightly ragged, shortish, grimy fingernails. I had a moment's doubt – his old fingernails had been so much a part of him that I couldn't believe he no longer had them. Maybe it wasn't him . . . Then I looked at his eyes again. It definitely was.

'Are you all right, Em?' Stella slid her arm protectively around my waist, and stood closely behind me. I nodded, without taking my gaze off the *Big Issue* seller.

The man looked at me blankly. 'That's a pound, please,' he said, nodding towards my clenched fist. Sunlight flashed and glinted off the diamond in my engagement ring, dappling his face with tiny dancing dots.

'Are *you* all right?' I blurted back towards the man, as if I'd taken the baton of Stella's enquiry and was passing it on. I was suddenly dying to know if meeting me had changed his life, in the same way he'd triggered the changes in my own.

He made a face at me. 'I'm all right. Are you all right?' He turned to Tony. 'What about you, mate? Are *you* all right?' He was mocking me.

Tony laughed uneasily. 'I'm all right.'

'Good,' said the man. 'We're all just bloody peachy then, ain't we? That's a pound, please.'

My hand finally unclamped enough to allow me to drop the pound into his own and, as if in a trance, I took the copy of the magazine. Its paper cover felt warm from where he'd been holding it.

I opened my mouth to say, 'I've seen you before,' when he beat me to it.

'Oi, I recognize you.'

I waited for him to mention that day on the tube, the hand-holding on the escalator, but he didn't. 'Yeah. Saw you on the telly. You was in that documentary, weren't you?'

Stella hugged me tighter. 'She certainly was.' Then she added, with considerable smugness, 'So was I, actually.'

'Didya find her, then, your mum?'

I felt blood rush to my face. 'No. But I found him' – pointing at Tony – 'and he's my dad.'

I didn't think the man would be interested in hearing that, via my search, I'd also found a husband and a soon-to-be stepdaughter with coffee-coloured skin and the sweetest nature imaginable. And a new best friend, Ruth, and her gorgeous daughter Evie. And had managed to extend the circle of my other friends considerably, including Mack and Katrina and Greg and Denise. And had totally changed my life around. I was tempted to explain how this was all due to our original, inauspicious meeting, but thankfully decided that it was best left unspoken.

'Excellent,' said the man, with more than a trace of sarcasm in his voice. 'Well, we're all happy then. Good luck to you.'

I tucked the *Big Issue* into my bag, and we moved off, Stella and Tony talking to each other across me; and I realized that it didn't actually matter that I'd never know whether I helped that man or not. I thought again about how we weren't steered onto the paths of our lives by anybody else: not I, not Stella, not Ann, Tony, nor anybody. They were our own paths, created by our own choices.

As my sister chatted to my father about what a completely innovative and show-stopping wedding dress she planned to make me, I tried to work out when would be the best time to tell her that, actually, I'd seen this gorgeous one in the window of a little shop off the Portobello Road. In my head I began to rehearse my defensive speech: it was my wedding, I was very grateful for the offer, etc., but . . . and then I thought, For God's sake . . .

'Stella,' I blurted, 'sorry, but I've found the dress I want already.'

'Oh,' she said. 'Oh well. Actually I didn't really want to make it anyway, not *your* dress – it'd cost a fortune and take me for ever, and I really have to knuckle down to my degree project next year. But just wait until you see what I'm planning for my brides-maid's dress! It's going to be so outrageously fab. I thought perhaps a mini, with a fishtail at the back and a really tight basque top; maybe we could use some really interesting fabric – there's a great sort of silvery hologram-type material you can get now . . .'

Stella's words washed through me and over me, and then away into the wide sky over our heads, mingling with all the other words that had ever been said, and all the choices and decisions ever made, good, bad or indifferent. Tony looked up, following my gaze. Then he pointed at something, a small scrap of primrose fluttering away over the rooftops.

'Did you see that?'

Stella stopped. 'No. What?'

'Little yellow bird. Must be a canary or something that's escaped from someone's house.'

We carried on walking.

'Maybe he's just learned to fly,' I said.

THE END

TO BE SOMEONE
Louise Voss

'BEAUTIFULLY WRITTEN . . . BY TURNS COMIC AND
POIGNANT, ABOUT FRIENDSHIP, LOVE AND REDEMPTION. I
LOVED IT!'
Marian Keyes

Helena Nicholls — ex-world-famous pop star and prime-time DJ —
wakes up in hospital to find her looks, her career and her personal
life in tatters. She has been abandoned by her boyfriend, and the
person she loved most in the world — her best friend since the age
of five — is dead. She feels that she belongs nowhere, and her
sense of identity, fragile at the best of times, is in pieces.

As Helena begins the painful path to recovery, she casts her
mind back over the events in her life which have brought her
here. Those memories, good and bad, combined with the songs
forever associated with them, are milestones on her journey.
When her world is rocked by a chance meeting with an old
friend, she sees a glimpse of the future she could have. But if she
is to have a chance at that happiness, she must first conquer her
troubled past and work out what it means to be someone. . .

'A SAD, FUNNY BOOK ABOUT FRIENDSHIP, LOVE AND
GETTING A NEW LIFE'
The Big Issue

'A GREAT FIRST NOVEL. LOUISE VOSS IS AN EXCITING NEW
NAME WITH A REAL TALENT FOR STORYTELLING. HER
BOOK IS DEFINITELY A MUST READ'
Woman's Journal

'IT IS LOUISE VOSS'S VOICE THAT YOU REMEMBER AT THE
END: CONTEMPORARY, FEMALE, AUTHENTIC'
Independent

'A STUNNING DÉBUT'
Heat

'MY FAVOURITE BOOK THIS YEAR. A BEAUTIFULLY
WRITTEN STORY WHICH I DIDN'T WANT TO END'
Cerys Matthews, Catatonia

0 552 99902 4

BLACK SWAN

I'M A BELIEVER
Jessica Adams

Is there love after death?

Read it and believe!

Mark Buckle thinks he's an ordinary bloke. He teaches science at a junior school in south London. He'd rather read Stephen Hawking than his horoscope column, he's highly suspicious of Uri Geller, Mystic Meg and feng shui, and he wouldn't be seen dead at a séance. Most importantly, he absolutely, positively doesn't believe in life after death. Then, one terrible night, Mark's girlfriend Catherine dies in an accident and his whole world is thrown into chaos.

Within days of the funeral Catherine appears by his bedside and he finds himself communicating with her from beyond the grave. Then, just when he's beginning to adjust to life with his ghostly girlfriend, she decides to send him someone new to love. . .

I'm a Believer is a funny, moving and compulsive novel about love, life and what lies beyond.

0 552 77083 3

BLACK SWAN

LOVE IS A FOUR LETTER WORD
Claire Calman

Sex. Yes. She remembered that.

Wasn't that the thing that happened somewhere between the talking-and-going-out-to-dinner bit and the sobbing-and-eating-too-many-biscuits bit? Still, Bella was sure she could handle some – preferably before her as yet unopened packet of condoms reached their expiry date. She must be practically a virgin again now, all sealed over like pierced ears if you don't wear earrings for too long.

But the 'L' word? Uh-huh. No way. She never wanted to hear it again. There were things in her past which needed to be put well away, like the 27 boxes of clutter she'd brought from her old flat. And having changed her job, her town, her entire life – the one thing she wasn't about to change was her mind.

'SIMPLY WONDERFUL! I WAS TOTALLY ENCHANTED'
Fiona Walker

'A WARM AND FUNNY FIRST NOVEL'
Elizabeth Buchan, *The Times*

'FUNNY, CLEVER AND MOVING'
Sunday Mirror

0 552 99853 2

BLACK SWAN

OUT OF LOVE
Diane Appleyard

It has been an idyllic summer, Tess reflects, as she packs up
the Cornish holiday home in preparation for plunging back into
the cold reality of normal life. An idyllic summer, and there will
be more – so why does she feel awash with a nameless fear about
returning home?

Alone at the holiday cottage for one last night with her young
daughter – Mark and the boys have already returned home to
London – she has the time, and the silence, to take stock of her
life. A life, which, on the surface, has everything a woman could
want. So why, now the children are growing up, does she want
more? The dramatic decision she takes that night sets her off on a
quite new journey – but one for which she may need the courage
to travel alone. . .

'VERY, VERY TRUE AND TOUCHING . . . PACKS A HUGE
EMOTIONAL PUNCH'
Sarah Harrison

0 552 99933 4

BLACK SWAN

THESE FOOLISH THINGS
Imogen Parker

In the hottest summer for twenty years, the lives of three women collide.

Alison – sophisticated, successful, married to the ideal husband, but still wondering what the future holds.

Lia – serene, beautiful, living in blissful contentment with the man she loves.

Ginger – chaotic, effervescent, unable to hold down a relationship for more than a few weeks.

Three women with nothing in common, nothing at all, except that they are all about to become mothers for the first time. In the year that follows their first, fateful meeting, their lives will change irrevocably.

These Foolish Things is an unforgettable story of sexual passion, maternal love, true friendship and the choices that confront us all.

'PARKER WRITES WITH SYMPATHY AND WRY HUMOUR'
The Times

'AN UNFORGETTABLE NOVEL OF PARENTAL LOVE, PASSION AND FRIENDSHIP'
Woman's Weekly

0 552 99993 8

BLACK SWAN

LIFE ISN'T ALL HA HA HEE HEE
Meera Syal

'A MAGICAL MOSAIC OF FRIENDSHIP, BETRAYAL AND CROSS-CULTURAL INCONGRUITIES. BY TURNS SPICY, HILARIOUS AND SAD, IT UNFOLDS THE TIES THAT BIND YOUNG WOMEN TO THEIR EAST END PUNJABI ROOTS EVEN AS THEY HEAD WEST FOR TRENDY CAREERS, CAFÉ BARS AND SEXUAL FREEDOM'
She

On a winter morning in London's East End, the locals are confronted with the sight of a white horse skidding through the sooty snow, carrying what looks like a christmas tree on its back. It turns out to be a man covered in tinsel, with a cartoon-size turban on his head. Entrepreneur Deepak is on his way to get married. As he trudges along, he consoles himself with the thought that marrying Chila, a nice Punjabi girl (a choice which has delighted his surprised parents) does not mean he needs to become his father, grow nostril hair or wear pastel colour leisure wear.

Life Isn't All Ha Ha Hee Hee is the story of Deepak's bride, the childlike Chila, and her two childhood friends: Sunita, the former activist law student, now an overweight, depressed housewife, and the chic Tanja, who has rejected marriage in favour of a high-powered career in television. A hilarious, thoughtful and moving novel about friendship, marriage and betrayal, it focuses on the difficult choices contemporary women have to make, whether or not they happen to have been raised in the Asian community.

'EXTREMELY FUNNY, WONDERFULLY INSIGHTFUL . . . BIG, AMBITIOUS BOOK WITH SERIOUS POINTS TO BE MADE ABOUT THE CHOICES WOMEN FACE TODAY . . . SYAL MIXES HER MESSAGE WITH HILARIOUS SET PIECES'
Sunday Express

'THE STORY SURGES ALONG ON A RIP-TIDE OF WISECRACKS AND WISDOM . . . EXCELLENT'
Sunday Telegraph

'A SUPERBLY CRAFTED, PAGE-TURNING COMEDY WHICH ISN'T AFRAID TO TACKLE THE BIG SUBJECTS . . . HEARTFELT, HEARTWARMING AND VERY, VERY GOOD'
Mirror

'AN ENGROSSING AND PROVOCATIVE BOOK, BOTH FUNNY AND SAD'
Big Issue

0 552 99952 0

BLACK SWAN

A SELECTED LIST OF FINE WRITING
AVAILABLE FROM BLACK SWAN

77083 3	I'M A BELIEVER	Jessica Adams	£6.99
99822 2	A CLASS APART	Diana Appleyard	£6.99
99933 4	OUT OF LOVE	Diana Appleyard	£6.99
14764 8	NO PLACE FOR A MAN	Judy Astley	£6.99
99950 4	UNCHAINED MELANIE	Judy Astley	£6.99
99734 X	EMOTIONALLY WEIRD	Kate Atkinson	£6.99
99860 5	IDIOGLOSSIA	Eleanor Bailey	£6.99
99853 2	LOVE IS A FOUR LETTER WORD	Claire Calman	£6.99
77097 3	I LIKE IT LIKE THAT	Claire Calman	£6.99
99910 5	TELLING LIDDY	Anne Fine	£6.99
99898 2	ALL BONES AND LIES	Anne Fine	£6.99
99890 7	DISOBEDIENCE	Jane Hamilton	£6.99
99887 7	THE SECRET DREAMWORLD OF A SHOPAHOLIC	Sophie Kinsella	£6.99
99737 4	GOLDEN LADS AND GIRLS	Angela Lambert	£6.99
99959 8	BACK ROADS	Tawni O'Dell	£6.99
99993 8	THESE FOOLISH THINGS	Imogen Parker	£6.99
99938 5	PERFECT DAY	Imogen Parker	£6.99
77003 5	CALLING ROMEO	Alexandra Potter	£6.99
99952 0	LIFE ISN'T ALL HA HA HEE HEE	Meera Syal	£6.99
99872 9	MARRYING THE MISTRESS	Joanna Trollope	£6.99
99902 4	TO BE SOMEONE	Louise Voss	£6.99
99864 8	A DESERT IN BOHEMIA	Jill Paton Walsh	£6.99
99835 4	SLEEPING ARRANGEMENTS	Madeleine Wickham	£6.99
77107 4	SPELLING MISSISSIPPI	Marnie Woodrow	£6.99